The

QUARTER NOTE

Tales

By ARTHUR WENK

The Quarter Note Tales

By Arthur Wenk

WINGATE PRESS
Ontario, Canada

Library and Archives Canada Cataloguing in Publication

Wenk, Arthur B., 1946-
    The quarter note tales / written by Arthur B. Wenk.

ISBN 0-9738565-1-3

    I. Title.

PS8645.E47Q37 2006   C813'.6   C2006-901139-7

Layout design by Wingate Press
Cover Design by Wingate Press
Edited by Stacey Lynn Newman
Cover photograph courtesy of the author

Published by:

Wingate Press
www.wingatepress.com

Printed in Canada.

We acknowledge the support of the Canada Council for the Arts
which last year invested $20.0 million in writing and publishing throughout Canada.

**Canada Council
for the Arts**

**Conseil des Arts
du Canada**

For Patti

The Quarter Note Tales

AN

UNFALTERING

TRUST

... sustained and soothed

By an unfaltering trust, approach thy grave

Like one who wraps the drapery of his couch

About him, and lies down to pleasant dreams.

—William Cullen Bryant

CHAPTER 1

I first heard about Grant Jarman's suicide in *The Bowser*. The Chihuahua State College student newspaper devoted virtually every column of its special edition to the death of the popular English professor. A front-page photograph, evidently taken during one of Jarman's writing seminars, had been cropped to include only the teacher, in full pontifical mode, and one of his students, Deirdre O'Donahue, looking on adoringly. The paper, unable to extract a comment from Jarman's wife Melissa, gave ample coverage to the curvaceous O'Donahue, who eagerly took on the role of grieving widow. According to her breathless account, not only had she been Jarman's lover, bringing him real sexual fulfillment for the first time in his life, but she had planned to bear his child. (Ms. O'Donahue offered a few unflattering comments about the childless Melissa, whom she claimed Grant had planned to divorce in order to marry her.) And, to hear Deirdre tell it, she was the inspiration for Jarman's yet-unpublished second novel. (Yes, she dared to call herself his muse.) It was to have been a romantic tale about an English professor who falls in love with one of his students. No, she hadn't seen any of the work in progress, but she was certain that it would be a best-seller.

Somehow the paper had obtained a copy of Jarman's suicide note, composed in the form of a long poem concluding with the lines:

> I go not, like the quarry-slave at night,
> Scourged to his dungeon, but, sustained and soothed
> By an unfaltering trust, approach my grave
> Like one who wraps the drapery of his couch
> About him, and lies down to pleasant dreams.

Grant Jarman struck me as a man quite pleased with himself, and I suppose he enjoyed the idea of departing this world with a literary flourish.

Jerome Chowning, editor of *The Bowser*, delivered himself of an editorial celebrating Jarman's suicide as a heroic gesture. Professor Jarman, taking control of his own destiny, had made death a matter of choice, not chance. Like an athlete who knows when to quit, Jarman went out in his prime, leaving us to remember a man at the peak of his powers rather than an ailing decrepit wreck. Head held high, Jarman courageously faced what lay on the Other Side. The editor judged Jarman's suicide poem to be the finest thing he ever wrote.

An unabashed pothead, Chowning typically responded to the greeting "Hi" with a grinning "Yeah!" He considered it his duty to bait the administration whenever possible and discovered to his delight that they invariably rose to take it. Lest his panegyric seem too one-sided, Chowning invited a comment from Maxwell Kent, the chairman of the chemistry department who had been engaged in a bitter competition with Jarman to replace Clive Pembroke, the retiring dean of Arts & Sciences.

Not surprisingly, Kent characterized the suicide as a cowardly act of passive-aggressiveness, unfairly placing a burden of guilt on those left behind. Kent considered it an obvious sign of mental instability and shuddered to think what might have happened had such a deranged person been given a seat of power in the administration of this august institution.

Cal State Chihuahua, when I began teaching in the music department in the fall of 1970, suffered from a split personality. The California State College system to which it belonged envisioned CSC as an all-purpose institution with a projected student body of around 15,000, and recreational facilities were built with this size in mind. A vast area north of Chihuahua had been paved with parking lots and connecting roads. Academic buildings were gradually added as needed, much in the style of a suburban subdivision.

The "Founding Fathers," as they liked to call themselves, had quite a different vision. Inspired by their own education at the University of Chicago and dissatisfied with the run-of-the-mill offerings at neighboring state colleges, they came to Chihuahua with the intention of creating the "Swarthmore of the West" (alternately, the "Dartmouth of the West"). There would be a College Reading Program where students would sit under the olive trees and discuss the Great Books. There would be stringent foreign-language requirements and departmental examinations administered by outside examiners.

Students would take only three courses a term for five credits apiece in order to assure an in-depth mastery of each subject. Every student would enrol in General Studies courses covering the great ideas of Western civilization. Of course transfer students would be discouraged since the program presupposed four full years of participation.

Say what you will about the merits of the vision, Chihuahua simply was not the place to found the "Swarthmore of the West." Chihuahua, California was what used to be called a lunchbox town, a blue-collar community of

100,000 in which couples divorced at the usual rate but no one ever left, so that while shopping for groceries in the Alpha Beta one would constantly encounter ex-spouses, ex-parents, ex-significant others. Local stores advertised "Total Discount", a phrase which I found mystifying, laundries advertised "Sudden Service," the St. Thomas Aquinas School claimed "Lux Et Veritas Since 1955," and every other store window contained a sign reading "Like It? Charge It!" So-called traditional values took on a slightly skewed perspective, as in "Celebrate Springtime With Artificial Flowers" and "Eastertime Is Familytime—Woolworth's Is Open On Sundays."

After high school, most local students went on to Valley Junior College, many of whose graduates would normally be expected to transfer to the local state college. Daunted by the language requirements and other academic paraphernalia, they instead opted to attend more distant branches of the state college system, with the result that enrolment at CSC in my first year there was only 2000, dropping in the following year to 1800. At that point the Glenn Butkus, chancellor of the state college system, intervened and threatened to replace the entire administration if they failed to improve their response to local educational needs.

Grant Jarman, the golden boy of the English department, had a genius for making a little go a long way. His brief first novel, though still lacking in progeny, provided dozens of opportunities for readings at other institutions in the state college system and served as the basis for Jarman's well-attended writing seminar. The sale of the movie rights prompted a second round of readings, this time accompanied by confidential off-the-cuff speculations as to which Hollywood stars might portray characters in the novel, giving the audiences an unexpected, and thoroughly unmerited, frisson of delight at insider knowledge.

The success of the eventual movie brought more publicity to the author, who hinted mysteriously at a new work in progress without furnishing any evidence of its existence. Other members of the department occasionally grumbled at the attention garnered by their colleague. Paula Rogers, in particular, didn't hesitate to claim the superiority of her unpublished poetry over Jarman's modest fiction. My friend and handball partner Wayne Tutworthy, who taught 19th- and 20th-century literature in the department, reported actual cries of dismay when Jarman revealed that he had been engaged to write the "novelization" of the movie script, the film-makers evidently considering the original novel beyond the grasp of their target audience.

It was widely suspected that the attractive Jarman carried his sexual activities beyond the bedroom that he shared with his wife Melissa. This was, after all, the permissive era between the advent of The Pill and the onset of AIDS. But until Deirdre O'Donahue's soul-baring account in The Bowser, I had never heard specific details of any of Jarman's extramarital liaisons.

Francis Weatherington, the chairman of the English department, asked to share his thoughts with the readership of *The Bowser*, began with a pedestrian recital of Grant Jarman's contributions to the college. Jarman had created the writing seminar, which became the department's single most popular course. Weatherington could scarcely imagine how the department would have gotten on if Jarman had been selected as the dean of Arts & Sciences. Then, as if compelled to rhetorical gesture, he imagined Jarman's body floating on a metal shield. "And which of us would not hesitate to avoid being the last to light the flame of the pyre of our fallen friend," evidently forgetting for the moment that Jarman had taken his own life, but pushing on in a spasm of redundancy, "as it moves inevitably westward toward the decline of the setting sun."

Stanley Hopkins, the president of the college, maintained his reputation for a near-total disconnect from reality with an encomium that made one wonder whether he actually realized that Grant Jarman was dead. "This young teacher, revered by students and colleagues alike, has made a unique contribution to the stature of this college that will resound in years to come like thunder echoing on the hills surrounding our fair campus."

The Bowser offered up a few more brief appreciations of Grant Jarman by students and colleagues and concluded with a paid advertisement for one of the area's most flourishing businesses: "Acme Exterior Decorators, Landscaping Southern California With Concrete." That afternoon I happened to pass an example of their handiwork, a green asphalt lawn.

At least concrete had the advantage of being fireproof. Shortly after my arrival in southern California a huge brush fire burned for more than a week about a mile and half from CSC campus. Experienced faculty members took a blasé attitude: "Let me know when it hits the second parking lot," one colleague said. We easterners just weren't used to this sort of thing. In eastern cities a big fire might take 10, 18, even 24 hours to burn out, but then it was over. In Apache Canyon, not far from the campus, a brush fire broke out and fire-fighters were saying they didn't expect to have it contained for four days. Then Santa Ana winds took over and even after a week the fire was only 80% contained. The day that I arrived, toward the end of August, winds carried the smog away and revealed preternaturally sharp mountains like something out of a science fiction movie. You felt as though you could extend a finger and lightning would jump from it to the mountain top. But when those same winds got behind a fire, nothing could stop it until it reached the sea.

In earlier, less secular times, one might have expected Grant Jarman to receive some kind of memorial service, but of course there was no chapel at Chihuahua State College, nor any other indication that religion had ever played a part in the development of western civilization. President Hopkins announced hours of viewing at a nearby funeral home but declined any further involvement with Jarman's passage to the hereafter. Individual students and colleagues were left to deal with the loss in their own way. As far as the college was concerned, life went on as usual.

For me, Axel Crochet, assistant professor of music and Director of Choral Activities, this included teaching counterpoint exercises in the first-year music theory course, supervising research projects in the nineteenth-century history course, and holding afternoon rehearsals with the College Choir. This, my first teaching position since leaving graduate school, kept me fully occupied. I had no way of guessing that the contents of *The Bowser* would completely change my life.

CHAPTER 2

President Hopkins had once visited Paris and insisted that CSC have its own kiosks to add an international flavor to the campus, never imagining that their charm lay as much in the content of the advertisements as in the cylindrical shape of the structures. While Parisians read about concerts by Charles Azvenour or Yves Montand, or farewell appearances by the retiring Maurice Chevalier, CSC students learned about lectures by visiting professors, macramé classes, and concerts by student rock bands.

The upward thrust of the kiosks gave them a disproportionate prominence in a setting otherwise devoted to the glorification of the horizontal. As if deliberately rejecting the majestic example of the mountains that served as backdrop to the campus, the architecture of the college, with the sole exception of the athletic complex tower, confined itself to sprawling ranch-style buildings.

In this respect alone Chihuahua State College harmonized with the town from which it took its name. Arriving from the East, I had entertained the dream of living near my office and walking to school each day. To my chagrin, the only habitation within several miles of the campus consisted of one-room shanties waiting to be torn down for an extension of the freeway. I ended up renting a bungalow in a subdivision six miles from the school. Its street address, 25553, made correspondents back home inquire whether there were really twenty-five thousand identical houses in a row.

There might as well have been. The subdivision spread out like the tiled floor of a bathroom with a design based on two room plans and their reverse images. Whenever I washed dishes in the kitchen I could look out at a woman across the way doing the same thing, her gesture of placing plates in a drying rack to the right of the sink exactly mimicking my own, so that I felt as if I were re-enacting the Marx Brothers' famous "mirror" scene in "Duck Soup."

On the day after Jarman's suicide the information kiosks dotting the campus bore stencilled copies of a cryptic message: "Grant Jarman Did Not Write That Poem!" I didn't know what to make of the words, so after my classes were over I walked back to my office in the trailer behind the library and telephoned Melissa Jarman. After expressing my condolences over Grant's death I mentioned the signs I had seen. I had never been close to Grant, but when I first arrived at the college Melissa had gone out of her way to introduce me to people at faculty functions, perhaps sensing that a recently-divorced easterner coming to California for the first time might have difficulty fitting into a close-knit, couple-oriented college community.

"I haven't been on campus," Melissa said, "but the message is essentially correct."

"How do you mean?"

"The police seem to think that Grant didn't kill himself."

"I don't understand."

"An officer came to the house yesterday asking me questions about how I'd spent my time Wednesday afternoon. When I asked him what that had to do with Grant's suicide, he told me they'd found traces of a drug in his bloodstream and that his body appeared to have been dragged into the garage."

"How do you feel about that?" I asked.

"I'm not sure whether that makes it better or worse," Melissa said. Her hesitation contrasted with her usual decisive speech, a style I sometimes found intimidating.

"But there was a suicide note," I persisted. "The poem."

"It was sitting on his desk, typed, with his initials GJ written on the bottom."

"So it seemed authentic as far as you were concerned?"

"It was a bit stuffy, perhaps, but Grant did have a pompous side to him." Melissa seemed to have mixed feelings about speaking ill of the dead.

"If you don't mind my asking, how do you think it got into *The Bowser*?"

"They published it?" she exclaimed.

"You mean you haven't seen the special edition they put out yesterday?"

"This is the first I've heard of it."

"I think you'll want to be sitting down when you read it. There are some fairly inflammatory disclosures about Grant's love life."

"I see." Melissa's voice sounded cold, but I kept on.

"Did you give the note to anyone?"

"The police wanted to keep it when they took Grant's body, but I insisted they let me make a copy."

"You mean you re-typed that whole thing yourself?"

"No. I had them drive me over to the college so I could make a photocopy."

"But you just made the one copy?"

"That's right."

"Then I wonder how it got circulated. I doubt that Jerome Chowning got it from the Chihuahua police."

Melissa's laugh was more like a grunt, as if to acknowledge the unlikeli-hood of "Chowning" and "police" even inhabiting the same sentence, then she went on. "Wait a minute. There was a student using the copy machine when I arrived—Sheri Kimball, I think it was. I asked her if she'd let me in to make one copy and she agreed. I photocopied the poem then hurried off and got halfway down the hall before I realized that I'd forgotten to pick up the original, so I went back and got it. I suppose she could have run off another copy, because when I went back, she said 'You forgot your original' and handed it to me, so I knew she'd seen it. Don't people have any respect for privacy?"

"I'm afraid you're probably going to be in for some unwelcome public-ity," I said.

"I refused to talk with Jerome when he called," Melissa said.

"Newspapers have to print something. If they can't get information from one source, they'll try another."

"So you're saying I should have bared my soul for *The Bowser*?" Melissa asked bitterly.

"When something like this happens, there probably isn't any way to avoid unpleasantness," I said.

"Well thanks for warning me about the paper; I guess I'll have to read it for myself."

I spent the rest of the afternoon correcting counterpoint exercises, made myself a quick dinner then went to the movies. Local theatres showed double features and I was still enjoying the unaccustomed pleasure of get-ting two films for the price of one. My ex-wife once accused me of not lik-ing movies at all: I just liked the sensation of images moving in front of my eyes. Naturally I rejected the idea, but in truth I often enjoyed the second, or "B" feature, as much as the first.

Over the weekend I had time to study Jarman's suicide poem more closely and I spread the pages of the student newspaper open on my desk. Though not expensive, the simple slab desk conveyed a certain solid au-thority and when I sat behind it I sometimes permitted myself to imagine what it would be like to write words that mattered, to be, say, a judge in a large city rather than an underpaid college professor in an insignificant town on the edge of the desert.

Jarman's opening lines made it sound as if he were offering a final tes-tament:

Yet ere I leave this world I would bestow
A few last words on those I leave behind.

The flowery language continued with a section about a girl:
> She has a voice of gladness, and a smile
> And eloquence of beauty, and she glides
> Into my musings, with a mild
> And healing sympathy, that steals away
> Their sharpness, ah, she was a lovely lay.
> And when last bitter hour come like a blight
> Upon my spirit, of all within my class,
> She was the comeliest and most willing lass.

Given the context of the disclosures in *The Bowser*, I imagined the lines probably referred to the remarkably forthcoming Deirdre O'Donahue.

The poem continued:
> Earth, that nourished me, shall claim
> My growth, to be resolved to earth again,
> And, radioactive trace, surrendering up
> My individual being, shall I go
> To mix forever with the elements;
> To be a brother to the insensible rock,
> And free at last from all malign retorts
> Of academe and other deadly sports.

There seemed to be a bit of word-play here, for "retorts" could be understood not only as "pointed replies" but also as containers for chemistry experiments. Similarly, "earth" and "elements" could refer not only to the interment of a body but also the preoccupation of a chemist, and with that thought in mind I surmised he must be talking about Maxwell Kent, who had been vying with Jarman to be dean of Arts & Sciences. Given Kent's single-minded devotion to his career, a would-be adversary could well think of opposition as a "deadly sport."

The poem went on:
> So shall I rest; and what if I withdraw
> In silence from the living, and no friend
> Take note of my departure? All that breathe
> Will share my destiny. She'll surely laugh
> When I am gone, no more our love to hide
> From plodding husband's unsuspecting gaze,
> Yet even one as young as she shall leave
> Her mirth and her employments, and shall come
> And make her bed with me in my new home.

This appeared to be a confession of another affair but I was unable to identify the "one as young as she" or the "plodding husband." If Jarman had
been planning to leave his wife, had he contemplated moving with a lover
to a "new home"? And did these words belie Deirdre's claim that Jarman
had intended to marry her? More likely it was just another reference to
death, a destiny that "all that breathe" will share.

The next section of the poem presumably contained an unforgiving jab
at Jarman's wife, Melissa:

Go forth into the open classroom, see
At last how thou hast been deceived and list
To earth and her waters, and the depths of air—
Comes a still voice—Yet a few days, and then
The all-unfaithful sun shall see no more
In all his course; nor yet in the cold ground,
None colder than thy nonexistent love
Nor gladder from thy household to remove.

The "open classroom" might be a literal reference to the local community
college where Melissa taught remedial English. By law community colleges
had to accept any resident of California above the age of 18, regardless of
previous academic performance. Referring to oneself as a "sun ... in his ...
course" seemed rather grandiloquent, but who could tell what thoughts
might pass through one's mind just before committing suicide?

Yet the stencilled notes insisted that Jarman himself had not written the
poem, and Melissa claimed that the police did not accept his death as a
suicide, which seemed to lead to the unavoidable conclusion that he had
been murdered. The poem, whoever had written it, offered a list of possible suspects. Take Deirdre O'Donahue, for surely the opening section referred to her. The "comeliest and most willing lass" of the poem testified to
Jarman's pleasure but the words suggested no plan to leave his wife and
run off with his student, much less have a child by her. Suppose Deirdre
somehow discovered that Grant considered her to be no more than a
"lovely lay"—her reaction might more closely resemble that of the woman
wronged than that of the grieving widow, and if to a male musicologist
murder seemed like an extreme response, who was to say where emotion
might carry an overwrought eighteen-year-old?

As for Maxwell Kent, identified by the several chemical references in the
second section of the poem, I had heard rumors about his ruthlessness and
vague warnings to avoid making an enemy of a man determined to let
nothing get in the way of his success. No sooner had Clive Pembroke an-

nounced his retirement as Dean of Arts & Sciences than Kent had begun his campaign for the position. But did he really consider it worth killing for?

The third section did not point specifically to any suspect, as far as I could see, though that "plodding husband" might have grounds for murder if he ever learned about his wife's apparent dalliance with Jarman. By the same token Melissa, the subject of the fourth section of the poem, might be considered a suspect if she had learned about her husband's philandering. Or, if this really was a loveless marriage, she might have tried disguising murder as suicide in order to collect on Jarman's life insurance in addition to inheriting an estate of which divorce would have brought her only half.

I reckoned that the police would probably solve the murder, if murder it was, on the basis of physical evidence, but the poem, along with the stencilled signs, posed an intriguing puzzle and I decided to test my ideas on Wayne Tutworthy when I next saw him for our weekly handball game.

CHAPTER 3

The largest, and only multi-story, building at Chihuahua State College began as an athletic complex, complete with a double gym for basketball, squash courts, weight room, indoor running track, and the largest swimming pool in the area. When the administrators examined the architect's plans and compared the relatively interesting shape of the athletic center with the squat boxes they were expected to occupy, they gave a cry of protest and forced a design change whereby administrative offices would occupy several levels on top of the athletic complex. The resulting five-story tower boasted an observation deck from which one could see Los Angeles on a rare clear day.

On Wednesday afternoons Wayne Tutworthy and I got together after classes for a few games of handball and an opportunity to let off steam about the frustrations of teaching at CSC. I was introduced to Wayne at the president's reception for new faculty members. Wayne was the first person I heard refer to the chancellor of the state college system as "butt-kiss." Rightly or wrongly, most of the faculty members held the chancellor responsible for the decline of the once-heralded California State College system.

Wayne's irreverent attitude appealed to me, and we soon became friends. His blond, curly hair and guileless expression gave him an innocent air that often allowed his subversive comments to pass unnoticed. The uninitiated would simply assume that they had misheard him when he passed a particularly outrageous statement. We turned out to share an interest in American history of the colonial period, and we identified ourselves with the Yankee sharpshooters who hid behind trees and stonewalls and sniped at the British regulars in their scarlet coats. It didn't take much of a leap to associate the British redcoats with the CSC administration. "Proud" would not be a strong enough word to describe their bearing at the new faculty reception. "Vainglorious" might better suit their attitude. One could easily imagine them polishing the gold buttons on their uniforms before appearing on parade.

The attitude of the "Founding Fathers" of CSC toward the town of Chihuahua could also be understood in terms of nobility bringing proper manners and institutions to the rough-shod colonials. Just as the royal governors had considered their domains to be simply an extension of the British realm, so the president and vice-president of the college, along with most of the deans, thought of themselves as administering a branch campus of the University of Chicago. Relations with the local population were expected to be strictly unilateral, the emissaries of excellence bearing truth to the unwashed masses.

Darryl Cooper, the music department chairman, summarized his dissatisfaction this way. "You know, Axel, if the administration were really representing our interests, they'd be standing with their backs to us, facing the chancellor down and defending the faculty. Instead, they stand with their backs to the chancellor, taking his part against us. No wonder we consider them the enemy."

The second week of the term, Wayne offered to teach me handball. Wiry and agile, Wayne had superior hand-eye coordination, but as a marathon runner I had the edge in endurance, so once I had mastered the mechanics of the game we were more or less evenly matched. When I removed my gloves at the end of the match, I was dismayed to see the way my hands had swollen.

"Oh, didn't I tell you that your hand might swell up?" Wayne said with a smile.

"No, you didn't, Wayne," I replied, wondering what was to become of my piano career.

Wayne assured me that my hand would eventually adapt to the stress of handball the same way that the rest of me had become accustomed to the stress of working at the college. The next morning my hands seemed to be fine, albeit a little stiff, but I couldn't move another muscle in my body. Well, Wayne did tell me that in handball I would run around more than in tennis.

This week's game had been postponed until Thursday because of Veterans Day, but we noted that the excitement surrounding Grant Jarman's death had scarcely abated in the seven days since the appearance of the special edition of *The Bowser*. I mentioned my conversation with Melissa Jarman, and Wayne told me she was having difficulty establishing an alibi. On Wednesday afternoons Melissa held office hours at the community college. The police had located students at either end of the period in question, but evidently there was a critical gap during which she could theoretically have driven home, administered a knock-out drug, dragged her husband to the garage, connected a vacuum cleaner hose from the exhaust pipe to the driver's side window, turned on the engine, then raced back to her office in time to meet the last student.

"Why the attention on Melissa?" I asked.

"As I understand it, their marriage wasn't doing too well," Wayne replied.

"Then why wouldn't she just seek a divorce?"

"Do you consider yourself well off?" Wayne asked.

"Not on an assistant professor's salary," I said.

"Grant wasn't doing much better," Wayne said.

"But what about the novel and the movie and the novelization?" I objected.

"You haven't had any experience with the movie industry, have you?" Wayne asked.

"I go to the movies a lot," I said.

"That's not what I mean. Hollywood accountants have learned to fiddle with the numbers until even a blockbuster movie doesn't show much of a profit, and that means people like Grant Jarman see only niggling fees."

"Although they get the glamor of being associated with the stars."

"Glamor the studios will give away for free."

"So what does that have to do with Melissa?"

"When Grant's novel was first published, he told me he took out a large life insurance policy for Melissa. So while she wouldn't have gotten much from a divorce—that nice house of theirs is pretty heavily mortgaged—she stands to make quite a tidy sum from his death."

"That's interesting. When I talked with Melissa on the phone, she didn't seem to show any feelings about Grant's death. So it could have been that any love between them was long past or that she was a cold-blooded murderer."

"Or that she was in a state of shock and hadn't let everything sink in yet. It doesn't pay to be too confident in analyzing women's feelings, Axel."

"You can say that again," I replied, thinking about my lack of success with my ex-wife. Wayne and I played two games, each winning one, and the hollow pong of the ball bouncing against the walls chased the memories of my ex-wife's complaints, just as the active engagement of arm and leg muscles dispelled the tensions accumulated during the week.

"How have you made out with the College Chorus?" Wayne asked when we paused for breath before finishing out the set.

"I had great plans for that group," I said. Here was a subject about which I could speak with enthusiasm. "I worked it all out before coming here: there would be a large chorus of sixty voices and a madrigal group of twenty-four. I planned the programs and purchased all the music."

"How did you recruit singers?"

"I had someone in the art department make up signs, and for two days I sat in the gym at registration listening to messages blaring on the PA system." I held my fingers on my nose to produce a nasal sound and imitated the registration announcer: "3804, Biology 101, is closed. Please consult the board at your right for the list of closed courses. If you are unable to resolve your schedule, consult the faculty advisors to your left. 6107, Physics 311, is closed. Richard Walters, you left your cards at Station 2; please come back and pick them up. 3402, History 271, is closed. Please form three lines at Station 3, Fee Assessment. Form three lines. 6103, Business 405, is closed. A new course has been opened, 2023, French 101. Cards for this course will be available in half an hour. 3003, Art 210, is closed."

"So did you accept sixty singers from those who auditioned?"

"Not exactly. Only twenty-eight kids signed up for chorus so I had to take them all."

"But you had the cream of the crop for the madrigal group?"

"I'm afraid not. Only eight students had that period free so I took all of them—they weren't even the best singers."

"I imagine you'll have to simplify the Christmas program for them?"

"Well actually, I already planned a program of eight-part music for the madrigal singers."

Wayne looked at me as if I were crazy, then he suggested that I talk with the Music Consultant.

"I've got a Ph.D. in musicology, Wayne," I said defensively.

"No, the Music Consultant is the local god—he administers the overall music program in all the schools in Southern California. I really think you ought to talk with him."

I promised to let him know how it worked out. We played a third game, showered, packed up our gym bags and got ready to go home. On the way out we passed Deirdre O'Donahue and several other girls entering the gym. "Hello, Professor Crochet," Deirdre called out in a sing-song voice. "Hi, Wayne," called out one of the others.

"You let your students call you by your first name?" I asked him wonderingly.

"Sure; what's the problem with that?"

"Well, I mean ..."

"What do you wear to class?" Wayne asked.

"A jacket and tie. Don't you?"

"I wear a jacket the first day, to let the kids know that I own one. After that, I just wear blue jeans."

"But ..."

"Come on, Axel; don't sound like one of the redcoats."

"How's that?"

"A few weeks into term, Gerry Siebel passed me in the hall and asked why I wasn't wearing a tie."

"You mean the vice-president of the college?"

"Do you know any other Gerry Siebels?"

"No."

"When I asked him why I needed to wear a tie, he got all huffy and asked how else we were to tell the students from the teachers."

"What did you say?"

"I told him that if a necktie was the only way we could tell the teachers from the students, we should fire the teachers, buy neckties for a few of the students, put them in the front of the class, and save a bundle of money."

"What did he say to that?"

"He couldn't think of anything to say. He just stalked off."

"But don't you think ..."

"Axel, there's a Latin proverb you need to learn: *Illegitimis non carborundum est.*

"I'm not sure ..."

"Don't let the bastards grind you under. See you next week." And Wayne walked off toward his car.

CHAPTER 4

The following Wednesday Wayne and I were leaning against the wall of the handball court, breathing heavily after a particularly energetic game, when he mentioned that the police had visited his house to ask questions about Jarman's death.

"Surely they don't think you had anything to do with it!" I said.

"Actually, that's exactly what they think," he said. Wayne's habitual irony had vanished before this worrisome intrusion into his life.

"I don't get it—you and Grant got along well enough, didn't you?"

Wayne hesitated. "I guess I might as well tell you," he said. "Caroline had an affair with Grant."

"Oh," I said and paused, searching for appropriate words. "I'm really sorry."

Wayne looked toward the floor. "I guess it shouldn't have surprised me. She's such a vivacious woman, other men have always been attracted to her, and I guess she hasn't always spurned their advances."

"So the police imagine that you might have murdered Grant in a fit of jealous rage?"

"Something like that."

"But we were playing here the afternoon he died. Doesn't that give you an alibi?"

"That's what I told them, but they found someone who saw me leaving the gym around 3:30 after our game. According to their timetable, that would have given me enough time to drive to Jarman's place, assuming I'd already made plans to meet him there, then dope his drink and set up the suicide scene."

"That sounds pretty strange."

"It gets stranger." Wayne seemed to have recovered his composure because he turned to me and said in a mock-conspiratorial tone, "About a week before Grant died, I received a stencilled note—it looked pretty much like the signs that went up around campus a couple of days after his death."

"What did it say?"

"It didn't have any words: it was one of those heart shapes that you sometimes see teenagers put on trees and inside the heart the initials CT + GJ."

"Presumably neither Caroline nor Grant sent you the note, so who could it have been?"

"I've been trying to work that out myself. It doesn't seem like Melissa's style, but I can't think of anybody else who would know or even care one way or another."

"You don't have any enemies?'

"None I can think of. At my previous college we got an unlisted number after I received a threatening phone call from a football player that I'd failed in a composition course, but I can't imagine that has any connection with this."

"How did the police find out about the affair?

"Apparently Melissa told them. Their questioning took a sudden turn into Grant's romantic life and she blurted out what she knew without thinking about the consequences. Later she called to apologize—one aggrieved spouse to another, so to speak."

We played a third and final game then retired to the locker room to shower and change. I mentioned studying the so-called suicide poem and finding references in it to several suspects, including Maxwell Kent. My friend's involvement in a police investigation had altered my attitude toward the poem, which had now become more than just an intriguing puzzle.

"Is someone taking my name in vain?" Came a bass voice from the next row of lockers, and Kent came around to join us. Dressed in a tight-fitting black bathing suit and black swimming cap, with tiny goggles pushed above his forehead, he was evidently headed for the pool. At the first general faculty meeting of the fall, Kent had introduced himself to me by saying that he was something of a sportsman. "Squash, skiing, horses: I like to keep trim." Judging from his physique, I wouldn't be surprised if he worked out with weights as well. Tall and muscular, he seemed to show even a greater preoccupation with his body than most other Californians. I suspected that his perfectly even tan had received artificial assistance. His wife, whom I met at the same gathering, despite looking like a former cheerleader, was a caring mother who didn't seem entirely sympathetic to Kent's playboy lifestyle. "Next summer he wants to drive his motorcycle across the country," she told me. "I just want him to stay home and be my husband."

"Don't be surprised if you get a visit from the police," I told Maxell, half jokingly. "According to Jarman's suicide poem, you had a motive for killing him."

"You can't be serious!" Maxwell said, his deep voice dropping even lower.

"Weren't you heard saying that you wouldn't let anything come between you and the deanship?" Wayne baited him.

"I don't think the administration took Jarman's candidacy very seriously," Maxwell said condescendingly. "And a good thing, too, wouldn't you say?"

"Well, just playing devil's advocate, what were you doing at around four o'clock on November 4th?" Wayne teased.

"I left the lab at four, as my assistant can verify," Kent said somewhat sniffily.

"Melissa didn't discover the body until 4:30. You could have gotten to Jarman's by 4:05, spiked his drink, planted him in the car and gotten away in time," I suggested, "though I admit you would have needed a fair amount of advance planning."

"Like a well-designed chemistry experiment," Wayne chimed in.

"I don't have to listen to this poppycock," Kent said testily, and headed for the pool.

"His alibi's no better than mine," observed Wayne.

"His motive's just as good," I said. "You play a heck of a game of handball, but somehow I don't picture you as the murderous type."

"I wish you could convince the police of that," Wayne said.

"But Maxwell, on the other hand, is something else. Did you notice that he never denied it when we suggested he'd murder anyone who got in the way of his becoming dean?"

"I'm glad I'm not competing with him for anything," Wayne said. "Did you hear what he did when the chairmanship of the chemistry department become open?"

"No."

"One of his colleagues was interested in the position. The story I heard was that Kent arranged to have a student alter the data on one of the chap's experiments, then he alerted a friend at a journal where the results were to be published. The man's reputation wasn't completely ruined—he'd published a fair amount before this—but now all that was thrown into question. Kent made it look as if the man had been faking the data in order to make the results come out right, and the department decided that until the questions were resolved, it might be a mistake to name the man as chairman. Kent was the only other candidate, so he got the job."

"Is that what the academic world is really like?" I asked.

"You thought it was just a community of scholars toiling in the ivory tower?"

"Something like that."

"You have to remember, Axel that academics are basically social misfits. If they got along with other people, they'd be doctors or lawyers."

"And if they got along with other people, they'd be able to resolve issues openly, instead of knifing them in the back."

"That may be putting a little too much faith in human nature, but it's basically the idea."

"Remind me not to make an enemy of Maxwell Kent."

We put our sweaty clothes in our gym bags and headed out to the parking lot.

That night the city was attacked simultaneously by wind, fire and earthquake. Up in the pass, next to the college, winds hit eighty miles an hour. The fires were the worst in local history, devastating forty thousand acres around Big Bison Lake and coming for the first time within a mile of the house where I lived. The earthquake felt to me like a mere shudder, but further to the west the tremor demolished a Veterans Administration hospital, forced fifty thousand valley-dwellers to seek higher ground when a dam threatened to break, and toppled highway overpasses up and down the Golden State Freeway. One had the feeling that all we needed was one good pestilence and Southern California would fold up and die. You just needed to take a deep breath and keep on going, but in this part of the country deep breathing could be hazardous to your health, and an entire generation of children would find the expression "disappeared into thin air" meaningless. As my colleague Charlie Purcell advised, "If you can see it, don't breathe it."

I'd known people like Maxwell Kent before. When I was in seventh grade, two of the older boys would pin me by the arms in the schoolyard and begin punching me. "Who's hitting you harder?" they'd ask. Of course there was no safe answer, since whichever person I didn't choose would just increase the intensity of his blows. When bullies got older, without actually growing up, they seemed to find other means for getting what they wanted, and the pain for their victims could be much longer-lasting.

Not all adults opted for indirect methods. A year earlier I had gotten nightmares after watching the scene in "Easy Rider" where a man in a sleeping bag is bludgeoned to death with baseball bats. What was it about people like Maxwell Kent that made them put their own success ahead of every other consideration? And what was Kent's real goal? A man his age probably wouldn't be content with spending the rest of his career as Dean of Arts & Sciences at Chihuahua State College.

Somehow Kent had managed to maintain his ambition despite the notorious southern California disease of laid-backness. Even before moving here I had heard stories of productive scholars from Princeton or Yale moving to the Golden State and abandoning scholarly activity altogether. When reproached by eastern colleagues they would utter vague remarks about finally seeing the light, turning away from a driven life (the term "Type A" hadn't been invented yet, but that's what they had in mind), embracing trees and becoming One with the All. One of my friends from graduate school used to keep a list of every book he read. Even while completing his dissertation he'd gotten through more than a hundred books. The year after accepting a position at Cal State Fullerton he reported that his total had dropped to fewer than fifty. The next year he read a couple of dozen books and before I lost track of him he'd sent me a semi-coherent letter declaring that words really weren't up to the task of conveying truth. I guess I shouldn't have been surprised that those were the last words I had from him.

CHAPTER 5

"You know, I think that might be fun," Melissa Jarman said when I invited her to join me at the Gourmet Club dinner on the Saturday evening before Thanksgiving. The coordinator of the event, stuck with an imbalance when one couple had to back out at the last minute, called me to see whether I'd fill in, and bring a date to keep the numbers right.

The idea of the Gourmet Club appealed to me. In the course of a year you made one dinner for three other couples, then attended three other dinners, with the group changing each time so that you ended up meeting eighteen new people. Even trenchant criticism from Darryl Cooper failed to dampen my enthusiasm. "My wife and I went once," he growled. "Drove all the way to the top of the mountain for tacos. That was the last time for us."

We didn't have to drive up the mountain. The dinner took place in a large ranch-style house across the street from the golf course. I guess I would have called it a boulevard rather than a street, since opposing lanes of traffic were separated by a wide median strip containing a row of evenly spaced palm trees. In contrast to the "desert coolers" in my subdivision, large rooftop cubes of straw kept moist by an internal water circulation system, the resulting cool air being forced downward into the house by a large fan, this house boasted a central air-conditioning system rather unusual for the time. Word had it that our host had married into money; a house like this didn't fall within the range of college professor's salary.

The Chihuahua real estate market was recovering from a down cycle. Darryl Cooper told me about folks who had gotten fed up with California life and headed back East. They'd paid only a tiny down payment for their house, but the market was so bad that they would have taken a considerable loss if they'd actually succeeded in selling. Since California law prohibited banks from foreclosing until sixty days had passed since default on mortgage payments, they'd simply stopped paying their mortgage then tossed the keys to the house into the pool when they moved out. Those days had passed by the time I was looking for a place to live.

Melissa was wearing a dark grey wool dress that clung attractively to her body, showing off her well-developed figure and slender hips. Her light brown hair lay flat against the side of her head then curled under as it reached her chin, not an easy coiffure to obtain, I guessed. She moved among the other guests with the physical assurance one associates with those who have been taught proper posture at an early age. I admired the way her high cheekbones and somewhat narrow face produced a striking profile.

The food was completely satisfying: duckling à l'orange, homemade bread, Greek salad and lemon chiffon cake for dessert. And I might have enjoyed the company of colleagues from the psychology and French departments, whom I'd known only by name. Unfortunately, the host, perhaps emboldened by an excess of wine, spent the dinner publicly criticizing his wife's sexual performance. Perhaps nowadays I would feel strong enough to intervene, but as a first-year teacher in an alien culture I just felt embarrassed, and the other couples seemed no less timid.

"What a disaster!" Melissa exclaimed as we drove away, as early as politeness would permit.

"So this kind of thing doesn't happen very often around here?" I asked.

"Not at any party I've attended," she said.

"Well that's a relief, I guess." I was new not only to California life but to the academic world in general, and was still trying to figure out what constituted normal behavior. One of my colleagues in the art department seemed quite unabashed about sleeping with his students. When reproached by his wife, he told her she was free to do the same. She complained that she didn't want to sleep with other men; she just wanted him to stay home.

I ventured upon the question of the stencilled notes and mentioned that Wayne Tutworthy had received one.

"That's funny; so did I, but my heart said 'GJ + DO.'"

"And you were able to figure out her identity?"

"I had to do some asking around. I'll tell you, I was ready to kill Grant when I learned about Deirdre!"

"But she wasn't the first?"

"No, she wasn't the first." Melissa took a deep breath, as if trying to keep her feelings under control. "There was a woman at our previous college. When I learned about the affair and confronted Grant, he swore it was a mistake and promised it would never happen again."

"And then?"

"When I learned he'd been carrying on with Caroline, he claimed that she'd seduced him. Well, you've met her; it sounded plausible, but I've got to say, I'd lost a lot of my love for Grant by that point."

"But Deirdre made you angry?"

"Damn straight! It didn't matter whether we had much of a marriage anymore. If he was going to sleep with some eighteen-year-old bimbo, what did that say about me? Caroline Tutworthy was one thing—at least we're in the same generation. But Deirdre! Yeah, I could have murdered him on that one."

"So the police still consider you a suspect?"

"No, thank goodness." Melissa's tone brightened perceptibly. "They finally found a student who had been with me at four o'clock that afternoon, and they calculated that nobody could drive fast enough to get to the house and back to the school in time."

"I'll bet that's a relief. Could I ask you just what happened that day?"

"I suppose I should consider that impertinent, but in point of fact I've been looking forward to telling somebody, and everyone else has avoided the topic like the plague."

"So try me."

"All right." She paused, perhaps arranging her recollections in proper order. I sometimes wondered what Melissa was doing teaching remedial English. I could picture her as a formidable litigator. "I saw what had happened the minute I arrived. We have a two-car garage, and there have been a lot of auto thefts and break-ins in our neighborhood. You know the way our driveway curves around behind the house."

"And you live on a cul de sac, don't you?"

"Right. So Grant and I make it a practice to put our cars away as soon as we get home. When I opened the door, the engine of Grant's car was running and the garage was full of fumes. I saw him lying there in the front seat but there was no way I could get in. I thought he might still be alive, so I called for an ambulance then went back to the garage. By then enough of the gas had escaped that I could get to his car and open the door. At that point I didn't know whether he was dead or alive."

"There was a hose connected to the exhaust?"

"Yes, with the driver side window rolled up to hold it in place, but there was enough of an opening in the window that after the inside of the car had filled up with fumes, they kept pouring out until they filled the whole garage.

"What happened then?"

"Well the ambulance people arrived very quickly and took Grant to the hospital. I rode along with them, but the paramedics weren't able to revive him; I hope I don't ever have to listen to another siren at close range. The doctor at the hospital pronounced him dead. Then I had to sign papers to authorize an autopsy."

"Why's that?"

"Evidently suicide is treated as an unnatural death. Did you know that it's against the law to take your own life?"

"But then they found out that it wasn't suicide, after all."

"They didn't exactly tell me that. Some police officers came by the house to talk with me, and their questions began sounding rather strange, but it wasn't until I asked them point blank that they told me about the drug they'd found in Grant's body."

"So what has it been like for you?"

"At first everybody was sympathetic, but then people started acting kind of funny, as if they thought I had something to do with Grant's death."

"That must be awkward."

"It isn't fun, I'll tell you that." Melissa's voice took on a bitter edge.

When we arrived at Melissa's house she invited me in and since it was still pretty early, I accepted. As I sat on the sofa of their living room, I couldn't resist imagining the scene two weeks earlier. The murderer may well have been sitting where I sat, waiting for an opportunity to pour a few knock-out drops into Grant's drink. Would the murderer have observed the quantity of books lining the walls, or the absence of a television set? Would the murderer have commented on the artwork, evidently original paintings, or the lack of a swimming pool in the yard behind the house?

Then Melissa came in and sat beside me. We talked briefly about our differing perceptions of the college as faculty member and faculty wife, then Melissa turned to me and said, "Would you hold me? I suddenly feel all alone." I put my arm around her and she snuggled against my body. It felt comfortable for me, too, to have a woman in my arms for the first time in more than a year. It felt very quiet, too. Wall-to-wall carpeting absorbed the usual mechanical sounds of a refrigerator recycling or even the drip of leaky faucet. No sounds came from outside, either. The dead-end street precluded the usual sounds of passing traffic and the house was set back a fair distance from the roadway. A murder could have taken place here with no one the wiser.

A few moments passed quietly and then we were kissing each other, at first tentatively, then more insistently. Lips and tongues had more power to express intimacy than all the books on the shelf. A short time later we were in Melissa's bedroom making love.

Afterwards she pressed her body close to mine and I said, "That was nice."

"It was more than nice," she said. "At first I was just trying to escape—it's been more than a year since I've had sex—but toward the end I was glad it was you."

"I felt the same way," I said. "It's been a long time for me, too."

We continued to lay together comfortably then Melissa asked, "Can you stay the night?"

"The only one waiting for me at home is my cat," I said, "and I guess he can manage without me."

"Good," she said. We turned off the lights and snuggled together, but before long we were making love again, more deliberately this time, and at the end I felt a great sense of peace.

"That was for us, wasn't it?" Melissa said.

"Yes," I said. "I hope that means we'll get together like this again."

"I'm afraid we can't be seen in public," Melissa said. "It wouldn't look right. But we can do this for awhile—what do you think?"

For answer I pressed my lips against hers and we went to sleep in each other's arms.

CHAPTER 6

Toward the end of November I made an appointment to see the Music Consultant, and on the day before Thanksgiving I drove to his office in downtown Chihuahua. After several months I had become more or less accustomed to the palm trees, whose unfamiliar silhouette at twilight had so disoriented me when I first arrived, but I still found it amazing that bougainvillaea plants could serve as median dividers and that just behind the walls that surrounded every property grew exotic plants I had seen only in botanical gardens, or never at all: jacaranda, camellia, jasmine, flowering pear, bird of paradise, fig, eucalyptus.

Free parking downtown continued to surprise me. The Chihuahua area had recently experienced its first mall—not a strip mall, mind you, but the full-fledged "take the family and spend the afternoon" indoor mall—and removing the parking meters had been one of the first steps in the futile campaign by downtown merchants to hold onto their customers. Some strange kind of centrifugal force seemed to drive everything in southern California away from the center so that small towns exploded into small cities whose downtown area, for all intents and purposes, ceased to exist. The urban structure resembled the educational philosophy of the Founding Fathers: when you finally penetrated to the core, you found nothing there.

The Education Department occupied part of one floor of the Municipal Affairs building, a modern structure whose design must have delighted the bureaucrats who thought it up. Seen from the air, it probably looked as simple as a square with two intersecting lines running through its center. Seen from the point of view of a hapless citizen, the place seemed like an impenetrable maze.

A plethora of signs and instructions sustained an illusion of navigability. According to the main directory I could find the Education Department on the 3rd floor, and I rode the elevator to that level confident that I was close to my destination. When I got off the elevator a second directory said that the Music Consultant could be found in room 3W25. Now things got interesting. Imagining that W might mean west, I headed in what I thought was that direction but the numbers on the office doors gave no reference to the compass. Room 325 turned out to be Accounts Payable and when I asked the clerk for directions, she'd never heard of the Music Consultant and didn't think the city even had one.

I reversed direction, passed the elevator banks for a second time and found a 325R: Central Purchasing. The secretary explained that 3W25 was located in one of the corridors that criss-crossed the main structure. I turned right, turned right again, turned right for a third time, and sure enough, there was 3W25.

The Music Consultant, Raymond Felch, was a large man with dark hair and a five o'clock shadow. His shirt was open at the collar and he'd rolled up his sleeves. He didn't seem particularly happy to see me.

"So you've come down off your mountain, eh?" he began.

"I was hoping to find out what we could do to attract more music students to Chihuahua State," I said.

"New at CSC, are you?"

"This is my first year."

"I thought as much. And I suppose somebody in the administration decided to send an emissary to the little folk in the valley?"

"No. It wasn't like that. I decided on my own."

"That's impossible. You didn't even know I existed."

"Well, that's true, but a friend in the English department told me about you and ..."

"English, eh? And what do they teach there, 'literary criticism,'" he pronounced the last words in a mocking falsetto voice.

"I'm not sure about that. All I know is that there seems to be a disparity between the number of music students graduating from high schools in the valley and the number who come to CSC."

"Disparity! I'll say there's a disparity. Have you ever visited a high school in the valley?"

"Well yes, as a matter of fact." I didn't like the way this interview was going. "I've been sitting in on choir rehearsals for the past two weeks."

"And what did you think?"

"I'm really impressed by the quality of the students. I wish we'd get students like that at the college."

"And why do think they're not coming to 'California State College at Chihuahua,'" again in that mocking tone.

"That's what I hoped you'd tell me."

"I'll tell you," he fairly roared. "They don't come because I tell them not to come."

"You ..."

"That's right. And I'm going to keep on telling them the same thing until your airy-fairy college decides to join the real world."

"But ..."

"You think we ordinary people haven't heard of the 'Dartmouth of the West'?" His voice fairly dripped with disdain. "You won't accept transfer students because they won't get the full benefit of the 'Dartmouth experience.' You won't teach students the practical skills they need because it doesn't fit in with your 'educational vision.' Well screw your educational vision!"

"That's your official position?"

"You got it, mate."

"Don't I get any credit for coming in to see you?"

"Wield a lot of influence up there on the hill, do you?"

"Not really, I just ..."

"Then save your breath for the people who can make a difference."

I thanked Mr. Felch for his time and left his office as quickly as I could.

When Wayne and I met for our weekly handball session later that same afternoon, he asked me whether I'd had any luck with the Music Consultant.

"I've discovered there really is a conspiracy against me."

"How so?"

"There's no shortage of students: the local high school turn out upwards of fifty kids a year who plan to become college music majors."

"But they're not coming here."

"You said it! The high school music teachers, in agreement with the Music Consultant, advise their students to attend Valley College, Fullerton State, San Diego State, L.A. State, anyplace but Cal State Chihuahua."

"Why's that?"

"Where do our graduates in English and music go for jobs?"

"Most of them become high school teachers."

"Right. So why don't we give them the kind of practical preparation they need?"

"Because it doesn't fit the vision of the Founding Fathers."

"Right again. And the Music Consultant said that until we start giving more consideration to the needs of the public schools, he has no intention of changing his policy."

"So what are you left with?"

"Transfers from out of town and students who can't afford to leave. One of the music majors told me that nobody would be here if they could go anywhere else."

After handball we walked back to the locker room to shower and change. "By the way," I asked, "have you completed your 'Annual Report of Faculty Activities'?"

"I could practically recite it to you: 'Please complete this form in duplicate and submit it to your Division or Department Chairman by November 21. Report all activities since your last report and include work in progress as well as completed work. Attach additional sheets where more space is required; where possible, append copies of articles, book reviews, reviews of your publications, programs, etc. All information which you feel appropriate in reviewing your accomplishments should be included in this report.'"

"Sounds just like a fan-club scrapbook."

"Except for the work-in-progress clause."

"You don't like that one either?"

"I object in principle to having to describe 'future activities.' I'd like to be able to abandon a project without having the RPT Committee looking over my shoulder and questioning me about it at year's end."

"I wasn't even here last year. I tried to argue with the Division Secretary about it but she said I still had to file the form. So I wrote "Not applicable" for every category and mailed it in."

"I'm not sure you can get away with that for long. The wheels of bureaucracy grind slowly but they grind exceeding fine."

"But don't let the bastards grind you under?"

"You're getting the idea."

As we walked toward the parking lot Wayne said, "I've been thinking some more about that so-called 'suicide poem.' You've talked about it with Melissa and with me, and last week we even got Maxwell Kent to put in his two cents' worth, but I've been wondering about Deirdre."

"Because the poem seemed to refer to her?"

"Right."

"She sings in the College Chorus—in fact, she's even on the executive committee. I'll see if I can find an opportunity to talk with her."

"You're going to ask her if she killed Jarman."

"Well I don't expect I'll probably put it as baldly as that."

"She certainly hasn't made any secret of her affair with him."

"I don't understand that. Wouldn't she be embarrassed to confess having an affair with a professor?"

"It's just the opposite, Axel. This is her moment of glory. Does Deirdre strike you as an exceptional student?"

"Not particularly."

"Has she ever expressed any ambitions?"

"Not to me."

"What Deirdre has going for her, aside from that extraordinary body, is a gift for taking advantage of situations?"

"How do you know all this?"

"She's been taking my modern lit course."

"Isn't that pretty challenging?"

"No, Deirdre's the challenging one. She's actually read the documents that the Founding Fathers put out."

"And?"

"When I announced that there was going to be a term paper, she asked whether she could put on a skit instead."

"That sounds pretty irregular."

"That's what I told her. Then she showed me some obscure regulation about alternative forms of assessment for students in special situations."

"What's her special situation, aside from not wanting to write the term paper?"

"She claims to have an identified learning disability."

"Did you make her produce documentation?"

"Heck, no. I don't really care if she writes a term paper or not. I figure the skit might even be entertaining. Perhaps she'll do a dramatization of her interview in *The Bowser*."

"So you think she might have killed Jarman?"

"I can't tell you that, but I know she can create opportunities when she needs to."

As we walked to our respective cars I tried to imagine how I might broach the subject with Deirdre.

CHAPTER 7

Two-hour rehearsals for the College Choir took place three afternoons a week in the all-purpose rehearsal room. Levels of risers had been arranged against three walls so that the conductor looked up at tiers of singers or instrumentalists. We didn't have enough singers to go beyond the second level, but I was impressed with the ingenuity of the arrangement.

Since September the choir had been working on the Christmas program, which included Gregorian chant and a Charpentier oratorio (both in Latin), two carols (in French), and cantatas by Buxtehude, Lübeck and Bach (all in German): not one word of English. In retrospect, I see that the Founding Fathers didn't have a monopoly on insensitivity to local needs. On the other hand, they'd been operating the college that way for years and this was just my first experience at the place.

The choir exec met after the rehearsal, drawing chairs into a circle on the lower level of the rehearsal room to talk about the Christmas concert. For concert dress the executive committee had decided in principle on long-sleeved Renaissance-style shirts for the guys and long blue gowns for the girls. Now it was a matter of selecting a specific design and fabric. Deirdre volunteered to form a committee of singers to choose an official choir costume. Then Sheri Kimball asked about printed programs.

"Last year I took care of typing the programs and getting them printed. I'd be happy to do that again."

"That's great," I said, "but I'd like to be sure that the audience has English translations of the texts we're singing. Why don't I type that part and we'll stick it in as an insert."

"That okay," Sheri said, "but I had a question. Should we list the names of the soloists?"

"I think it's important to have the soloists' names in the program," said Doris Hayes, the soprano soloist.

"I agree," said Jackie Basinger, the alto soloist.

"But what about the names of the officers?" Sheri asked.

"We should list those, too," said Doris, who was also secretary of the chorus.

"Definitely. Be sure to list the officers," said Jackie, who was also president of the chorus. Since nobody else had a strong opinion one way or another, the names of soloists and officers went into the program.

When the meeting adjourned, I asked Deirdre if she'd stay behind for a few moments. She called to several of the others that she'd catch up with them at the student union, then turned and looked at me expectantly. Those wide eyes, the long hair, that amazing figure, emphasized in a T-shirt that read "Make Love" on one side and "Not War" on the other: I could see why Grant Jarman found her attention appealing.

"Thanks for offering to take care of the choir gown," I began.

"That's all right," Deirdre responded.

"I haven't had a chance to talk with you since you gave that interview to *The Bowser*." Deirdre looked at me a bit warily, as if uncertain how I felt about the whole thing. "I was particularly interested in Grant's poem. Part of it seemed to refer to you."

"' she glides/Into my musings, with a mild/And healing sympathy,'" Deirdre smiled as she quoted. "Wasn't that nice of him?" She looked as if she were still basking in the warmth of public attention.

"But then I was puzzled by the signs the next day that said Grant hadn't written the poem."

"You didn't believe that, did you?" she said ingenuously. "Who else could have written lines like that?"

"I wasn't thinking so much about the message as the medium: those stenciled letters. I didn't know anybody still used stencils. All the rest of the signs I've seen around here look as if they've been produced with stick-on type."

"I guess," Deirdre said uncertainly.

"I don't suppose you received a note with stenciled letters?"

Deirdre turned pale and her mouth dropped. Then she recovered herself and asked, "How could you possibly have known that?" She thought a moment then demanded, "You haven't been talking to my roommate, have you?"

"No. It was just a guess. I don't know what was written in the note, but I was hoping you'd be willing to tell me."

Deirdre hesitated briefly then gave in to a rush of emotions at the memory that message. "It said 'GJ thinks you're a bimbo.'"

"Did that seem likely to you?"

"At first I didn't believe it, but when I accused Grant I was amazed that he actually admitted it."

"Why did that surprise you?"

"Well, it's not the sort of thing you're going to tell a girl, is it? I was expecting him to try to weasel out of it the way he always does. But I think he thought that I'd actually talked to the person he'd talked to. He must have decided there was no point in trying to lie to me if I really had the goods on him."

"And how did you feel about that?"

"At first I was just hurt, but later I felt ready to kill him. Here he'd been claiming that I was his muse when all he really cared about was balling me!" The ingénue had suddenly turned into savvy young woman.

"Did you kill him?"

"Come on. How could I have done that?"

"What were you doing that afternoon?"

"I was getting my psych term paper photocopied. Sheri saw me leave and come back." Deirdre had evidently prepared a response in advance.

"It's not my business to ask this kind of question, but don't be surprised if the police eventually ask you for an alibi."

"The police!"

"They'll think you had a motive, and they'll probably figure that you could have photocopied the term paper the day before, then used the time to get over to Grant's house and back before his wife came home."

"That's not my style. If I'd had something handy, I would have bashed Grant over the head right away. If you want something, go for it: that's my motto." Everything I knew about Deirdre so far suggested a strong loyalty to that principle.

I let Deirdre join her friends while I tried to decide whether she was really as dumb as she pretended to be. Then my thoughts were interrupted by a telephone call from Melissa Jarman.

CHAPTER 8

"This is fun," Melissa said as we hugged under the covers after making love at my apartment. I wasn't used to looking around my bedroom. Ordinarily I just fell into bed at the end of an exhausting day. Now, with Melissa in my arms, I cast my eyes about the white walls, white bureau and white framed mirror, contrasting with the blue comforter on the bed and the 20"x30" framed photographs I had mounted on the walls. California had made such an impression on me that I felt the need to hold on to favorite bits: a cactus plant in Joshua Tree National Monument, the Golden Gate Bridge photographed from an unusual angle, the green hue of the ocean viewed from the Pacific Coast Highway near Big Sur, the mountains behind the campus on a rare clear day. The scenes reminded me that California contained great beauty in addition to all the frustrations I'd been experiencing.

"It feels a little like being a teenager hiding from parents," she continued, "but better than that, I guess because we know more."

"More about hiding or more about making love?" I asked.

"Oh, you!" she laughed, and threw a pillow at me. "Tell me about your week," she said, "and then we'll do this again."

"Okay. After the choir rehearsal Thursday, I asked whether there was anyone who wouldn't be coming back next term. I figured I might have a couple of spots to fill and thought it would help if I had some advance warning."

"What happened?"

"Fifteen out of nineteen said they didn't want to sing with me anymore."

"Sounds like a vote of no confidence. What did you do?"

"I just finished the rehearsal then went to Darryl for advice."

"He's kind of taught you the ropes around here, hasn't he?"

"It helps that he came from the East, too. For example, he once said that at faculty parties back home, people would make a play for each other's spouses, but at the end of the evening, everyone would go home with the right person. Whereas in California, he told me, there are just no limits. You flirt with someone at a party and next thing you know you're meeting them outside the Alpha Beta for a tryst."

"Not exactly the way we got together, was it?" Melissa said with a smile.

"Darryl said he'd talk to the kids. Seems as if one of my problems was working the singers too hard. I'd just start a rehearsal at full speed and keep on going for two hours."

"Didn't anyone ever teach you about pacing?" she asked.

"Performance practice, technical skills, ear training, instrumentalists, early music, making editions, program planning—but pacing? Guess I missed that."

"So what are you going to do?"

"We changed the schedule so that instead of having two-hour rehearsals after school, we'd have fifty-minute rehearsals during the day. And I promised to adopt a more relaxed rehearsal style, so it looks as if we've weathered the storm."

"What about your other group, the Madrigal Singers?"

"Their program is coming along pretty well, although we lost one of our key sopranos due to bronchitis, laryngitis, an aged parent and a delinquent teenage son. I've noticed that troubles never come one at a time around here."

"What kind of singers do you get here, anyway?"

"Ah, let me tell you about the singers we don't get. During the last couple of weeks I've been visiting early morning choir rehearsals at a number of high schools in the valley. After a rehearsal of one *a cappella* choir I stayed on to hear the girl's choir rehearse. This was a select group of thirty-six, you understand. They were working on their procession, and as each singer passed by I could hear the individual voices—all pure and accurate. They began in two rows on opposite sides of the gym singing 'Angels We Have Heard on High' in four parts in perfect coordination despite the distance separating the two groups."

"That must have taken a lot of practice."

"You have no idea. Later they performed the 'Carol of the Bells.' You tend to forget just how active energetic teenagers can be. There was so much pulsating, rhythmic movement that I had the impression of a gale force wind sweeping through the choir, threatening to drive the singers off the risers."

"I take it your singers perform without accompaniment from a tempest?"

"Nary a breeze," I said.

"What do you do for accompaniment, anyway?" Melissa asked. "Does someone play the piano for you?"

"I advertised for an accompanist in *The Bowser* and put up a large poster outside the music office."

"Any takers?"

"One sweet little old lady came to inquire, so I took her across the hall to one of the practice rooms and placed a score in front of her. 'Where's the piano reduction?' she demanded. 'There isn't one,' I explained. 'Then how can you play all four lines at once?' she asked."

"Seems like a reasonable question," Melissa said.

"'Some people play the soprano and alto with the right hand and follow the lines with their right eye, while playing the tenor and bass lines with their left hand and following with their left eye,' I suggested. 'But how does this tenor line fit in? Doesn't it get in the way of the upper two?' she wanted to know. 'You have to transpose the tenor line down an octave,' I replied. She looked at me incredulously. 'That's impossible.' 'I know,' I agreed, 'but somebody has to do it.'"

"You're just making this up," Melissa protested.

"Swear to God," I said. "I reckon I'll have to keep on being my own accompanist until we can find someone who can read from score."

"But the singers—it sounds as if your students aren't any better than what we get at the community college."

"I don't know what it's like for other departments," I said, "but most of the music students have transferred from the local junior college." I leaned up on one elbow and looked down at Melissa's merry eyes. "They live with their parents or in trailers on the edge of town, hold part-time jobs as manager of the local Burger King and regard the few hours they spend at CSC as just one more stop in their day, usually not the most important stop. But it's a comfortable way of life and a chance to see their friends as long as they don't graduate. There's no pressure to complete their studies, since after achieving their B.A. they'll still be working as manager of the Burger King. If they come too close to graduating, they just drop their courses— you wouldn't believe the dropout rate just before exams—or change majors. Since the state system is practically free, they can be students as long as they like."

"Haven't you gotten awfully cynical in one term?"

"I'm just totally amazed at the way the system operates."

"Let's see if we can't get your system operating again," Melissa said with a wicked grin as she reached for me under the covers. Enough time playing with Melissa and I'd forget all about the inanities of Chihuahua State.

CHAPTER 9

Cal State Chihuahua, like the rest of the state college system, operated on a central purchasing system designed to reduce costs. When the music department put in an order for a Steinway piano, the central purchasing system checked current specifications—88 keys, three pedals, wooden lid— against those used in acquiring an instrument for, say, the State Rehabilitation Center recreation room, asked for bids, then sent us a Kawai.

Eager to maintain my career as a pianist, I inquired of dealers in the area whether it was possible to rent a grand piano. "Not in Southern California," I was told. "The population is so mobile that people just disappear with them." (I enjoyed imagining midnight departures. "I've loaded the piano into the pickup, Sid; let's make tracks.")

So I chose to purchase a five-foot, two-inch Yamaha grand piano, scaled after the renowned Bechstein piano, combining a full resonant sound with a stiff even touch. It was the first time in my life I'd ever purchased anything on credit, and as I signed the necessary papers I observed that the piano cost almost exactly the same as a Volkswagen Beetle, the official car of the city of Chihuahua.

Along with the piano came a descriptive pamphlet, "All About Yamaha Piano," that included the following useful information: "A piano is an object of distinction in any home. It also has a valuable educational function. For the young girl it is an expression for her dreams. With tenderness she caresses each key to tell of the man she loves. For her whose love is lost, its vibrating strings spell out the sadness in her heart, the gentle regrets, and the melody that once was his." Clearly not an instrument for practising scales.

My office at CSC was in a trailer right behind the library. In contrast to the practice rooms, the faculty offices were superbly equipped: Thorens Turntable, Dynaco Stereo preamp and amplifier, KLH Model 17 speakers, Sony TC 355 tapedeck (called a "tapecorder" rather than a "tape recorder," presumably to let you know that you were getting the original, not some cheap imitation), Superex Professional Headphones, and a horrendous Baldwin spinet piano. To make the place a little bit homier, I added a day-bed, a long columnar lamp, and a mobile that I'd bought on an excursion to San Francisco. But in these innocent times it was never necessary to lock the door.

Other employees in the state system weren't so fortunate. Three office typewriters were removed from the local high school and placed in a warehouse when it was discovered that according to state-aid calculations the school was entitled to only nine typewriters. They could keep their twelve secretaries but only nine of them could have typewriters. The State of California giveth and the State of California taketh away.

On the first Monday in December President Hopkins assembled the faculty in the Faculty Assembly Room, not, as the name might have suggested, a lounge where teachers could gather for conversation and perhaps refreshments, but a formal hall that would not have been out of place in the United Nations building. A round table at the lowest level served as the focal point for high-backed chairs arranged in a series of successively higher concentric circles. Banners emblazoned with the emblems of the college, the state college system and the sovereign state of California extended from ceiling to floor around the chamber. The room had been elaborately soundproofed so that so that conversational tones could be heard only a few inches away and even a shout would not carry across the hall. To compensate for the dead acoustics microphones had been installed at every chair. I leaned over to ask Wayne why the room had been arranged this way. "Think about it, Axel," he responded. "If you need a microphone to make yourself heard, and the administration controls the microphones, nothing can ever get out of hand."

President Hopkins asked us to listen to some important announcements from the chancellor, which he helpfully numbered for us:

1. The 5% cost of living salary increases—approved for all other state employees—had been rescinded for teachers in the California college system. The state legislators considered the toleration of anti-war protests to show a lack of discipline on the part of the teachers. "If those pointy-headed intellectuals can't keep the campuses in order, they won't get any more money," was the clear message.

2. Starting immediately, each state college employee must certify in writing that he had met all of his responsibilities during the month past in order to collect his pay check.

3. The budgets of all the colleges had been cut. This naturally led each department to spend all the money in its budget right away lest there be further cuts.

4. There was to be no experimentation with grading procedures while the chancellor and the Board of Trustees decided on a unified grading system for the entire state college system.

5. The grievance procedure had been changed so that instead of a faculty committee from the state faculty senate having final say, the chancellor

had final say. This came about as a result of an incident last spring when the chancellor tried to dump some professor and the faculty committee ruled that proper grievance procedures had not been followed. The chancellor, with the aid of the state assembly, simply turned the faculty committee into an "advisory panel." The same principle could be observed in the workings of the Nixon administration. During this period, the L.A. Times displayed the headline, "ABA Scores High Court Nominees," followed the next morning by "Mitchell Ends ABA Screening of Supreme Court Candidates."

6. There had been a cut in funding for sabbatical and creative research leaves. According to college publications, every faculty member was eligible for a sabbatical at the end of six years, but the catch was in the word "eligible." In fact, there was funding for only one sabbatical leave each year at Cal State Chihuahua, where the faculty numbered 150 and was increasing.

7. We now had computer time with a tie-in on the big mainframe in Los Angeles. At least we would have computer time once they worked the bugs out of the system. It seems they had purchased the computer software on a low-bid basis, with the usual results.

8. The chancellor of the state college system, Glenn Butkus, had cancelled a convocation on the Indochina War to have been held at Sacramento State College. There were to have been speakers representing a variety of viewpoints followed by a poll of participants on some position statement. The chancellor, justifying his action, explained that he had cancelled the event in order to preserve academic freedom. If a scholar takes sides on an issue, the chancellor explained, he ceases to be a scholar.

"Can you imagine where we'd be without the chancellor to save us from ourselves?" Wayne Tutworthy whispered to me. After the meeting a professor from the math department proposed Butt-Kiss's Paradox: you could continue to lose half your academic freedom indefinitely, but you could never lose it all because you would always have one-half of the last increment.

Not to be left out, President Hopkins had a policy statement of his own to announce: henceforth "The Green," the area north of the present library and northwest of the administration building/athletic complex, would be the official Free Speech Area of the College, the Student Affairs Committee having voted to change the former Free Speech Area to a table area.

"The administration as usual doing its part to keep our First Amendment rights safely circumscribed," my colleague Charlie Purcell observed. We went home to read in the Los Angeles Times that the president of each college in the system must submit to the chancellor a quarterly list of all outside speakers brought onto the campus, along with the topics of their addresses and how much they were paid, so that a "balanced presentation" might prevail.

Someone transmitted the announcements to Jerome Chowning and the following day *The Bowser* announced, "Chancellor Slaps Wrists of Permissive Professors." In an editorial Chowning exhorted his fellow students to get off their asses and get themselves arrested, like their outspoken colleagues to the North. CSC students seemed too laid back or ill-informed to get involved in the anti-war movement sweeping the rest of the country's campuses.

I spent the night with Melissa, who helped me put aside visions of a bleak future at Chihuahua State. "Have you made any progress deciphering Grant's poem?" she asked me during one interlude. In an adventurous moment she had bought black silk sheets for her bed and added tiny accent lamps around the room. The effect was rather theatrical, so that I almost felt like a detective in a Victorian melodrama rather than an underpaid college professor trying to get a friend off the hook.

"I'm interested in the person who claimed Grant didn't write it," I said.

"But we all know that," Melissa said.

"No, I mean the person who posted the stencilled signs around campus. It turns out you weren't the only person to get a note written that way. Deirdre got one, too."

"Oh, her," Melissa said flatly.

"Hers didn't have a heart the way yours did," I continued. "Hers read 'JG thinks you're a bimbo.'"

Melissa brightened at these words. "Maybe Grant had some taste, after all. How did the bimbo respond to this news?"

"She didn't take it well. In fact, she said she wanted to kill him."

"Well, there you go," Melissa said.

"But you know these California girls: instant gratification takes too long. Deirdre said she would have bashed him on the head with whatever came to hand, but it appears that setting up a fake suicide would have required too much patience."

"And you believed that?"

"Well ..."

"Honestly, Axel, I sometimes wonder whether it's you personally or men in general."

"How do you mean?"

"You seem so willing to accept what women tell you."

"But ..."

"I guess you're just used to talking with other men. And you and I have been pretty straightforward with each other."

"I'm grateful for that."

"But when it comes to doing battle, a woman's arsenal has a lot more variety than a man's."

"Including the art of deception, I take it?"

"You're the most transparent person I've ever met, Axel."

"Is that good or bad?" I asked.

"You tell people what you think. It doesn't matter whether I think it's good or bad. I'm just saying that you tend to assume that other people are the same way, and let me tell you, they're not!"

"I guess I see what you mean."

"But even you wouldn't say you trusted Deirdre, would you?"

"No, I haven't been able to figure her out yet."

"There's not much to figure out, Axel. That girl's mind is totally in the service of her body."

We left off further talk of minds and devoted our efforts to the service of our own bodies.

CHAPTER 10

"Sorry I couldn't make the Christmas concert," Wayne said when we met for our weekly handball session. "How did it go?"

"Surprisingly well, all things considered," I said, "but I'm going to have to do something about Deirdre."

"What's the problem?"

"You know when someone's singing a solo, the rest of the choir is supposed to maintain a neutral pose, to keep from distracting the audience."

"That makes sense."

"Well Deirdre, when someone's singing a solo, listens attentively."

"What's wrong with that?"

"Sometimes she gives the impression that she's putting more energy into listening than the soloist is into singing. Pretty soon everyone in the audience is watching Deirdre listen."

"Sounds as if that's just what she wants."

Wayne set the ball in motion for our first game. While southern California didn't have the dramatic changes in season that I was accustomed to, the shortening of days in December made a perceptible difference in the way light entered the court through the windows near the ceiling. Now fluorescent bulbs provided the major illumination for our game. We finished one game, then another, then took a break, but my mind was still on the choir concert.

"Did I tell you about the choir gown?" I asked Wayne.

"This is the one that Deirdre picked out?"

"That's right. You know what Deirdre looks like. The design she chose looks stunning on her and a few of the others but a lot of girls are unhappy with the way it makes them look."

"But does she sing all right?"

"No problems there, but I do spend a lot of time answering her questions."

"How do you mean?"

I tried to imitate Deirdre's breathy manner. "Oh Mr. Crochet: should the "e" in "Domine" be pronounced "eh" or "ay"? Oh Mr. Crochet: where do you want us to put the cut-off? And could you play that passage on the piano? I'm having trouble getting the intervals."

"She sounds like a pretty high maintenance soprano."

"But the Christmas concert wasn't the biggest musical event of the week. Monday we invited high school students and teachers from all over the area for the First Annual High School Day at Chihuahua State College."

"And they came?"

"In droves. We gave them a tour of the electronic studio, showed them the view from the top of the tower, and offered them up a potpourri of instrumental, choral and solo music and a free lunch."

"So maybe they'll decide CSC isn't such a bad place after all ..."

"And next year when I hold choir auditions instead of twenty I'll have a hundred ... "

"And David his ten thousands ... "

"In saecula saeculorum amen."

"As good as that, huh?" Wayne asked.

"The Opera Workshop outdid itself with a scene from 'Madame Butterfly,' complete with costumes and a simple set. After the concert the chairman rushed back to the music room next to his office and banged discords on the piano. The chairman doesn't like Puccini."

"It sounds like a great success."

"We had to do something. Did I tell you about Butt-Kiss's latest?"

"What's that?"

"There's a new policy for instrumental lessons. Up to now, when someone wanted to learn oboe, say, he would study with me or with Charlie or with Darryl, who would be paid extra for this added teaching duty. The state assemblymen, who keep a close watch over the state college system without understanding it very well, decided that this constitutes moonlighting. So a directive came from the chancellor's office ordering that no student could be required to pay for private lessons in order to meet applied music requirements, and that all teachers must be regular members of the staff who would simply take on instrumental lessons as part of their regular duties.

"So who's going to pay for all the additional teachers?"

"That's the whole point: the chancellor isn't offering any more money to fund the program. Cal State Los Angeles just abolished its entire applied music program."

"What are you going to do here?"

"It's a real problem. If we decide to abolish applied music, we'll be doing a disservice to prospective education majors, which make up most of our students, while playing into the hands of the Founding Fathers, who can't see why you should have applied music in the first place."

"I can just hear Stanley Hopkins now: 'The purpose of the music department is to train music historians and scholars. This isn't a conservatory.'"

"These guys just can't believe that the kind of student coming to CSC is simply not the same as that entering Swarthmore or Michigan State or UCLA or whatever." I suppose my frustration carried over in my voice.

"I don't imagine things will be any different now that Maxwell Kent has taken over as Dean of Arts & Sciences."

"I've never heard him express any great enthusiasm for music."

"What do you think? Did he kill Grant Jarman to get the job?"

"I don't know. You'd think the police would have solved the case by now. I imagine they've worked out the timing of the murder and finished checking alibis."

"If there were fingerprints or some other physical evidence, there probably would have been an arrest. My guess is that they're stumped."

I had held my own for the first two games but perhaps I was tired out by the concerts, because Wayne whipped me handily in the third. As we left the athletic complex Wayne said, "You know, I'm still bothered by that poem. Whoever wrote it linked Jarman and Kent in that 'deadly sport.'"

"It's an interesting point. Aside from suicide itself, that's the only reference to violent death in the poem. Perhaps we should tip off the police."

"On a note with stencilled letters." We laughed and headed for our separate cars in the parking lot.

I found Chihuahuan Christmas to be a pretty dispiriting affair. Homeowners in the development where I lived unanimously decorated their tract houses with rows of Christmas lights outlining the lower rooflines, transforming the area into one gigantic used-car lot.

When I asked the madrigal singers whether they'd be interested in going carolling, they gave me a mystified look. Finally Doris Hayes raised her hand. "You mean going from house to house singing carols, like the pictures on Christmas cards?"

"That's more or less the idea," I said.

"But don't you need snow for that?" asked Jackie Basinger.

Finally someone showed a spark of imagination. "There's snow in the mountains," said Jerome Chowning, who had joined the group late in the fall. "We could go up there."

Other singers began to find the idea appealing, so one evening we all drove up to Crestline to sing carols in the snow, and everyone had a fine time except for Jerome, our resident pothead, who nearly had a heart attack when he realized that one of the houses we visited belonged to the county sheriff. Afterwards we returned to my house for a potluck supper and more singing, and at long last I was able to feel a bit of Christmas spirit, although I still found the sight of palm trees unnerving.

I flew back East to visit family over the Christmas holidays and welcomed the opportunity to put everything Chihuahuan, whether music students or murdered colleagues, out of mind for a couple of weeks.

CHAPTER 11

Wayne Tutworthy and I resumed our weekly handball game after the Christmas break. Invigorated by the vacation, we put a lot of energy into the first game, and as we leaned against the walls of the court catching our breath Wayne said, "Did you hear about the poetry festival that Paula Rogers has organized."

"I think I saw a poster somewhere. What's happening?"

"I'm not sure. Evidently instead of going through the chancellor's office she's just gotten in touch with a number of her friends in other state colleges and asked them to come read their work. Francis gave her a bunch of money to cover expenses: evidently he feels that the suicide of his star teacher is putting the English department in a bad light."

"Or murder."

"Even worse."

"So what are they calling it: the Association of Spinster Poets?"

"Something like that. But the event seems to be more than Paula can handle by herself. I don't think she really thought through what was involved in putting on a festival."

"Surely her colleagues are willing to help."

"She won't accept any assistance from us. She seems to have the idea that we don't take her seriously."

"Imagine that."

"But she does have a groupie, Dale Cochrane, who's volunteered to organize a session of student poets."

"I'm pretty sure they won't be reading anything by Maxwell Kent?"

"Why do you say that?"

"After our conversation before Christmas, I visited the archives of *The Bowser*, to see if I could find any more information about him. I had an interesting conversation with Jerome Chowning, too. He acts as if he's perpetually stoned, and maybe he is for all I know, but he really does take the newspaper seriously. He set up the Bowser Annals and persuaded some computer geek to create an index, so it was pretty easy to find the poem that Maxwell Kent composed for the retirement party when Greg Peabody left here two years ago."

"A modest effort?"

"Well the newspaper article made it sound as if Kent thought of himself as something of a bard."

"Did they have the poem?"

"Indeed they did."

"And I suppose you made a copy of the magnum opus."

I pulled out the small sheet of paper that I'd stashed in my gym shorts and recited:

Gregory Peabody, known for his pendulum,
Refraction gratings and tests for "Big G,"
Einstein would smile at a fellow cosmologist,
Grinding his lenses assiduously,
O for a smog-free night in December, when
Rugged astronomer peers into heaven, and
You can be sure that the coming of asteroids,
Predicted by our ingenious Peabody,
Enter earth's atmosphere, glowing like fireflies,
Attracted by gravity, preoccupation of
Bearded professor intent on a mission
Or drawn to the stars by an inner obsession,
Devoted to teaching astronomy
Yet, a regular guy whom we all call GP.

"It doesn't always scan, does it," Wayne observed, "but I detected an actual simile. Who would have thought of describing asteroids as fireflies?"

"Was that supposed to be a sexual reference in the first line: 'known for his pendulum?'"

"No, there really is a pendulum. I'll show it to you when we leave. Peabody insisted on having a Foucault pendulum installed in the atrium of this building, and I have to admit it does lend a touch of class to the place."

"You may not have caught it when I read the poem aloud, but the first letters of each line spell out the name G-R-E-G-O-R-Y P-E-A-B-O-D-Y."

"Aha—an acrostic! Our friend Maxwell is a clever gent."

"But not much of a poet."

"I don't think Paula would think too highly of his efforts." Wayne put the ball back into play and I began to weave a pattern of shots, gradually trying to get the ball beyond his reach rather than looking for an immediate put-away shot. "Have you been practicing or something?" Wayne asked at the end of the game.

"No, but I think over the break I finally assimilated a bunch of the things you've taught me. I have a good teacher."

"Something else has been bothering me about that poem."

"What's that?"

"You keep looking at people mentioned in the suicide poem as suspects, but why would the murderer mention himself in the poem?"

"For that matter, why have a poem at all?"

"That part's clear: the murder was supposed to look like a suicide, and the murderer figured that an English professor and novelist would leave a literary note."

"Right. Now why bother mentioning names? Why not just a flowery poem saying, in effect, 'To hell with it all'?"

"I suppose to generate suspicion in several different directions."

"Right again. Now it doesn't take a genius to come up with a list of possible suspects. What happens if you write a poem and mention everybody except yourself? Doesn't that make you even more obvious?"

"I guess I see your point," Wayne admitted. "It seems like a peculiar way of going about a murder investigation, but so far traditional police methods haven't gotten much further."

When we resumed play, the rubber ball, rebounding off walls and floor, almost seemed to defy gravity, and I recollected why I enjoyed this sport so much: all the exertion and calorie-burning of tennis in about one-third the time. Deirdre – Maxwell – Melissa – Wayne: the names bounced around in my mind and I had a sudden vision of Grant Jarman himself standing in the middle of the handball court as little balls with faces on them caromed off the walls toward him. One of the balls had struck him a lethal blow, but which one?

CHAPTER 12

My teaching schedule prevented me from attending the morning ses-
sions of Paula's poetry festival but as I walked past the English department
classrooms late in the afternoon I felt an atmosphere of intensity despite a
very low attendance. Serious ladies in tweed suits read their poetry, or
criticism of other poet's works, in near-empty rooms. But either Paula or
Dale had done a fine job with the preparations. Each room had a sign on
the door announcing the name and institutional affiliation of the speaker
along with the title of the presentation, and English majors wearing arm
bands stood around ready to help visitors find their way.

"I didn't know you were interested in poetry, Professor Crochet," said a
familiar voice from behind me. It was Sheri Kimball, looking for all the
world like a lollipop, with brightly-colored tights, her trademark short skirt,
and a pastel sweater.

"What, you think musicians don't read?" I asked in mock reproach.

"I didn't mean that, exactly."

"Where do you think the texts come from that you sing in the choir?"

"I hadn't thought about it."

"And what about the song that Doris sang at the last noon recital?"

"You mean 'Drink to me only with thine eyes'?"

"Sure. The melody is a British folk song but the words are by Ben Jonson, one of the finest English poets of the seventeenth century."

"I guess." Sheri's eyes began to glaze over. "You're going to come tonight, aren't you?"

"You mean to hear Deirdre's poem? Yes. She asked me to come, and I'll
be there."

"Then I guess I'll see you later." Sheri wandered off to join a group of
friends, and I found my way to a presentation on "T. S. Eliot: A Poet for
Our Times?"

Friday evening, the student poetry session, was another matter entirely.
The room assigned to the reading proved altogether inadequate for the
crowd. Dale Cochrane, evidently acting on her own responsibility, since I
didn't see Paula Rogers anywhere in attendance, changed the venue to the
ballroom in the student center, and I joined the throng of mostly young
people headed in that direction.

Though the name summoned up images of cotillions and formal proms,
the ballroom had in fact seen nothing more elegant than rock concerts and
discotheques. The circular room had walls made of floor-to-ceiling panels

alternating between glass and California redwood, giving the impression of a gigantic zoetrope that, if set spinning, would produce stroboscopic images.

Several student poets offered predictable treatments of adolescent love, the joys of marijuana, the death of a beloved dog and the metaphoric qualities of butterflies. How had this event attracted so many people? Whenever the student literary magazine came out, copies mostly sat in stacks around the campus, unread by any except its contributors. Then I thought about why I was there—Deirdre O'Donahue had asked me to come. Did she really have that many friends?

A buzz of anticipation went around the room when she finally approached the microphone. This was clearly the event everyone had been waiting for. Deirdre gave a good imitation of a shy smile—I was beginning to realize just how much of this girl's presentation was a carefully calculated act—and began her poem. "Grant and Me," she announced breathily into the microphone and a murmur of approval came back from the audience. She took a breath and then began reading her poem in a tone of confidentiality, as if sharing a passage from her diary with her roommate.

When he put his arms around me
It felt like nothing bad could ever happen.
The minute our lips touched
I started to get excited.
Pointing to my breast I said,
Touch me there, and he did,
And oh, it was nice.
I was really getting hot
So I took off my skirt,
Pointing between my legs I said,
Touch me there, and he did,
And oh, it was nice.
So I slid off my panties and pointed again,
And I didn't even need to say
Touch me there, because he did,
And oh, it was more than nice,
It was fireworks and candy and
Chocolate syrup and I made him
Lick me there until I came
And nobody will ever do it better.

When Deirdre finished there was a stunned silence for a few seconds, then applause and shouts of approval. Eventually she had to read the thing again, after which there was even more applause. When Deirdre left the room virtually everyone followed. As the crowd streamed past me I felt a hand squeeze my arm and heard Sheri Kimball say, "Wasn't she wonderful?" before she disappeared into the crowd. A mere handful of hard-core poetry enthusiasts remained to listen to the students who had the misfortune of being scheduled after Deirdre on the program.

The next morning, the lead story in *The Bowser* bore the headline, "'Grant And Me' Hit Of Poetry Festival," accompanied by a photograph of Deirdre not, as one might have expected, standing at a microphone, but dressed in a negligee leaning against the post of her bed. The clever girl had obviously seized the opportunity of the ASP poetry festival and turned it to her carefully orchestrated advantage. What a terrific publicist she would make! But for the time being, it seemed that she was using her considerable skills in the service of a single client.

As I crossed the campus at lunchtime I ran into Dale Cochrane, who gave me a look that I had difficulty interpreting. Was it anger, or fear? I could imagine Dale being upset with Deirdre for making a mockery of her favorite professor's project, but what did that have to do with me? I decided that since Deirdre sang in my choir, Dale somehow figured that I had allied myself with the enemy. I shrugged off the baleful look and went on my way.

That evening with Melissa I wasn't sure how much of the previous day's events I could comfortably discuss with her. After all, it had been her late husband and his student lover that had engendered the most memorable event in the poetry festival. But she had already seen the photograph in *The Bowser* and seemed more titillated than perturbed by the whole situation.

"So what do you think, Axel?" Melissa asked when we were comfortably seated on her sofa. "Could you have resisted the charms of the formidable Miss O'Donahue? Or does she prefer 'Ms'?"

"To tell the truth, I've never had to worry about resisting the advances of students."

"You mean you always yield to temptation?"

"No, I mean temptation doesn't often present itself."

"All the better for me, I guess," she said as she snuggled into my arms. "Now tell me about this poem."

"You mean Deirdre's poem." I was beginning to feel a bit uneasy.

"It's all right. I'm finished being angry with Grant. We weren't even sleeping in the same bed by the time that trollop came along."

"I take it your forgiveness doesn't extend to Deirdre."

"She's just so blatant. Do men really like that kind of thing?"

"I guess the men who hang nude calendars in auto repair shops aren't looking for a lot of subtlety in a relationship."

"Hell, Axel; they don't even use words like 'relationship.'"

"I suppose you're right."

"So I understand that the distinctive features of this poem didn't include worn-out clichés like rhyme or meter."

"It was also a little light on imagery or metaphor. But it did have a haunting refrain: 'I said Touch me there, and he did,/And oh, it was nice.'"

"You're joking. She said that in public?"

"It got pretty graphic."

"I think I need to hear more," Melissa whispered in my ear and began to nibble on my earlobe.

I ended up reciting as much as I could remember of the poem. Perhaps 'reciting' isn't the right word—more like 're-enacting,' with Melissa serving as a more than willing surrogate for the author.

"How was that?" Melissa asked when we finished, "And if you say 'More than nice' you'd better be prepared to protect your private parts." Under the circumstances I decided a non-verbal response to be the safest, so I led her into the bedroom for an anatomy lesson of my own devising.

CHAPTER 13

For the second term I had planned, and already purchased the scores for, a concert of music for double chorus and brass, yet we had scarcely one chorus. The obvious solution was to invent another, and so we created the Choral Society. In contrast to the College Chorus, this ensemble had an auspicious beginning. While only twelve people gave advance notice, twenty-one came to audition and twenty-six showed up for the first rehearsal, including a number of experienced singers and a few high school students from the Chihuahua area. The first week the group quickly covered all the ground that the College Chorus had traversed, then went on to begin new music.

At the second rehearsal of the Choral Society, singers came up to me complaining that their cars had been ticketed by the ever-vigilant college police. This seemed ridiculous, since the parking lots stood empty at night, but it turned out to be so. I checked with the police chief the next day. He explained that official state college policy required that anyone benefiting in any way from the college must pay for those benefits. It made no difference that the college profited from having a chorus. Nor did the college feel any sense of service toward the community. If you used our parking lot, even only once a week, you had to pay. We eventually worked out a compromise whereby I would supply the chorus members with slugs that they could use in the pay parking lot.

I was pleased that my friend Wayne Tutworthy saw fit to join the tenor section of the Choral Society, and when we got together for handball the following Wednesday, he expressed satisfaction at making music within a group. Then our conversation turned to the poetry festival. "I understand I missed quite a show Friday night," he said.

"Deirdre really outdid herself. It looks as if once having tasted the thrill of publicity, the girl doesn't want to let it go."

"Paula Rogers was furious. You know how she always felt underappreciated in comparison with Grant Jarman. This was supposed to be her moment in the sun, but the way Deirdre hijacked the affair, nobody is paying attention to Paula."

"But she had a chance to get together with all the other ASPers."

"That doesn't count. She was hoping for some real publicity, the kind of thing you get when you sell the movie rights for a book."

"I guess they don't make many movies about poetry."

"And technically she doesn't even have a book."

"Then how did she get to be an associate professor?" I asked.

"That's what I asked Francis Weatherington. He said it was different in the 60's. The college was new and they had trouble filling positions. Paula was not only a woman but also part of a minority."

"Which one is that?"

"She claims to be Croatian on her mother's side."

"And what about this book of poetry?"

"She refers to it every time you speak with her, but it never seems to get published."

"I'm supposed to have a visit from the Retention, Promotion and Tenure committee in two weeks. Didn't she have to go through that?"

"Nah. RPT didn't even exist until two years ago. As I say, it was different in the 60's. There was plenty of money, a shortage of teachers, and the dean had a pretty free hand with hiring and promotion."

"One thing's sure after Friday night."

"What's that?"

"Deirdre O'Donahue could never have written Grant's suicide poem."

"And you've eliminated Maxwell Kent on literary grounds," Wayne said.

"Either you or Melissa would have had the skill to write it, but I'm ruling both of you out."

"That's generous of you."

"So a literary approach doesn't seem to have led to a murderer."

"On the other hand, the police investigation hasn't led to any arrests either."

"But none of us believes that Grant himself wrapped 'the drapery of his couch about him and lay down to pleasant dreams.'"

"No, he definitely received assistance as he 'approached his grave.'"

The next morning the wind was blowing fiercely as I got dressed, so I put on a vest in addition to a coat and tie and donned my ski parka as I strode out into the January chill. Except this wasn't an eastern winter wind but a California Santa Ana. The wind speed approached forty miles an hour but the temperature was nearly seventy. I went back inside to change my clothes, hoping that the neighbors hadn't seen me making an idiot of myself once again and wondering whether I would ever get used to this strange place.

CHAPTER 14

Early in the fall I had looked around for a church where I might feel comfortable, not imagining how difficult such a quest might be. One Sunday I attended First Presbyterian Church, offering the sight of a modern, attractive building and the sound of an ancient pipe organ badly played. At the appointed hour a young minister—jet-black hair, deep tan, vaguely resembling Ronald Reagan—came on like the warm-up man for a TV show. "Good morning," he said in a resonant, carefully modulated voice, which emerged from concealed loudspeakers all around the church. He asked us to greet our neighbors in the pew, and for thirty seconds the air was filled with introductions and greetings. With the audience, that is, congregation relaxed he went into a preview of the Sermon Feedback, to be held after Coffee Hour (at First Congregational Church they called it the Iced Tea Hour). Then a Call to Worship, Prayer of Confession, and Assurance of Pardon, delivered with the reassuring confidence of an experienced group leader from the Esalen Institute.

They brought on a second minister for the Scripture Lesson, a friendly, white-haired, patriarchal gentleman who read with an exegetical voice of experience. After a wretched performance of a forgettable anthem "Let There Be Peace on Earth (And Let it Begin With Me)", the young minister crossed the chancel to the high pulpit.

The sermon, entitled "The Family and Leisure," while devoid of any message represented a brilliant use of the medium. No actor could have made a smoother, more appealing presentation. Twice during the sermon a third minister appeared on the opposite side of the stage, that is, chancel to inject some humor into the proceedings with a brief "Dear Diary" monologue, written from the point of view of a harried housewife. Presumably this was to avoid any sense of levity from spoiling the confident young counselor image of the smooth minister. The sermon concluded with a few more prayers, addressed in upbeat, colloquial language to an upbeat, colloquial God who wanted his flock to get more out of life. Then came a Charge, a Benediction, and a Congregation Response which enabled the ministers to recess to the narthex, shaking hands with all the parishioners who happened to be trapped in the aisle seats. (This apparently did not excuse them from shaking hands again at the door of the church.) I didn't return.

Then, not long before Christmas, I received a call from Francis Weatherington, chairman of the English department, one of the wardens of St. Peter's Episcopal Church, who explained that the church was in need of a music director, the incumbent having been so unhinged by the recent earthquake that he had announced his intention of leaving immediately after the holidays.

I invited the search committee to attend one of my rehearsals with the College Chorus, and after a successful interview I began my stint as organist and choirmaster on Epiphany Sunday. On the Wednesday after the Super Bowl, I reported my experiences to Wayne at our weekly handball game.

"The minister, Jeff Healy, is something of a jock," I began.

"I suppose you've been getting your fill of sports metaphors."

"Wait till you hear. Last week he began by saying 'Today is Super Sunday, and I imagine that most of us will hurry home after the service to watch Super Bowl VI.'"

"This is an Episcopal church you're talking about?"

"That's what the sign on the lawn says. Anyway, first he gave us a capsule history of football. Then he went into a discourse on the Great Football Game of Life. 'The Christian that can't take it shouldn't be in the line-up' he proclaimed from the pulpit. 'But we have a Quarterback who has never lost a game.'"

"You're putting me on!"

"Those were his exact words. My first Sunday there they had a dedication replacing the wooden cross with a new aluminium version. It seems the crucifer was having trouble carrying the old one. I'm having trouble getting used to Christianity California style."

As we headed toward the parking lot, Maxwell Kent emerged from the pool locker room, almost as if he'd been lying in wait for me. "Could I have a word with you, Crochet?" As I waved farewell to Wayne I wondered whether a reversion to last names was a concomitant to taking a job as dean. We stepped around the corner of the hallway to an alcove in sight of the outdoor "Free Speech" area. Kent gathered himself to his full height and arranged his face into a glare before continuing. "I understand that you've been asking questions about me." I made a gesture to indicate that I had no idea what he was talking about, but he barrelled ahead. "If I hear an inkling of any remark linking my name with the death of Grant Jarman, you will regret the day you ever came to CSC." Without waiting for a response, he turned on his heel and strode briskly around the corner.

Who had been talking with Maxwell, I wondered. Could he have had some contact with Jerome Chowning after my visit to the *Bowser* archives? Or had my friend Wayne been less trustworthy than I imagined? I didn't suppose that Kent had anything to do with Melissa, but I hadn't shared my thoughts with anyone else. Life around here seemed to be a confusing mixture of the ludicrous and the nasty. Perhaps the suicide poem had been right in describing academic life as a deadly sport.

CHAPTER 15

Toward the end of January, Wayne and I met again for handball. Although he was limping a bit after spraining his ankle in a ski accident, his unerring placement of shots kept me on the move and the score was pretty close when we finished our session and headed for the showers.

"How did your RPT visitation go?" Wayne asked.

"Pretty well, I thought. Your chairman was a member of the committee, along with someone I didn't recognize from the social sciences."

"Francis is chair not only of your committee but of the entire RPT committee."

"Does that mean he has a special interest in my case?"

"No. It's probably just the luck of the draw."

"None of them knew anything about music, they told me at the outset, but they were intrigued that anybody could hold the kids' interest in a subject as boring as species counterpoint."

"What did you do?"

"The students write counterpoint exercises every night, and the next day I put a Rogues Gallery of errors on the board, without identifying the composers, and let the class point out where they've made their mistakes. Actually I think the students are glad to have a situation where the rules are clear and you can actually decide whether a solution is right or wrong."

"So you think species counterpoint is an essential skill for the 'educated man'?"

I groaned at the phrase. An article in the Los Angeles Times, "College Innovations Proposed to Produce 'Educated Man,'" described the changes envisioned by the California State College system, formerly one of the finest educational enterprises in the world. Under the new system, comprehensive exams testing a broad grasp of an entire body of knowledge would largely replace the old system of piling up credits to win a degree.

One might suppose that this would encourage students to take more courses or organize their studies in a number of areas, the better to become "educated men." (It didn't say anything about "educated women"—this was still 1970). But that wasn't the idea. Students who elected courses in excess of the minimum required for a degree would be charged full costs. According to the article, "The chancellor estimates that state colleges could be collecting $10 to $15 million a year by 1974 from students who amass

too many credits or stray from their degree objective." The article continued:

> The state currently spends $1,520 a year on each student in the
> tuition-free state college system. So the student ad-
> judged to be an academic dilettante would have to pay
> whatever proportion of this is accounted for by his "un-
> necessary classes"—probably on a per-unit basis.

The chancellor also proposed to get more work out of the teaching staff.
Under the new plan:

> At the start of each academic term (the professor) would meet
> with each student to outline the area of knowledge the
> student was to cover and furnish specific help like a
> reading list As the term unfolded, the professor would
> spend much time in his office, available for consultation
> with his students. His other big assignment would be
> developing and administering the all-important exami-
> nations by which each student's progress would be
> measured.

So a faculty member might spend four hours teaching a class and eight
"adjusted hours" as tutor to dozens of students, each working "independ-
ently" to become an "educated man." Madness.

"But at least the chancellor backed down making us sign a loyalty oath in
order to receive our pay checks," I said. "I guess his lawyers told him it
would never stand up in court."

"But it did establish one interesting point?"

"What's that?"

"That state college professors are quite willing to perjure themselves for
money."

"So how is the enrolment limit policy going to affect you in English?" I
asked.

"We're supposed to reduce the number of students in the humanities
and social science since students in these areas are 'without clear career
goals.'"

"What does that mean?"

"It's just a code. It means students in those areas are more likely to be
troublemakers."

"So they've recruited the registrars into the campaign to contain free
speech."

"What bothers me even more is the proposal that the University of California sell its rare books (after photocopying them, of course) in order to raise money. The waters are rising, the ship is sinking, and the captain has lost his head."

"Who said that?"

"I did," Wayne replied.

"Nice turn of phrase," I said. "Maybe we should send it to *The Bowser*. Speaking of which, if the administration can confine all student discontent to the Free Speech Area, why haven't they clamped down on Jerome Chowning?"

"I was wondering when you'd ask that. A few years ago they tried. The editor at that time somehow found out that the contract for paving the north parking lot had gone to the dean's brother-in-law. One of the other bidders may have complained; I'm not sure. In any case, when *The Bowser* printed the story Jerry Siebel ordered all the copies seized."

"Sounds typical."

"But in this case a bad miscalculation. The editor's father was a lawyer who sued CSC. Of course the college threw its legal team into the fray, but the judge ruled that First Amendment protections extend to university publications."

"So the college backed down?"

"Not exactly. These guys really hate to lose. They discovered that the editor hadn't turned in an assignment for a chemistry course ..."

"Chemistry!"

"He had to take it to satisfy distributional requirements. Anyway, they declared that he wasn't in good standing and tried to get him expelled."

"How did that go over?"

"A terrific mistake. The lad's father was able to quote the college's own internal regulations against them, and the judge gave the vice-president a stern warning against frivolous dismissals when he forced them to reinstate the editor."

"Who I don't suppose was sitting quietly by the sidelines."

"No way. Throughout the process—and it took quite awhile to get it all settled—he kept publishing editorials lampooning the administration. He had the support of all the students and most of the faculty: the Founding Fathers ended up looking like fools."

"I don't suppose Maxwell Kent was the chemistry professor in question?"

"Ah, my friend, you're beginning to understand how this place works. It wasn't just ruthless ambition that got Kent the job as dean of Arts & Sciences: it was payback time for loyalty to the administration."

"But the newspaper isn't any more supportive than before?"

"No. Jerome Chowning has taken a keen pleasure in being a thorn in the administration's side, and so far nobody knows what to do about him, though if I were in his shoes I'd be a little more discreet with marijuana: it's still illegal even if everybody does it."

CHAPTER 16

Along with an athletic facility many times too large for the actual size of the college, CSC boasted an extremely well-equipped art department. There were pottery wheels in abundance and a state-of-the-art kiln, multiple darkrooms for photography, and spacious studios for painting and sculpture. The gallery included works by a number of California artists in addition to full-size reproductions of works by the Old Masters for teaching purposes. A small area was reserved for travelling exhibits and an annual display by members of the faculty and artists from the Chihuahua area.

The student art exhibition in early February might have passed without notice had it not been for an entry by Deirdre O'Donahue entitled simply "O." She had evidently enlarged a photograph, using either darkroom techniques or just a photocopier, until its original source had become quite unrecognizable. There did seem to be a vaguely circular quality to the image that might connect with its title, but beyond that one could tell nothing. But with her gift for self-promotion, Deirdre had spread the word that the "O" stood not for "O'Donahue," but for "orgasm" or "organ," and that the source belonged to the anatomy of Grant Jarman.

At that point, the actual image ceased to have any importance, though it seemed as if virtually every student at the college passed by the picture to render judgment or attempt to verify the rumor. Once again Deirdre had single-handedly turned an exhibition from a marginal event into major happening, with her contribution at the center.

The administration responded in typical fashion. Without ever bothering to inspect the picture in question they fulminated about the decline of culture, the negative effects of student art on the moral climate of the college, and the unfortunate consequences of allowing students too much freedom, culminating in a spectacularly ill-considered edict. Effective immediately, all representations of any part of the unclothed human anatomy were to be banned.

Jerome Chowning welcomed the announcement as a god-sent relief from a drought of newsworthy material and published a merciless mockery of the new policy, predicting the moral collapse that would surely result from a salacious display of elbows or the titillation of naked toenails. Half a dozen new entries were placed on display, including a rather ingenious photograph of a line of coeds, cropped to show only "Soft Shoulders," and a close-up photograph of the indentation at the base of the throat entitled "Manubrium." The most provocative entry was a close-up photo of a forearm, enlarged to the point that it could have been any part of the body, bearing the title, "Buttock."

The administration looked like a collection of fools, and Deirdre O'Donahue had again become a cause célèbre. I began to wonder whether I hadn't underestimated this young woman. I remained convinced that she could never have written Jarman's suicide poem, but she was good friends with Jerome Chowning, who probably could have managed the task for her. With Jarman alive, she had a lot to lose when he inevitably dumped her. But his death gave her a kind of permanent celebrity status which she seemed to be going to some lengths to preserve.

That same week the president of the college assembled the faculty to announce more bad news, again in numbered points:

1. The building fund had been cut from $160 million to $19 million.

2. The building utilization standard had been increased.

3. There would be 250 fewer faculty state-wide than in the previous year, instead of the 1300 more which had been requested, but there would be 20,000 more students.

4. Educational Opportunity Programs had been scrapped state-wide.

5. The creative leave program had been scrapped, but there was still one (count it, one) sabbatical leave assigned to Chihuahua State.

6. The 10% cost-of-living wage increase had disappeared, just like its 5% brother of last year.

7. Auditors would visit each campus in the state college system in the fall to check faculty classroom loads.

8. Classes with fewer than six students registered would be cancelled. Faculty members whose classes were cancelled would replace lecturers. Lecturers would be dismissed.

As a relative newcomer to the college, I didn't fully understand the implications of these changes. Wayne Tutworthy, who seemed better connected to the college grapevine than I, filled me in at our weekly handball session.

"How does the building fund affect us," I asked. "I thought we had all the buildings we needed."

"Where did you say your office was?" Wayne responded.

"Out in a portable behind the music building."

"I rest my case. As for the other colleges in the system, next year faculty members will have to double up on office space and the year after, students will be sitting in each others' laps."

"What's this about auditors? Aren't our financial affairs in order?"

"It isn't that kind of audit. Governor Reagan is convinced that the state is wasting too much money on professors' salaries."

"I'm not exactly getting rich on what I make."

"Nor is anyone else, but that's not the way they look at it. How many hours a week do you meet your students?"

"I have three courses that each meet five times a week, so let's say fifteen hours."

"Right, same as everybody else. But they consider a normal work-week to be forty hours, so by their calculations, you're spending most of your time goofing off."

"But what about all the hours it takes to prepare lessons and grade papers?"

"You don't have to tell me. Anyway, they're planning to send people to each state college to add up the number of hours that you can be shown to be making an active contribution. They'll divide that into the number of students you teach and end up with an efficiency factor. Then they'll start firing the least efficient and everybody else will start working harder."

"And what's this about canceling small classes? I have over a hundred students in my General Studies course but only five in the 20th-century music course."

"My guess is that 20th-century is history."

"That's right: we're studying historical trends ..."

"That's not what I meant: your 20th-century course is a thing of the past."

"Well sure, most of the 20th-century has already gone by."

"Axel, they're going to axe the course."

"Oh."

CHAPTER 17

We had a successful choir rehearsal on Thursday. With just a month to go before the March concert, the kids seemed to be getting the music firmly in control. Afterward, as the singers dispersed, Jerome Chowning passed me with a big smile on his face.

"High again, Jerome?" I asked.

"Well that, of course," he said, "but I'm just amazed at the way things go around here."

"You're referring to the art exhibition?"

"And the administration's response!"

"I suppose it sometimes seems as if they were put on earth just to play straight man for your newspaper."

"I couldn't have put it better myself."

"Saves you a lot of work."

"You said it. I just have to sit back and watch them make fools of themselves."

"I guess it doesn't hurt to have someone like Deirdre around as a catalyst."

"That's for sure. By the way, did you hear that Dale Cochrane tried to tear her picture down?"

"No. Does Dale have such delicate sensibilities when it comes to the male anatomy?"

"I don't think that's it. I think it has something to do with Professor Jarman specifically." Then he hurried off to join some friends for a toke in his trailer. I thought about the way Dale had looked at me the day after the poetry festival, but couldn't make a connection.

The room emptied and I found myself alone with Sheri Kimball. She had volunteered to serve as music librarian, but I suspected she enjoyed my company as much as the satisfaction of seeing that all the chorus binders found their places on the appropriate shelf. Though not as strikingly attractive as her roommate, Sheri was cute in her light brown bangs, short skirts and easy smile. Strict eastern prohibitions about romantic involvement with students had placed her off limits as far as I was concerned; otherwise I might easily have been tempted. I had been taught that one would rot in hell for holding lascivious thoughts about female students, at least one's own students, and lose one's job for acting on those thoughts, in light of the obvious inequality of positions and the conflict of interest for the instructor. Still, one couldn't be prosecuted for admiring female pulchritude. Sheri's speech patterns fascinated me, the way she'd pronounced "dawn" as "don," and made the "o" in "office" sound the same as the "o" in "top."

I tried to adopt a casual tone as I gathered my things together and Sheri filed choral binders. "I've been rereading that poem in *The Bowser*," I began.

"You mean 'Grant and Me,'" Sheri said with a slight blush.

"No, I meant that so-called suicide poem. Weren't you one of the first to see it?"

Now the girl reddened considerably. "Oh, that." She stared intently at one of the binders as if looking for words that would get her off the hook. "I guess I shouldn't have done that. Professor Jarman's wife came into the copy room while I was there, carrying a piece of paper. I let her interrupt what I was doing, but she was in such a hurry that she left it in the machine after copying it."

"Go on," I prompted.

"I saw it when I started doing my work again. I only took a quick glance, but certain words kind of jumped out at me: 'She was the comeliest and most willing lass,' and then later that bit about her coming to bed with me. I don't know. I was just really curious, and a little bit turned on, I guess, so I copied it without thinking about it and hid the copy with my things. When Mrs. Jarman came back I handed her the original."

"What did you think when you had a chance to read the whole poem?"

"That was really weird. It sounded like some kind of farewell. At that point I didn't know that Professor Jarman had killed himself. Or not killed himself. You know what I mean."

"What did you do then?"

"Well naturally I showed it to Deirdre, and that's when she said that it was about her, at least the first part."

"Did you know that she'd been having an affair with Jarman?"

"'Affair?' That sounds so sordid. I knew they'd been sleeping together. Every time Deirdre came back she was so dreamy-eyed. She kept telling me how Professor Jarman was going to leave his wife and marry her."

"So she really believed that?"

"Oh, yes. At least until she got that note that said Professor Jarman thought she was a bimbo. She told me they had a real fight."

"What did you do with the poem after that?"

"Deirdre persuaded me to show it to Jerome, and he thought it was so important he printed it in *The Bowser*."

"But Deirdre didn't say anything about her fight with Jarman in her interview with Jerome."

"I guess by then she'd decided what people needed to hear and what they didn't."

"Deirdre has really made things go the way she wants. Is she acting all the time?"

"Any time you see her, I'd say yes. She talks to me like a normal person."

"Let me ask you one more thing. Do you think that Jerome could have written that poem?"

"Jerome?"

"Well evidently Grant Jarman didn't write it."

"No way. I mean, he's probably good enough with words, but I saw his face when I showed him the poem. He's not a good enough actor to fake that kind of surprise."

"Thanks," I said. "I'll help you with the rest of those." As we put the remaining binders away in the cabinet we accidentally bumped into each other. Sheri leaned over and gave me a quick kiss on the lips, which I instinctively returned, then, in embarrassment, I tried to explain what seemed to me to be quite obvious.

"What planet do you come from, Mr. Crochet? Nobody around here thinks that way."

"But the obvious disparity ..."

"I'm over twenty-one. How old are you?"

"Twenty-eight."

"Well there you have it," she said conclusively, as if all my arguments had been answered.

"In point of fact, my affections are otherwise engaged."

Her face fell. "Well why didn't you say so? That's completely different." Then she batted me on the nose with her index finger and left the rehearsal room.

I drove down to the church for the regular Thursday routine of Junior Choir rehearsal, organ practice, and senior choir rehearsal. I'd worked out a deal with Mrs. Healy whereby I'd give her daughters piano lessons in exchange for dinner on Thursday nights so that I wouldn't have to drive home and back.

St. Peter's Episcopal Church seemed to represent a bastion of the traditional, or as traditional as one could be with an aluminum cross and an electric organ. In contrast to the angled planes and glass walls of First Presbyterian Church, the dark wood and narrow nave of St. Peter's could have been transported directly from the New England churches of my college days. The chancel followed the conventional layout of choir pews on either side of the altar, with half the choir watching the organist in a large mirror mounted on the wall.

The senior choir, numbering about a dozen, sang with fervor and embraced my direction enthusiastically. They were open to learning new music, even in languages other than English, and sang lustily during rehearsals but had an unfortunate habit of freezing in performance, which of course meant every Sunday.

The Junior Choir consisted mostly of young teenaged and pre-teen girls, who managed to sing two-part harmony quite nicely. They performed with confidence but only sang in church every fourth Sunday.

I was working out the fingerings on a Bach prelude and fugue when Jeff Healy stuck his head through the door and asked whether I could see him for a moment in his office. I followed him down the hall and into the minister's study. In contrast to the minister's office in the church where I grew up, which resembled a library reading room, Jeff's office seemed awfully light on books. There was *The Interpreter's Bible*, of course, and a large concordance, along with enough theological tomes to fill several shelves, but certainly not enough to fill a bookcase. On the wall, in addition to a framed diploma proclaiming Jeff to be the holder of a Bachelor of Divinity degree, with all the rights and privileges pertaining thereto, hung a photo of Jeff in full football gear, to which had been attached a photocopied headline describing his most memorable touchdown.

Jeff beckoned me to a seat and sat his own ample body behind his desk. He maintained the barrel-chested physique of his days as an athlete but his face had become fuller than the image in the photograph, his ready smile now curving gently into a double chin.

"You seem to have made a good start here at St. Peter's," he began. "Members of the Senior Choir have spoken enthusiastically about your rehearsals."

"I'm glad to hear it," I said. "I've enjoyed working with them."

"How about the Junior Choir?" Jeff asked.

"They're terrific!" I said, thinking about the performance they'd recently given of a Healey Willan anthem. "It's been a pleasure getting to know them."

"So you've been working closely with the choir members?"

I thought about the energy that these young people put into singing, and I said, "It's been a great experience. They've touched me as much as I've touched them."

Jeff squirmed a bit in his chair then asked, "Are there any you're particularly fond of?"

"I don't like to play favorites," I replied. "I love them all."

Jeff gave me a long look, then pulled out a mock-up of the bulletin for Sunday and went over the list of hymns with me. We finished a few minutes later and I returned to the organ.

CHAPTER 18

The following day Darryl Cooper called me into his office. One wall served as a huge window on the rehearsal room, evidently so that the chairman could keep track of what went on there, but it was fitted with Venetian blinds, frequently closed during lunch hours when Darryl reportedly entertained favorite female students. A door on the opposite wall led to the music office, with a second door opening on the corridor. In addition to bookcases full of books and scores, a piano, and the standard-issue sound system, the room contained a number of Indian instruments brought back from Darryl's visit to the sub-continent several years earlier.

Darryl's moods varied from twinkle-eyed humor to black cynicism, so I wasn't sure what to expect. Darryl was a big man who occasionally felt defensive about his size. "In the East," he once told me, referring not to our common background in upstate New York but to his experience in India, "people have a certain reverence for size. Not like here," he said disdainfully, referring to the California cult of fitness. Darryl tended to move slowly, his craggy, bearded visage looking down on the rest of the world.

Yet at other times, he expressed a concern about loss of stature. "Every year I've been here, Axel, I've felt smaller than the year before. This place wears you down. Sometimes I feel as if I'm eventually going to be reduced to a piece of shit. Then someone from the administration is going to come along and say, 'What's this piece of shit doing here,' and kick me into the trash barrel, and I'll be gone for good."

After asking how the choir was coming along Darryl told me that he'd composed a piece of music that he wanted me to perform on the March choral concert.

"We're getting pretty close to concert time," I said. "I think it might be better to put it off until June."

"I'd really like you to do it in March, Axel."

"I don't think that's going to work. It takes the kids a fair amount of time to learn new music."

"Axel, let me give you some practical advice."

"I'm listening."

"I don't know what they taught you back in those Ivy League schools, but if you want to keep your job, you do what your chairman tells you to."

71

"But what about academic freedom?"

"Screw academic freedom. Got it?" I nodded. "And now I'm asking you, *as your chairman,* to perform this piece on the next concert with the College Choir."

"Yes, sir," I said.

"That's more like it."

"Now may I ask you a question?"

"Go ahead."

"Why do we have to do this?"

Darryl sighed and abandoned his drill sergeant stance. "Axel, everybody has skeletons in their closet. Paula Rogers discovered one of mine."

"What does she have to do with this?"

"She wrote an elegy on the death of her father and asked me to set it to music for choir."

"I see."

"Don't worry—I've made it as simple as I could." Darryl showed me the score which at first glance didn't seem to present any major difficulties for the College Chorus. "You can even help them along with the piano if you want," he added.

"Any place special where I should put it on the program?" I asked.

"Why don't you put it first and get it out of the way. Then you can go ahead with your music for chorus and brass."

"Okay. When did you get the text, anyway?"

"About three week ago. Why?"

"Just wondering. You compose quickly."

"Don't you usually try to get unpleasant tasks out of the way as soon as possible?" Darryl said in a confidential tone. "My second string quartet—I've been working on that for more than half a year."

"Golly."

"There is one other thing I wanted to see you about, Axel. That girl who you accused of plagiarizing on her Chopin paper, what was her name?"

"Linda Selden. She just copied whole paragraphs out of a popular biography without any attribution."

"I understand. Where you and I come from, she would have been expelled, or at least failed the course. But there's a lesson to be learned here."

"What's that?"

"If you ask students to do something they can't do, but you force them to do it, they have no option but to cheat."

"But ..."

"No, let me finish. I have no doubt that you considered the assignment to be within the capabilities of your students. But in at least one case, it wasn't. I'm not going to tell you how to run your course, but just ask that instead of thinking about the assignments in terms of what you did when you were an undergraduate, think about them in terms of what these kids can do given their background and intelligence. That's all."

Darryl handed me the score of the elegy as if returning an unwanted brochure to a traveling salesman and shambled over to the piano to resume work on his string quartet.

As I walked out of the office I recalled Linda Selden's class presentation in which she trotted out all the old myths—that Chopin couldn't orchestrate, that he was a failure in large forms, that he never amounted to anything until he met George Sand—and wondered whether it was really such a good idea to treat my nineteenth-century music class like a graduate seminar.

After dinner I decided to go to a movie and invited Melissa to join me. We still avoided being seen together in public locally, but figured there wouldn't be much risk in the next town. In the East I would never have thought of driving forty miles to a movie theatre. Out here such excursions were commonplace, thanks to the freeway system.

California was justly famous for its network of highways. You could travel everywhere on six- and eight-lane freeways, yet the building continued. In 1970 the Los Angeles area had 555 miles of freeway and was master-planned for 1550. Paul Ehrlich predicted that by 2020, 50% of California's best farmland would be paved over. But since you still couldn't get in or out of Los Angeles during rush hour, highway engineers came up with new measures to speed traffic: aerial surveillance, electronic sensing devices and distant early warning systems. The L.A. Times bragged about the program in a headline that cynics might interpret as prophetic: "Crash Program to Speed Traffic."

The source of the problem was no mystery: there were simply too many cars. The family across the street from my house had four cars: one for papa, one for mama, one for junior and one which they were trying to sell. Since their garage had been converted into a family room, all four cars had to live outside, two in the driveway and two in the street. The house next to theirs had one car, two pickup trucks and a house trailer. The fellow next to me had a car and two house trailers. No one knew for sure what he kept in the garage because it was always locked, but some speculated that it might be bomb shelter.

After the film Melissa came to my house to spend the night. As we were getting ready for bed, she asked, "Axel, are you holding onto any lingering thoughts about my involvement in Grant's death?"

"I thought the police accepted your alibi that you were with students all afternoon."

"I'm not talking about the police, I'm talking about you."

"You mean, do I think you might have found a hired killer to do the deed?"

"Something like that."

"Melissa, I don't think I've been sleeping with a murderess, if that's what you mean. But you have to remember that I've been approaching this strictly from a literary point of view. I give you credit for having been capable of writing the suicide poem."

"Oh, that again. Well, I don't write poetry, and if I did, it certainly wouldn't be in that style. Who else is on your list?"

"The poem seems to mention four people. In addition to you there's Deirdre—I think we can safely eliminate her now—and Wayne Tutworthy. He probably could have written it, but I don't like to think of my friends as murderers."

"Who else?"

"There's a veiled reference to Maxwell Kent."

"Why would he want to kill Grant?"

"You remember they were competing for the deanship."

"Grant didn't take that seriously; at least, not the way he talked about it to me. The glory of the title paled when he considered that he'd have to spend most of his time working with Jerry Siebel."

"I think I've been able to eliminate Kent on stylistic grounds, too," and I told Melissa about the retirement poem that Kent had composed.

"What about Wayne?" Melissa asked.

"What about him?"

"You've ruled him out as a candidate?"

"Well, he's my friend."

"How well do you really know him?"

"I've only been here for half a year. How well do I know anybody?"

Melissa hesitated for a moment then spoke. "I'm not sure whether I should tell you this, but you seem pretty persistent in trying to solve this problem, even if your methods are a bit strange."

"What are you trying to say?"

"Grant wasn't the first person to cuckold Wayne Tutworthy."

"That seems like a rather old-fashioned way of putting it. You mean Grant wasn't the first to sleep with Caroline?"

"I said it that way on purpose. Wayne and Caroline were at Chico State at the same time Grant and I were, before coming here. Caroline was just as rapacious in those days and she had an affair with someone in the art department."

"What happened?"

"Wayne found out about it and while he didn't actually kill the guy, he came close enough for assault charges to be preferred. Eventually the administration intervened and the charges were dropped."

"This is Wayne, the person I play handball with every week?"

"I'm not saying he killed Grant, but so far as I know he doesn't have an alibi and in spite of the quiet side he's shown you, he's capable of being rather violent if provoked."

"I don't know what to say."

Melissa took my hands in hers. "I don't know how much experience you've had with women, Axel, but a man married to a woman as attractive as Caroline is apt to regard her as something of a treasure to be guarded. I don't say that other people take adultery casually, but a man in Wayne's situation is likely to react very strongly."

I must have had a strange expression on my face because Melissa said, "Life is always more complicated than you think, Axel." Then she kissed me lightly on the cheek and said, "But enough of murder. Let's talk about us. We've been seeing each other for three months now. Is it just fun and games for you, or are you interested in building a serious relationship with me?"

"You know, if someone had asked me that, as a hypothetical question, when I first met you, I would have answered completely differently."

"How's that?"

"To tell you the truth, I always found you intimidating."

"Me?"

"Yes. You're so self-assured and beautiful, and you're not afraid to wade into an argument."

"But what do you say now?"

"Now that I've seen another side of you, I have to say I really like being with you—no matter what we're doing—and I'd like to carry that as far as we can. Did you want to talk about a relationship now?"

"No. I was just checking. Right now I'm more interested in fun and games."

Melissa pushed me over on my back and began doing things that could only lead to one conclusion.

CHAPTER 19

Through the second term both choruses struggled against a variety of obstacles. The College Chorus of nineteen voices, including one tenor who couldn't sing in concerts because he played in a rock band every Sunday night, lost its lead soprano and secretary, Doris Hayes, who couldn't resolve a registration problem. Our lead alto departed for a period of practice teaching, along with a reliable bass for the same reason, and one of the tenors defected to the mountains to build a house for his wife and newborn son.

The Choral Society eventually found an accompanist, but a crisis arose when she lost her job as organist due to a budget cut by a failing church. In order to meet the family budget she now needed to be paid. She could not be hired, however, since her husband taught in the biology department and the college, among other practices, maintained a strong anti-nepotism rule. She would probably have been willing to continue unpaid, but her husband wanted her to stay home and take care of the kids so that he could work in the lab. Male chauvinist pig!

There seemed to be no consensus on the nepotism issue. The women in charge of the Faculty Wife Bulletin refused to publicize efforts by other faculty wives to form an Ad-Hoc Committee to End Discriminatory Hiring Practices at Chihuahua State, whose anti-nepotism policy worked to their detriment. Those in charge of the bulletin explained that their constitution represented them as a "friend of the College," and it would be unfriendly to suggest that there was anything wrong (not to say illegal) with the college's hiring practice (notwithstanding a citation against the college by the Department of Health, Education and Welfare).

"Is this place crazy, or is it just me?" I asked Wayne as we returned to the locker room after several exhausting but exhilarating games of handball.

"You're the sanest person I know, Axel," Wayne said. "What's the matter?"

"We're just a three-man department in music—Darryl, Charlie and me. Darryl's three-year term as chairman is up but we're happy to let him keep on being chairman."

"So?"

"So last week I was working in the photocopy room when Gerry Siebel wandered in and muttered that he was having difficulty getting the music department faculty (all three of us) together for a meeting with himself and

Maxwell Kent to choose a music department chairman. I asked him why we needed a meeting. After all, Darryl's just going to keep on being chairman."

"I can imagine what he said to that. Of all the tight-asses in the administration, the vice-president of the college is the tightest."

"He said that our department had to elect a three-man election committee to conduct a department-wide search."

"Oh Axel! You have to realize this guy takes his job extremely seriously."

"I gathered as much. So, eager to be helpful, I suggested that the three of us had a department meeting every Friday; why didn't he and the dean just drop in sometime. Gerry sniffed and said that it was all a question of whether your meeting came to us or our meeting came to you; then he left the room. I knew I had him because we'd spent the better part of two hours at the beginning of the quarter determining that Friday afternoon from two to three was the only hour in the entire week that all three of us had open."

"So what happened?"

"A little while later Gerry wandered back in. 'What time did you say that meeting was?' 'Fridays from two to three,' I said. He disappeared. In a few minutes his stern face reappeared at the doorway to announce that he had decided to have a meeting the first Friday afternoon that the Dean had free. 'Good thinking,' I said."

"So did you have the meeting?"

"This is where is really got silly. The following Friday Gerry and Maxwell arrived and asked whether we'd appointed a nominating committee. We were supposed to have a committee of three members drawn from the department to nominate a chairman."

"I can see where this is going."

"It gets worse. This committee is supposed to have at least one tenured professor (we don't have one) or full professor (we don't have any of those, either.) Maxwell allowed as how we could waive that requirement, but we really did have to have the meeting."

"Then what?"

"Then Gerry had to give a little speech about how he didn't think there were sufficient funds to bring in an outside candidate and that we would have to confine our search to within the department."

"So what did you do?"

"He and Gerry actually left the room so that Darryl, Charlie and I could nominate Darryl to be chairman."

"And then?"

"We waited till they had closed the door, then laughed ourselves silly, counted to twenty, and let them back in again."

"I think Robert Frost has a poem that fits the occasion: 'It couldn't be called ungentle/But how thoroughly departmental.'"

"Then we went home. By way of the bank, of course."

"Oh yes. I heard about the uproar that took place a couple of years ago when the state comptroller discovered that he could save California millions of dollars by holding onto salary funds one additional day and giving us our pay checks on the last day of the month. After the banks close."

"Last payday I heard Charlie muttering that he could no longer afford to exist."

"He has a point. The state of California takes awfully good care of your survivors."

"Small comfort."

"Hey, around here you take what you can get."

As I drove home, I thought about Melissa's description of the violent incident in Wayne's past and wondered why I hadn't asked Wayne about it. Was I beginning to get paranoid?

A letter from the church awaited me in the mailbox. I opened it and read:

The recent downturn in the economy, combined with the deficits run by the church for the past two years, have compelled us to re-think every aspect of worship at St. Peter's, including the music program. We have reluctantly decided to scale down the church's commitment to professional staff in this area, with the result that your services will not be required after Easter Sunday, March 29. Please understand that this decision in no way reflects upon your considerable musical gifts. We trust that you will soon be able to find another position commensurate with your talents.

(signed) The Wardens of St. Peter's Episcopal Church

Funny. No one had mentioned that the church was in financial difficulty when they'd hired me, although the regular disaster warnings from the president of the college signalled economic troubles generally in this state. I felt suddenly bereft. St. Peter's had become more than just a job for me. Though I joked with Wayne about Jeff Healy's football sermons, I felt a certain attachment to the church, and it hurt suddenly to be excluded.

That evening I was scheduled to meet Melissa for dinner. I left early in order to make a stop at the orange grove near the foothills in hope of relieving the pain I felt inside. The fragrance of the orange blossoms at twilight was something so foreign to my experience before moving to California that its beauty still took my breath away. The ugliness of human culture and human behavior seemed to disappear in this magical place. Let Jerome Chowning keep his hallucinogens; I felt as if I could escape to a different world just by breathing in this extraordinary perfume.

Yet even as I enjoyed the aroma that surrounded me, I realized that such pleasures might be short-lived. One of my students recounted the visit of her aunt from back east. Impressed with the orange grove across the street from her house, the aunt had taken practically a whole roll of photographs then driven into town to have the film developed. They had lunch and did a few other errands. When they returned home, the orange grove had disappeared, bulldozed to make way for yet another housing development. As a crowning touch, my student told me, the film hadn't turned out.

The oranges sat silently in the grove, exhaling their perfume for my delectation, in contrast to the high-pressure hawkers at last month's Orange Show, selling electronic bibles, computerized character-analysis kits, and an adjustable torture rack billed as a rejuvenator-exercisor, within sight of an exhibit claiming that Walt Disney proved the scientific accuracy of the bible. It all made me understand why Chihuahua was described as unique—it offered so many experiences that you wouldn't want to try more than once.

I reluctantly left the orange grove and drove to Melissa's house. I'd been looking forward to an amatory encounter but she seemed strangely distant. When I asked her what the matter was, she hesitated for a moment and then said, "Axel, I haven't been entirely honest with you." My heart sank. Melissa was going to tell me that she'd fallen in love with someone else, or that after deep reflection, she didn't think we were right for each other. The expression on my face must have conveyed my fears because she continued, "It isn't anything about us, or at least not directly. But all this time I've been giving you the impression that I had nothing to do with Grant's death. That's true enough as far as it goes, but there's more to it than that."

"I see," I said, not seeing at all.

"The day I received that note about Grant and Deirdre I tried to kill him."

"You what?"

"When he came into the kitchen from the garage, I confronted him, he confessed, and then I grabbed a kitchen knife and tried to stab him with it."

"What happened?"

"He dodged and I ended up putting a long gouge in his expensive leather briefcase."

"What happened then?"

"He put his arms around me, the way he used to when we still cared about each other, and for a brief moment I had a glimpse of the feelings I used to have for him. Then the moment passed and I realized I no longer felt anything at all. So we kept on sleeping in separate bedrooms."

"Oh my."

"I was afraid to tell you because I thought you'd be scared away."

An older part of me said in a nagging voice that I should have nothing more to do with this unstable woman. But the part of me that was beginning to fall in love with Melissa Jarman silenced the objections and pushed me into an embrace. I felt Melissa give a brief sob—perhaps relief, perhaps just an overflow of emotion. Then without another word we took hands and walked toward the bedroom.

CHAPTER 20

The last time we'd met for handball, I just hadn't been able to confront Wayne with Melissa's revelations, but I couldn't go on week after
week wondering whether I was playing with a murderer. I began rather
awkwardly. "We don't really know that much about each other. You
know that I come from the East; I know that you taught at Chico State
before coming here."

Happily, Wayne helped me out. "Uh oh; I think I know where this is
going."

"You do?"

"You've been talking with Melissa and she told you about my fracas
with the art professor that screwed Caroline."

"Well ..."

"And so you've been wondering whether maybe I'm a murderer, after
all."

"I ..."

"And considering that I'm an English professor, you figure I could
have written Grant's suicide poem."

"It's just that ..."

"And I haven't been able to come up with a convincing alibi for the
afternoon of Grant's murder."

"You have to admit ..."

"Okay. Let's clear the air." Wayne had abandoned his usual relaxed
posture and stood erect, his weight balanced over the point midway between his feet, the way my debating coach taught us in high school. "I
can't think of another time in my life when I've experienced the sheer
rage that I felt when I learned about Caroline and Kevin. For some reason it never occurred to me to blame her, but I went after Kevin, and if
they hadn't pulled me off him I might have killed him."

"But you didn't feel the same way when you heard about Caroline and
Grant?"

"Maybe it's different the second time, or maybe I knew what would
happen to me if I attacked Grant. Or maybe it's just that he was such a
charming, likeable guy. I really don't know. But I can assure you that I
did not murder Grant Jarman."

Something in Wayne's voice went inside me, and I realized that if I'd
ever harbored suspicions about him, they had now vanished. You can
only go so far in treating people like parts of a puzzle; at some point you

have to trust your feelings. I shook his hand solemnly then we both laughed and began another game with a deepened sense of camaraderie.

After the game Wayne asked how I was doing with my choral conducting students.

"I can't understand it," I said. "I don't think the students have spent more than an hour collectively working on anything outside the classroom since the term began. They seem to expect that I'm going to tell them everything they need to know so that they can write it down in their notebooks."

"That sounds like our students."

"But it doesn't make sense. Nobody was required to take this course, but it has a lot more practical application to their careers than anything else they study. What's more, I took their questions and interests and made that the syllabus for the course. But when they say they're interested in finding out about something, it appears that they take 'finding out' to be a passive rather than an active verb."

"Have you considered taking them out of the classroom?"

"We did that last week. I wanted them to see the real world of high school classroom teaching, so we made a field trip to visit one of the local choral directors. He was happy to share his expertise with this promising group of future teachers, and he gave them a lesson in classroom management that they'll never forget."

"That must have been instructive," Wayne said.

"Wait till you hear. 'The other day,' he told them, 'a boy passed by my desk and said "Hi, John," using my first name. 'What did you say?' I demanded, and called him back to my desk. Then, without raising my voice or showing the slightest emotion, I marched him to the opposite side of the room and began banging his head against the wall. The rest of the class got the message: if this is what I did when I was calm, they didn't want to see what might happen if they ever made me angry." My awestruck students nodded appreciatively. I think they remembered the field trip more than anything I've tried to teach them about choral conducting."

"That must get discouraging."

"These kids are unbelievable. One week, temporarily giving up the fight to expect the students to do any of my assignments, I wrote a half-whimsical list of skills and activities that I thought might interest them: write your own music dictionary; sing a 12-tone row; cultivate deep breathing; investigate the choral history of a particular country; take a field trip to the library; prepare a piece for chorus; compose a madrigal; write a canon and teach it by rote; learn how to pronounce a language you don't know; learn to play the recorder; take a tenor to lunch; beat 3/4 with one hand and 4/4 with the other."

"Sounds like fun."

"I also asked some questions: what would you most like to be doing in ten years? Why aren't you doing it right now? What would you need to know in order to be able to do it? How do you intend to find out? What could you become really enthusiastic about doing? If music is inherently so exciting, why is music class so dull? This really turned them on. For about fifty minutes. Each one thought that several of the items on the sheet would be fun to do. Then I learned what the conditional 'would' meant. It meant 'fun to do if I were going to anything, but of course I'm not.'"

"Have you ever thought you might be happier teaching somewhere else?"

"All the time. The problem is, there isn't that much demand for musicologists. What keeps you going in English?"

"I keep waiting to see another piece of creative writing like the poem that Deirdre read at the ASP festival."

"Speaking of Deirdre, I was wondering whether she could have gotten Jerome Chowning to write the suicide poem for her."

"It's a thought." Wayne frowned and nodded thoughtfully.

"Her roommate was the one who originally gave a copy of the poem to Jerome. She thinks he was genuinely surprised to see it."

"But you still suspect Deirdre?"

"I have to confess, girls like Deirdre scare me a bit." We closed our lockers and began to walk toward the parking lot.

"How's that?"

"All that self-assurance."

"And you find that scary."

"Let me try to explain. The other day Darryl was trying out one of his theories on me. He claimed that the reason that virtually all composers are men is that men feel compelled to create knowledge whereas women, I guess by virtue of their reproductive powers, can simply embody it."

"And that didn't strike you as rampant bullshit?"

"It sounded pretty convincing the way he said it."

"So you think Deirdre embodies knowledge? Come on, Axel."

"The theory somehow seems less attractive when you move from the abstract to the specific."

"That's the sign of bullshit."

"All I know is, Deirdre is easily Maxwell Kent's equal when it comes to getting what she wants, even though she may use different methods."

"I can't argue with you on that point." We had reached our cars and exchanged the motto that had become our watchword, "Illegitimi non carborundum est." Wayne closed his car door and I was struck again by the way the thin desert air turned the sound flat and empty, existing only in the immediate moment with no resonance, no future. It seemed like a metaphor for my existence at CSC and, a few hours later, my love life.

That night I had a telephone call from Melissa. "I know I was planning to come over tonight," she began, "but I was afraid to tell you this in person." I had a sinking feeling in my stomach as she continued. "You know I've really enjoyed the time we've spent together, and please believe that I think the world of you, but I'm finding that I'm just not ready for a long-term relationship at this point."

"I see."

"Please don't be angry with me. I've tried to persuade myself that we could become partners, but it isn't any use. Something inside me is telling me not to go ahead, and I have to listen."

"I'm really disappointed, Melissa," was the best I could muster under the circumstances, "but I guess you have to do what you have to do."

"We can still be friends, can't we?" Melissa asked the question women always ask in these situations.

"I'm sure we can," I lied the way men always do in these situations. We said good-bye and I spent the rest of the evening thinking of might-have-beens, but then decided nothing good could come of it and went to a late movie.

CHAPTER 21

Early in March I received a note asking me to meet Jerry Siebel in his office so I made my way to the top floor of the athletic/administration tower, with no idea of what lay in store. Jerry's office looked like a conscious effort at recreating a faculty lounge from the University of Chicago. No other room at Chihuahua State had dark panelled walls hung with oversize photographs of Lake Michigan, Rockefeller Chapel and Hyde Park. Window shades and Venetian blinds blocked out the view of southern California scrub oaks, palm trees, and smog.

As usual, Jerry made no effort at small talk but got straight to the point. "I'm disappointed to have to tell you, Axel," he began, "that you have been non-reappointed."

"You mean fired?" I asked.

Jerry didn't so much as smile. "Both of your colleagues, with whom you seem to enjoy such levity at the expense of your superiors, have expressed dissatisfaction with your performance. Professor Purcell was unhappy that you asked his advice on a point of performance practice but then evidently ignored it. And Professor Cooper asked you to assist the college by changing textbooks and you refused."

Was this all it took to get fired at Chihuahua State College? I recalled the incident with Darryl clearly. He had ordered too many copies of a music anthology and asked whether I'd consider using it instead of the one I had chosen. I took a look at his choice, found it completely unsuitable to my purposes, and told him I'd just as soon continue with the anthology I'd been using. Nobody had told me that this was a capital offence. As for Charlie, I'd gone over a score of Baroque music with him in detail and adopted virtually every one of his suggestions. Perhaps he only remembered the exception.

"You will have an official appointment with the president in due course, but I thought you would appreciate the favor of advance notice."

I managed to control my gratitude, but when I met Wayne later that afternoon for handball, he commented on the ferocity of my play and invited me to unburden myself. When I finished the story, he said, "That's a lot of crap. There's something else going on here."

"I'm beginning to wonder the same thing. I know we're living in troubled times in the middle of a disaster area, at least according to President Hopkins, but lately it's beginning to seem personal."

"How so?"

I recounted my dismissal as music director from the church and Melissa's telephone message breaking off our relationship. "I don't see any connection among these things, but it sure seems like an awful lot of bad luck all at once."

"Naw, this is too much to be a coincidence."

"But how ..."

"I'm not sure. Is there anything else you haven't mentioned?"

"Well, last month I had that threat from Maxwell Kent."

"You didn't tell me about that."

"He said he would make life untenable for me if I did anything to link his name with Grant Jarman's death."

"Do you think he could be behind all these other things?"

"It doesn't make sense. What does he care about my relationship with Melissa? And I don't know that he has any connection with the church."

"But what about your investigation of Jarman's death?"

"I'd hardly call it an investigation. I've just been trying to work out a puzzle in order to get you off the hook as a murder suspect."

"Go back to Kent for a minute. Did he tell you to stop trying to find out who killed Grant?"

"No. He didn't seem to care about that. He just didn't want his name to be involved with it."

"So do you see him as the murderer?"

"You'd think he would have forbidden me to investigate at all if he'd been the killer."

"That's the way it looks to me. You've already concluded that he didn't write the suicide poem himself, and he doesn't strike me as the kind of person who would delegate a detail like that to someone else."

"So what are you suggesting?"

"If Kent isn't the murderer, someone else could be upset by the questions you're asking. The connection between the church and the college and Melissa doesn't have to be the murderer, you know: it could be you."

"I don't get it."

"Suppose someone is really serious about stopping you. Short of killing you, what could be more discouraging than to have you lose your jobs and your girlfriend?"

"Well I don't expect to hang around here long once the spring term ends."

"Exactly. If the trail has gone cold for the police, and you can be persuaded to give up the chase, the murderer will have gotten away with it."

"So how am I going to find out who's behind this."

"I suggest you make a formal request to see your RPT file. You're entitled to do that under college regulations."

"You mean you think there's something in there that Jerry isn't telling
me?"

"It doesn't hurt to look."

With Wayne's encouragement I was able to turn my anger into construc-
tive play and succeeded in beating him two games out of three.

Having the administrative offices right above us seemed almost like an
invitation, so I proceeded there directly from the locker room and, to my
surprise, the president's secretary didn't require me to fill out a form in
triplicate or to wait for three weeks or to get a letter of permission from my
department chairman or the Dean of Arts & Sciences. Instead, she simply
handed me a file along with a warning that none of the documents could
leave the room.

"Am I allowed to photocopy them?" I asked.

"Oh, sure. State law requires that personnel files be open to employees."
She went back to her work while I perused the material in the folder. There
were copies of reports of RPT visitations to my classes as well as letters
from my colleagues, which didn't seem nearly as harsh as Jerry had made
out, along with a letter from the chairman of the RPT committee, Francis
Weatherington, to the president of the college, recommending that I not be
reappointed. "Despite Professor Crochet's promising academic credentials
and satisfactory teaching record, this committee, taking into account the
subject's inability to accommodate himself within his academic department, along with certain improprieties in the community, cannot recommend that he be reappointed."

I made a photocopy of the letter, drove home, and immediately telephoned Wayne to tell him what I had found.

"So what improprieties are they referring to?" he asked.

"I haven't any idea. They don't mean my relationship with Melissa, do
they?"

"I don't think that's public knowledge, and besides, nobody cares about
that sort of thing."

"But I don't have anything to do with the community," I said.

"Except the church."

"The church?"

"Have you had any problems there?"

"No. Everything was working out great. But one evening Jeff called me into his office. He seemed particularly interested in the Junior Choir, for some reason."

"What exactly did he say?"

I tried to recall for Wayne the particular wording of Jeff Healy's questions and my responses.

"You told him you touched the children and that you loved them all?"

"I meant that they moved me with their singing."

"I know what you meant, but that's not the way he construed it."

"Doesn't that seem kind of twisted, to turn that into improper behavior?"

"Exactly! It's been twisted."

"I don't understand."

"If this were just an ordinary conversation, nobody would have thought twice about what you said. So obviously there was something else going on."

"I still don't get it."

"I think I'm beginning to get the picture. Imagine that you're the minister, and that you've just received an anonymous letter suggesting that your new choir director has been getting too friendly with the little girls in the choir. What would you do?"

"If it's anonymous I can't talk to the sender, so I'd call in the director to find out what's going on."

"Right. And then he tells you he's touched the girls, even though he hasn't done anything wrong. How would you understand those words?"

"I guess I'd start preparing the tar and feathers." Wayne chuckled. "But how can I clear my name?"

"You can't. It's very easy to accuse somebody of sexual impropriety, but virtually impossible to disprove it. What would you do? Call every parent of every girl and ask to be exonerated? Any parent is going to think that where there's smoke, there's fire."

"So what can I do?"

"Find the person who sent the letter."

"Or letters. Somebody had to make the link between Weatherington the church warden and Weatherington the RPT committee chairman."

"What about Melissa?"

"Do you think she got a letter, too?"

"You'd have to decide that one. Has your relationship gradually cooled off, or did this seem like an abrupt end?"

I thought about Melissa and our love-making, and my disappointment when she'd broken things off. "It seemed pretty sudden to me."

"Well, I think you should assume that somebody else may be behind that, too?"

"Does that mean I can get Melissa back?"

"What are you going to tell her? 'I'm really not a pervert'?"

"Oh. I see what you mean." My situation seemed even worse now than before. A string of incredibly bad luck you just had to take in stride. But an enemy who was deliberately trying to wreck your life—more than trying— who had succeeded in wrecking your life: that was something else. I was no longer in a position where I could simply lay the death of Grant Jarman aside. Now, to use Robert Frost's words again, I was in the game for mortal stakes.

CHAPTER 22

As the date approached for our concert of music for double chorus and brass, I began to look around for some brass players. Neither Valley Junior College nor the University of Redlands seemed anxious to assist us, at least not for free. Darryl suggested I make use of our own music majors, substituting clarinets for missing trumpets, bassoons in place of trombones, and so forth. Unfortunately, our students worked on Sundays (and every other evening, or so it seemed.)

Eventually I was able to recruit eight high school students to assist in the concert of music by Gabrieli, Schütz and Bach. The concert attracted a fair-sized crowd to the concert hall. In contrast to the art studios and gallery, designed to be something of a showplace for the college, the auditorium seemed to have been built with an eye to cutting corners. The walls were plain grey concrete, which actually wasn't all that bad acoustically but looked distinctly utilitarian. Rows of seats sloped down toward a lectern at the front when the room was used for large lecture courses. A grand piano took up most of the space in one of the wings, and the curtains at the sides didn't actually close but only provided an extremely meager aesthetic touch. Apart from risers to accommodate the singers, the stage was utterly bare.

Unfortunately I'd never worked with really inexperienced instrumentalists before and it never occurred to me to be sure that they had all tuned up before the performance. So the auditorium resounded with the splendour of Gabrieli in eight different keys. I still had a lot to learn.

We had non-musical problems as well. Sheri Kimball had again volunteered to take care of the programs if I supplied her with all the information of titles, composers' names, and so forth. I was preoccupied with finding brass players and grateful for a little assistance. Not having looked over the copy before letting her take it to the printer, I was as surprised as anyone when the dedication of Darryl Cooper's elegy, instead of reading "In memory of my father," appeared as "In memory of Grant Jarman."

In the great scheme of things, nothing could have been more appropriate than for the College Chorus to sing a piece composed by the music department chairman on a text by the English department's resident poet to honor a recently deceased colleague. But Paula Rogers was fit to be tied and Darryl had to improvise an explanation to the audience to the effect that music could express emotions but not specific ideas, so an elegy created with one man in mind could well serve as a general expression of grief for the recently departed. I'm not sure this cleared things up for the audience, but they had evidently come to see friends and children perform, not to wrestle with problems of musical aesthetics.

Knowing my weakness for ice cream, the College Choir held the after-concert party at Farrell's, an establishment the size of a large restaurant, devoted exclusively to serving ice cream concoctions. The *pièce de resistance* was called the Zoo: fourteen scoops of ice cream in a silver bowl, served with a forest of spoons. Whenever someone ordered this creation sirens went off, lights blinked, a bass drum boomed and two waiters raced around the restaurant carrying the bowl in a special contraption with four handles.

In the party room I was in the process of consuming a Pig's Trough—a double banana split with two bananas, six scoops of ice cream and six toppings—when Jerome Chowning joined me at my table. We laughed about the administration's miscalculation over the nudity in art issue and I suggested that Jerome had a problem with authority figures. "I don't have any objection to authority," he replied. "I just have a problem with the people in authority being such complete idiots."

"You mean this isn't the first time they've messed up?" I asked.

"Didn't you hear about the proctor campaign?" he said.

"Must have been before my time," I said.

"They used to have a disciplinary officer here called the proctor. His job was to listen to charges, gather evidence, and render judgment."

"Sounds like judge, jury and prosecutor all rolled into one."

"That's the way this student's lawyer presented it. The kid had been charged with demonstrating against the war outside the Free Speech area. The proctor heard the case, listened to the arguments, and then placed the student on disciplinary probation."

"I take it the student didn't go quietly."

"No. His father brought in a lawyer. They sued the college and got the boy reinstated."

"That must have made the administration look bad."

"Worse than bad. Along the way the vice-president issued a statement of support for the proctor while the students started a button campaign."

"How's that?"

"They printed up large yellow badges with the words 'I am not yet convinced that' in very tiny letters, and 'The proctor is a horse's ass' in very large letters superimposed over an image of an equine derriere. The college became such a laughing stock that they finally had to abolish the position of proctor altogether."

"Somehow I suspect you had a larger role in this than you're saying."

"Who, me?" Jerome just chuckled. "But there is something I wanted to ask you."

"What's that?"

"This piece we sang tonight, the Elegy. According to the program, it was dedicated to the memory of Professor Jarman, but then Professor Cooper explained that it was really for Professor Rogers's father. What gives?"

"How do you mean?"

"Well, it makes sense for the College Choir to be singing a piece in honor of a deceased faculty member, but why would we have to perform an elegy for somebody's father?"

"What do you think?" I was getting uncomfortable with Jerome's questions but was trying not to show it.

"I think Professor Rogers is trying to get some publicity?"

"Why should she want to do that?"

"I don't know, but if you look at her poetry festival and then this concert—both times she's had the limelight stolen from her by your soprano with the Irish name. Yes, Sheri told me—that wasn't any mix-up with the dedication: Deirdre persuaded her to change the wording in the program."

Suddenly I realized what had been bothering me about Darryl's piece during the time that I'd been rehearsing it with the chorus: the text sounded familiar. I needed to get home, but first a Farrell's ritual had to be observed. As I finished the last bite of my ice cream, an alert waiter jumped up on a chair and shouted, "Professor Crochet has just made a pig of himself!", then ran over to pin a commemorative ribbon on my jacket while everyone else in the room pointed at me and shouted, "Pig! Sooey! Sooey!"

I smiled, gave a victory wave, and excused myself. As I left the restaurant and head for my car, I heard rapid footsteps behind me. I turned to see Sheri Kimball, looking quite fetching in her blue satin choir gown.

"Mr. Crochet," she said, quite out of breath from her sprint.

"Relax, Sheri," I said, putting my hands on her shoulders. "Just take your time, and then tell me what you have to say."

She took a few deep breaths, collected her thoughts, and spoke. "I want to apologize for messing up the program."

"I don't know," I said. "In some ways you may have improved it."

"That's sweet of you to say, but I had no business doing what I did."

"I understand it wasn't exactly your idea."

"So somebody already told you?"

"Jerome explained what happened."

"Oh good. I didn't want to betray my roommate, but I feel loyal to you, too."

"I appreciate that."

"But evidently more than one person has gotten upset. I overheard Dale Cochrane saying nasty things about the choir and when I asked her whether she didn't think we sang well she said, 'What difference does it make if you can't even get the program straight?'"

"I wouldn't let it upset you. But Deirdre really loves publicity, doesn't she?"

"Is that what you think?"

"Isn't that what's going on here? She got a taste of the spotlight and decided she really enjoyed it?"

"No, that's not it at all."

"Suppose you explain."

"Deirdre doesn't want publicity; she wants Grant."

"But ..."

"No; let me explain. She had this fully-formed vision of life as the wife/muse/lover of a famous writer, and she set about realizing that vision. She still hasn't accepted Grant's death. As long as she keeps his name alive, it's almost as if he's still alive."

"So you're saying that's the reason for her 'O' photo, and her erotic poem?"

"Right. And that's why she made me change the dedication in the program. It makes Grant seem alive so she doesn't have to abandon her dream."

"It isn't for me to tell Deirdre what to do, but if you really care about her, I think you should try to persuade her to get some counseling."

"Do you think Deirdre's crazy?"

"Not a bit. But we all go off the rails once in awhile and sometimes we need help getting back on."

"That makes it sound a lot different, the way you say it." She took a half step toward me and kissed me on the lips. I let my hands fall from her shoulders to her back and pressed her body against mine. So many things had been going wrong in my life, I felt relieved to have this attractive young woman thinking positive thoughts about me.

"Golly," she said when we paused for breath. "You were certainly serious about that kiss."

"I'm sorry," I said. "I've been a bit upset lately."

"You don't need to apologize," she said. "I liked it. But I've got to get back or my friends will come looking for me."

I squeezed Sheri's shoulders one more time then watched as she disappeared inside the restaurant. A siren indicated that another Zoo was about to be consumed.

As soon as I got home I pulled my anthology of English poetry off the shelf and thumbed through its well-worn pages until I found what I was looking for, an elegy by Ben Jonson. As I compared Jonson with Rogers, I was amazed by the similarities. Paula's poem began:

Though virtue be the mark of praise,
And yours of whom I sing be such
As not the world can praise too much,
Yet 'tis your courage now I raise.
O'er death you triumph yet because
Despite the pains of flesh you use
The noblest freedom, not to choose
The easy course, against God's laws.

Jonson's read:

Though beauty be the mark of praise,
And yours of whom I sing be such
As not the world can praise too much,
Yet 'tis your Virtue now I raise.
Wherein you triumph yet—because
'Tis of your flesh, and that you use
The noblest freedom, not to choose
Against or faith or honor's laws.

Paula's poem continued:

And you are he—the deity
Who all my destiny designed
In whom my every value find;
Among which faithful troop am I—
Who as an offspring at your shrine
Have sung this hymn, and here entreat

One spark of your diviner heat
To light upon this love of mine.
While later in Jonson's much longer elegy I read:
And you are he—the deity
To whom all lovers are design'd
That would their better objects find;
Among which faithful troop am I—
Who as an off'ring at your shrine
Have sung this hymn, and here entreat
One spark of your diviner heat
To light upon a love of mine.

I telephoned Wayne Tutworthy to ask whether I could come over to talk with him, and ten minutes later we were in his study, comparing the two essays in verse. Some college professors keep all their books and do most of their work in their offices, to the point that you might not even guess their profession if you visited their homes. Wayne, by contrast, kept only the necessary textbooks in his office at the college. This study was clearly his workplace. Inexpensive bookcases went from floor to ceiling on three walls, even covering over the window of what I guessed was originally a guest bedroom. In some cases one row of books had been pushed to the rear of the shelf and another added in front, giving the effect of a child whose adult teeth have poked their way into prominence before the baby teeth have disappeared. A small work table covered with books and journals had been set up next to a desk that had probably been in Wayne's possession since university days. Other books lay in stacks on the floor creating an effect of ordered confusion. I had no doubt that Wayne could quickly locate any item but I could see no pattern to the piles.

"'Similarity' isn't a strong enough word," Wayne said after comparing the two poems. "'Cribbing' is what I'd call it?"

"But how could she do that?" I demanded.

"Not many people around here read Ben Jonson," Wayne said.

"Do you think maybe she was just too pressed for time to write something really original?" I asked.

"I have an idea," he said, as he rummaged through a stack of papers, brochures, programs, pamphlets, and scholarly journals precariously balanced at side of his work table. "Ah, here it is," he said.

"What's that?"

"The texts of all the poetry in the ASP festival. Paula is planning to have the college publish it as a pamphlet and Francis asked me to have a look at it before it goes to press."

"What are you looking for?"

"Paula's contribution. Here it is. It's called 'Recycle.'" He adjusted his glasses and began to read aloud:

Dump what shall I dump?

All waste is trash: compacting

The filtration and the pond, the knights of the trash disposal, the engineers,

O engineers! of urban sanitation,

The department heads (urban and suburban),

And the office of the City Council,

Dump dump what shall I dump?

A committee has been appointed to nominate a commission of engineers

To consider the water supply.

A commission is appointed

For smog control, chiefly the question of controlling toxic emissions.

Tell me,

May we not be some time, almost now, recycled,

If the regulations, conventions, by-laws, restrictions

Are now observed

May we not be

O protected

Protected in divisions and subdivisions,

O tell me,

What shall I dump?

We demand separation of organic, inorganic, and completely non-biodegradable

Compost   Compost   Compost

"Has a nice ring to it, wouldn't you say?"

"But that's T.S. Eliot!" I protested. "It's 'Difficulties of a Statesman.' I set it to music when I was in college. It's supposed to go:

Cry what shall I cry?

All flesh is grass: comprehending

The Companions of the Bath, the Knights of the British Empire, the Cavaliers,

O Cavaliers! of the Legion of Honor,

97

and it ends up with:

We demand a committee, a representative committee, a committee of investigation

Resign   Resign   Resign

"Paula's version is a bit more up to date, though, wouldn't you say?" Wayne asked facetiously.

"I can't believe this," I said. "Why hasn't anybody noticed this before?"

"Axel, from what you know of the English department, do you think many people have read Paula Rogers' poetry?"

"But what about her book?"

"Unpublished. And unpublishable, I would assume, given what we've seen here."

"But what about her ASP colleagues? Surely they know enough poetry to have spotted the source."

"What did they hear? Just that one poem. Heard in isolation, it seems like a clever parody, nothing more."

"But isn't this illegal?"

"Calm down, Axel. My guess is that Paula is doing the best she can. She's chosen literary models and imitated them—a bit slavishly at times, to be sure."

"Wait a minute." I pulled out a well-worn copy of *The Bowser*. "Have you actually read Grant Jarman's suicide poem in its entirety?"

"I can't say I've read the whole thing. All I know is what you've told me."

"Well take a look at it then." Wayne scanned the text, thought for a moment, then got up and walked over to a bookshelf, pulled out an anthology of American poetry, and leafed through it. "Here's what I was looking for."

"What's that?"

"'Thanatopsis,' by William Cullen Bryant." He began to read aloud:

To him who in the love of Nature holds
Communion with her visible forms, she speaks
A various language; for his gayer hours
She has a voice of gladness, and a smile
And eloquence of beauty, and she glides
Into his darker musings, with a mild
And healing sympathy, that steals away
Their sharpness, ere he is aware.

"Nothing about her being a good lay, I see."

"No, that appears to have been the good Paula's invention. No 'plodding husband,' either, nor 'deadly academic sports.' Well, Axel, I think you've finally found your poet."

"This is unbelievable!"

"Your department chairman is wiser than you may realize."

"How do you mean?"

"Didn't he tell you that if you ask students to do something they can't do, but you force them to do it, they have no option but to cheat?"

"Right."

"I think the same may apply to the distinguished Professor Rogers." Then he saw a look in my eye. "Hold on, Axel. Don't go trying to handle this on your own."

"Do you think the police are going to be interested in my literary theories?"

"Probably not, but there's a difference between theory and practice, okay?"

CHAPTER 23

On Tuesday *The Bowser* announced the death of Deirdre O'Donahue. It seems she had been trying to take a photograph from the top of the athletic complex tower when she lost her footing and fell. Her camera was found near her crumpled body.

Jerome Chowning came through with another trenchant editorial. After deploring the lack of safeguards around the observation platform he went on to speculate that Deirdre may have taken her own life, still distraught at the death of her lover. Was this not a tragedy worthy to be compared with the story of Eloise and Abelard, pupil and teacher and a love that transgressed social norms but was transformed by art? Or perhaps, the editor continued, Deirdre was the victim of an uncaring bureaucratic system that treated students as no more than numbers to be factored into favorable Full-Time Equivalent statistics. And while everyone seemed to know Deirdre the lover of the late Grant Jarman and darling of the recent poetry festival, not to mention the star of the art exhibition, did anyone really know this girl? Weren't her public presentations just pathetic cries for genuine intimacy? And since we all read or heard her words without responding to her desperate need, were we not all to some extent responsible for the death of this lonely, pathetic creature?

After classes Sheri Kimball came to my office, her eyes red from crying. She didn't say anything but just sat down on the daybed. When I sat beside her and put my arm around her, she pressed her face against my chest and began sobbing. "She was such a good roommate," she began when her convulsions eased enough for her to speak. "I know you may have thought she was crazy, but she was like a sister to me."

"You really miss Deirdre."

"Yes. She told me everything that was on her mind, and listened to everything I had to say."

"That's what a good roommate is for."

"She encouraged me when I needed support. She really made me feel good about myself."

"That's a special gift."

I kissed Sheri on the cheek. She looked up inquiringly and said, "But ..."

"It's over," I said simply.

"I'm sorry," she said and kissed me gently on the lips. "Thanks for being here for me. We'll get together again." Then she was off.

I telephoned Paula Rogers to ask if I might come over to explain the error in the program at the choral concert. She said "Certainly," and gave me directions to her house. As I walked to the parking lot, I saw a figure move furtively near my car, slide a piece of paper under the windshield wiper, then scuttle off. I stopped and studied the situation. As the figure drew nearer I recognized Dale Cochrane. What was all this about? I decided to follow her.

She disappeared into the passageway between the music building and the cafeteria, and then continued across the Free Speech area toward the library. I decided this was as good a time as any to have it out with her, and so increased my pace until I was right behind her.

"Dale," I called.

She turned in surprise, recognized me then gave me an evil look. "What do you want?"

"Why did you put a note on my car?"

"What are you talking about?"

"Dale, I watched you do it."

"Why don't you just go away!" she said angrily.

"'To him who in the love of Nature holds/Communion with her visible forms, she speaks/A various language,' I quoted. "You know that poem, don't you?"

"What if I do?" Came the sullen response.

"Do you know it as 'Thanatopsis' or as Grant Jarman's suicide poem?"

Dale's eyes widened.

"You've read Professor Rogers' poetry, haven't you?"

"Yes," Dale said defiantly. "I'm probably the only person at the college who has!"

"Then you're aware of her unique method of creating poems," I said as diplomatically as I could.

"Yes." Dale sounded a bit defensive.

"So you must have figured out what happened as soon as you read Professor Jarman's suicide poem in *The Bowser*."

"Yes." Dale's entire posture changed, as if she were gradually casting off the burden of the terrible secret she had been guarding. I gestured for her to take a seat and I sat beside her on one of the stone benches lining the sidewalk in front of the library.

"You realize that you've destroyed my career here." I looked directly into Dale's eyes and tried to keep any accusatory tone from my voice. At first she bristled again in defence of her mentor. Then she let my words sink in and her gaze dropped to the ground. "You know how it is with chemical reactions," I continued. "Sometimes they can be reversed; sometimes they can't. The things you've done can't be reversed." Dale still didn't say anything but a brief shudder went through her body and I thought I detected a tear.

"You haven't told Professor Rogers about any of this, have you? Discovering her secret, carrying on this war to protect her?"

Dale shook her head.

"How did you find out that I was trying to solve the riddle of the poem?"

Dale spoke quietly. "Jerome told me you'd visited the newspaper archives and when he said how excited you were to find a poem by Professor Kent, I guessed what you were doing."

"And how did you find out that I was involved with Mrs. Jarman? I thought we had been pretty discreet."

Dale looked up and gave a tentative smile. "I saw the two of you at the movies in Riverside. You seemed to be acting as if you were keeping a secret."

"You're something of an expert in secrets, aren't you?" Dale nodded. "But how could you know that Professor Weatherington was the chairman of the RPT Committee, or that he was a warden of St. Peter's Church?"

"Paula, that is, Professor Rogers helped me out with the first one. I asked her who decides which teachers get to stay and which ones get fired, and she explained the system to me. As to the church, I followed you there one afternoon, and while you were practicing the organ I snooped around. The names of the wardens were listed on a plaque near the entrance and when I saw Professor Weatherington's name I realized what a useful coincidence that was for me."

"So your first letter went to him as warden of the church?"

"That's right."

"Who else did you send letters to?"

"Just Professor Kent, Professor Weatherington, and Mrs. Jarman." That's all it took, I thought with a touch of bitterness. Dale turned and looked directly at me. "Professor Crochet, I don't have any right to ask a favor of you, but do you have to tell Professor Rogers about all this?"

"Dale, I have to admire your loyalty, but I can't say the same for your sense of judgment. This isn't a question of plagiarism, or whatever you call Professor Rogers' way of writing poetry. It's a question of murder." Dale looked to the ground again. "But no; I don't plan to discuss your behavior with Professor Rogers." I stood up.

"You mean you're going to talk with her?" Dale suddenly looked frightened.

"I have no choice," I said, and walked back toward the parking lot. A piece of paper under my windshield read, "Why don't you go back where you came from?", expressing in black and white a question I had been asking myself a lot in recent days.

Chihuahuan street addresses were notoriously unreliable due to the foothills that extended like great tentacles from the mountains into the city, disrupting the orderly array of numbers. Paula's house turned out to be mounted on one of these shoulders, not the expensive side, with its view across the valley, but the canyon side. I had to drive down a steep side road that curved past her house and then ended in a flimsy-looking barricade. The house itself occupied two levels, each with an exterior entrance.

I knocked at the front door and Paula greeted me with the words, "I've been expecting you, dear boy, please come in."

We sat in her living room, a room with tall ceilings, panelled walls, and sliding doors opening onto a deck with a view of the fire lanes running from the entrance to this National Forest land up into the mountains themselves. The modernity of the house's shape contrasted with its old-fashioned furniture. A small antique reading stand in one corner of the room held a large open dictionary. Between the sofa and the fireplace sat a rocking chair in classic design. Strangest of all was an old Victrola horn. When I looked more closely I saw that it wasn't connected to a wind-up record player but had been attached to a modern turntable. No doubt there were speakers concealed in the horn, preserving the appearance of an antique without sacrificing modern audio standards. Ah, California!

Paula quickly brushed aside my apology of the mistaken dedication in the program and said, "But that's not the real reason you're here, is it?"

I felt a little disconcerted that she had been able to read my mind so easily, but went on with what I had prepared to say. "I've been reading some of your poetry."

"Delighted to hear it. So few people at CSC have taken the trouble."

"If I had done so earlier, I might have been able to make sense of recent events sooner."

"What put you on my track?"

"Your elegy. Something nagged me about the text all during our rehearsals with the College Choir, but it wasn't until the performance that I realized I read a lot of those words elsewhere, in a poem by Ben Johnson."

"Ah, yes. Not many people read Jonson nowadays."

"But you ranged so widely—to T.S. Eliot and William Cullen Bryant, among others."

"You need to understand that I really love poetry. I've devoted my whole career to it."

"But largely unappreciated."

"Completely unappreciated!" Her tone turned bitter. "Even with that glory-hound Jarman out of the way so that I could organize a festival to Erato, that silly girl had to make a mockery of my efforts."

"How did you get her to meet you at the tower?"

"It was childishly easy. I told her that I wanted to put her picture on the cover of the festival booklet, and that a sunset silhouette from the tower would make a dramatic portrait. She swallowed the bait without a question."

"But at the end?"

"That was easier yet. I told her that the railing was getting in the way of her body and asked her to stand on that little step at the corner of the tower. When she mounted the step I told her to arch her back to enhance her figure, and when I came over to adjust her hair, it only took a slight push to send her over the edge."

"But the notes you sent to Deirdre and Melissa and Wayne? What was the point?"

"Everything in the department was 'Grant this' and 'Grant that' and 'wasn't Grant wonderful?' Nobody gave me any attention at all. When he announced that he was going to write the 'novelization' of the screenplay that he'd written for his own novel, that was the last straw. Grant had to go. I was just hoping that Melissa or Wayne might take care of it for me. I'm not really a violent person, you know."

"Or Deirdre," I said, thinking of the other stenciled message. "But how could you possibly have known that Grant had called her a bimbo?"

"If you listen carefully, Axel, you learn more than people suppose. Deirdre told her roommate about her affair with Grant. Then Sheri got into an argument with Dale, who said she didn't know the first thing about passionate love. Sheri borrowed Deirdre's experiences, which Dale reported to me."

"But wasn't Grant himself more discreet?"

"Your friend Wayne Tutworthy helped me with that."

"I don't believe it."

"Think again. After Grant announced his silly novelization, I complained to Wayne that Grant was getting all the glory, and in a moment of indiscretion, Wayne said 'And all the women, too!' That was when I guessed that Grant had been having an affair with Caroline."

"What about Deirdre?"

"Around this time Wayne had gotten into a dispute with Grant over the ethics of sleeping with one's students. Grant argued that the girls were 'begging for it,' and when Wayne asked whether he was planning to leave Melissa, Grant said, 'Don't be silly. They're just a bunch of bimbos.' Paula smiled; she was clearly enjoying this chance to show off the nuggets of information that she had been carefully hoarding all this time.

"Why would Wayne tell you this?"

"When I guessed that Grant had cuckolded him with Caroline, Wayne said 'I wish he'd just stick to sleeping with students.' I said, 'I suppose he idolizes them as muses,' and Wayne said, 'Nah, he told me they're just a bunch of bimbos.' It's as I told you: you only have to listen and remember."

"But Deirdre wouldn't kill Grant for you, either?"

"No, the spineless wench!"

"So you felt compelled to do the deed yourself."

"Why don't we have some hot chocolate?" Paula said abruptly, and went into the kitchen without waiting for a response. I heard a tea kettle whistle and in a few moments she returned with two mugs bearing the CSC crest.

Just as Paula claimed to have been expecting my visit, so I had been expecting the presentation of some kind of beverage. Keeping my voice as casual as I could under the circumstances, I asked Paula if she wouldn't mind adjusting the Venetian blinds, which were making a glare in my eyes. When she turned away I quietly exchanged cups with her. When she returned to her seat I resumed our conversation.

"I'm still a bit unclear about the suicide poem that you adapted from 'Thanatopsis.'"

"I never expected it to be published! I thought that Grant might write a literary note, something to express his bitterness at being in a loveless relationship. But I thought Melissa would be the only one to see it."

"Seems like an awful lot of work for an audience of one."

"We have our pride, Mr. Crochet," Paula said, then frowned and looked at me with glazed eyes. "Ah, of course. You switched the cups." Then she fell over onto the sofa. I had no way of knowing what she had planned for me—whether knockout drops or poison. I looked at her body more closely but couldn't detect any breathing at this point—it must have been poison. I reflected on Wayne's advice that I wait for proper back-up before confronting Paula. Sometimes he seemed like such a sissy.

I made my way to the desk in the study off the living room and observed another faux antique, in this case a lamp that from the outside looked like an Art Nouveau piece, with a long-haired maiden holding up a jade green shade, but inside a high-tech, high-intensity bulb.

All I had to go on up to now had been hunches based on comparisons of poems. This hardly constituted grounds to convict a murderer. I needed to find something more substantial. Nothing in the top drawer but the usual odds and ends. The second drawer contained upright file folders with labels for bills, bank statements, insurance information and the like. But at the back of the drawer, behind the labelled folders, Paula had stuffed some sheets of paper which I withdrew and examined. This was it: a photocopy of "Thanatopsis" with Paula's handwritten emendations in the margins, along with a template for making stencilled letters. I was about to look in the drawers on the other side of the desk when a slight change in the light attracted my attention. I turned and saw Paula with a wine bottle held in both hands over her head. Evidently there had been neither knockout drops nor poison in the mugs: she had been playing possum. I tried to dodge the blow but the bottle struck me on the side of the head and everything went black.

I half-woke to a comfortable rocking sensation and idly wondered how far Chihuahua was from the ocean. When I opened my eyes I found myself in my own car rolling down the road toward the embankment and the canyon below. A rush of adrenaline brought me to full consciousness. Time seemed to slow down as I reviewed my options. With no key in the ignition the steering wheel was locked. Only the camber of the road had brought the car around the slight curve and out of sight of Paula's house. The power brakes were also ineffectual. I tried the emergency brake and felt the car begin to slow down, but not nearly enough. I didn't want to trust the barrier at the end of the road to withstand the mounting momentum as the car picked up speed. My only recourse seemed to be to bail out. I opened the door, tried to roll like the stuntmen in the movies, and tumbled heavily against the dirt of the hillside, then watched as my car crashed through the barrier and down into the canyon. A few moments later I heard an explosion. The resulting fire must have ignited the tinder-dry canyon brush, for before long, flames were racing up the hill toward the spot where I was huddled.

My only choice was to head back up the road, but having underestimated Paula once, I didn't want to make the same mistake again. I needed to assume that she would be watching to make sure that her second car-bound murder had worked as well as the first. I examined the angles. As long as Paula was on the upper level she had no way of seeing me, but I also had no way of getting past her house on the road unseen. I wasn't going to get out of this without assistance and Paula's house had the only telephone. I crept toward the building, found the door of the lower level unlocked and entered as quietly as I could. A telephone rested on a small table and I dialled Wayne's number, hoping he'd be home. When he answered, I whispered, "Send for the police. I'm at Paula's," then hung up quickly.

Before long I heard the comforting sound of a siren and relaxed in the knowledge that rescue was close at hand. An image of Jerome Chowning flashed into my mind, and I felt relief at being on the right side of the law. Then I listened again and realized that the siren was coming from the wrong direction. It must have been fire trucks tearing up the fire lane of the canyon to extinguish the flames produced by the demise of my car. They weren't concerned with me at all.

Then I heard the doorbell ring and the sound of male voices, answered by Paula's gentle tones. Great! The police had finally arrived. I couldn't make out the words but the voices never became louder. Was she surrendering so easily? Then the male voices stopped and the front door closed. They must be coming in to search the house. I was all ready to come upstairs and greet my deliverers when I heard Paula's steps on the staircase. Where were the police officers? Surely they could not have left! I looked about for a place to hide then curled up as best I could under the table.

Through the narrow space between the table and the wall I could make out the glint of a revolver as Paula paused at the bottom of the stairs. She proceeded slowly across the room then stopped in front of the table. If I was going to make a move, I had to do it now. I reached out, grabbed her ankles and pulled with all my might. I didn't have much room to manoeuver, but the unexpected attack caught Paula off balance. As she tumbled to the floor the revolver discharged. I emerged from my hiding place, knocking the table over in the process, ran to the place where the gun had fallen, picked it up, and fired it three more times. I heard the squeal of car brakes being applied, and in a few moments the police officers were back in the house.

CHAPTER 24

After our weekly handball match I recounted my adventure with Paula Rogers to Wayne and asked what he thought would happen to her.

"She won't go to jail, at least not as such."

"How do you mean?"

"California has the death penalty. A lawyer will argue that a person would have to be crazy to commit murder given the consequences, and considering Paula's status as a college professor, she'll probably be sent away to a psychiatric hospital for the rest of her life."

Wayne turned out to be right. Paula proved eager to confess the details of her crimes, but her rant about being unappreciated and her obsession with Grant Jarman's success with made her sound like a complete loony.

As I walked to the car that I had rented until I could find a permanent replacement, I noticed a piece of paper stuck under the windshield wipers. Was this another poison pen letter from Dale Cochrane? Not this time. The note read, "Haven't you forgotten something in your office?"

Curiosity won out over prudence and I retraced my steps, passed the library, and approached the door of my office. I still had to consider the possibility that something nasty awaited me, but assumed it wouldn't be anything as drastic as an explosive. I gently opened the door and peered around inside before venturing further. A figure sat at the end of the day-bed but until my eyes adjusted to the reduced brightness I couldn't tell who it was. No revolver in sight. I took a tentative step forward.

"Were you expecting a cat burglar?" The voice belonged to Sheri. I took a relieved breath and entered the room. "I'm glad you found my note," she said.

"How did you know that my car was wrecked?" I asked.

"Jerome followed the fire truck when he heard the siren. When he recognized your license plate he was afraid that you were trapped inside the car. But considering its condition, it was easy to guess that you'd be driving a rental today."

"You'd make a fair detective."

Sheri just smiled. "But nothing happened to you?" she asked.

"No; I'm all right." I didn't particularly want to go into the details of my encounter with Paula Rogers, but I was glad to see Sheri and sat beside her on the daybed.

"After the choir party you asked if you could take a rain check on a kiss."

I didn't recall putting it exactly that way, but she had the idea right, so I leaned toward Sheri, put my arms around her and kissed her gently on the lips. She kissed me back but with greater intent of purpose.

"Perhaps I'd better lock the door," I said.

"Might be a good idea," she said.

We kissed for awhile then Sheri asked, "Do you want to stop?"

"No," I said.

"Me neither," she said. "Just checking." So we kept going.

Afterward Sheri gave me a funny look and asked, "Do you have anywhere you have to go right now?"

"No," I said.

"Then can I take you shopping?" she asked.

"If you'll let me buy you dinner."

"It's a deal."

So after eight months steadfastly maintaining my identity as an uptight Easterner, I went native: flair pants, wide belt, body shirt, apache scarf, and hair combed forward the way it had always wanted to grow, so that when just washed it looked not unlike a Pizza Hut. Soon thereafter I grew a beard, which added a note of incongruity with the orthodontic braces that I was putting on just as my students were finally having theirs removed.

Just as steel bands could gradually bring wayward teeth into submission, so the experiences of my first year at Chihuahua State tamed a bit of my fierce independence. Not all advice was misguided, I decided, nor every suggestion a threat to my autonomy. The painful process of shedding my defensiveness had begun.

Sheri continued to find reasons to spend time with me after choir rehearsals, and expressed amusement over the combination of metal on my mouth and mushrooms on my shirt. Wayne and I continued playing handball and complaining about the administration, notably a faculty meeting in which we spent three-quarters of an hour trying and failing to get a consensus on a question which, it later turned out, the administration had already decided.

One afternoon Sheri asked me what I was going to do. I hadn't made a formal announcement that I was leaving the college, but I'd indicated to Sheri that my position there was no longer tenable.

"I'm thinking about going to Boston," I said.

"Do you know anyone there?"

"Nary a soul. But it seems like a good place to be. You'll be graduating this year. What are you going to do?"

"I'm interested in becoming an editor."

"So do you think you might go to New York? That's where most of the publishing houses have their offices."

"I don't know. I was thinking maybe of going to Boston."

"There are a number of reputable publishers in Boston. Do you have friends there?"

"I think there may be one person I know." She smiled and gave me kiss.

So I ended up following Dale Cochrane's advice. It occurred to me that everything at CSC was so realistic: the mountains were realistic, the state college looked quite realistic, and the students—they were really realistic. Perhaps the most striking thing about Southern California was the verisimilitude of life there. As for me, I preferred the real.

MURDER

in the

MUSIC

DEPARTMENT

CHAPTER 1

At the heart of any great university stands its library. The buzz of activity at the library offers a kind of pulse of the life of the university. I have visited university libraries where the happy hum testified to the institution's basic health. I have taught in universities where the sullen silence betrayed malaise in academic life.

The music library at Brooks University was in the music building at one corner of the Arts Quad. The building originally housed the English department that had moved to larger and grander quarters. Thus the music collection occupied a space not originally intended for a library. One entered the music library through two glass doors at the end of the second floor corridor.

Rows of gunmetal gray bookcases contained the bulk of the library's holdings. A spiral staircase led down to the score collection, which occupied the space left over when classrooms had been converted to music studios. Books on music theory took up the middle level, comprising half the second floor of the music building. Taking the spiral staircase in the other direction brought one to the upper level, which occupied the entire third floor of the building. This area, described as "music literature" in the Library of Congress classification system, encompassed everything from biographies and historical studies to doctoral dissertations and interdisciplinary treatises.

On the left was the reference room with half a dozen long worktables and, behind them, tall free-standing bookcases containing reference works. Additional reference materials occupied waist-high stacks, cutting the room into several sections. One window looked out on the Arts Quad, where graduate students in music, spending Saturday afternoons doing their bibliography assignments, could envy those playing Frisbee on the grass.

At least the graduate students had a window. The undergraduate music majors on work-study spent their Saturday afternoons in the darkness of the stacks, loading books onto a dumbwaiter, raising or lowering the cargo to the proper level, then re-shelving the books according to their call numbers. (Some, impatient with the dumbwaiter's tendency to jam, preferred just lugging the books by hand.) On one occasion I had caught two of the undergraduates giving a third a ride on the shelving cart, but otherwise I hadn't seen them having much fun.

I was headed to the music library on the day after my return from a weekend conference. I hoped to check out several bibliographical references that a colleague at the conference had shared with me.

As I entered the building I saw the front page of the student newspaper stapled to the bulletin board. "MUSIC CHAIRMAN SLAIN," screamed the headline, followed by "Voice Teacher Suspected." I scanned the text.

"Music department chairman Edgar Frost was murdered early Friday afternoon, bludgeoned to death. Authorities have questioned Viola Mordent, the department's vocal instructor. Several witnesses reported an altercation between Professor Frost and Miss Mordent on the morning of the attack. Police investigators have refused to comment on the case."

My reading was interrupted by the sounds of an animated discussion coming from the graduate student lounge, actually a kind of alcove produced when the English classrooms had been converted into music studios. The grad students had taken over the space, furnished it with a second-hand sofa, some chairs and a table. The department had added some informal cubby-holes and a coat rack. Somebody had put up a poster for Oxford University and others had added posters for the Sorbonne, University of Florence, University of Geneva and other institutions of academic excellence that none of our students would ever attend.

I recognized the voice of Bonnie Pearson, a graduate student in musicology. "But I had a class with Prof. Frost Friday morning."

"Well," came another voice—it sounded like Eileen Shaw—"they say he was murdered early in the afternoon."

"The murder weapon was that bust of Brahms he had sitting on the piano," said Chad Brimley, a graduate student in organ.

"How do you know that?" Eileen asked. Perhaps she had absorbed our lessons about the importance of questioning one's sources.

"I saw the statue lying on the floor when the police came to his office."

"Did you see the body?" asked Bonnie.

"Just a leg," Chad said. "They closed the door pretty fast."

"Was there any blood?" Eileen asked.

"I didn't see any," said Chad.

"But why do they think Miss Mordent did it?" Bonnie asked.

"Didn't you hear about the fight she had with Prof. Frost Friday morning? She came back to his office in the afternoon and killed him. They found her brooch on the floor." Chad seemed to know a lot about the case.

"You mean the cameo of Mary Garden?" asked Eileen.

"I don't know, but they spent a lot of time in her studio then took her to the police station for questioning."

"That's horrible," said Eileen.

"What was the fight about?" Bonnie asked.

"You remember Stephanie Whelan?"

"Who could forget," said Eileen. "She felt so humiliated after Prof. Frost badgered her at her recital talk that she dropped out of school."

"On Thursday night she committed suicide: jumped into the College-town gorge. Miss Mordent came storming into Prof. Frost's office on Friday morning and said it was his fault."

"That isn't fair," said Eileen. "Prof. Frost may have been a little rough with his questions, but he's like that with everybody. You don't see the rest of us jumping into the gorge."

"Well, Stephanie did," Chad said.

"So what happens now?" asked Bonnie.

"Dean Manx named Prof. Mack to replace Prof. Frost as department chairman. I haven't seen Miss Mordent. She cancelled her lessons for today."

I continued in the direction of my office. As I passed the door of the department office, Cecilia Crawford called out, "Axel, you have a message from Maureen Chesterton. The telephone number is in your box." Cecilia Crawford had made it clear when she arrived five years ago that she would not be the music department secretary. The position had been upgraded to administrative assistant; Edgar Frost was quite content to give her full control over the day-to-day operations of the department, a task she carried out with efficiency if not warmth.

A call from the president's wife was not to be ignored, so I pulled the pink slip of paper from my cubby-hole and mounted the stairs to my office. The movement of air as I opened the door set in motion the vanes of a mobile, after Calder, a gift from a friend. My bookcases are filled with books, scores and three-ring binders. I like to write in books, a practice frowned upon by librarians, so I end up buying most of the books I use for research. My method when writing on any topic is to read everything that's been written on the subject, including journal

115

articles. These I photocopy and place in binders so that if I ever want to check on a quotation, I have the original source right at hand.

Atop the filing cabinet stand boxes of typed index cards. A simple braided rug lies on the floor. A hooked rug in an Escher design hangs on the wall beside framed prints by a local artist. On the worktable lie the notes for my current project, a book on Debussy's opera "Pelléas et Mélisande." At the edge of the worktable squats a small shepherd playing the flute, fashioned from nuts, bolts and bent nails.

I figured that the call from Maureen Chesterton must be connected to the murder. She and Viola Mordent had shared an apartment in New York when they'd sung at the Met after Maureen returned from an extended stint with European opera companies. There was no rivalry between the two sopranos whose voices dictated different roles. Maureen's unusually high range enabled her to portray the Queen of the Night in *The Magic Flute,* whereas Viola had made her name playing parts like Cherubino in *The Marriage of Figaro.*

Mrs. Forrester answered the phone. "Good morning, Axel, I'm glad you called. Doubtless you've heard."

"Just the general picture. The police suspect Viola because she had a spat with Edgar."

"It's more complicated than that. They found her fingerprints on the murder weapon."

"That doesn't make sense," I said. Viola Mordent had collaborated with me on a series of recitals covering the songs of Claude Debussy. Viola had a celebrated temper—the students nicknamed her "The Dragon"—but physical violence didn't fit with the woman I knew.

"No, of course it doesn't. Gerald has brought pressure to bear in the appropriate places, and so far Viola hasn't actually been arrested, but it's only a matter of time unless her name can be cleared."

"Sounds as if she needs a lawyer."

"That's exactly what I said, but she's determined that you are the only person who can help her."

"Me?" What could a musicologist accomplish in a murder case? I reflected on Viola's way of dealing with the world. In matters musical, be it her own career or the lives of her fledgling students, Viola oversaw every detail, from the shaping of a musical phrase to the proper length of a concert gown. Yet for problems outside what she considered her domain, be it her automobile or her income tax returns, Viola tended to call on an appropriate male figure and tell him, in effect, to "make it go away."

"Now listen carefully, Axel. Viola Mordent is my oldest and dearest friend. I want this matter taken care of and taken care of fast. For the time being I've respected Viola's wishes, but at the end of the week I plan to engage professional assistance whether she wants it or not."

"That's fine with me," I replied, "but couldn't we just start with a detective in the first place?"

There was a pause, then the voice took on a different tone. "I'm going to be frank with you, Axel. Much as I respect your work as an historian, I think you're out of your depth here."

"I couldn't agree with you more."

"Please don't interrupt. You've worked professionally with Viola, so you must have observed her, let us say, tenacity."

"Nice choice of words."

"And so you've probably discovered that the best way of handling these situations is going along with Viola, up to a point."

"True enough."

"That point comes at the end of the week."

"I understand."

"Do your best, Axel."

"You can count on me."

"And if you need any help, just give me a call."

Maureen Forrester believed in the iron fist within a velvet glove. A few years back, one of the star members of the Brook University basketball team had been suspended after an undergraduate student accused him of sexual harassment. Given the circumstances, with the team about to enter the NCAA tournament, Mrs. Forrester didn't wait around for due process but swooped down on the women's dormitory, talked to the girl, determined that she'd invented the story at the behest of an unscrupulous boyfriend at a rival school, and persuaded her to recant, all in the space of one afternoon. The basketball player didn't miss a game.

I didn't see any way of refusing her request. An untenured assistant professor would be crazy to claim that a murder investigation wasn't in his job description.

I couldn't see Viola as a murderer. She was generous with her time; she had served as advisor and confidante to dozens of students. On more than one occasion I had seen a singer enter her studio cloaked in gloom and emerge wreathed in smiles. Viola was forgiving of human faults, particularly her own appetite for sweets.

On the other hand, I could imagine the encounter in Edgar Frost's office. Frost had no patience for incompetence, and he had long resented the continual eroding of standards for performance majors. Where once the requirements for a Masters degree in voice had included the submission of a thesis, this burden had been watered down to the writing of a brief essay; and, even this proving too onerous a task to impose on voice students, the requirement now stood as an oral presentation on the musical works presented in the student's recital, after which the student was expected to respond to questions from the examining panel.

Stephanie Whelan had not been a gifted student, nor even a very talented singer; but she'd been able to pay her own tuition, which excused the department from finding a teaching assistantship for her. She prepared a recital with Viola on the songs of Berlioz and his contemporaries, a poor choice as it turned out. Frost numbered Berlioz among his many areas of expertise and had skewered the hapless girl in the interrogation.

Viola tried unsuccessfully to persuade Stephanie to remain in the masters program. When the girl took her own life, Viola would not have hesitated to storm into Frost's office and blame him for Stephanie's death. But murder? That didn't seem likely.

Naming Lewis Mack as the new department chairman made a certain amount of sense. Mack was well known in the city for his radio program, "In Your Ear," in which he perpetuated anecdotal misinformation about the composers whose works he played. Presumably he could be counted on to deal with the police diplomatically, an assumption that could not be made for many members of the music department, a notorious collection of misfits. Surely the appointment could not have been made on the basis of his scholarly pretensions. Edgar Frost had not hidden his disdain for Mack's program notes for the local symphony and the articles he wrote for piano teachers' magazines.

CHAPTER 2

Viola's studio was open; so I walked in and waited in the crook of her grand piano, idly stroking the bust of Mozart that lay atop the instrument, its base rubbed shiny by countless nervous singers. Viola's desk was pushed into the corner—she never used it as a barricade against students the way many of the faculty did. Above the desk hung photos of a younger (and thinner) Viola Mordent: on the stage of the Metropolitan Opera House; posing with famous conductors; or in costume as a rather hefty Cherubino. One wall held a blackboard painted with clef lines and another a set of low bookcases filled with opera scores in their familiar green bindings. In the corner stood a small refrigerator, on the table beside the sofa a bowl of cellophane-wrapped sourballs next to a box of Kleenex.

Viola came in looking a bit tired, but impeccably dressed as always. "I'm glad to see you, Axel. I've just had the most unpleasant experience."

"You mean an interrogation at the police station?"

"Worse. Do you know a Freddy Thatcher?"

"Never heard of him."

"He claimed to be a reporter for the *Brook Banner*."

"Surely Maureen has warned you to stay away from reporters."

"He's just this little kid with thick black glasses. I wanted to laugh."

"So what happened?"

"He explained that he thought the police were making a big mistake."

"And that made you listen."

"But after that it got rather complicated. He said he admired Mark Lane, who wrote *Rush to Judgment;* and he was sure there was what he called a 'second assassin,' whom I was covering up for."

"Second assassin?"

"He didn't see how a woman could lift that Brahms statue high enough to hurt anybody."

"So you decided to show him by throwing your Mozart statue at him?"

"He talked so fast I didn't get a chance to say much. The worst part was when he took out a camera and started taking pictures of me."

"Couldn't you get rid of him?"

"I tried, but he wouldn't leave. Eventually Mark Fillmore heard the commotion and rescued me. He picked the little twerp up by the belt and the collar and just heaved him out of my studio."

"I wish I'd been there to see it," I laughed.

"It wasn't a bit funny, Axel."

"No, I suppose not. You obviously won't talk to him again, but I have a feeling we're going to be seeing our young Mark Lane in Wednesday's edition of the Banner. I'd rather get the story from you. So far all I've heard are bits and pieces. Suppose you tell me what happened." She motioned me to an armchair and pulled her desk chair toward it.

"You remember the incident with the poor Whelan child, whom Edgar practically crucified during her oral presentation."

"I heard about it."

"Well, Thursday night she took her own life—they really ought to put up a suicide barrier on the Gorge Bridge; that's the second time in two years that someone has jumped."

I remembered with a shudder. I had crossed the bridge the morning of the previous suicide and had seen the body spread-eagled on the rocks while a parade of policemen and paramedics scrambled down the path toward it.

"I should have stayed in closer touch with Stephanie," Viola reproached herself. "After she left the university I may have talked with her once or twice, but I can't say I really knew how she was doing. I had no idea that things were as bleak as that for her."

"Hmm."

"I went to see Edgar on Friday morning, and I guess I lost my temper. You know how cruel he can be. You remember how he treated Owen Birtwhistle, who brought him to Brook in the first place."

"I remember," I answered. He took away Owen's graduate seminars and made him teach nothing but General Studies courses. For a serious musicologist, that constituted cruel and unusual punishment.

"It broke his heart when Edgar cancelled the Sweelinck organ."

"An organ in mean-tone temperament on which you couldn't perform Bach— it did seem a bit impractical."

"Stephanie wasn't that bad a singer, and so what if she hadn't gotten all of her facts straight about Berlioz?"

"So you blew up at him?"

Viola seemed calm enough now as she recounted the confrontation, but I knew another side of her.

"What about the murder?"

"I went back to Edgar's office in the afternoon to invite him to Stephanie's funeral. I thought it might smooth things over a bit."

"But you didn't kill him?"

"Of course not! I mean, everybody thought Edgar was a bastard, but you didn't see them killing him."

"But this time somebody did, and evidently managed it in a way that points to you."

Viola frowned and began to shake her head. "You've got to help me, Axel. I don't know anything about this sort of thing."

"Viola, I'm your friend, but it looks to me as if what you really need at this point is a good lawyer."

"That's what Maureen Chesterton said. But nobody beyond the department would understand this place. To an outsider, our colleagues would look pretty strange."

I couldn't contradict her on that point, but still couldn't see myself in the role of detective. "I don't know, Viola. I'm afraid of letting you down."

"I think you're mistaken, Axel," Viola said. "I think you're afraid of succeeding."

"What do you mean?"

"You're a fine scholar and you enjoy your work, but I've observed that you don't like getting too close to other people, aside from a few friends. If you take on this job, you're going to learn a lot about some people in this department that I suspect you'd just as soon not know."

"Am I that transparent?"

"Axel, when you get to be my age, men are easy."

"So you think somebody in the department killed Edgar?"

"A lot of people would have been quite happy to see him dead."

"That's true enough."

Edgar Frost enjoyed making enemies. He took arbitrary positions and didn't hesitate to point out shortcomings in the university's pursuit of excellence. His administration of the department seemed to some deliberately calculated to thwart their ambitions.

To my surprise, Viola wanted to work on the next program in our series, Debussy's settings of texts by Stéphane Mallarmé. We spent the rest of the morning working and talking about our recital. As I walked back to my office to grab a sandwich, I reflected on my relationship with Viola. It seemed inconceivable to me that she would ever hurt a fly. Yet the police would not have focused their investigation on her frivolously. And why did she refuse to get a lawyer?

If an insider had done the deed, I would probably see the murderer at the department meeting that afternoon.

CHAPTER 3

When I arrived at the Matthew Finson Seminar Room, named after a local linoleum dealer who, not coincidentally, had supplied the flooring, Lewis Mack was already seated at the head of the long conference table rapping impatiently with a pencil. A few people at the other end of the room took the hint and found their seats.

The door opened and in came Seth Chichester Nelson (he used all three names on his recital programs), the university organist and teacher of the graduate seminar in Baroque music and the undergraduate music survey. Nearing sixty, Nelson had a master's degree from Yale and a "certificate" in organ from France, the provenance of which no one had ever been able to trace. He maintained that it was the equivalent of a doctorate; and while all the rest of us hold genuine Ph.D. degrees, Seth was the only one who insisted on being called "Doctor."

Across the table sat Paavo Raine, the Ives Professor of Musicology, who bored us every year with "Aspects of Quatrain Theory in ___," the blank filled in over the years with the names of Haydn, Mozart, Beethoven, then Clementi, C.P.E. Bach, Czerny, Dussek, and Hummel. Now making a second round of composers from the Classic era, Paavo had been scheduled to present "New Aspects of Quatrain Theory in Haydn: What Is the Difference Between a Theme (=Subject) and a Transitional Development?" at the next meeting of the American Musicological Society.

I greeted Jonathan Whitby, the electronic composer, and took my place between him and Mark Fillmore, the department's senior ethnomusicologist.

"If we could get started please, gentlemen," Lewis said. "Naturally we all mourn the loss of our colleague. Dean Manx has named me as department chairman. Where's George?"

"I think he's sick," said Fillmore.

"More likely at the bar," muttered Jonathan.

"Miss Mordent has asked to be excused," Lewis continued briskly. "I've written the agenda on the blackboard and I'd like to follow it." Lewis seemed to be making a point of showing us who was in charge now. "Please remind your graduate students to see Miss Crawford to pick up their complimentary tickets to the Boston Symphony Orchestra concert Wednesday evening."

"What are they playing?" Nelson inquired.

"The Berlioz Requiem."

"Edgar gets his own Requiem?" Paavo observed sardonically.

"The program was set well in advance; but I believe that Prof. Frost had some input into the choice of selection, as befit his station," Lewis answered somewhat officiously. "Also, let me remind you that next Monday is the deadline for applications for university research grants. At my instruction, these applications will now go through the chairman's office." His tone suggested he had been contemplating this change in procedure for some time.

"Prof. Fillmore has made a proposal that ethnomusicology students be exempted from the harmony requirement on the grounds that the music they're studying often has no harmony," Lewis continued.

"How can they be expected to make meaningful comparisons with Western music if they don't understand the principles of Western music?" Nelson demanded.

"Suppose I respond to that," Fillmore spoke for the first time. "Contemporary practice in ethnomusicology studies the musics of different cultures on their own terms, not in comparison with what we in the West consider to be the norm. It would seem to me that our students would be better served by a course in melody, which the ethnomusicology department would be prepared to offer. Actually, a course in melody should be required of all graduate students."

"Now wait just a minute," objected Paavo. "If anyone teaches a course in melody, it should be me. I've devoted my entire career ..."

"I think we're departing from the motion on the floor," Lewis interrupted. "The proposal is an exemption from the harmony requirement."

The debate carried on for another ten minutes and the motion was tabled, the normal fate of any idea proposed in the music department. When I first came to the university, I listened to Edgar Frost talk about his vision for a more scholarly orientation to the music program and drafted a revised undergraduate curriculum. I took my ideas to each member of the department in turn, soliciting their suggestions and criticisms. Nobody raised strong objections; but when I finally brought my draft to a department meeting, they accorded it a perfunctory discussion, and then tabled it.

"I have another request to review the Master's degree requirements for voice majors," Mack went on. "The suggestion is that we replace the current oral exam with written program notes on the student's recital program."

"A bit like bolting the barn door after the horse has escaped," said Paavo.

This proposal was tabled in the absence of Miss Mordent, but only after a number of professors had expressed their opinions on the weakening of requirements in the music department and the decline of civilization generally, and Prof. Mack had to remind us again who was in charge here.

He moved to the next item. "I have an application from a Sigrida Salo in historical musicology. Has anyone read her file?"

"I read it," said Jonathan Whitby, who had a reputation for actually reading every document that crossed his desk. No wonder he had such a small output as a composer. "I didn't think it was very impressive." Of course, he also had a reputation for extreme misogyny and would probably have had something negative to say about any woman's application.

"I've received a note from Miss Salo," Prof. Raine said, "withdrawing her application."

"All right." Lewis continued making little tick marks next to each item on the agenda. "Now we need to appoint a committee for Chad Brimley's masters examination. Axel, I'm naming you to the committee, and of course Seth, as Chad's advisor. Would you please find another person from outside the department?" Seth nodded, but Lewis was busy making another tick mark on his sheet and didn't notice.

"We have a request from Leslie Spraggett for a fourth extension to the statute of limitations for submitting his doctoral thesis."

"What's the statute of limitations for?" Jonathan Whitby whispered in my ear.

"Musicology students have ten years to complete their doctorate after they pass their qualifying exam," I whispered back. I would have said more, but Lewis was already rapping his pencil at me.

"... no reason why he should be given another extension," Seth Nelson was saying. "What's his excuse this time?"

"It seems he lost the index cards containing his entire dissertation while on a visit to the Library of Congress," Mack said. "We have a recommendation from his graduate committee that the request be denied."

"Here, here!" exclaimed Paavo. The recommendation carried unanimously.

"You'll be glad to hear," Lewis said, "that I've accepted an invitation to write the music portion of the Open University's program on "Culture," to be published by World Academy Press."

"Way to go, Lewis!" said Jonathan.

"Good for you!" said Seth.

"Amazing!" I managed to choke out a response.

Over the weekend a colleague at another university, author of the most widely used undergraduate music history text in the country, told me about the World Academy Press, an enterprise devoted to purveying intellectual pabulum to the masses and luring unwary college professors to help cover the product with a veneer of academic respectability. Though unwilling to contribute to the "Culture" project, my colleague did propose a heraldic crest for the enterprise: education recumbent upon a field of bull rampant.

The meeting dragged on till after 3 p.m. When I was able to extricate myself, I headed to the Music Office.

CHAPTER 4

Cecilia Crawford considered it part of her mandate to protect the chairman from interruptions by students and, as far as possible, colleagues. The department office had once been a favorite hangout and center of gossip. While we never had a stove or a cracker barrel, the mail boxes served as an excuse to gather and exchange critical observations on student recitals, tidbits on the latest scandal, and futile proposals to the effect that if the administration couldn't give us a proper staff lounge, they might at least provide a coffee machine.

One of Cecilia's first actions had been to erect a counter which destroyed the kaffee-klatsch atmosphere, kept students and faculty out of her hair, and served as an additional barrier to the chairman's office.

I suppose I should not have been surprised that Cecilia gave no outward sign of having any feelings at all about the events of Friday. She answered my questions briskly and with a tacit acknowledgement that since I had been away over the weekend, I merited a certain amount of information, and naturally she would be its most authoritative source.

On Friday Cecilia had overheard the argument between Edgar and Viola. She would stipulate only that "voices had been raised." Viola had returned in the afternoon around 1:30, had entered Frost's office through the department office door and exited to the hallway. Cecilia had no idea what they had talked about.

"About half an hour later, I knocked on Prof. Frost's door. I don't like to interrupt him when he's working, but there were some letters requiring his signature that needed to go out that afternoon."

"So you were the one who discovered the body?"

"That's right."

"Did you hear a cry, a blow, anything?"

"No."

Cecilia declined to speculate on who had committed the murder. She glanced at the clock pointedly, as if to remind me that I had a graduate seminar that took precedence over idle questions.

"Don't forget that your course descriptions are due today," Cecilia reminded me as I left the office.

"Prof. Crochet?" A short fellow with light brown hair combed straight back wearing round black glasses: Freddy Thatcher. "Can I have a word with you?"

"Actually, I'm on my way to class."

"This will only take a minute. I heard you're investigating the Frost murder."

"Who told you that?"

"We reporters never divulge our sources," he said smugly. "I'm looking for a 'Deep Throat,' someone on the inside who can feed me clues."

"Look ..."

"Frederick Thatcher," he said, handing me a card.

"I really do have to get to class," I said. "And stop pestering Miss Mordent."

CHAPTER 5

An atmosphere of excitement filled the seminar room. We were supposed to be talking about Wagner's Ring Cycle. Edgar hated Wagner and had perennially denied me permission to enter a graduate seminar with that title into the course catalogue; but a master of politics, he had no objection to letting half a dozen graduate students register individually for independent study with me and coincidentally meet on Monday afternoons in the seminar room after the faculty meetings. I reminded the students to pick up their tickets to the BSO concert, and then asked them to discuss Wagner's use of leitmotifs at the beginning of *Die Walküre*, the second opera in the cycle.

"Oh, Prof. Crochet, how can you talk about leitmotifs when there's been a murder?" Bonnie Pearson was a second year musicology student, friendly, self-assured, with a modesty and openness that disarmed other girls who might otherwise have been envious of her good looks.

"And why would Miss Mordent kill Prof. Frost? It would be like Fricka killing Wotan." This was Eileen Shaw, a third-year musicology student and fine pianist with whom I had recently performed a recital of Debussy's four-hand piano music.

"Did you think of Prof. Frost as the king of the gods?" I asked her with some amusement.

"Well, he was department chairman. It's practically the same thing."

"I've always thought of Miss Mordent as Brunnhilde," Bonnie said.

"You mean riding through the skies on a horse and singing 'Ho-yo-to-ho'?" Eileen asked.

"No, I mean disobeying her father ..."

"Do you think Prof. Frost was Miss Mordent's father?"

"No, I mean being put on a rock and surrounded by magic fire and F# major chords until a young hero should come to rescue her." Maybe we were going to get to the music.

"And her sister Valkyries could be all the rest of the sopranos at the Met: do they always have to be so big?"

"But Prof. Frost was killed by a statue of Brahms—Brahms hated Wagner," Bonnie said.

"Who's going to replace Prof. Frost as respondent to Prof. Raine's paper?" Chad wanted to know.

"What's a respondent?" came the query from Marcia Tidd, a first-year theory student.

"At professional meetings, after someone gives a paper, he usually invites a colleague in his field to offer comments on it," Chad explained. More often someone to point out factual errors in the paper, undermine its basic assumptions, and brag about his own work, I would have answered, but decided to keep my cynicism to myself.

"I know," Bonnie went on excitedly. "Suppose Stephanie was really Prof. Frost's daughter, the way Sieglinde was Wotan's daughter."

"You're still thinking of Prof. Frost as a god, and Stephanie's mother as a mere mortal?" I would have liked to get the conversation back to Wagner's music.

"Do you think Stephanie was in love with her brother?" Eileen asked.

"I don't think she had a brother—she was an orphan," Bonnie said.

"That's not what orphan means," said Chad impatiently.

"Do you think Stephanie was pregnant? Maybe that's why she committed suicide." Eileen brought a critical mind to gossip as well as to scholarship.

"Maybe she was carrying Prof. Frost's love child," Bonnie said.

At this point I insisted on changing the topic. Chad's next question, while not related to Wagner, at least took us away from Edgar's personal life.

"Did you know Prof. Nelson is having a Festschrift?"

"What's a Festschrift?" Marcia wanted to know.

"We had to cover that in bibliography seminar," Eileen said. "When a famous scholar reaches seventy-five, a bunch of his colleagues write essays on topics that he..."

"Or she...," interjected Bonnie,

"... wrote about in their career," Eileen finished, inclusively if not grammatically. "Then the university publishes the essays as a book and they have a big party to present it."

This was news to me. I wouldn't have thought Seth was sufficiently old for a Festschrift, never mind sufficiently eminent. And did he really have a company of admiring colleagues? This bore looking into.

We were able to get to Wagner's music at last. I pointed out the tonal movement through the opera and we listened to the final act, scores open on the seminar table.

For the following week's assignment, I asked the class to examine the large-scale tonal structure in the third act of *Die Walküre* in greater detail, starting with the famous "Ride of the Valkyries" and ending with the

Magic Fire Music. But as the class left the seminar room, the conversation was not about the death of Siegmund but the death of Edgar Frost.

"You know," I heard Chad say, "if Prof. Raine murdered Prof. Frost, it would be like Fafner killing Fasolt: two giants in musicology fighting for the golden ring of scholarship."

Wagner's Ring Cycle incorporated many symbols of human interaction. The golden ring of the title supposedly conveyed absolute power to its bearer, but a curse on the ring brought death to those who sought it. Chad's comment might not have been so far off the mark. Paavo Raine held the Ives Chair but Edgar Frost held the respect of the scholarly community. It seemed a bit far-fetched. On the other hand, if Viola really had murdered Edgar in rage over his part in Stephanie Whelan's death, the Ring offered a counterpart for that, too. In *Die Walküre,* Hunding kills Siegmund in revenge for the death of his kinsmen.

CHAPTER 6

"I'm glad I caught you, Axel," Lewis said as I came into the hallway. "This just arrived in the mail and I thought you'd be the person to take care of it."

"What's that?"

"It's from the regional chapter of the AMS. Evidently it's our turn to host the next meeting."

"And you wanted me to organize it."

"Who better?"

Who indeed. Nobody else would take the job. I thought about the last regional meeting of the American Musicological Society I'd attended. The program had included an interesting talk on the Janko keyboard, a nineteenth-century attempt to rationalize the piano through the use of four interlocking keyboards, arranged somewhat like the manuals of an organ, each tuned in whole steps; an overlong disquisition on the inappropriateness of the term "nonliturgical" to describe a corpus of Baroque instrumental concerti; my own contribution on Debussy's *Children's Corner* suite; and a performance of a recent quasi-aleatoric piano composition based on a Chopin piano prelude, preceded by a quasi-intelligible analysis no less convoluted and even less interesting than the piece itself.

The most unpredictable portion of the meeting had been a paper by the chapter's unofficial crackpot, Hilbert Titcomb, who turned up at every meeting with a presentation distinguished by its breadth, originality and humility. While scholars habitually indulge in a ceremony of defensive backing and filling, this chap had no peer at grovelling, scraping, bowing and writhing. What his remarks lacked in substance, they more than compensated in qualifications: "We may perhaps be not entirely unjustified in supposing, at least as a temporary hypothesis, quickly to be superseded by superior hypotheses as its inevitable flaws come to light, as indeed they must..."

On this occasion, a twenty-five-page handout accompanied the talk, with musical examples drawn from every period of Western history, elegantly calligraphed, flagrantly misspelled. After twenty minutes of pointing out relationships, some legitimate, some specious, among widely disparate examples, our speaker turned to Beethoven's Eroica Symphony and proposed to treat the two opening chords as a motive. Working his way through the symphony, movement by movement, he pointed out a multitude of spots which might, *or might not,* have anything to do with those chords, inviting his audience to draw its own conclusions, and closing with the humble wish that his remarks, partly facetious, partly earnest (and wholly fatuous, one added silently) might possibly lead his audience to think differently about the Eroica Symphony and, dare he hope, about music in general, in order that his modest contribution might not have been in vain.

Did I really want to spend the next several months making all the arrangements for this meeting? Edgar Frost, bless his memory, had offered me an out.

"Lewis, I'm honored that you would think of me for this assignment, and I agree that it's high time we held a regional meeting here at Brook; but I think, under the circumstances of Prof. Frost's recent demise, that it might be considered insensitive on our part to celebrate musicology so soon after his death."

"Oh, good idea. I'll tell them we'd be happy to host the meeting next year." He walked down the corridor.

I continued in the opposite direction toward Paavo Raine's office, which hadn't changed appreciably since my initial visit as a new faculty member: clutter everywhere, scores opened on every surface, piano lid closed, covered with notes and file folders. The desk was also littered with piles of papers, scores, and books. Raine had a reputation for being continually at work. He wasn't unfriendly, just terribly busy. Nobody really knew what he felt or thought about anything, though he periodically reminded students and colleagues about the inferiority of university education in the United States compared with that in Europe.

Paavo looked up from his worktable when I entered and offered a smile that seemed to say "I'd be more than happy to give you sixty seconds of my time."

What he actually said, in response to my query, was, "Are you still thinking about the murder, Axel? I thought Miss Mordent had confessed."

"On the contrary. But the circumstances suggest that if it wasn't Viola, it would have to be someone else in the department."

"That's impossible," Paavo replied flatly. "Prof. Frost was beloved of everyone on the faculty. You know about Miss Mordent's temper. She's obviously an unstable woman. She could probably plead insanity and get away with it."

"I understand Edgar was to have been the respondent to your paper at AMS," I said.

"Yes, I was looking forward to Prof. Frost's comments. I'm sure they would have been as insightful and penetrating as always." He didn't actually say "Was there anything else?" but his body language shouted his desire to get back to work; so I wished him well with his paper and returned to my office.

I remember once being told that when people work incessantly they are usually trying to escape from something. I didn't know what Paavo might have been trying to escape, but he published more than anyone else in the department and gave annual lectures in which he would play the musical examples himself, badly, at the piano. I first heard the phrase, "plays like a musicologist," perhaps the ultimate insult for a pianist, directed at Paavo Raine.

Paavo always had difficulty filling his classes, mostly because he clung to archaic standards of academic excellence in an age of degrees by accumulation. As tenant of the Ives Chair in Musicology, Paavo only had to teach two courses a year, but getting enrolment for them was sometimes a struggle. Last year Edgar had arranged that in place of one course, Paavo would offer three public lectures on Schubert. After working all summer on the project, Paavo delivered an enthusiastically incoherent rehash of old scholarly opinions which provoked one of my junior colleagues to mutter, "If you or I had given this lecture, we never would have heard the end of it."

While Paavo's arguments may have been unconvincing, his rhetoric was compelling. Each paragraph started with an introductory "Now" and concluded triumphantly with a shouted "Yes!" The best part of the presentation was the musical illustrations, which had nothing whatever to do with the lecture proper. Paavo just thought it would be nice if we listened to some Schubert. One observed that Prof. Raine played the phonograph the same way he played the piano: loudly and badly. Tearing across the grooves, he would find the passage he wanted, turn the volume up until the loudspeakers threatened to give way, then scream to make himself heard, if not understood, over the din. Ah, the joys of tenure!

Eileen Shaw was waiting for me. I unlocked the door and invited her to sit down.

"Prof. Crochet, I'm really upset," she began.

I nodded and waited for her to continue.

"Everyone was talking about Prof. Frost's death as if they thought it was just a big joke."

"They did seem a bit unsympathetic. You know, Eileen, sometimes people make jokes when they're afraid to show their true feelings."

"Well, I'm not afraid," she went on resolutely. "I'm angry and upset."

"I see."

"Some stranger has come in here and murdered the chairman, one of our best teachers. Everything's all messed up." The girl seemed near tears.

"And you're angry."

"Yes! Prof. Frost knew so much. Did you know he could speak five languages? Anything you could think of, he could always talk about it with you. No matter what the subject was, he always knew something about it."

"You admired that."

"Yes. It's so unfair that somebody killed him!"

"You really feel this loss."

"That's right. He was my advisor. I was doing my thesis on the madrigals of Francis Pilkington, and now Prof. Frost is dead. What am I going to do?"

"Do you want to continue with that topic?"

"Yes. I've already done all the background research, and I've gathered the music I need, along with information on the poets."

"So you weren't planning to do a manuscript study?" On more than one occasion I had borne the criticism, either stated or implied, from colleagues who believed that the only proper task of musicologists was to examine watermarks or study handwriting or measure the distance between clef-lines in a manuscript. Since these were the subjects that the most prestigious journals seemed to prefer, I suppose they had a point, but I thought there should be room on the professional spectrum for a variety of ways of understanding music.

"No, I want to investigate the relationship between the poetry and the music."

"You mean word-painting?"

"Yes, that of course, but I'd like to see if there aren't deeper connections as well."

"I'd be willing to serve as your advisor."

"What?"

"I've done that kind of study with Debussy, and I've always admired Pilkington's madrigals.

"Is that all right?" Eileen looked doubtful. Edgar had been our Renaissance man in both senses of the term. My fields were nineteenth-century music and opera.

"I think, under the circumstances, the department will approve it."

"That would be super." She looked dubious but relieved.

"Sleep sweetly, sleep sweetly, let nothing affright ye, in calm contentment lie."

"That's Pilkington!"

"It's also good advice."

"Thanks, Prof. Crochet. You're a peach."

"You're welcome, Eileen. You know, there is something you could do for me."

"What's that?"

"I imagine you've been in Prof. Frost's office a good deal?"

"Sure, we met there every week to talk about my thesis."

"Could you try to remember if anything has changed in that office in the last week or so? Anything different that you might have noticed?"

"I can't remember anything different, but if I think of anything, I'll tell you. Why do you need to know?"

"Do you think Miss Mordent killed Prof. Frost?"

"No, of course not," she said with some feeling.

"If the murderer was someone in the department, rather than a stranger, your memory may hold a clue."

"Gee, I never thought about it like that. I'll try to remember. Thanks a lot."

After she left, I closed the office and went to the student union for supper.

CHAPTER 7

The chapel bells were ringing as I crossed the Arts Quad from the music building and past the library toward the student union. The bells had fallen into disuse by the time of the university's centennial celebration earlier in the year. A request had come to the music department from the administration asking whether someone could play the bells, and since I had done some bell-ringing as an undergraduate, I volunteered to take a look.

In contrast to the huge levers I had performed on at college, resembling a rank of rowboat oars, the Brooks carillon operated from a conventional keyboard. For the centennial I had played a medley of football songs but eventually I interested some of the graduate students in performing Bach organ preludes and fugues four-hands on the bells, and before long the students had taken over the operation entirely, organized a rotation, and offered a daily recital.

I caught sight of Seth Nelson coming toward me, returning from his office in the chapel. For someone who never published anything, he had made an astonishing number of research trips to France. He taught both his Baroque seminar and also his undergraduate survey from notes he had taken as a student at Yale, which is why none of the Brook undergraduates had ever heard about the music of Bartók, or that of any other composer writing after around 1930. (One would think that they'd have picked that up in the 20th-century music course; but that was taught by the early-music specialist, who took it on several decades earlier when he was chairman, in order to demonstrate his broadmindedness in teaching a subject he personally detested. He would begin the course with Stravinsky's *Firebird* and skip lightly over the rest of the century to arrive at the enormous corpus of extremely conservative music produced by one of his friends.)

Seth's contribution to the centennial was to have been the inauguration of a new rank of pipes, the State Trumpet, on the chapel organ; but for some reason the pipes were never installed, and instead we heard a group of student trumpeters, playing very loudly and very badly.

When our paths crossed, I congratulated Nelson on his upcoming Festschrift.

"Who told you about that?" he demanded.

"It's quite an honor," I said. "Who's editing the book?"

"I am," he said under his breath.

"Really? Who's publishing it?"

"None of your business."

He pushed past me. I wished him well, wondering at his peculiar behavior.

From the outside a great monolith, on the inside the student union building was a maze-like structure of halls and stairways. The first two floors held offices for student organizations and the university bookstore, the third floor a few hotel rooms for those who could not afford the pricey accommodations at the School of Hotel Administration. One descended a level to a cafeteria and yet another level to the university theatre.

The cafeteria offered quirky short order fare including a "Boburger," a cheeseburger with a fried egg on top, and milkshakes made with real milk and real ice cream. The Sunday morning brunch—omelettes, hotcakes, hash browns, bacon or ham—was a campus tradition, if a dietary disaster.

As I entered the dining area, Bonnie and Eileen saw me and beckoned for me to join them.

"We meet again." I smiled at Eileen.

"Chad's just gone back for dessert," Eileen said, when I glanced at the third place at the long wooden table.

"You hang around together a lot, don't you?" I observed. "Can't Chad make up his mind?"

"It's not like that," Bonnie said.

"Why not? You're both very attractive young women."

"Chad's gay," Eileen said quietly. "We like being with him because he's smart and funny, and because it's relaxing to be with someone who's not always propositioning you."

"Sounds like a nice threesome. It's a shame Chad's leaving."

"Leaving?"

"Prof. Nelson told me that Chad was applying to the doctoral program at Boston University for next fall."

Chad returned to the table with a three-colored ice cream parfait.

"You didn't tell us you were going to BU!" Bonnie said.

"It isn't official," Chad said. "There's still more paperwork to do, and Prof. Lewis still has to write me a letter."

"But why BU?" Eileen demanded.

"I've gotten really interested in the mechanics of organ construction. That goes beyond Prof. Nelson's expertise, but Graham Twillinger told me that the president of the Organ Historical Society teaches at Boston University, so I talked to him and he said he'd welcome me as a student."

"Why do you need a letter from Prof. Lewis?" I asked.

"Prof. Nelson said that Prof. Lewis had his masters and his doctorate from BU, and a letter of recommendation from an alumnus carries a lot of weight."

"But he hasn't written it yet?"

"No. He said he'd do it a couple of weeks ago. I guess he's just busy."

That struck me as odd. Writing recommendation letters takes a high priority for any university teacher and most of us try not to let the sun set between a request and a submission. The conversation shifted to the death of Edgar Frost.

"I'm going to miss Prof. Frost," Chad began. "I don't know about the rest of you, but I think he was the best teacher I've ever had."

"How so?" I asked.

"Well, he always liked to throw out ideas rather than just telling you stuff you should know. One time he stopped in the middle of a lecture and said he wondered whether harmony hadn't been a grand mistake, whether Western music hadn't taken a monumental wrong turn around the 11th century."

"That must have stirred things up."

"I'll say. The class started shouting 'What about Bach?' and 'What about Mozart and Beethoven?'"

"What did Prof. Frost say?"

"He didn't give them any answer. He just smiled, told them to think about it, and went on with his lecture. I was blown away."

"I liked him too," Eileen said, "but right now I'm more worried about Miss Mordent. She seemed really upset when I talked to her this afternoon."

"I'm not surprised," Chad said. "I mean, how would you feel if you'd not only been accused of murder, but all the evidence was directed at you, too?"

"It doesn't look too good for her right now," I said. A bunch of freshmen entered noisily and made their way into the cafeteria section.

Bonnie looked at each of us in turn, then said, "I have a confession to make."

We looked at her in surprise.

"Miss Mordent wasn't the last person to see Prof. Frost alive."

"The murderer was presumably the last person," Chad observed logically.

"I mean besides the murderer," Bonnie said. "On Friday afternoon I was standing in the hall trying to get up the nerve to see Prof. Frost; and as soon as Miss Mordent came out of his office, I went in."

"What for?" Eileen asked

Bonnie hesitated, reddened a bit, and continued. "I was really upset about the mark I got on my term paper—it counted for practically the whole grade for the course—and I was hoping I could persuade Prof. Frost to change it. Friday was the deadline for grades to be posted."

"But Bonnie," Eileen said, "Prof. Frost has a reputation for never altering a student's mark."

"Well," Bonnie reddened even further, "I wore a really low-cut blouse and no bra, and I said that I'd be willing to do anything to get the mark changed."

"So you were more interested in preserving your GPA than your virtue?" I asked.

"You sound like my father."

"Ouch."

"So he turned you down?" asked Chad.

"Yes. He just said that I should put as much thought into my essay as into my chicanery, and then turned his back to me and went to work. I was so mad I could have brained him."

"You don't know him well enough, Bonnie," said Eileen. "If he'd accepted your proposition and changed your mark, it would have given you a hold over him. He likes to have the advantage over other people, but he's extremely careful never to be at a disadvantage himself."

Eileen showed a good deal of insight. All the same, I'm glad Bonnie had aimed her wiles toward Edgar and not toward me.

"So you see," Bonnie concluded more confidently, "Miss Mordent couldn't have killed Prof. Frost."

"Have you told this story to the police?" I asked.

"They haven't even asked me. They never talked to any of the students."

I could understand the reluctance of the police to seek complications in a case that looked cut and dried.

I asked the students whether they were planning to go to the concert Wednesday night and Bonnie asked whether I thought it was a good idea to listen to a recording of the Berlioz Requiem beforehand.

"I'll tell you about an experience I had," I replied. "When I was an undergraduate, the Boston Symphony played the Prokofiev Fifth Symphony on a concert series; and since I'd never heard the work before, I listened to it over and over on a recording by another orchestra. I became so familiar with their interpretation that when I finally heard the live performance, it sounded wrong just because it was different. Then, one summer at Tanglewood, I had a chance to hear the BSO rehearse the piece; and by then I knew it so well that most of the time when the conductor stopped the orchestra, I could predict what he was going to tell them."

"Which recording should I listen to?" Bonnie asked.

"Why don't you listen to several and pick the one you like?"

"What if I can't tell the difference?"

"Then I guess it doesn't matter which one you pick."

I returned to my office to work on the textbook on nineteenth-century music that I was writing for the External Studies Program.

Brook University, in addition to providing instruction for the twelve thousand students on campus, had developed a program of what used to be called correspondence courses and was now called "The Uncollege." With the aid of an editor provided by the ESP, I was developing a text for use by this distant audience. The writing had to be so clear that no one could possibly have any questions. The format called for a preview at the beginning of each chapter, a summary at the end, and a set of review questions.

When I raised the issue of listening assignments, the editor at first seemed perplexed. "If they read your text, they'll learn everything they need to know," he assured me. I told him that unless the students actually listened to the music I was describing, the whole exercise was pointless. He suggested that we broadcast the music over the radio, but the local radio station had already filled its quota of classical music with Lewis Mack's inane program and had no interest in cutting into its more relevant offerings (i.e., right-wing talk shows). When the editor asked whether we couldn't work with Prof. Mack, I asked him whether he could keep a confidence.

"Sure," he said.

"Lewis Mack is an idiot."

"Can I tell you something, Axel?"

"Sure."

"That isn't a secret."

I felt a measure of relief in learning that the university included people with sound judgment and a reasonable amount of insight.

"Even if I agreed to play your selections on my program, which I haven't said I'll do," Lewis had complained, "I'm far too occupied with more important matters to write the introductions. I mean, you can't expect people to just listen to classical music without a proper introduction."

"I'll write the introductions, Lewis," I said.

"Always looking for an opportunity to show me up, aren't you, Axel?"

"On the contrary, I know how busy you are and I wouldn't think of presuming on your time." I hated to grovel before this *poseur*, but sometimes the end justifies the means.

Eventually we arrived at a compromise whereby Lewis would play the selections for my course on his program, introducing them with several paragraphs that I would write and that he would repeat without attribution, thus confirming the rule that there is no limit to what you can accomplish if you don't care who gets the credit.

It was just after nine o'clock when Eileen Shaw returned to my office with an excited look in her eyes. "Prof. Crochet, you know how you were asking if I'd noticed anything different in Prof. Frost's office? Well, I did."

"What's that?"

"Last week when I went in for my thesis meeting, there was a volume of JAMS on Prof. Frost's desk, along with a photocopy of an article in some language I couldn't read—maybe it was in Dutch."

The Journal of the American Musicological Society exercised great discrimination in selecting the articles it published. Of the legion of scholars who had never published there, a fair proportion dismissed the journal as stodgy or overly conservative. Those whose work appeared in the journal considered it a bastion of excellence.

"And that surprised you?"

"Yes. It was a bound volume from the library. Miss Shaw would never let one of those volumes out of the reference room."

"Was the volume still there this week?"

"No. Prof. Frost must have taken it back to the library. Is that a helpful clue?"

"I can't tell you, Eileen, but it's something to think about." Edgar had probably brought the volume of JAMS down to his office after hours, (faculty members have keys so they can work late), so there wouldn't be any record to determine the year in question, much less which article had attracted his attention. The photocopy might supply more of a lead.

"Who do you think killed Prof. Frost, Eileen?"

"I've been trying to think about that, but it's hard for me to believe that any of my teachers is a murderer. You trust your teachers."

"A trust that one of them has betrayed."

"Do you have time to play some piano duets? I really enjoyed reading the Dvorak Slavonic Dances with you last week."

"That's nice of you to say, Eileen, but I can't tonight. We can play when you come to show me your Pilkington notes," I suggested. "I've just bought the four-hand transcription of the Brahms symphonies and they look as if they might be a challenge even for you. Anyway, thanks for stopping by."

As I listened to her footsteps down the corridor, I reflected that I'd rather be playing duets with a pretty graduate student than writing prose for an anonymous audience, but with another half-hour of work, I managed to finish off the ESP chapter and went home to bed.

CHAPTER 8

Mid-morning Tuesday I returned to my office after a trying hour-and-a-half with my grad seminar on 19th-century music. Two students had given reports, the second discussing an organ piece by César Franck.

"César Franck was born in France in 1822."

"Well, no." I'd had to interrupt. "Actually he was born in Belgium and lived there until he was nearly fifteen."

"In 1862 Franck became organist at St. Clothilde."

"But by then Franck was forty years old. What had he been doing all that time?"

"Well, he'd probably been playing a lot of chamber music and basketball and stuff."

Finally we got to the analytical portion of the presentation. "Franck begins with this theme, and it goes on like that for awhile. Then another section begins and it goes on like that for awhile, then ..."

"Can you comment on Franck's melodic and harmonic practice and how these elements are treated in this piece?"

"Well, Franck uses a lot of chromatic harmony."

"Where?"

"Well, here and here and here."

"But everybody in the mid-nineteenth century used chromatic harmony. How did he use it?"

"Well ..."

"May I ask what resources you used to prepare this talk? Did you consult *The New Grove Dictionary*?"

"No."

"Did you read any of the classic biographies on the composer?"

"Uh, no."

"Did you look up this work in the periodical literature?"

"I'm sorry, Prof. Crochet," interjected another student. "You've used up all three of your questions." The laughter relieved the tension.

"I didn't have time to go to the music library; but I heard Prof. Mack's radio program on Franck, and I took careful notes. I might have gotten some of the facts wrong."

No, I imagined she had written down exactly what she heard. A dozen years ago in Boston I accepted a part-time job correcting tests for a music professor at a university I'll leave unnamed. At first I was surprised to see how many students described Tchaikovsky's naval career as the inspiration for one of his pieces. How could so many of them be making the same mistake? Then it occurred to me—it must have been their teacher who had mixed up Rimsky-Korsakov and Tchaikovsky, and the students were simply repeating the misinformation. On the essay portion of the same test, in writing about Debussy's "Prelude to the Afternoon of a Faun" (a two-legged satyr), these students persisted in evoking the image of a four-footed fawn walking gracefully down to the river to drink. Would you be surprised if I told you that the teacher in question was one Lewis Mack? And now he was my chairman.

It was a relief to get back to my office. I nodded to the bust of Debussy perched on a bookshelf. (Assistant professors don't rate a grand piano.) I guess most of us possessed some physical embodiment of the composer at the center of our research. Viola's bust of Mozart commemorated the creator of the roles that made her famous at the Met. Edgar had a framed facsimile of a Berlioz manuscript. (The Brahms bust came with the office and Edgar never bothered to get rid of it.) The music department even had an icon. The widow of industrialist Harold Witherspoon not only gave the building his name and, it goes without saying, the money to convert it, but also a large, heavy bust of her late husband, so ugly that immediately after the dedication ceremonies, it was banished to the top floor of the music library.

The telephone rang. A friend and colleague, Chairman of the Music Department at Cleveland State University, called to confirm the arrangements for my visit there a month hence. In the morning I would give a talk on Debussy's piano music to his undergraduate history course and, in the afternoon, present the music faculty a paper called "Debussy and the Pretentious Maidens," referring to a remark the composer had once made concerning his piano etudes.

"I'm sorry to hear about Edgar Frost's death," he said. "We were in grad school together, though he was several years older. I talked with him just last week. I complained to him, in jest, that one of my teachers was spending so much time writing his contribution to the Nelson Festschrift that he wasn't able to attend my recital. I hadn't realized that Seth Nelson was such a giant in the field that he merited a Festschrift. I hope I'm not giving offence."

I allowed as how perhaps the standards for Festschrifts for organists were like the standards for performance among organists.

"Don't get me started," he said. "I had to sit through the most appalling recital last night. Well, I'd better get to my class. I'm looking forward to seeing you."

This Festschrift business seemed more and more peculiar. Chad Brimley, one of "Dr." Nelson's organ students, was just passing outside my door and I beckoned to him to come in for a moment. "Hi, Chad. I'm curious about Prof. Nelson's Festschrift."

"What did you want to know?"

"How did you learn about it?"

"Oh, he had pages for it spread all over the worktable in his office. It looked as if he were correcting page proofs."

"Did you happen to notice the publisher?"

"Sure. It said Scholarium Press. That seemed like a pretty strange name for a music publisher. Well, I'd better dash." Chad concluded as he headed off to class, nearly bumping into Lewis Mack.

"Glad I caught you, Axel," he said. "I've just looked at the teaching schedule for next year and it seems you're teaching most of the same courses you have now."

"Well, yes..."

"That means you'll have time to be the department's representative to the Faculty Senate."

"The chairman has always represented the department."

"The chairman or his appointee. I looked it up. You're my appointee. Now that I'm chairman, I'm looking forward to having more time to spend on my radio program."

"I didn't know you disliked me that much, Lewis. Have you ever attended a Faculty Senate meeting?"

"Once. Boring as hell. They spent the entire afternoon debating whether to lengthen March Break so that if the basketball team made it to the NCAA tournament again, they wouldn't miss so many classes. After an hour and a half I gave up and left."

Thus missing the real business. I'd once attended a Faculty Senate meeting, more or less out of curiosity. The institution was created during the era of student unrest and, in principle, represented every part of the university from the administration and teaching staff to the graduate assistants, undergraduates, secretarial staff and maintenance crew. After the novelty wore off, most people decided they had better ways to spend their time; but through a fluke in the constitution there had to be a quorum or the university more or less shut down, so the administration put a lot of pressure on the academic departments to insure regular attendance.

The day I went, they were trying to decide whether the Centennial procession should start with all the tenured faculty, followed by the lesser orders, or should proceed by department, and if so, whether the departments should line up in order of seniority of their formation or in alphabetical order. They finally settled on alphabetical order by the last name of the current department chairman. Then, about fifteen minutes before the end of the meeting, a flurry of parliamentary activity took place too fast for me to follow what was happening. I later learned that this was the rule for every meeting. The department chairmen would get together beforehand to decide all the important issues. They would allow the rest of the representatives to carry on some pointless debate for the most of the meeting, then pass the important business in the last few minutes when everyone was eager to get home.

"But why me?" I asked.

"Who else am I gonna send, Axel? George would sleep through the meetings." That seemed to be more of a recommendation than a disqualification, but it didn't pay to say so.

"You'll do a great job, Axel," Lewis said and left the office.

CHAPTER 9

Scholarium Press was just the sort of name you might expect a vanity press to adopt: it wasn't even proper Latin. With the threat of "publish or perish" over their heads, scholars incapable of passing the peer-review process of a respectable university press might succumb to the temptation of paying to have their work published.

If Seth Nelson was really using a vanity press to publish a Festschrift in honor of himself, it could be considered contemptible, pitiable, or ridiculous, depending on your point of view, but not criminal. Obviously he would become the laughingstock of the scholarly community if the knowledge ever became public, but he must have known the risk he was taking when he started the project. Nonetheless, the situation merited a bit of further probing, so I located the offices of the publisher Chad had named and telephoned them.

"Scholarium Press, 'If it's good enough for you, it's good enough for us.' Good morning."

"Good morning. This is Axel Crochet from the Brook University Accounting Department."

"Hello, Mr. Crochet. What can I do for you?"

"We recently switched over to a computerized accounting system ..."

"... and all your records are in a complete mess. Don't I know it!"

"Well, there have been a certain number of problems, and we've had to check several of our accounts by hand for verification purposes. I understand you're publishing the Nelson Festschrift. Would you mind looking up that account for me?"

The pause in conversation was filled with the sound of fingers typing letters on a computer keyboard.

"Yes, here it is, 'Essays in Honor of Seth Chichester Nelson on the Occasion of His 60th Birthday by a Coterie of His Esteemed Colleagues.'"

"That's the one. Have payments been made to invoices on that account?"

"Oh, yes. We require half the money up front, one-quarter on completion of the proofs and the balance on delivery of the printed volumes. I have the most recent check right here, charged to the Organ Maintenance Fund. The check is good, isn't it?"

"I have no reason to doubt the validity of the check."

"That's a relief. So what information can I give you?"

"You've already told me everything I needed to know. Thank you."

"Well, if Dr. Nelson gets the proofs back to us on time, we should be able to deliver the book right on schedule."

"I'm sure he'll do his best," I said.

I was trying figure out how all this fit together when I heard a gentle knock on the door and Patricia Makefair came in. A graduate student in French literature, she was studying voice informally with Viola Mordent. Last year she'd attended the program that Viola and I had given of songs by Debussy and Fauré set to texts of Paul Verlaine and had caught several errors in my French translations.

We had become friends two years earlier when she had enrolled in my General Studies opera course. After classes, we would frequently walk to the Hotel Administration School, sit in a corner of an out-of-the-way lounge and talk for hours. Only a few years separated us in age but she was going with someone else at the time. I drew the line at becoming involved with my own students so nothing came of it; but I'd always been attracted by her inquiring mind as much as by her easy smile, fine figure, low-pitched voice, and the air of amusement she had about life. Today she was wearing a light blue ribbed sweater over a navy wool skirt, and I felt my pulse beat faster when I saw her in my office.

"Hi, Patricia. How's the thesis going?" I began, somewhat lamely.

"Hi, Axel. Prof. Morrison is serving as my advisor, and working with him is like taking an advanced course in composition."

"How so?"

"Each week I bring him a new chapter, and each week he gives me back the previous one, all marked up with that exquisite handwriting of his. Honestly, Axel, I'm writing as well as I know how, but I get the feeling that he's reading even more carefully than I'm writing."

"I've heard that about him. Brook is really lucky to have a teacher of his calibre.

"And yet he says it's almost impossible for him to write anything of his own."

"I know. He's published less than anyone else in the French department; but his classes are always overflowing; and he directs more theses and dissertations than the rest of the department put together."

"Listen, I talked to Miss Mordent about the trouble she's in and she said that you were trying to help her."

"I've been asking a few questions, but I still haven't been able to figure out why she chose me rather than a professional investigator."

"Maybe she really wanted an amateur."

"Why?"

"Well, suppose there's something she doesn't want discovered, something that would make a lawyer refuse to defend her?"

"Lawyers will defend anyone who pays them."

"That's just a man's way of looking at it," Patricia responded. "Viola may be afraid that if someone thinks she's guilty, he won't look further."

"That seems to be the position of the police."

"Well if you're going to stop them, I have some information that I think you should know about."

"Tell me."

"When I came to see Prof. Frost to complain about Prof. Collins missing his General Studies classes, he seemed really interested in my thesis on the treatment of nature in Chateaubriand's *Atala*. The story takes place in North America. Did you know that?"

I had to confess that I hadn't read *Atala*.

"Prof. Frost compared Chateaubriand's description of the Mississippi with the grandeur of the great landscapes by 19th-century American painters. You know the ones I mean, with those huge palisades and forests and so forth."

"Mmm."

"Well, he was really quite charming, and when he asked me to do a little job for him, I was flattered."

"What sort of job?"

"He asked me to keep attending Prof. Collins' class, and to write him a note every time Prof. Collins wasn't there. By the middle of the term, I'd written quite a stack of notes."

This had Edgar's signature all over it—gather information surreptitiously then seize the moment of greatest impact to take decisive action.

"Don't tell me. Edgar decided to replace George, and he gave his annual farewell address."

"Yes, but how did you know?"

"This department has certain recurring events, and the replacement of Prof. Collins is one of the most predictable. What did he say to the students?"

"It was quite an address. Only about two-thirds of the class was there—we'd been using it as a kind of study hall—and I guess they were pretty surprised when Prof. Collins put in an appearance."

Patricia drew herself into George's somewhat hunched over posture and began in a pretty good imitation of his gravelly voice: "Well, class, it looks like this is the end of the road for Old George. I've given you my all, and you know me to be the most generous and devoted teacher you've ever had. I promised you the Big Apple on your report cards, and Old George doesn't forget his promises. But now they want to send in some young punk to replace me. I have nothing personal against him. But he's going to treat you all like music majors, or graduate students, or worse, while I've always understood how hard music is for you General Studies students. You can't say I've asked too much of you."

"I can't recall George ever having asked anything of his students."

"Don't interrupt." She continued the speech: "So the choice is yours: you can go along with this new teacher and kiss your grade point average goodbye, or you can stand by Old George in his hour of need and march to the chairman's office to let him know that there are still a few people in this world who care what happens to Old George. I know you won't let me down." A few students sniffed and then they all applauded.

"Did they go to the music office?"

"Every one. It was like a parade."

"And what did Prof. Frost do."

"He was very diplomatic. He thanked the students for bringing the situation to his attention and promised to investigate the problem and take appropriate action."

"So?"

"Well isn't it obvious? Miss Mordent didn't kill Edgar at all—it was Prof. Collins! I hadn't thought of him as a murderer; but it just goes to show, you can never tell about people."

"I guess that's true. I'm glad you came to tell me about this, but when am I going to see you again?"

"Could be sooner than you think," she said with a mischievous grin. She gave me a quick kiss on the cheek and glided out of the room.

Could George really have murdered Edgar? Parallels from Wagner's Ring cycle sprang to mind again. George wanted to keep his job, just as the Rhinemaidens had wanted to keep the gold. In *Götterdämmerung*, the fourth opera in the cycle, Hagen tries to take the gold, and the Rhinemaidens drown him in the river, fitting aquatic imagery for a man of liquid lunches and the chairman who wanted to take his job from him. I was about to head for the university pub when the telephone rang.

CHAPTER 10

The voice at the other end of the line said, "Hello, is this Mr. Crochet? They told me you give lectures on opera."

"That's right."

"Well perhaps you could answer a question for me."

My heart sank. "Perhaps. I'll try."

"Can you tell me why *Die Fledermaus* has 'Die' as a prefix. I spent two hours in the library this morning without being able to find the answer and my music teacher, who has a Ph.D., doesn't know either and has assigned me to find out."

"'Die' is the German definite article, feminine gender, singular number. *Der Freischütz* is masculine, and *Das Rheinhold* is neuter."

"Then what about *Die Meistersinger*?

"*Die* is also the plural form for all three genders."

"But what makes *Die Fledermaus* feminine? It's only a mouse."

I didn't have the heart to tell him that a Fledermaus wasn't a mouse but a bat. Instead, I suggested he might want to talk with Lewis Mack.

The university pub, located in the basement of the Arts Building, had the name "The Down Under," and featured Australian décor. Or at least the impression of Australia by someone in upstate New York who had probably never been south of the Mason-Dixon line, much less the equator. The walls were covered with posters from "Mad Max" movies, advertisements for Qantas Airlines, photos of surfers and pictures of koalas, kangaroos and emus. A few boomerangs hung over the bar, along with an incongruous frisbee, and the grad student bartender liked to address visitors as "mate."

I found George at the bar. In a previous age, George would have been called the department drunk. In this PC era, I guess you could call him "sobrietally challenged." He motioned me to a vacant stool and listened with a vague half-interest when I told him the story about the spy in his class.

"Who was it?"

"Would it matter?"

"I guess not."

"So Frost was really going to can you this time?"

"That's what he threatened. He said he planned to talk to Dean Manx on Friday afternoon."

"What's happening now that Mack's in charge?"

George brightened visibly. "He wants me to teach a second section of the course—the enrolment has really boosted the department's statistics."

Count on Lewis to keep his priorities straight.

A bus boy brought a plastic container of clean glasses from the kitchen and began sliding them into their racks over the bar.

"But that gave you a motive to kill Frost. What were you doing on the afternoon he died?"

"Aw, Axel, you can't ask me that."

"Memory that bad, eh?"

"You have no idea. But it keeps my mind open for other purposes."

"Such as?"

"I've been thinking about the murder."

"And?" I prompted.

"I think Edgar brought it on himself."

"You think he dropped a bronze bust on his own head?"

"I didn't mean it that way. It seems to me that if you really want to solve this thing, you should look at everything that Edgar has done or said during the past week."

"So you don't think Viola killed him?"

"Viola may be a dragon, but she's no murderess." He emptied his shot glass and lined it up beside the others on the bar.

"Well, if Viola didn't do it and you didn't do it, does any other name come to mind?"

"Why couldn't you have done it, Axel," George said with a mischievous look.

"I was out of town."

"You were?"

I could see this conversation wasn't going to lead anywhere so I thanked George and walked back toward the music building. Up to now I'd thought of George's drinking problem in abstract terms. This was the first time I'd actually seen first-hand the effects of alcoholism on someone who had once been an accomplished musician. Maybe Viola was right about me. I felt queasy being forced to confront other people's flaws at close range.

Something about George's look when he suggested I examine Edgar Frost's final week alive made me wonder whether I shouldn't try to learn more about the way he had spent his scholarly life. We all know each other's major fields of interest; but unless we've been privy to a tenure file, we haven't actually read each others' curricula vitae. But I reckoned I could obtain a list of Edgar's publications at the music office. I'd forgotten to reckon with Cecilia Crawford.

"That's restricted information."

"Cecilia, these are publications. What could be more public than that? I could obtain this information by spending a couple of hours with the Music Index, but it would be an awful lot easier if you just gave me the list."

"I can't give you the original. That's an archival document."

"A photocopy would be fine."

"Wait here."

Cecilia gave me a stern look and went into Edgar's office. I glanced around the office and noticed a stack of printed sheets with Edgar Frost's name at the top. It appeared to be an obituary, due to be released to the local newspapers. I tucked a copy into my notebook.

Cecilia returned with a file folder from which she extracted a document, ran it through the photocopier, handed me the copy, then returned the document to the folder and the folder to the file cabinet in Edgar's office. I thanked her and headed to Viola Mordent's studio.

"Your course descriptions were due yesterday," Cecilia called after me.

I promised to get to them right away.

CHAPTER 11

Viola was on the phone when I arrived; but she motioned for me to come in, so I returned to the comforting crook of her piano and found my hand going once again to the bust of Mozart. The muffled sound of a student pianist came from the practice room below. I couldn't quite make out what was being practiced, but it was evidently giving the student some trouble. Viola hung up and I asked her if she could help me recreate Edgar's murder.

"You don't know how different it feels to hear that question coming from you rather than from a police officer."

"They're still hounding you?"

"It's awful. They say 'we've got your prints, we've got your brooch, we've got motive, we've got opportunity. Why don't you just confess and save the taxpayers the cost of a trial?'"

"And your loyalty to the taxpayers doesn't extend that far?"

"Axel!"

"Sorry. Okay. Edgar kept his bust of Brahms on the piano, the same as you do; and his desk faced the wall, the same as yours."

"That was his way of ending a conversation. He'd just turn around and go back to work."

"His idea of non-verbal communication."

"When I went into his office on Friday afternoon, I put my hand on the base of the statue, just the same way you're doing now. That's how they got my fingerprints."

"What were you doing there in the afternoon?"

"Paavo suggested I invite Edgar to Stephanie's funeral Saturday afternoon, and I thought it would be a chance to smooth over the morning's blow-up. Edgar wouldn't even listen. But I was determined not to lose my temper again, so I grabbed the base of the statue even tighter in order to keep control."

"Suppose I'm Frost," I said, moving over to Viola's desk. "I'll sit here at the desk with my back to you. You come and try to cosh me with the bust."

Viola walked over to the piano, grabbed the Mozart statue by the head and approached me. I turned to watch her.

"But you're holding the statue by the head," I objected.

"How else would you do it?"

"Let's switch places."

I went to the piano, seized the bust by the base, and strode towards Viola's desk.

"You're shorter than I am. Is that the way you'd hold the statue?"

"I guess I could pick it up the other way, but it would be awkward."

I tried reaching for the head, but had to stand on tiptoe to get a proper grip on it. "But your fingerprints were on the base."

"Because I was trying to keep my temper. If I'd been trying to kill someone, I'd have grabbed the head—better leverage."

"So it was probably a taller person—like Lewis, or Seth, or Paavo or Mark or George."

"... or Chad, or Jonathan or even Eileen. But not Cecilia or Bonnie or you."

I was still puzzled. "That explains how your fingerprints could have been on the statue. But what about the brooch?"

"It's been missing for over a week. I hadn't been in Frost's office for several weeks before Friday morning, and I know I wasn't wearing it then. It's one of my most precious pieces. My voice teacher received it from Mary Garden herself." Viola invoked the name of a Metropolitan star from the turn of the century.

I tried to work out the schedule. "Cecilia found the body at around 2:00. You saw Frost around 1:30. You must have come in just before the murderer."

"He, or she, might have been lurking outside the door."

"How did you come in?"

"From the department office. I checked my mail, then went in to see Edgar."

"His door was open?"

"No. I knocked. He told me to come in, then I closed the door."

"How about the door to the corridor?"

"That was open. Seems strange—ordinarily he'd close it when he was working."

"You left it open when you left?"

"Yes—he pulled his 'going back to work' routine. I was so annoyed."

"So the murderer could have been in the hallway."

"Or on the stairs coming up from the basement or the stairs coming down from the 2nd floor."

"Or even in the grad lounge around the corner."

"I didn't see anyone except students on their way to classes." Viola had probably thought about that a number of times. "Who could it have been?"

"Patricia Makefair's convinced that George did it, but after talking with him, I'm not sure he could have remembered enough of the details to dream this up. What's the story with George, anyway?

"How do you mean?"

"Well, how did he get to be George?"

"You know, Axel, he always was George. It's the university that's changed."

"And that made him an alcoholic?"

"In a manner of speaking, yes. George was a pretty fair trumpeter—he played in the army band when he was in the service. When he got out, he took a job at the teacher's college. When it turned into Brook University, he was grandfathered into tenure."

"But he was basically still just a trumpet teacher?"

"That's right. While his wife was alive, he could overlook the fact that he didn't really have a place in this academic community; but when she died about ten years ago, he started drinking in earnest."

"I don't see him as a murderer in any event. The more I learn, the more I'm suspicious of Seth Nelson."

"Why is that?"

"He's been acting awfully funny about his Festschrift. I congratulated him on it, and he behaved as if I'd stumbled on some big secret. It's not a real Festschrift, anyway. It's being published by Scholarium Press, for goodness sakes. That means Seth is paying for it himself."

"But Seth doesn't have any money. The department has paid for all his so-called research trips to France. He moved into an apartment after his wife left him. It was a pretty expensive divorce, as I recall."

"Scholarium Press said the checks were drawn to the Organ Maintenance Fund."

"Aha! The non-existent State Trumpet," Viola exclaimed. "My head is still ringing from those awful student trumpeters that Seth hired for the centennial celebration."

"I'll try to talk with the organ technician this afternoon. He might be able to clear up the State Trumpet situation. And maybe there's some way I can look at the financial files in Edgar's office."

"Cecilia would never let you in there."

"That's true. Maybe I can get Bert to help me."

"Edgar shooed me out that afternoon, saying he had a meeting with Dean Manx. Do you think the dean can tell you anything?"

"That's a thought. I'm sure the police have already questioned him, but it's worth a try. You really want me to keep doing this rather than a professional investigator?"

"You've worked on it this long, Axel. Do you really imagine that a stranger came into the music building in broad daylight, walked into the chairman's office and killed him?"

"It does sound pretty improbable."

"And you have no shortage of suspects."

"That's true, even if George is out."

"Please do your best, Axel. I don't think I could face another grilling at the police station; and if they actually arrest me, I don't know what I'm going to do."

I promised to persevere.

CHAPTER 12

Getting to see a Dean is difficult in the best of times; getting to see a Dean without an appointment unthinkable. But I felt justified in using the cliché "a matter of life and death" and managed to get past the secretary.

Dean Manx's office had a bird's eye view of the Arts Quad. When the university library had been constructed—the tallest building on campus at the time, surpassing even the bell tower next door—-the administration had twisted some arms and an administrative floor was placed at the top of the building, a kind of penthouse for deans. This room held a long conference table, no files, no books; although Manx reportedly kept another office in the physics building.

Creighton Manx, Dean of Arts & Sciences, former head of the Physics Department, was considered handsome by those who weren't frightened of him. The sharp nose, black-rimmed glasses and silver hair could have supported either response. Where some people refuse to suffer fools, Dean Manx refused to suffer frills. He liked facts, disliked imprecision, and dealt with every issue, from grade inflation to date rape, with the same detached, unemotional attitude that gave him a reputation for having no feelings, an attribute that could be considered positive or negative depending on the speaker's perspective.

"Sit down, Axel," Manx said, gesturing to one of the straight chairs opposite his desk, not to the easy chair beside the sofa. He evidently intended to keep this interview brief.

"I'm glad you stopped in, Axel; I was planning to give you a call. There's been an official complaint from one of your students." This surprised me since, as a rule, I got along pretty well with my students. "It seems that someone in your General Studies course on 19th century music is unhappy about the way you've treated his attempt to withdraw."

I remembered the chap. He came to class irregularly then turned up around mid-semester with a petition to drop the course. This was the kind of form which included all the pertinent regulations as well as lines to be completed. It explained that while a student could drop a course at whim during the first six weeks, after that time a student could drop the course, with the instructor's permission, only for "specific, non-academic, extenuating circumstances." The petitioner was required to detail these "specific, non-academic, extenuating circumstances" on the back of the form.

Ordinarily I just signed whatever students put in front of me, but on this particular occasion something impelled me to read through the form; and I found myself fascinated by the carefully-wrought language which, while lacking the resonance of, say, "one holy, catholic and apostolic church," nonetheless had a certain ring to it, as if someone really wanted each word to carry its weight.

After inspecting the blank reverse side of the form, I asked the student to enumerate his specific, non-academic, extenuating circumstances. He said he hadn't done too well on the mid-term, needed a B to get into business school, and thought he'd better drop the course to save his grade point average. I remarked that this sounded like an entirely academic reason and that, as far as I could see, the language of the form did not permit me to sign it; but I offered to consult with higher authority.

I called the office of the Dean of the School of General Studies, mentioned the form, and asked how I could sign it, given the careful wording of the condition. The secretary said, "If you want to sign the form, sign it; if you don't want to, don't." I tried to explain that it wasn't a question of inclination or disinclination but the interpretation of a phrase that someone had presumably spent a good deal of time formulating. She wouldn't have any of it and transferred me to another bureaucrat who didn't want to touch the question either, and he transferred me to another fellow who explained that the Faculty Senate had inserted the phrase to prevent students from dropping courses just to preserve their grade point averages. Then he concluded, "If you want to sign the form, sign it; if you don't want to, don't."

I sought the counsel of a more experienced tenured colleague. Seth Nelson said, "Hell, tell the student to study harder; with luck, maybe he'll even pull a B for the course." The student went away sorrowfully, and didn't appear in class again until the final examination.

Meanwhile, the rest of the students had continued to attend class without fail, doing their best to master the intricacies of chromatic harmony and the like. Come the review session, when I read them the previous year's version of the final exam, it became obvious that one of the students, for all his diligence, just wasn't going to make it. When I asked him why he had enrolled in the course, he pointed to the fellow next to him and said, "Fred persuaded me to take the course with him." Well, Fred wasn't doing all that well either, but I told him, "Look, you got your buddy into this; I think you've got a responsibility to help him out of it."

I then asked whether they'd be willing to collaborate on the final exam; neither was sure he could even pass it, but perhaps working together they might scrape by. It was only a General Studies course, after all; I was happy to do what I could to let them pass. Then I asked whether the other students had any objections, and they all assented to the procedure, which wasn't going to affect their grades in any event since I wasn't marking on the curve.

On the night of the final exam, my erstwhile petitioner turned up for the first time in weeks, wrote his exam, then departed after half an hour. Reading his exam, I found that he had attempted the first few questions, scribbled "my mind's a blank" on his paper, and quit. Now he was complaining to Dean Manx that "two students were allowed to collaborate on the exam," in the hope of overturning his failure on procedural grounds.

After hearing my summary, Dean Manx thought for a moment, then spoke. "Would you have any objections to the following plan: we'll offer him the option of taking the exam over again or getting a retroactive withdrawal from the course on a specially-made form from which the word 'non-academic' has been expunged?"

"Capital idea," I said, noting Solomonic wisdom as a useful qualification for deanship.

This wasn't the first time that Dean Manx had bailed me out. One afternoon in January I was working late in my office when a student from the previous term's music appreciation class came in with her father. "Excuse me for bothering you, Prof. Crochet," she said, "but I came to see you about the grade I got for the music course."

"As I recall, you failed the course didn't you?" I asked.

"Yes. That's why I came to see you. I'm student teaching this term so I can't take the course over again, but I have to graduate in May, so I was wondering whether I could write a paper or something to raise my grade, even to a D-."

"That sounds a bit irregular to me."

"I told you there wasn't any point in wastin' words," said her father.

"Be quiet, Daddy," she said, and began to weep softly.

"How did she fail the course?" her father wanted to know.

I looked over the grade sheet. "Well, she had a D on the mid-term, failed all the quizzes, and scored 31 on the final."

"31 out of what," asked the father.

"Out of 100," I replied.

"What would you have to do to get such a low grade," he asked.

I pulled out the girl's exam. "You'd have to get a lot of wrong answers—listening, identification, and here she only wrote one sentence for each of the essay questions." (The weeping grew into a wail.)

"One sentence on an essay question!" the father exclaimed. "After all yer ma and me have done to increase yer word power!"

"Is it really so important that you graduate in May?" I asked the girl.

"Yes." She sobbed. "The year after I entered Brook they changed all the requirements, and if I don't graduate in May I'll have to take a bunch of other education courses and calculus!"

I suggested they talk with the dean, and that I would support waiving the requirements if she wanted to take the music appreciation course over the summer, presumably with a different teacher. They went away more or less mollified.

I turned to the matter that had caused me to come to Dean Manx's office, explaining my interest as Viola Mordent's friend and colleague, and my personal conviction that she had not killed Edgar Frost.

"You know, Axel, I admire your loyalty, but I think this matter really calls for the professional expertise that the police can bring to it."

For a moment I felt an almost irresistible impulse to accept the counsel of this wise administrator and abandon my unhappy snooping into the private lives of my colleagues. Then I recalled Viola's plight and reluctantly returned to my questions.

"I understand Prof. Frost was to have seen you the afternoon he died."

"As I told the police, Edgar was scheduled to come to the weekly chairmen's meeting Friday afternoon but asked to speak with me beforehand about two matters that might have been embarrassing to the music department if they'd been aired publicly."

I thought about Edgar's decisions to discharge George and presumably to do something about the non-existent State Trumpet, and reflected that the other chairmen might have enjoyed a laugh at the music department's expense.

"I'm sorry I can't help you further, but I have a meeting with the provost," he said, rising to his feet. "I'll be seeing you again at three."

"I'm sorry?" I said in some confusion.

"Interview and decision meeting," he explained.

"I thought that was on Monday," I said.

"Change of schedule," were the dean's last words, as he ushered me out of his office.

I wasn't sure how this interview had helped me, but the Dean had made it clear that it was over.

A crowd of people had gathered at the corner of the Arts Quad nearest the music building. As I approached I could see they were watching a performance of some sort. Mark Fillmore stood a bit apart from the rest of the crowd and I walked over to join him.

"What's this all about?" I whispered.

"A bit of performance art, it appears," he answered. "These young ladies call themselves the Sisters of Viola, and it looks as if they've been reading *Hamlet*."

"Why do I detect the hand of Freddy Thatcher behind this?"

"He was the one who introduced the performance."

As I watched, a girl evidently intended to represent Viola approached a figure whose head was resting on a desk. Was this supposed to be Edgar Frost? She was carrying a great placard on which a picture of a bearded man, presumably Brahms, had been crudely drawn. Just as she was about to whack the sleeping figure on the head, a young man rushed forward, pushed her aside, and, taking out a vial, poured a dark liquid into the sleeping figure's ear.

"Who's that?" I whispered to Mark.

"I'm afraid it's meant to be you," he answered.

"Oh no!"

Meanwhile the two figures had begun wrestling for the placard, which slipped from their grasp and fell on the head of the figure at the desk.

"It's a theory." Mark observed.

All three actors left the stage area, to be replaced by a group of half a dozen or so young women carrying signs that read, "Free Viola," and "Viola was framed," and "It isn't over until the fat lady sings."

"I hope Viola can't see this." I looked toward the music building, calculating the angle to the window of her studio.

"I'm sure she'll hear about it, though," Mark observed.

Some cheering from the crowd marked the end of the performance, which itself had been completely silent. The group dispersed and I walked upstairs to my office.

CHAPTER 13

At three o'clock the music department faculty filed into the Matthew Finson seminar room for the second time in as many days. I greeted William Fuddy, whose imminent retirement had produced the vacancy we were now trying to fill. His short stature, bald, bulbous head and heavy brows went with a proclivity for bow ties.

Fuddy had rendered forty years of faithful service to Brook University, going back to the days when it was still a state teachers college, giving several generations of college students lessons on the electronic piano. The classroom contained a dozen of these bastard instruments which the students would listen to through headphones while Fuddy would switch from one to another at the master control panel.

Edgar Frost had seized on this opening as an opportunity to raise the standard of the department. The first candidate for the position, a pleasant young lad from North Central Colorado University, had been Fuddy's choice from the start, a man just like himself: bland, methodical, untroubled by any conception of music as an academic discipline. His paper on fingering problems in Mozart's piano concertos had given an exhaustive treatment to a pedestrian topic. Frost had vetoed his appointment.

The second candidate, a Princeton man, came with glowing recommendations and strong credentials. Had he failed to show up for the interview, he might well have landed the job. In the event, he talked himself out of it. All through his lecture, Fuddy kept turning to one member of the department after another to ask, "What did he say?" At least Fuddy gave an honest response. The rest of us just nodded sagely as if we'd heard it all before.

After the lecture, the Princeton man entertained questions.

"What do you consider to be the goal of analysis?" he was asked.

"The purpose of analysis (or of a composition) is to reconstruct (or construct) a musical structure. We bother to reify 'analysis' (and 'composition') and 'analytic methods' ('compositional methods' or 'techniques') because of the conviction, reinforced by confirming practice, that, beginning from the simplest levels of intersubjective auditory experience, pieces are constructible most favorably up to a certain point through hierarchical functional paths that may be considered to be shared by all, then, beyond that point, through increasingly divergent, coherently subdivided paths, up, finally, to the singular stem: the individual piece."

"Do you know of any other approaches to the problem?"

"The second of the suggested approaches, in particular, may save us from the necessity of Procrusteanism with respect to some pieces we have cared enough about to be willing to force them into some system or other, often by ignoring certain kinds of evidence that we normally regard as crucial signalogy for the invocation of the particular systematic-model-type involved, and by accepting a degree of interlevel opacity that, especially when it occurs at lower levels, would be decidedly unacceptable to us in an analysis of almost any of the other pieces we have subsumed in that literature."

"How do you think you would fit into this department?"

"Were it not for this radical contextuality, the generalizing kind of activity would be more 'scientifically interesting' than 'musically crucial;' for our musical stake is in discovering as many respects as possible in which pieces can exhibit particularity of choice among alternatives, as many dimensions as possible of significant variability (where, hence, choices make a difference) and, thus, of individuality of identity."

"Do you have any questions about our program?"

"Can we in fact make use of super-syntactical structural observations in one systematic domain to assist cognitively the explication of structures defined as being in another?"

The faculty sent him off with the kind of effusive greeting you give someone you know you're never going to see again. Now we had gathered to hear the third, and presumably final, candidate, after which we would make our decision.

Creighton Manx called the meeting to order. "Prof. Mack has requested me to chair this meeting in order to allow him to participate fully in the discussion."

What a magnificent liar he was! Must be one of the prerequisites to being dean. I was convinced that the dean, lacking confidence in Lewis Mack's ability to prevent the department from getting completely stalled, had stepped in to take command.

The third candidate, a graduate of nearby Colgate University, came in and heard the names of his listeners and eventual judges. He acknowledged Paavo with a kind of bow and said with an engaging smile, "Of course I know your work, sir."

His paper on expressive elements in the piano accompaniments of the songs of Hugo Wolf made a number of interesting points, gracefully illustrated at the keyboard. The chap could play, he could talk, and his letters of reference said that he could teach. He gave relaxed, competent answers to the questions put by members of the department, then left to catch a plane while we proceeded to our deliberations.

"I thought on the whole it was a good presentation," Lewis Mack opened the discussion, "though I thought he could have said something about the relationship between Wolf and Schubert." A typical academic criticism—attacking someone for not answering a question that he hadn't asked.

"Do you think he might be too brilliant for our students?" Prof. Fuddy worried.

"Seemed clear enough to me, Bill," said Mark Fillmore, "and I don't even know Wolf's songs."

We heard several more expressions of approbation, though always couched in reservations of one sort or another, to demonstrate the speaker's sharp, critical mind.

Then Paavo spoke. "I'm sorry, gentlemen, I won't have this man in the department."

"He seemed all right to me, Paavo," said Seth Nelson. "What's the problem?"

"I am the Ives Professor of Musicology, and I refuse to countenance hiring this man."

No one pushed him further for reasons. Everyone, or at least every tenured professor, had the right to blackball a prospective candidate; but the finality of such a privilege meant that it was seldom invoked.

"Perhaps we could interview a fourth candidate," Jonathan Whitby ventured.

This was the moment Creighton Manx had been waiting for, the inevitable moment in which the music department would show itself once again incapable of making a decision. This was the reason he had come.

"I'm afraid that's out of the question, Jonathan," he said firmly. "You had more than two hundred applicants for this position, from which you selected the three most promising candidates to interview. The moment has come to decide."

"Might I suggest," Mark Fillmore said, "that we reconsider the first candidate. As I recall the discussion, we were all favorably disposed except Edgar..." he let the sentence hang.

With a bit of skilful but discreet shepherding by the dean, the department offered the position to the pleasant chap from Colorado.

As the faculty members made their way out of the room, I took a look at the file for the candidate we had just heard: B.A. from Colgate, summer internship in piano at the University of Helsinki, M.A. from Cornell. He'd acted respectful toward Paavo. What had made him issue such a categorical refusal?

CHAPTER 14

I headed back to my office to call Graham Twillinger who maintained the university organs in the chapel, the concert hall, and in the organ practice room in the basement of the music building. He was out tuning an organ but would be back soon. I was about to leave when I heard a knock at my door and looked up to see Marcia Tidd. I invited her to come in and sit down. The only first-year student enrolled in my Wagner seminar, she had caught on quickly and had contributed interesting insights.

"Hello, Prof. Crochet," she said. "I came in to talk with you about my term paper."

"Have you thought of a topic?"

"I think so. I'm really interested in the Sword motive in *Die Walküre*. It's so exciting in that part just before Siegmund pulls the sword out of the tree. At first the orchestra just hints at the motive, and then when he pulls it out the music seems to explode."

"So you want to study Wagner's orchestration?"

"No, I'm interested in the harmony. The Sword motive itself is just a C major triad, but Wagner doesn't use that harmony by itself very often. It's usually a resolution of another harmony."

"That's right."

"What I'd like to do is trace all the uses of the Sword motive in *Die Walküre* and see how Wagner harmonizes it each time."

"That would make an interesting catalogue."

"But that's only part of it. Then I'd like to group them by type to see whether they have anything in common."

"I don't quite follow. In common with what?"

"I want to see if the harmonies are linked to the drama, to what's happening each time the motive appears."

"So you're really asking whether Wagner makes symbolic use of harmony."

"I guess you could put it that way."

"That sounds very promising. There are some motives, like the Magic Fire Music, that always come with the same harmony. But the Sword motive, as you've noticed, isn't like that."

"Do you think someone has already used this idea?"

"I've never read anything like it. If it pans out in *Die Walküre*, that idea could take you a long way into a masters thesis or even a doctoral dissertation."

I hoped that my enthusiasm for Marcia's idea had not been prejudiced by the fact that I was attempting a comparable investigation for Debussy's opera, *Pelléas et Mélisande*.

"I thought doctoral dissertations had to be about manuscripts," she said, a bit cautiously.

"That's what some musicologists want you to think. But aren't you doing your degree in music theory?"

"I thought I'd do a masters in music theory and a doctorate in musicology, the same way you did."

"So you've been checking up on me?"

Marcia just smiled. "And I brought you something," she said, handing me a small, narrow box.

"What's this?" I wondered.

"Open it and see."

Inside the box was a silver letter-opener, about eight inches long, on which Marcia had had inscribed the word *Nothung*, the German for sword.

"This is marvelous," I said. "May I show it to the rest of the class?"

"Sure, but why don't you keep it to yourself where you got it."

"If you like."

"I'm really enjoying the seminar, but I wanted to tell you something else, Prof. Crochet."

"Mm hmm?"

"I think it's really great what you're doing for Miss Mordent."

"I don't know that I've done anything yet."

"Well at least you're trying. She needs someone to help her right now."

"I'll do what I can, Marcia," I said, "and thank you for Nothung. This is really nice."

"You're welcome." She left the office. A letter-opener disguised as a sword. Is that what my efforts represented? I placed the object next to my flute-playing shepherd and hoped it might bring me more luck than it had to the ill-starred Siegmund.

I walked home to get my car and drove out Barleycorn Road, following the winding course of Spring Creek to the white clapboard house that evidently served as residence as well as the office of Twillinger Organ Services.

From the driveway I had a view across the valley to the houses on the other side of the lake. The area around Brook University was dotted with small villages disproportionately populated with Brook graduates, many of whom postponed taking jobs in their chosen fields in order to prolong their time in the region. Some of them who never did manage to leave supplied towns in the area with highly overqualified clerks, postmen, and gas station attendants.

Graham Twillinger had graduated from Brook, nobody knew quite how long ago, and had made a living tuning and repairing the organs not only in Tioga proper but in surrounding towns as well. He refused to have anything to do with electronic instruments.

His truck pulled into the driveway beside my car and he got out.

"Hi, Axel. Hear you've had a little murder in the music department." He ushered me into his office, pulled some magazines off a dusty chair and invited me to sit down. "I'm just back from First Methodist. Did you know that's the only organ in Tioga with direct electric action?"

"I didn't realize that," I said, knowing that I was about to hear more about direct electric action than I would have dreamed possible.

"You don't need big wind chests, and you never have to worry about releathering. Instead of leathers, the pipe valves are made of felt with lambskin on top. When the key is depressed, an armature connected to a threaded valve opens the valve; when the key is released, a spring closes it. Easy to maintain. But that organ is a brute to tune. They don't really have enough space in the organ chamber, so all the tallest pipes are bent over and around till there's hardly any place to work."

"Amazing."

Twillinger's technical talk had begun to make the birds twittering in the eaves of the house sound to me like high-pitched flute stops. "I was wondering if you could tell me a little bit about the plans for our chapel organ."

"Oh, sure! You know we installed a Zimbelstern for Christmas Vespers?"

That part at least I understood. The Zimbelstern seemed to be the latest addiction for organists. Once they had heard the high-pitched, untuned bells rotating on a star-shaped frame, they had to have one for their own church; and if anyone raised questions, the self-righteous insistence that "Bach had a Zimbelstern" could usually be counted on to lay them to rest.

"But the real coup is the State Trumpet."

"That's the rank of trumpet pipes pointing out directly toward the congregation instead of up and down like the rest of the pipes?"

"That's right. They sometimes call it a *trompette en chamade*. It really socks a punch. You can hear it above the whole rest of the organ. Of course, I'm not sure how the singers in the Chapel Choir are going to feel about having that blasting into the backs of their necks. Do you know how they manage to achieve the high air pressure to ..."

"But there is no State Trumpet." I felt compelled to break in.

"No. Prof. Nelson cancelled the order."

"But I thought I saw you on campus last week."

"Yes, I was there tuning the organ on Thursday morning. Prof. Nelson was helping me locate a cipher on the swell ..."

"What was it, a wind leak?"

"No, there was a problem in the valve under one of the pipes. Now if they converted to direct electric action the way I suggested ..."

"This was Thursday morning," I said, trying to pull Graham back on track.

"That's right. I was up inside the chamber when Prof. Frost arrived. I don't think he even knew I was there."

"What happened?"

"Well, they had this terrible row. Prof. Frost called Prof. Nelson an embezzler, and Prof. Nelson called Prof. Frost a busybody who didn't understand anything, and Prof. Frost said he'd have Prof. Nelson's job, and Prof. Nelson said he had tenure, and Prof. Frost said that didn't excuse malfeasance and that he planned to take the matter up with Dean Manx the next day."

"Sounds pretty nasty."

"It didn't stop there. Prof. Nelson said he'd given thirty years to the university and he deserved to be recognized even if he had to do it himself, and he wasn't going to let Prof. Frost take it away from him. I can't say I understood much of what they were saying; but I could sure hear them clearly enough, the way they were shouting at each other."

Before I could get away, I had to hear about the tracker action organ in the Presbyterian church with a wind system built with schwimmers fed from a static wind regulator. It was nearly five p.m. before I was able to escape.

On the way back I picked up a student hitching a ride to the university.

"Hi, how's it going?" I greeted him as I pulled back onto the road.

"Hi. You teach at Brook, don't you?"

"Yes, I'm in the music department."

"I thought I recognized you. I've seen you on the Arts Quad."

"Are you in English?"

"You guessed it. What's happening in the music department, anyway?"

"How do you mean?"

"You know. The voice teacher who whacked the chairman."

"What do you make of it?"

"Well, my girlfriend says that if a woman kills a man, he probably had it coming." Radical feminists had a disconcerting way of simplifying situations.

"And how do you feel about it?"

"I don't know. I'm more interested in the basketball team. I think we could make it into the Sweet Sixteen this year."

I slowed down behind a lumbering truck. "Isn't it awkward for you living so far from campus without a car?"

"Oh, I have a car. My girlfriend had to drive to Virgil."

"So you're going to have supper at the university." I guessed. "Don't you like to cook?"

His look said, "You've got to be kidding, man."

"I do the same thing." I continued. "Living alone, I don't cook for myself a lot."

He just grunted, as if to suggest that the thought of living without female companionship made even less sense than the thought of cooking.

I pulled into the parking lot behind the music building.

"Thanks a lot," he said as he gathered his backpack.

"Don't mention it. Have a good evening."

CHAPTER 15

The percussion room in the basement of the music building had been a source of irritation ever since it was installed. The faculty, who never agreed about anything else, were unanimous in wishing that the percussion room could have been installed somewhere off campus, but if you were going to give academic credit for an instrument, you had to provide practice space for that instrument. Soundproofing had made the piano practice rooms tolerable to those teaching in the classrooms above them, but no amount of acoustical tile could absorb the sound of the lowest drums. A high-tech solution—suspending the entire percussion chamber inside another room—was felt to be prohibitively expensive, so we arrived at a compromise whereby each member of the staff would have to take a turn teaching in the dreaded classroom above the percussion chamber.

We each devised some strategy for dealing with the din. Lewis Mack, impatient and self-righteous, had tried stamping his foot on the floor when the noise level became too great to bear. The drummer below had simply picked up the beat of the stamps and proceeded to improvise an elegant riff on it that of course did nothing to relieve Mack's ire. I made it a point to schedule a listening session whenever my turn arrived, and would turn up the volume so that the subterranean beat was muffled.

By five o'clock all the students had departed and Bert Crowley, the custodian for the music building and the neighboring arts building, had taken up residence in the percussion room. Bert was of the old school, and had no use for fancy titles like plant engineer. He knew the buildings inside and out and seldom encountered a problem he couldn't solve one way or another.

Bert enjoyed jazz and had developed into a pretty fair self-taught drummer. He would bring a boom box into the percussion room, seat himself behind the drum set, and play along with the recorded combo. "Evening, Bert," I said as I entered the percussion chamber. "What have you got tonight?"

"I'm doubling Ed Thigpen with the Oscar Peterson Trio playing the Canadiana Suite."

"Does that give you much of a challenge?"

"The drumming is pretty basic, but I really love the way Oscar plays."

"I'm with you on that. Listen, when you get a break, could you let me into Prof. Frost's office. I lent him a score of *La Mer,* and I'd like to get it back before they clean out his office. I don't want it to get lost."

"Well, they've taken down the police tape, so I guess it's all right. Prof. Nelson had the same request, except he wanted to get back some book on the history of the organ. So it should be okay for you."

Bert preceded me up the stairs to the corridor entrance to Edgar's office and unlocked the door. "I've set it to lock again as soon as you close it."

"Thanks, Bert," I said, "I shouldn't be long."

Though I had been in Frost's office before, it always felt uncomfortable to me: the celebrated bronze bust of Brahms on the grand piano, the desk facing the wall, above it a framed facsimile of the title page of Berlioz's "Harold in Italy." On another wall hung a framed page of Gregorian chant. Frost had books not just on music but on French literature, American and European history, history of science, and philosophy, books not just in English but also in French, German, even Russian. (I've always found the Cyrillic alphabet an impenetrable barrier to learning the language of Glinka, Tchaikovsky, and Rachmaninoff.) One straight chair sat beside the desk and above it a window covered with a heavy curtain. This was not a room intended to make visitors feel at ease.

Against one wall stood a bank of half a dozen filing cabinets neatly labelled, most of them devoted to Frost's research. I looked under "departmental affairs," and eventually found the financial files. The department chairman wasn't responsible for salaries or benefits, which were administered by the Dean's office, or for expenses having to do with the physical plant; but a fair number of areas still fell under the chairman's jurisdiction. Some items, such as the chapel, were divided between the music department, which handled the choirs and the organ, and the religion department, which took care of hiring guest preachers for the weekly services.

I looked in the folder marked "chapel" and found a number of records having to do with choral activities but nothing for the organ. So I started working backwards through all the files, looking for the records for the Organ Maintenance Fund. I flipped through Travel, Recruitment, Publicity, Professional Development, Part-Time Instructors, Insurance, Instrument Repairs, Guest Lecturers, Concert Series, but nothing at all on the organ.

Surely Frost must have known about Nelson's little scheme, but it looked as though Nelson, preceding me, had simply cleaned out not just the documents concerning the State Trumpet but everything having to do with the organ. To my eyes, the absence of those papers told nearly as much as their presence. Seth must have thought that he'd covered his steps pretty well. Evidently he'd forgotten about Twillinger in the organ chamber. Seth Chichester Nelson was going to have some explaining to do.

As I came out of Edgar's office, a high-pitched voice said, "Returning to the scene of the crime, eh, Prof. Crochet?"

Of all the people I didn't want to see right then, Freddy Thatcher would have to head the list.

"How did you like our play this afternoon? I saw you lurking over at the edge of the crowd."

"I wasn't lurking ..."

"That sounds awfully defensive, Prof. Crochet. Could it be that I've touched a sore spot?"

"Freddy, are you seriously suggesting that I killed Edgar Frost?"

"Accomplice is the way I think I'd describe it."

"Freddy, I was in a different city on Friday. At the time Prof. Frost was murdered, fifty people were listening to me talk about Debussy."

"Some people might find such a convenient alibi pretty suspicious."

"And some people should learn the legal meaning of the words 'slander' and 'libel'."

"Okay, I was just trying to spread a bit of confusion—perhaps throw the killer off stride."

"And what book did you learn that from?"

"Oh no, that's my own invention," he said proudly.

"Your contribution to investigative journalism?"

"Speaking of contributions, wouldn't this be a good time for us to compare notes on our investigations?"

"You persist in imagining that we're working together."

"Aren't you trying to uncover the truth, Prof. Crotchet?"

"That doesn't mean sharing my thoughts with a reporter."

"Everything you say would be completely off the record, sir. Hey, maybe you could be my Deep Throat."

"Don't tell me we're back to that again."

"What were you doing in Prof. Frost's office, anyway?"

"Looking for a book I'd lent him."

"Not removing evidence that would make you an accessory after the fact?"

"Where have you been getting this lingo, Freddy?"

"I watch a lot of television."

"Well, this has been very interesting, but I'm going home." I walked toward the front door.

"But the parking lot is in the other direction," Freddy said.

I increased my pace as I crossed the Arts Quad, hoping Freddy wasn't following me, unwilling to turn around in case he was still watching.

CHAPTER 16

I crossed the Arts Quad to the university chapel, trusting that Nelson would still be there. The sounds of a Bach fugue could be heard from the organ as I peered into Nelson's office. On the wall I saw the framed diploma, in French, that Seth claimed was the equivalent of a Ph.D., hence his insistence on being called "Dr." Nelson. Around the diploma hung framed photographs of Nelson dramatically posed at large three- and four-manual consoles of unidentified organs.

The space was rather cramped, in contrast to the spacious quarters of those who had studios in the music building. An old wooden desk looked second-hand rather than antique. The only nice piece of furniture in the room was a special file for organ music, which allowed one to pull out a drawer tab for the music of each composer. The chair next to the desk, upholstered in plastic, had evidently been borrowed from somewhere.

On top of a battered filing cabinet sat a display of sample organ pipes: a square, wooden stopped flute, with its knobbed top; a gray metal gemshorn, looking like two thin cones joined in the middle; a cylindrical trumpet pipe, and a tiny piccolo pipe.

I heard the windy sound of the organ being turned off and pretty soon the footsteps of Seth Nelson clomped slowly down the stairs from the organ loft. "Hello, Axel; is the boy sleuth hot on the trail of a murderer?"

"It's funny you should put it that way, Seth, since everything I've seen in the past couple of days points toward you."

"Me! You've got to be kidding."

"Seth, this so-called Festschrift of yours is a mockery. You've commissioned your friends to write essays; you've gone to a vanity press to publish the thing; and you've paid for it all by checks drawn on the Organ Maintenance Fund, presumably from money that had been budgeted for the non-existent State Trumpet."

"My, my, my, we have been doing a bit of research, haven't we?" Seth Nelson had never taken my scholarly work seriously, and it irritated me.

"Your argument with Frost was overheard. We're not talking about your Festschrift here. From what I can see, you had a splendid motive for murdering Edgar. So far, no one has come forward to place you anywhere but at the scene of the crime."

And if Seth had been the murderer, the Ring cycle offered another appropriate comparison. Siegfried, the hero of the third opera in the cycle, learns from a bird, represented in the orchestra by a flute, just like the organ pipe, that Mime plans to poison him; so Siegfried kills him. Almost self-defense, I could imagine Seth saying, thinking about saving his job from Edgar's poisonous intentions.

Seth's face turned ashen. "I'm not sure what to say," he said softly.

"Did you kill him?"

"Axel." Nelson hesitated. "I was with Chad."

"What do you mean 'with'?"

"Do I have to spell it out for you?"

"Oh," I said.

"Yes, oh. So far the police have been so interested in Viola that they haven't bothered me for an alibi. But if you feed them all this stuff about the argument with Frost and the money for my Festschrift, I don't know what will happen."

"Just how were you planning to pay back the money from the Organ Maintenance Fund?

"I don't know," he moaned weakly. "But I didn't kill Frost."

"No, I suppose you didn't. Chad would back you up?"

"You're not really going to make him do that, are you?"

"Probably not."

"And you're not going to tell the police?"

"Not unless it's necessary. It seems as if you're in enough of a pickle as it is. Lewis sounded a bit suspicious about the State Trumpet at the department meeting yesterday."

"I know."

"Maybe you could pawn the Zimbelstern."

"Don't joke with me." Nelson had entirely lost his attitude of dismissive amusement.

I left Nelson to his misery and went to get some supper before marking the tests from my undergraduate opera course. Not that I had much of an appetite after talking with Seth. I've always thought of myself as liberal when it comes to other people's relationships, but now that the liaison between Seth and Chad had been forced into my consciousness I began to imagine the physical details and found the whole affair nauseating. People sometimes used the phrase "ivory tower existence" as a criticism; to me it seemed more like a haven. But I had gone too far with the investigation to withdraw now. Neither George nor Seth seemed like reasonable suspects any longer; but somebody had killed Edgar, and I still couldn't believe that Viola had done it.

After supper I returned to the music library, where I could look up any of Edgar Frost's publications if it seemed appropriate. There were a few students going in and out of the stacks, but the place was mostly quiet.

I took a moment to read the obituary I'd picked up at the music office.

"Edgar Frost Mourned," the heading read. "Brook University lost one of its most distinguished scholars with the death of Edgar Frost last Friday. Dr. Frost came to Brook University fifteen years ago and served as music department chairman for the last five years. Born in Evansville, Indiana, Prof. Frost attended Earlham College and Harvard University. During World War II he served in the Army Intelligence Corps, with special assignments in Germany and Russia. After the war, he taught at Wittenburg University before coming to Brook. Frost's scholarly interests covered a wide range including the vocal music of Hector Berlioz, the subject of his master's thesis, and rhythmic practice in Renaissance sacred music, the focus of his doctoral dissertation and a number of subsequent publications. Prof. Frost was awarded the Otto Kinkeldey Award by the American Musicological Society for his book, *Nicholas Gombert, Opera Omnia, Vol.II*, published by the AMS Press. Dr. Frost is survived by his sister, Eustace Frost McInnes."

"What are you looking at?" Mark Fillmore had quietly entered the reference room.

"Edgar's publications. He really was a Renaissance man."

"Why do you say that?"

"Well just look at the breadth of his interests: Berlioz, Gombert, performance practice in the Renaissance ..."

"I'd call that pretty restricted: it's all Western European art music by dead white male composers."

"Well I guess it all depends on your frame of reference."

"And what is your frame of reference, Axel?" Mark cocked his head with an amused look.

"How do you mean?"

"In this so-called murder investigation of yours. Have you figured out the identity of the murderer?"

"There certainly seem to be a lot of candidates so far. Yours is the only name that hasn't come up. Were you on such good terms with Edgar?"

"He hired me. I always did everything he asked of me. He never gave me any trouble. Isn't that 'good terms'?"

"That's strange. Everyone else on the faculty seems to have borne Edgar a grudge for one thing or another."

"Look at who's on the faculty. Edgar was a Harvard man. Those are the standards he wanted to be associated with. Now Brook University has an excellent reputation in a number of fields, but would you rank our music department in the top twenty in the country, or even the top fifty?"

"I see what you mean."

"Look at you. You're always going off to give papers at conferences and at other universities. Do you see us ever inviting anyone here?"

"Well, you've had a couple of regional meetings of the Society for Ethnomusicology."

"What does that tell you, Axel?"

"You're thinking of Lewis and Seth ..."

"... and George and Paavo. What have they really contributed?"

"Paavo's productive."

"But what he's produced is drivel. Why do you suppose Edgar was so incensed at not getting the Ives Chair? Edgar really didn't have a big ego, Axel, but he did have a healthy sense of his own self-worth. You don't win the Kinkeldey Award unless you've done something pretty special. And for a real scholar to be passed over in favor of that Scandinavian scanty-weight left him pretty bitter."

"A bitterness he's expressed by thwarting all the people he considered to be dead wood."

"You can't get rid of a tenured professor. Mediocre people don't like to be reminded of their mediocrity."

"What about Viola?"

"That depends on where you place her on the excellence scale."

"Or rather," I suggested, "where Edgar placed her."

"Now you're catching on. You know, Axel, you've begun to come out of your shell as a result of this investigation."

"How do you mean?"

"Well, I think I've gotten to know you better in the last day or two than I have in the entire five years that we've been colleagues."

"You may be right about that."

"I think you've gotten a raw deal here, Axel."

"Tell me about it."

"But a lot of it you've brought on yourself."

"How's that?"

"Take your revision of the undergraduate curriculum."

"But those were all Edgar Frost's ideas. I went over every detail of the plan with him beforehand. I thought I'd get ahead by pleasing him."

"Axel, do you know the phrase 'stalking horse'?"

"How does that apply here?"

"When you presented the plan to the faculty, did Edgar show a lot of support?"

"Not really."

"And when the faculty voted to table the motion, did he express any displeasure?"

"Not that I recall."

"He was just using you, Axel, to see how things stood with the others."

"But that issue more or less got me fired. That and others like it."

"Edgar never cared a lot about other people's welfare, Axel."

"But I consulted every member of the faculty individually about that plan?"

"And when they didn't offer specific objections, you assumed they approved."

"Well, yes. Doesn't that make sense?"

"Axel, people always know what you're thinking because you say whatever is on your mind. They usually don't know what you're feeling—up to now you've seemed pretty detached, and that makes them uncomfortable. With most of the faculty here, the reverse is true: you know what they're feeling, but they guard their thoughts. That was your undoing."

"So if it hadn't been for that fiasco, I might have had tenure?"

"No, that just showed the senior faculty what kind of person you were, and they felt threatened. You give the impression that you care more about ideas than people. You know the way tenure really works: if they like you, they'll find a way to keep you; if they don't like you, they'll find a way to get rid of you. And in your case, they didn't have to look far for ways to get rid of you."

Mark departed, and I was left alone in the reference room. Even empty the room seemed to retain the purposeful energy of those who had worked there earlier in the evening. No one came to the music library except to work.

I returned home to mark the tests from my symphony course. We had just finished studying Beethoven's Eroica Symphony and I had showed the class how Beethoven used an anomalous note in the opening measures as the basis for an enormous first movement that was longer than an entire Mozart symphony. I was interested to see what they would make of the examples I had chosen from later movements in the work.

At around 8:30 the telephone rang. It was Maureen Chesterton wanting to know how the investigation was coming along. I told her the story of Seth Nelson, the "Festschrift," the State Trumpet, the row with Edgar, and my conclusion that Seth hadn't killed him.

After an extended silence Maureen spoke. "I'm not sure how to put this, Axel. I don't want to hurt your feelings; but as I told Viola, I think you're just too nice for this kind of work."

"Too nice?"

"You believe what people tell you."

"How do you mean?"

"Take Seth Nelson. You've just told me that he's a liar, an embezzler and an intellectual fraud. Does that inspire confidence in his words?"

"But a man's intimate life ..."

"Oh come on, Axel. Don't be so squeamish. Do you think he and Chad are lovers?"

"Well, it would be hard to prove, but I don't have any reason to doubt it."

"If Seth asked Chad to provide him with an alibi, do you think he'd do it?"

"I've never doubted Chad's integrity, but I suppose he might, under duress."

"But Seth was counting on you not to ask him."

"True."

"So what's the value of his alibi?"

"I see your point. How do you feel about Edgar's death?"

"Harold always considered him a trouble-maker, but I found him rather charming."

"So why did you intervene for Paavo over Edgar for the Ives chair?"

183

Maureen paused for several seconds. "That was a long time ago, Axel."

"With respect, that doesn't answer my question."

She paused again. "Viola has probably told you that I spent a number of years in Finland early in my career. I've always felt a debt of gratitude toward the people of that country; and so when the choice came between a troublemaker and a compatriot, even a compatriot once removed, I went with my sympathies. I'm going to have to let you go now. Good luck, Axel."

Maureen's answer to my last two questions didn't seem compatible with each other, but her objections to Seth's alibi seemed to have validity.

It looked as though Chad would be heading to Boston University. Had he really developed a passion for organ building, or might he have had a lover's quarrel with "Dr." Nelson? Then I remembered Chad's words from Monday morning, that he had been just outside Frost's office when the police arrived. I decided to risk embarrassing him and made a phone call.

"Hello, Prof. Crochet."

"Chad, I think I overheard you say that you were at the scene when Prof. Frost's body was removed."

"Even before that. Eileen and I went to the library right after lunch to work on our bibliography assignment. I came down to the music office to pick up our tickets for the BSO concert—Miss Rockwell had just posted the announcement—and I was there when the police arrived."

So Seth's sob story had been concocted for my benefit. Perhaps Maureen was right. Maybe I was too trusting for this kind of investigation. But Seth's embarrassment had seemed genuine. Was he using a liaison with a grad student to cover up an even more damning secret? I decided to push Chad a little further. "Chad, this may be awkward for you, but I need to ask it anyway. Did you see Prof. Nelson Friday afternoon?"

"What do you mean?"

"Miss Mordent's life may be at stake here, Chad. That's the only reason I would ask you to break a confidence."

"He said he would torpedo my application to BU if I told anyone. Could he do that?"

"No, Chad," I said. It might not have been true, but it should have been true, and I believed it to be true.

There was a silence at the other end of the line. "All right," he said softly. "I saw him."

"Prof. Nelson?"

"Yes. He was coming out of Prof. Frost's office."

"When was this exactly?"

"Just before two o'clock. I remember looking at my watch when Miss Crawford came out of the music office. He said that Prof. Frost was dead but that he hadn't killed him. He made me promise not to say anything or I'd never get to go to Boston University."

"Did he offer a reason for being in Prof. Frost's office?"

"No. That's what's made me so worried. Do you think he killed him?"

"I don't know, Chad, but I know you did the right thing to tell me."

"I hope so." He didn't sound too convinced. I thanked him and hung up.

If I were to go back to Seth with this information, he would likely direct his wrath against Chad with nothing gained. I tried to imagine why Seth would go to Edgar if not to kill him, and came back to the question of Edgar's unfulfilled meeting with the dean.

Once Edgar revealed Seth's wrongdoing to Dean Manx, a process would have been started that could not easily be halted. This would have been Seth's last opportunity to resolve the fight with Edgar and plead for mercy. Finding Edgar already dead, he might have thought he was in the clear, except for the incriminating financial documents. He might even have been trying to cover his tracks when Cecilia knocked on Edgar's door. Seth would have beat a hasty retreat, only to find that his exit had been observed. On the other hand, Seth murdering Edgar also fit the facts.

If Chad's story was correct, and I couldn't think why he would invent such a tale, the hallway outside Edgar's office must have been a busy place the afternoon of his death. Viola had visited him briefly around 1:30. Bonnie saw Viola coming out of the office, say around 1:35, and immediately went in herself. Edgar rebuffed her advances so she was probably out again in another five minutes or so. If the murderer had been basing his attack on Viola's return visit, he had probably been lurking nearby during Bonnie's visit and must have gone into the office as soon as she came out. Seth, if he were not the murderer, could have gone into the office shortly before 2:00, his intrusion interrupted by Cecilia's knock at around 2:00. A crowded timetable but possible,

brought about by the coincidence of Stephanie's funeral, Edgar's intended meeting with Dean Manx and the deadline for grade changes: a
triple witching hour.

My meditation was interrupted by the doorbell. It was Patricia. I
invited her in and asked whether she'd like some fruit juice. "That
would be nice," she said with a smile.

I've never developed a taste for alcohol, but I do like to experiment
with fruit juices. My current favorite, Orange and Tropical Fruit, contained a blend of pineapple, apple, orange, mango and passion fruit.

When I came into the living room I saw Patricia examining my book
collection: on one wall literature, including more or less complete col-
lections of John Barth, Joan Didion, Richard Ford, Garrison Keillor and
John Updike, as well as Margaret Atwood and Robertson Davies. On
the facing wall, books on science, history, film, humanistic psychology
and recreational mathematics, all in white bookcases matching the
white sofa, loveseat and, around the corner, white dining room table and
chairs. Color came in the form of a large print of Henri Rousseau's "The
Sleeping Gypsy" hanging over the sofa, as well as the varied hues of the
book bindings.

"This place is so clean!" Patricia exclaimed.

"It's my response to the double standard. A woman can have dust
kittens the size of mountain lions and people will say she was just too
busy to vacuum that week. If a man has so much as a hair in the bathroom sink, it's 'See what I mean? Men live like pigs.'"

We sat down beside each other on the sofa.

"I owe you an apology," Patricia began.

"I didn't mean you personally."

"I'm not talking about that. This morning, in your office, you didn't
really think Prof. Collins murdered Edgar Frost, did you?"

"Not really, but I talked with him anyway. I'm not a detective,
Patricia, but I do take a mathematical approach to problem-solving. I
find one way to get the correct answer is to eliminate all the incorrect
ones."

"You mean like Sherlock Holmes' rule that once you have eliminated
the impossible, then whatever is left, no matter how improbable, must
be the solution?"

"Something like that. An awful lot of people disliked Edgar Frost,
several of them intensely, but it remains a finite number."

"So you plan to eliminate them one by one?" Patricia asked with an amused laugh.

"Unless a better plan comes along. George Collins had some interesting things to say, nonetheless."

"Really?"

"He thought that in a sense Edgar had brought the murder on himself, and that we would do well to look at what Edgar said and did during the past week."

"That's what I wanted to tell you," Patricia said, drawing closer to me on the sofa. "Last Tuesday as I was walking to class, Prof. Mack came out of the chairman's office. He didn't even see me, but the look on his face—if the phrase 'murderous gaze' ever meant anything, that was it."

"What happened then?"

"Well, I was on my way to the music library and Prof. Frost came out of his office and greeted me but didn't stop to talk. When I got to the library, he was already there talking with Miss Rockwell."

Lewis Mack, eh? None of us took him seriously as a scholar, but he took himself extremely seriously. Perhaps Edgar had thwarted him once too often. At last Monday's faculty meeting, Edgar had announced the distribution of graduate assistants for the coming year, and Lewis hadn't seemed too happy when his request was turned down. This might bear investigating.

"I'll look into that." Then I recalled Viola's words. "Pat, do you think I'm emotionally distant?"

"What brought this on?"

"Viola said that I'm detached from people."

"So?"

"Well, do you think I keep my feelings inside?"

"I'd say the same for most of the men I've dated. I figure it goes with the territory. If I want to know what you're feeling, I just ask."

"But don't you think ...?"

"Don't think so much." Patricia, now quite close, was looking at me with an air of expectancy that probably didn't have anything to do with the murder case. I put my arm around her.

"Look, it's getting rather late," I said, finally getting the message. "Would you like to spend the night?"

"I thought you'd never ask," Patricia responded, and kissed me warmly on the lips. With one graceful gesture Patricia turned off the light and drew me close to her. The symphony students would have to wait another day for their tests.

CHAPTER 17

A new issue of the Brook Banner appeared Wednesday morning, and someone had already fastened the front page to the bulletin board when I entered the music building. Under the headline "ARREST IMMI-NENT" appeared a large picture of Viola, her head bent over and her hands covering her face, with the caption, "Who is she shielding?" Out of all the photographs Freddy had taken of Viola, he'd managed to get one picture in the classic pose of a mobster being taken away by the police.

The story, under the by-line of Frederick Thatcher, read, "Information obtained by this reporter suggests that murder suspect Viola Mordent was not acting alone in the brutal slaying of music department chairman Edgar Frost. A second assassin is being sought for questioning, though authorities have refused to comment on these developments. Prof. Crochet, conducting an independent investigation within the department, claims to have been out of town on the day of the incident. Asked if he thought he would ever confess the truth in this matter, Crochet gave an evasive shrug and said 'What is truth?'"

The clever wording made it sound as if the police themselves were on the trail of a mysterious accomplice who, in fact, was purely the invention of Freddy Thatcher's overactive imagination. And his weasel words made me look like a henchman. As I headed up to my office, I wondered whether one ambitious but misguided writer could be called a "media circus."

I had scarcely hung up my coat when Lewis Mack burst into my office, carrying a bunch of file folders. "Good morning, Axel. I've decided to make you director of graduate admissions. Here are all the folders. You're to read and summarize them and report to the full faculty at the next meeting."

"Well, that's always been the responsibility of the chairman up to now, Lewis. After all, as chairman, you get a reduction in your course load."

"And I also get the authority to delegate responsibility, and I'm delegating this responsibility to you."

"Sounds as if you thought Edgar worked too hard?"

"Frost, work? Listen, pal, all he ever did was put people down. I requested travel funds to visit Europe to record myself playing on the pianos that Liszt might have played on."

"I didn't know you played Liszt, Lewis."

"Well, I can't play the stuff myself—Liszt made it too hard just to show off—but I was going to record a piece I've written myself, and that bastard Frost just turned me down. Then I asked for release time to compile a discography of all the records I've played on my radio program, and Edgar said that that wasn't 'appropriate scholarly activity.' Then last year I asked to go to Switzerland so that I could get a feel for the countryside that Liszt wrote about in the first volume of his 'Years of Wandering,' and Frost nixed that, too."

"That must have been disappointing." My irony was wasted. Mack paused only for breath then went right on. "Then this year I asked him to give me a graduate assistant to transcribe my lectures on music for publication."

"You mean your off-the-cuff remarks?"

"Frost just laughed in my face. He never took my scholarship seriously."

My regard for Edgar Frost rose several notches.

"That was the last straw." Lewis was really getting worked up at this point, his hands clenching into fists and his face turning red. "I was tired of being thwarted. Frost had to go. So you know what I did? This is the really clever part. I stole that Mary Garden brooch from Viola and planted it in Edgar's office—brilliant, huh? I was all ready to make my move when she beat me to it."

"Wait a minute. You're telling me you were planning to kill Edgar."

"The bastard had it coming!"

"But why did you want to implicate Viola?"

"I'm sick of hearing about Viola Mordent, 'formerly at the Metropolitan Opera,' sick of her students always getting awards. Songbird to jailbird—it's not so far, is it? And it looks as if I picked the right person anyway, since she ended up offing Edgar."

"But ..."

"And you know what? Friday wasn't the first time Viola had threatened Edgar. Two weeks ago I overheard her telling Ruth Rockwell, 'I could just kill that man!'"

"I suppose you felt compelled to communicate this to the police?"

"Damn straight. I know my civic responsibility. This whole murder thing is hurting the reputation of the music department, not to mention my radio show."

"I was hoping you wouldn't mention it."

"What's that?"

"Now that you mention it, exactly how were you planning to kill Frost?"

"I was going to strangle him with my bare hands, that's how."

"And if you'd succeeded, were we to believe that Viola Mordent could have done that?"

"Are you kidding? Have you seen the muscles on that broad? She could bench-press you!"

I wondered whether Wagner had managed to anticipate this scenario, too. As Lewis Mack would have had it, he was Siegfried slaying the dragon who blocked him from getting his much-deserved scholarly recognition, in the form of the Rhinemaidens' golden treasure hidden in the dragon's cave. "Well this is all working out pretty well for you, Lewis."

"Yeah, I guess I owe Viola a big thank-you. Anyway, I want that report by next meeting." Lewis left my office without waiting for any further objections on my part.

Only after I sat down did I realize how smoothly Lewis had manipulated me. Under the guise of confessing his murderous intention, he had begged the question of Viola as the killer. But if she hadn't killed Edgar Frost, why couldn't it have been Lewis after all? Perhaps all these extra responsibilities he was loading on me stemmed not from his colossal laziness but from a desire to keep me occupied.

What had I learned about Lewis since Edgar's death? He was supposed to have written a letter for Chad Brimley but hadn't done it. He'd raged out of the chairman's office, after which Edgar had gone directly to the music library to consult with Ruth. The library might not be the repository of all knowledge, but I suspected I could learn more about Lewis Mack there. Then the telephone rang.

CHAPTER 18

Cecilia Crawford had lost patience with me. "Those course descriptions were due Monday, Axel. You should have written them before you went away for the weekend. The deadline for printing the new catalogue is this afternoon. I really must have them right away."

"I'll type them out right now and have them in your hands within the hour," I promised.

Cecilia considered that teaching constituted the only proper activity of a university professor. Research, as far as she was concerned, was simply a recreational activity for overeducated men with far too much time on their hands. A trip to attend a conference or to deliver a paper, to her mind, had about as much importance as a golf tournament or a fishing trip, expensive and frivolous.

The musicologists held the opposite point of view. By their reckoning, anyone who had fulfilled the prodigious task of completing a doctorate (or in Seth's case, what he claimed to be its equivalent), should be entitled to compensation for life. They considered teaching a course now and then an act of *noblesse oblige* rather than the fulfillment of a contractual agreement with their employer.

My enthusiasm for teaching, though welcomed by most of the students, was looked upon with suspicion by the tenured faculty as one might look askance at someone who smiled while completing his income tax return. In fairness, the theory teachers, to whom pedantry came as second nature, had little use for the condescending attitude of the musicologists.

I set about typing the course description for the Wagner seminar, which under Lewis Mack's chairmanship would have no difficulty entering the catalogue. Not that Mack was any fonder of Wagner than Edgar Frost had been, but he was even less fond of work of any kind and had no interest in monitoring what went into the catalogue.

"Richard Wagner continues to excite passionate disputes even a century after his death. His detractors consider Wagner an anti-Semite, a proto-Nazi, a wife-stealer, and worse. Yet musicians consider him to be the most creative innovator in large-scale structures since Beethoven. The seminar will focus on the relationship between large and small forms in *Die Meistersinger von Nürnberg*, Wagner's only comedy, and the use of harmony as an organizing force in *Tristan und Isolde*."

One down, one to go. Next year I was scheduled to teach a nine-teenth-century music course in the General Studies program, always a challenge, especially since many students considered George Collins as the exemplar for offerings by the music department.

"Music from the nineteenth century occupies a preponderant position in contemporary concert life. Symphony concerts, piano or song recitals and opera productions all draw on music from this period for the largest part of their repertory, and classical radio stations reflect this predominance in their programming.

"This course will focus on several genres of the period: symphonic poem, concert overture, piano concerto, song, and character piece for piano. We will listen to and discuss representative examples of each genre, after which students will write a one-page paper comparing the works they have heard."

These five or six one-page papers would prove a challenge to students accustomed to taking multiple-choice tests on facts they had been told to memorize but would offer an opportunity to the Patricia Makefairs of the world to learn to form and articulate distinctions in an area they had not explored before.

I took the descriptions down to the music office and apologized for their tardiness.

"I should think so," Cecilia said. "I reminded you about this yesterday."

"That you did."

"What about the choral conducting course? You didn't give it last year."

"I know we generally offer that course every other year, but there were so few students enrolled last time, I think we'll wait another year before offering it again."

The undergraduate music majors had persuaded me to offer the course in the first place. They said that since many of them were going to be high school music teachers, this was something they should know. Made sense. So over one summer I put together a choral conducting course which absolutely bombed.

Students apparently thought that the hand gestures of beating time embodied some kind of sleight of hand that would make a chorus materialize out of thin air. (Evidently they had taken the orchestral conductor seriously when he had explained the process to them: "You wave your hands in time to the music," he had told them facetiously, "and whenever you hear someone make an entrance, point to him and smile.")

I thought about Debussy's harrowing experiences as a conductor of his own music, an unwelcome assignment he was compelled to take on for financial reasons. Facing an orchestra for the first time in concert, he raised both hands high above his head, thus immobilizing himself for all practical musical purposes. Looking around desperately, he finally caught the eye of the sympathetic concertmaster who, summoning the attention of the rest of the orchestra, gave a strong up-bow followed by a strong down-bow, starting the piece on its way and releasing the hapless composer from his state of imprisonment.

My choral conducting students, faced with instructions and assignments in ear training, breath control, warm-up exercises, rehearsal technique, repertoire and programming, recruitment, performance practice and music editing, had responded the same way as the daughter of a colleague starting piano lessons. Upon learning that there wasn't going to be a simple "trick" which would allow her to play the piano, she just quit.

I left Cecilia to finish compiling the catalogue and headed to the music library. Ruth was working at her desk and no one else was in the immediate vicinity, so I could speak to her confidentially.

"Good morning, Ruth. I'm going to ask you commit an indiscretion."

"Right here in public?"

"Well, sort of. You know I've been asking questions about Edgar's death. I'm trying to find an alternative to Viola."

"Quite right. Viola couldn't possibly have murdered Edgar."

"That's what I think, too, but the police have put together a pretty strong case against her, and it's going to take more than my personal convictions to clear her."

"What do you want me to do?" Ruth sounded eager and conspiratorial.

"I understand that Edgar came here last Tuesday. From what I gather he may have been looking for information about Lewis Mack."

"And while Edgar is dead, Lewis is still alive, hence the indiscretion."

"You got it."

"Tell you what, Axel. You ask your questions, and I'll wrestle with my conscience."

"Sounds good to me." I tried to phrase a question that wouldn't end the inquiry before it started. "Did Edgar ask to look at a reference work?"

Ruth smiled at me. She understood exactly the game I was playing and was taking delicious pleasure in it. "Yes, he asked to see *Who's Who in American Musicology.*"

"You wouldn't happen to have a copy of that handy, I suppose."

"Right here," she said as she pulled the volume from a shelf behind her desk. "In addition to the regular reference collection in the reading room, we have a small group of what we call 'ready reference' books here at the desk."

"To deal with all those telephone questions like, 'Can you tell me who wrote this tune?'"

"We'll make a reference librarian out of you yet, Axel," Ruth said.

I opened the book to the M's, and consulted the entry on Lewis Mack: "B.A., Thackery College; M.A., Ph.D., Boston University," followed by a list of the places where Mack had taught, and passing reference to his publications, most of which the editors of *Who's Who* did not deign to acknowledge.

"Nothing particularly surprising here. Did Prof. Frost ask to see any other reference works?"

Ruth nodded; I was following the correct trail and she still hadn't been required to violate any of her professional standards. "I believe he went to the Dissertation Abstracts next," she said.

I could have found them unaided but Ruth was enjoying this little game far too much to quit now. We went into the stacks together, climbed to the third floor where I stuck out my tongue at the hideous face of Harold Witherspoon, and proceeded to the shelves containing the abstracts of every dissertation in music published in the United States.

I went unaided to the final volume, an alphabetical index of names, updated annually, and once again turned to the M's. "That's funny," I said, "there's no entry for Lewis."

"Those were practically Edgar's exact words," Ruth said.

"But how ...?" I began. At this, Ruth turned and pretended to align several volumes of the abstracts, as if to tell me that while she could assist me with the facts, I would have to reach the conclusions on my own. Then she turned to me and said, "Can I ask you a personal question, Axel?"

"Shoot."

"You're a published scholar yet you didn't even get your initial three-year appointment renewed here. Then after leaving you fired for a few months the senior faculty changed their mind and rehired you only to deny you tenure a couple of years later. That approaches academic abuse in my book."

"So what else is new?"

"Why do you stay here and take it? Why don't you go somewhere where your talents would be appreciated?"

"It's not as easy as that. I've checked the job listings every year and filed applications for every position I could, but nothing's come of it."

"Have you been active in the American Musicological Society?"

"I've organized a number of symposia."

"That's not what I mean. When you go to the annual meetings, how many people do you seek out to talk with?"

"Oh, I don't know. Four or five maybe."

"It should be four or five dozen. It's not enough to publish articles, Axel, you have to make the personal connections, too."

"Why are you telling me all this, Ruth? And why now?"

"I don't know, Axel. I just think highly of you and hate to see you getting hurt. And now that you've been talking with me it just seems easier to tell you what's been on my mind for a long time."

"Well I appreciate the advice, Ruth. I'll think about what you've said. But right now I've got a murderer to catch." I returned to my office, knowing where I'd find the answer to the question.

CHAPTER 19

If you're ever trying to locate someone, the best source of information is not the police or the postal system but the alumni office of the person's university. Their investigative talents rival those of a detective agency, I can say having tried several times to cut off my trail from those eager to solicit my donations.

A telephone call to the Boston University alumni office received a courteous response. "Good morning, Prof. Crochet. Ordinarily I would need to check our database to answer your question; but, as it happens, yours is the second call we've received about Lewis Mack in less than two weeks, so I can tell you confidently that no such person ever did graduate work at Boston University."

"I suppose you've checked with the registrar of the School of Music and ..."

"Prof. Crochet," the voice interrupted, "nobody escapes from our checking department."

You don't build and maintain an institution the size of Boston University without squeezing every possible dollar from those who have passed through its ivied gates. I had no reason to doubt her confident answer.

That explained why Lewis had put off Chad's request. It also gave him a much better motive for murder than his whining about being turned down for travel grants. All the evidence suggested that Lewis's scholarly career was a fraud. The man had no credentials beyond a B.A. from an obscure school in Boston. No wonder his radio program was so banal: the information he disseminated came not from respectable scholarly sources but from popular books and record liner notes.

For this information to become public would end his easy academic life. Planting Viola's brooch in Edgar's office was part of a genuine murder attempt. Correctly calculating that Dean Manx would most likely turn to him to replace Frost, Lewis counted on the position of department chairman to insulate him from further inquiries. Manx, scientist that he was, would assume that Frost had vetted his faculty; but Frost knew how many of his deadwood professors had been grandfathered into tenure when Brook University came into being. Lewis had joined the staff in an era before the demand for physical evidence of every credential claim became common. With nerve and a good story, Lewis Mack had managed to secure a comfortable existence. I wondered what had tipped Edgar off in the first place.

"Prof. Crochet!" Freddy Thatcher rushed in without bothering to knock. "I've decided on a great new approach to this murder. I'm going to write a non-fiction novella, like *In Cold Blood*."

"You fancy yourself in the company of Truman Capote?"

"That way if I don't know some of the details, I can just make them up."

It seemed to me that that's what he had been doing from the outset, but I held my peace.

"I really have a lot of work to do right now," I said before realizing that subtle messages weren't going to have any effect.

"Prof. Lewis said you'd give me your full cooperation," Freddy persisted. "What I need from you is the story of the 'real' Viola Mordent. What's the secret persona behind her public mask?" Freddy reached into his book bag to pull out his notebook, stumbled into the corner of the worktable, and in the process knocked the stack of grad applications on the floor.

"That's enough!" I shouted. "Get out of here!"

"The people have a right to the truth," Freddy shouted back as I pushed him into the corridor and locked the door.

I had planned to spend the morning on Debussy, but I couldn't just leave the grad application folders scattered all over the floor. As I got things back in order, I reflected on the process by which we admitted our graduate students.

The music department had established a formal examination procedure for prospective graduate students in which they had to take musical dictation by ear, answer a three-page test of historical knowledge, and identify a piece of music and discuss its musical style. For those who couldn't come to the university to take the examination, we had a kit of materials to be administered at their home institution. Trouble was, of late very few applicants could pass this examination, so we were compelled to rely on letters from their teachers and transcripts of their undergraduate courses.

Going through the files I came across a name I'd heard before: Sigrida Salo. Oh yes, that was the woman whom Paavo had said had withdrawn her application. Still, it might be interesting to see what we were missing. Undergraduate degree from Helsinki University. High marks in all of her courses.

Here was a hand-written letter. I skipped past the summary of her academic work to the end of the letter. "In thinking about a topic for my graduate work, I went through some papers written by my father before his accident. They were the basis for an article published in the *Finnish Journal of Music* whose English title would have been, "Quatrain Theory in Classical Music." He was working with Professor Raine at the time of his death, which took place when I was only two. I would consider it an honor to work with Professor Raine and to carry on my father's work."

"Quatrain theory?" Paavo certainly had been getting a lot of mileage out of the idea. But this Salo fellow must have been awfully ambitious to cover all of Classical music with this article. You'd think Paavo would have guided him into something more manageable.

Then I stopped to calculate. This article was supposed to have been published twenty years ago. That was even before Paavo's first article in JAMS. Of course, you could never tell with delays in publication. Still, it might be worth checking. I headed off to the music library.

On the way down the hall I bumped into Jonathan Whitby, who pushed me into a corner and demanded, "Axel, just what are you doing?"

"Going to the music library."

"I mean this investigation of yours, turning the department upside down to play detective."

"Actually, I'm trying to clear Viola's name."

"That's just what I mean. You get this foolish notion into your head and stubbornly refuse to look at the facts."

"I guess it all depends on how you look at the facts." I was beginning to get impatient.

"Axel, I saw her do it."

"You what!"

"I saw Viola kill Edgar Frost."

"Well this is a fine time to tell me. Why didn't you speak out sooner?"

"You keep acting as if you have some kind of official capacity. Have the police suddenly slapped a deputy's badge on your chest?"

"Not exactly."

"So what makes me accountable to you?" Whitby was one of these annoying people who liked to poke you in the chest to underline their pronouns.

"Well I would have thought that ..."

"This play-acting of yours has gone far enough. It's gotten to the point that the sponsor of Lewis's radio program wants to pull it off the air because of the publicity."

"It's not my fault that Edgar was murdered."

"No, but you're prolonging the controversy. The police solved the case right off the bat—it didn't take a lot of thought—and should be arresting Viola any time now. End of story. But you come along and start accusing one member of the department after another so that when the story's safely moved out of the headlines, you keep fanning the flames."

"What has this got to do with Lewis's radio program?"

"The sponsor is Ernest Shackleford of Shackleford Electronics."

"And?"

"And his niece, Marcia Tidd, is one of our students. I think you have her in your seminar."

"I'm still not following this."

"Shackleford said he thought being connected with a murder was bad for his business, but as long as the murderer had been caught, the public might not be so upset."

"So?"

"So Marcia tells him that you're trying to make people think that Viola Mordent didn't do it."

"I don't think she did."

"But that means there's a murderer running loose in the same music department whose new chairman is being sponsored by Shackleford Electronics. People don't like that sort of thing. So now he wants to pull the plug on Lewis."

"What's your interest in all this?"

"I just want to see justice done, that's all, and put that banshee behind bars where she belongs."

"I suppose you've told your story to the police."

"Actually not. I was visiting my sister on Saturday and Sunday when they were doing interviews, and nobody's seen fit to talk with me since then."

"You don't think an eye-witness account is something they should hear?"

"What's the point? They've already identified the killer."

"But you thought it important enough to corner me here?"

"Because you're the one that's creating the fuss. Viola hasn't been bothering anybody. She's just marking time until she's arrested and tried."

"And you say you saw her kill Edgar."

"That's right. I was passing the chairman's office when I saw her come into the room from the department office, pick up the statue, and club him with it."

"And you just kept on walking?"

"I didn't think she'd killed him. Anyway, he had it coming."

This was beginning to sound awfully familiar. Was there nobody on the faculty whom Edgar Frost hadn't managed to antagonize? "How do you mean?"

"For five years I've been trying to upgrade the electronic studio, and every time I talked to Edgar he'd come out with some cute comment that one bloop or bleep sounded pretty much like another and look what Karlheinz Stockhausen managed to do with nothing but a few oscillators and a couple of tape recorders."

I thought of Stockhausen's early work, *Gesang der Jünglinge*, an evocative piece from the mid-50's, combining the sound of a boy's voice with purely electronic sounds. Frost really did know the repertoire.

"So you didn't feel any need to rush to Edgar's aid?"

"No. Let the bitch maul him if she had a mind to. I wasn't going to stop her."

"This certainly puts a new light on things."

"So I can tell Lewis you've decided to call off this witch-hunt?"

"I don't think his radio program has anything to fear from me."

"All right, Axel. I hope this is the end of the story."

I moved past Jonathan and continued on to the music library. This sudden "eyewitness account" sounded rather dubious, and I suspected that Jonathan's new-found interest in Lewis Mack's radio program would eventually be linked to a *quid pro quo* involving an upgrade to the electronic studio. Still, I couldn't rule out the possibility that, despite his personal unpleasantness, Jonathan might be telling the truth.

CHAPTER 20

I greeted Ruth and asked if it would be possible to request an article from the *Finnish Music Journal* on interlibrary loan.

"Which article did you need?"

"'Quatrain Theory in Classical Music' by Einar Salo. But don't you need the volume number or at least the year in order to order a particular article?"

"In general, yes, but the article you want is right here."

"I don't understand."

"Edgar Frost ordered a copy of it some time ago and it came in just last week. I kept a photocopy for our files." She looked pleased with her own efficiency.

"You're going to miss Edgar, aren't you, Ruth?"

"You have no idea, Axel," she said, and paused a moment to regain her composure. "I think I may be the only one in the department who appreciates what he's done for this library. Take that new acquisitions shelf beside you."

I looked down at the row of books, each with a protruding card.

"Edgar started the buck-slip system, so that any new book entering the library would stop on this shelf for a week before disappearing into the stacks." Those interested could put their names on a card, then sign out the book after it left the new acquisitions shelf.

"I've found that system very helpful," I noted.

"Edgar's name appeared on more slips than anyone else's. I've never known another man with his breadth of interests. And whenever the central library threatened to reduce our budget for periodicals, he always found some way to preserve it."

"You helped a lot yourself," I observed, "by keeping records on frequency of use for each of the journals. I wonder what will happen now that Lewis is chairman."

"Pardon me for saying so, but Lewis Mack is no Edgar Frost."

I agreed with her and took the photocopied article to one of the work tables and hunted for Paavo's article. Bound volumes of Journal of the American Musicological Society were consulted so often that they were housed right here in the reference room. I had no difficulty tracking down Edgar Frost's maiden article.

I couldn't read Finnish, but I could compare the musical examples— with respect to notation, at least, music is a universal language. They were the same! How could Paavo have allowed a graduate student to plagiarize his work this way? You would have thought that the *Finnish Music Journal* would very likely call on Paavo to give an opinion on Salo's work before publishing it.

Then it struck me. Could it have been the other way around? Suppose Paavo had stolen his student's ideas, then published them as his own after the student's untimely death. I would have loved to know more about that "accident." No doubt Edgar had wondered about that, too. Paavo was already on the faculty when Edgar came to Brooks. Had Edgar hired Paavo himself, he would have uncovered every detail of his past.

I returned to my office and telephoned a colleague in Ann Arbor who was to preside over the session at which Paavo was scheduled to present his paper. As I expected, Edgar's request to serve as a "respondent" had come very recently. My friend was a bit surprised since this hadn't been one of Edgar's areas of research, but you wouldn't turn down a department chairman if he wanted to respond to the work of one his professors. "I telephoned Paavo, of course, as a courtesy, and he was very cordial, said he would be honored to hear Edgar's thoughtful remarks."

But how had Edgar been so sure about the plagiarism? He wouldn't have proceeded just on the basis of musical examples. He knew a lot of languages, but Finnish?

The only person I knew who could speak Finnish was Maureen Chesterton. She had spent her apprenticeship with the Tapiola Opera Company and returned to Finland regularly later in her career. I telephoned Maureen and found her at home. "Good morning, Axel. I hadn't expected to hear from you so soon. Don't tell me you've solved the murder already."

"I've discovered more secrets about people in the music department than I really wanted to know."

"So what happened to Prof. Frost?"

"I think you may be able to help me on that. Did you talk with Edgar the week before he died?"

"Yes, I did. He brought over an article in Finnish that he asked me to read for him. He didn't want a formal translation, he just wanted to know the gist of it."

"Did he say anything about the article?"

"Well, it was sort of peculiar. While I was giving out a rough translation of the Finnish, he was following along in a book of some sort, actually it looked like a bound periodical, now that I think about it. He kept muttering something like 'They're the same, the same.' But what does this have to do with his death?"

"I can't tell you just yet, but you've been a great help."

The other telephone call took some calculation—it would be evening now in Finland. Happily, Sigrida Salo was at the number she had listed on her application.

"Hello. This is Axel Crochet, calling from Brook University."

"Ah, hello. Then you received my application."

"Yes, we did. It looks like a very strong application."

"Thank you."

"There wasn't any question of your withdrawing your application, was there?"

"I'm sorry. I don't understand. Did I do something wrong?"

"Not at all. You're still interested in coming?"

"Yes, of course. I thought I explained in my letter."

"Yes. It's very well written. We'll be in touch with you. Thank you."

So Edgar's master plan came clear. He hadn't intended to confront Paavo at all, but to expose him, and not just before the department, but before the assembled musicological community. He had intended to use his "response" to Paavo's paper to discredit, humiliate and destroy him. And all because he'd been passed over for the Ives chair in favor of the man who now turned out to be a complete impostor. Paavo must have realized the trap that was being set for him as soon as he'd received the call from Ann Arbor and planned to kill Edgar before he could carry out his plan.

Paavo had cleverly sent Viola into Edgar's office, and once Viola had laid her hand on the bust of Brahms, he was all set. Knowing that Edgar would have his back to the door, Paavo had only to strike quickly. A daring plan, but a shrewd one.

I'd had the wrong Ring analogy. Paavo murdering Edgar wasn't one giant killing another, the way Chad had suggested. Rather it was the cowardly Hagen murdering Siegfried to get the ring, and concocting a tale that Seigfried had been killed by a wild boar, in this case, Viola Mordent.

CHAPTER 21

As soon as my afternoon seminar was over, I went to Raine's office. "It wasn't Seth at all, it was you," I began.

"What are you talking about?"

"You know very well: Edgar discovered that you had published Einar Salo's ideas as your own; and when you realized that he planned to expose you at the AMS meeting, you killed him."

"Axel, you're totally mistaken. Viola killed Edgar, not out of pity for that wretched Whelan girl, but to get the money."

"What money?"

"Edgar's fortune. By academic standards, Frost was a relatively wealthy man, and Viola stood to inherit everything."

"What do you mean inherit?"

"She was his wife, Axel. Don't you know anything?"

My head was reeling as I left Paavo's office. Viola married to Edgar? The obituary hadn't mentioned a wife. I wondered if I'd had this upside down from the very start. All the negative feelings I'd had about poking into people's private lives gathered into one paralyzing knot. Before I'd always pushed them aside and concentrated on my commitment to Viola. Now it looked as if my loyalty had been misplaced. The possibility that all this unpleasant prying had been a charade made me feel sick.

Viola had classes for the rest of the afternoon so I decided to go for a run to see if I could get things worked out. From my apartment I ran along Grange Avenue, behind the women's dormitories, across Cogwheel Footbridge, around Brook Lake (evidently the Development Office hadn't yet located a donor willing to re-name the prosaic pond for a price), and down the path heading into the gorge, feeling the temperature go down with each step.

When I first came to Brook, the gorge path had consisted of broken slate and gravel, hazardous under normal conditions and perilous in wet weather. Recently the university, leery of lawsuits, had constructed a paved path along the river at the base of the gorge and protected it with guard-rails. This mile-long stretch at the bottom of the gorge was my favorite part of the run. Ragged stone walls extended up on either side of me, occasionally decorated with a hardy bush or clump of wildflowers.

As I came around a corner I practically bumped into Marcia Tidd.

"Prof. Crochet!" she exclaimed.

"What are you doing down here?" I asked.

"It's a project for the electronic music workshop. I'm gathering sounds from nature."

"That must be the 'found sounds' project that Prof. Whitby mentioned at the last faculty meeting."

"That's right. This is my last sound, but the microphone isn't very good. I'm having trouble getting close enough to the water. Can you help me?"

"What would you like me to do?"

"Well, if you could hold onto me, I could hang out over the river." Marcia slid under the guard rail and I followed suit, then held onto the wooden railing with one hand and Marcia's waist with the other while she leaned out over the running water, tape recorder in hand. We stayed in that position long enough for me to reflect that our graduate students were entirely too attractive.

"That should be enough," she said, just when I was going to ask for a break. I pulled her back from the edge in what in other circumstances would have been a romantic embrace; but she scarcely seemed to notice as she scrambled back under the guard rail, then offered a hand as I followed.

"Thanks a lot," she said. "I'm sorry to interrupt your run."

"It was my pleasure," I said. As I continued along the gorge path, names ran through my head in a rhythmic mantra: "Ed-gar, Le-wis, Paa-vo, Seth, George," with an occasional cross-rhythm, "Viola, Patricia, Cecilia, Eileen, Ruth."

"Follow the money," Paavo had implied. I didn't really know anything about Viola's financial circumstances. She lived alone and had drawn a regular salary from the university for years. I assumed she was adequately provided for. Could she have some great need for money that would have led her to a desperate act like murder? If so, why would she have chosen a method that pointed so directly to herself? Surely she could have found a more subtle method than bashing Edgar over the head with a statue.

The path ascended out of the gorge and followed Yeoman Drive behind fraternity row and the freshman dormitories. I braced myself for the steep hill that lay ahead of me. Perhaps Viola was trying to shield someone else. That would explain why she wanted me to help her and not a real detective who might have uncovered secrets she preferred to leave concealed.

I turned up Campus Road and followed it past the Law School, up past the baseball and football fields and tennis courts. The road curved past the Synchrotron Lab into the College of Veterinary Medicine, with its small animal hospital, large animal isolation facility and poultry virus isolation facility, then turned left onto Schoolhouse Lane. This was my least favorite part of the run—too many cars—but I kept to the left shoulder of the road and hoped for the best.

Perhaps I was just making this too complicated. If what Jonathan said was true, there may never have been an issue of money. Viola simply lost control of her temper again and instead of grabbing onto the statue to keep control, had grabbed it, raised it, and hit Edgar on the head.

But Bonnie claimed to have seen Edgar after Viola left his office. In her embarrassment at being rebuffed, could Bonnie have confused Viola's second visit with the first?

One thing I knew: someone was lying. Viola had been trained as an actress as well as a singer, and even after her operatic career had ended she had regularly demonstrated her ability to dramatize the meaning of a song. Were her protests of innocence just another act? Schoolhouse Lane led into Barleycorn Road; and I was on the home stretch down hill.

What about Jonathan? Like Lewis, he had been regularly thwarted by Edgar Frost; but with a new department chairman in place, the request for a new electronic studio might reach a more receptive ear. And why this sudden preoccupation with Lewis's radio program? I didn't know Jonathan that well, but Lewis's lack of moral fiber was well established. I wouldn't put it past him to arrange some kind of deal with Jonathan, a noted misogynist, for false testimony against Viola in return for department funding for his studio.

As I turned the corner to my apartment, I knew I had a method of determining whether Jonathan was telling the truth. My body felt refreshed and my mind clearer.

I took a shower, put on slacks and a pullover, and telephoned Jonathan Whitby's office.

"What's up, Axel?" he said.

"Hi, Jonathan. Look, Lewis has dumped this pile of grad applications on me, and I'm trying to find a good way to process them. Applicants are supposed to indicate which program they're applying for, but there's no space to differentiate the composers who want to work in electronic music from those who write traditional music."

"They both take pretty much the same courses their first year."

"Yes, but I'm thinking more about the entrance requirements. For instance, we might not want to weigh the harmony requirements as heavily if they're mostly interested in electronic composition."

"I see your point."

"Suppose I pull the composer files and let you see which ones you'd recommend if they mention electronic music in their letter."

"That sounds okay. Thanks."

"Listen, I've been thinking about our conversation this afternoon. Didn't that shake you up at all, seeing Edgar die last Friday?"

"Well, like I told you, Axel, it wasn't till later that I learned he'd actually been killed. I know one thing—I sure don't want to have a muscular voice teacher mad at me."

"Edgar didn't stand up, did he?"

"Naw, he was sitting at his desk with his back to the door, the way he always does. She just grabbed that statue by the head and let him have it."

"Sounds pretty gruesome."

"Well, better him than me, is what I thought."

"Right. Well, I'll drop those files off to you in the morning,"

"Right-o."

So Viola may have been an actress, but Jonathan was a liar. The fingerprints on the base of the statue made his story impossible. Then I realized I might have another way of refuting his story. I checked the department directory and called Marcia Tidd. Her roommate said that she was in the shower but would call back. I made myself a light supper and just as I was about to sit down, the phone rang.

"Prof. Crochet?"

"Hello, Marcia. Thanks for calling back. I was thinking about your electronic music course. When does that course meet, anyway?"

"Monday, Wednesday and Friday, 1:00 to 2:30. Why?"

"So you had a class last Friday?"

"Oh yes; it was awful. We came out of the studio, and there were policemen taping off Prof. Frost's office."

"Thanks, Marcia. You've been a big help."

"And thanks for helping me this afternoon."

"Don't mention it."

So much for Jonathan Whitby's 'eye-witness account' of Edgar's death. I finished supper and headed back to the music building.

CHAPTER 22

Viola wasn't in her studio. I left a note on her desk, and returned to the music library to compare the two articles in greater detail.

Viola entered the room around eight o'clock. The place was deserted—all the graduate students had gone to the BSO concert. I brought Viola up to date on everything I'd discovered: the comparison of the articles, the call to Maureen Chesterton, the phone call to Sigrida Salo that had shown Paavo to be lying, Edgar's evident plan to discredit him at the AMS meeting.

"So that's why Paavo suggested I invite Edgar to Stephanie's funeral. He wanted to get me into the office just before him."

"And when you left your fingerprints on the Brahms bust, you strengthened his case—he had already implicated you through your two visits to the office. The fingerprints made it even better for him."

"We've got method, motive and opportunity, but no proof. Paavo will just deny everything." She stood thinking. "Quiet a minute," she said suddenly.

"What?"

"Did you hear something?"

"No."

"It was probably nothing," she concluded.

"But there's one thing I don't understand. Paavo said that you were Edgar's wife."

"That was a long time ago. We divorced quietly years ago."

"But his obituary never mentioned a wife."

"I wrote that."

"You?"

"It seemed like the easiest way. I just put a few copies on Cecilia's desk and the rest took care of itself. Everything I wrote was the truth."

"But not the whole truth."

"Axel, you can never write the whole truth about anybody."

"But how could Paavo have known about it?"

"He probably heard from a colleague who knew us when we were married, and filed the information away for future use."

"That sounds like Paavo."

"I admit I was dismayed when Owen Birtwhistle brought Edgar here eight years ago, but we've mostly managed to stay out of each other's way."

It seemed to me that Viola was putting a fairly optimistic spin on the relationship if Friday's blow-up was any indication. But now I had apparently answered the other mystery, "Why me?" Viola had evidently been counting on me not to discover the damning evidence of her former marriage to Edgar. "The only way we're going to get Paavo to confess is to set a ..."

A subtle movement in the shadow on the wall in front of me made me turn around—the wall seemed to be moving. I grabbed Viola's arm and tried to pull her out of the way as the huge bookcase came crashing down on the place where we'd just been sitting.

I wasn't fast enough. The bottom of the bookcase caught Viola's leg and pinned her in place. I heard the sound of footsteps going into the stacks. "Go after him—I'll be all right," Viola whispered.

The lights were out in the stacks. Paavo must have turned them off at the junction box, because the light switch didn't work. "Paavo!" I shouted. I heard footsteps on metal. He must be going up the spiral staircase to the third floor.

I stopped to think. It had been foolhardy to confront Paavo the way I had that afternoon. If I simply chased him now, it could be fatal. While I had the edge in age, Paavo was bigger and stronger than I was, and had more to lose. Paavo liked to drop heavy objects on people. Where would he go? Then I thought of the bust of Harold Witherspoon resting on a stand on the third floor of the library. I would wager that Paavo had it in his hands right now, just waiting to drop it on my head as I came up the stairs.

Was there another way? In the darkness I tripped on the edge of the book cart filled with volumes waiting to be shelved. Just beyond it was, yes, the dumbwaiter. Happily, it had never been electrified. But Paavo might be expecting me. I took off my shoes in order to approach him quietly, then took several books, threw them down the spiral stairs to the first floor, and swore loudly. "What's the matter, Axel? Lost your way?" came a voice from above. If I could just squeeze into the compartment. It was going to be a tight fit.

I managed to cram my body into the narrow space, but manipulating the pulley was going to be tricky. The mechanism hadn't been designed to be operated from inside the compartment. I felt around in the dark for the pulley cords and began my ascent.

Each pull of the cord made such a small difference. My awkward position in the compartment made my hands cramp; but I didn't dare let go of both ropes at once. I stretched my hands as best I could, one at a time, then began pulling again. The cart crept upward.

The cart stopped. I reached out, expecting to find the opening on the third floor but my hand ran into a wall. I pulled on the rope with both hands at once. No dice. Suppose I move the cart down a little and try again. Nothing doing. The cart would go neither up nor down. This was the curse of the dumbwaiter that the work-study students had described.

Now what? I considered the situation. In here I was safe but helpless. Nothing was to prevent Paavo from going back down the stairs and attacking Viola. I had to get out of the compartment.

I felt around at the top of the cart. It would have been needlessly expensive to weld the pieces together. There must be screws somewhere. In the upper corner I felt the round curve of a nut and soon located the slot for a screwdriver. Of course, I didn't have a screwdriver. I pulled out my keys and eliminated them one by one: car key, apartment key, office key, building key were all too wide. The only hope was my mailbox key.

As I maneuvered the thin sliver of metal I realized screwdrivers have handles for applying sufficient torque. And screwdrivers, unlike mailbox keys, are made of tempered steel so that they won't bend under the pressure of turning. I bit my lips and continued pushing on the key. At last I felt the screw budge.

I reversed the position of the key in the slot and pushed again. The screw moved a little more easily this time. Reverse and repeat. At length the screw came out completely. I felt around at the next corner, hoping that the dumbwaiter had been made cheaply. My best-case scenario was a screw in each corner. Luck was with me. Another few minutes of finger-numbing labor and I was able to lift the entire steel plate off the compartment and place it quietly on its side.

A slight variation in the darkness indicated the opening for the third floor, above me out of reach. "Now what, smart guy?" I could imagine Paavo saying were he to look into the opening at this moment. The only obvious procedure was to shinny up the pulley cord, but shinnying requires the coordination of hands and feet, I discovered when I tried it; and feet without sneakers can't get an adequate purchase to allow the hands to move to a higher position.

Every problem contains the seeds of its solution, my fifth-grade teacher used to say. I doubted that my fifth-grade teacher had ever found herself stuck on a dumbwaiter in the dark between floors in a music library with a mad musicologist primed to drop a bust of Harold Witherspoon on her head. Still, the principle had merit. The shaft of the dumbwaiter was so cramped, I found that I could press my back against one wall and my feet against the other, raise my upper body using the pulley cords, wedge myself into a higher position, and by repeating the process, bring the third-floor opening within reach. I hoped that my exertions had not alerted Paavo. I let myself out of the opening and onto the linoleum of the third floor.

If I had calculated correctly, Paavo would be just around the corner, with his back to me. The light spilling in from the reference room gave only the feeblest illumination. There he was. I tip-toed most of the way, then rushed as fast as I could and pushed with all my might.

Under ordinary conditions, Paavo might have recovered by grabbing the railing at the top of the staircase, or even the handrail. But his hands were encumbered with the heavy bust with which he had intended to kill me. Thrown off balance, and top-heavy, he fell down the stairs. The statue made a terrible clangor. Paavo ended in a crumpled heap at the bottom of the staircase.

I waited in silence at the top of the stairs. Would Viola be able to notify the authorities before Paavo regained consciousness? Minutes passed. Still no sounds of any kind except my own breathing. I heard the tower clock chime the half-hour, then the lights came on and I saw the welcome badge of a police officer.

CHAPTER 23

On Thursday I stayed at home, unplugged the telephone and refused to answer the doorbell.

On Friday morning I mounted the steps to the music building. As I entered the building I saw the front page of the Brook Banner, stapled to the bulletin board. "MUSIC PROF ARRESTED," screamed the headline, followed by "New Chairman Named" and "Electronic Music Studio Announced." I moved closer and scanned the text. "Prof. Paavo Raine, Ives Professor of Musicology, was arrested Wednesday night for the murder of Edgar Frost, the late music department chairman. Miss Viola Mordent, previously a suspect in the case, was hospitalized after a scuffle involving Prof. Raine. In another development, Dean Manx of the College of Arts and Sciences named Prof. Mark Fillmore as acting chairman of the music department to fill the vacancy left by the sudden departure of Prof. Lewis Mack."

My reading was interrupted by the sounds of an animated discussion coming from the graduate student lounge. "That's wonderful, Chad," I heard Bonnie Pearson say, "but Eileen and I are really going to miss you."

"I'm going to miss you, too," said Chad, "but you can come and visit me. I hear Boston's a great city."

"Why did Prof. Mack leave in such a hurry?" asked Eileen.

"Didn't you hear?" said Chad. "It turns out the reason he never wrote a letter to BU for me is that he never went there. The only degree he has is from Thackery College."

"What's he going to do?" asked Bonnie.

"I heard somebody say he was going back to Thackery to teach."

I continued on in the direction of my office. As I passed the door of the department office, Cecilia Crawford called out, "Axel, you have a message from Maureen Chesterton. The telephone number is in your box."

On a hunch I asked Cecilia, "Did you happen to find any notes among Prof. Frost's papers regarding his meeting with Dean Manx?"

"I can't see that that's any of your business."

"Well, if you had found such notes, wouldn't your efficiency as an administrative assistant have led you to insure that the information reached its intended recipient?"

Cecilia started to smile, stopped herself, and said "I don't know what you're talking about, Axel."

So I'd been wrong about the two items that Edgar had wanted Dean Manx to know about. It wasn't George and Seth at all. Those were small matters that Edgar could handle without the dean's intervention. He'd needed the dean's advice on dealing with Lewis and Paavo, whose academic fraud combined with their status as tenured professors would require the power of higher authority.

When I got to my office I telephoned Maureen Chesterton, who asked what I'd learned about Einar Salo.

"I understand the police are getting in touch with the authorities in Helsinki to reopen the file on Einar's 'accident.' I talked with Sigrida Salo again. She's very proud of her father, even though she scarcely knew him. From what she told me, I wish I could have had him as a colleague.

"How do you mean?" she asked.

"He started out as a violinist and had an active career as second violinist in the Tapiola Sinfonietta. His first-hand knowledge of the orchestral literature and an inquiring musical intellect gave him the idea for 'quatrain theory,' and he'd started working on his doctoral thesis with Paavo at the University of Helsinki."

"So he might have become an eminent musicologist. Whereas our 'eminent' Dr. Raine had a past we didn't know about."

"What's the word on Paavo?"

"His father was a distinguished musicologist at the University of Helsinki. I had heard his name mentioned more than once during my years with the opera company there. Those associations influenced me when the decision came to give the Ives Chair to Paavo."

"So Paavo himself wasn't so distinguished?"

"No. Everybody had high expectations for Paavo, but he didn't like to work and tried to take shortcuts. After he was dismissed from Helsinki University for cheating, Paavo took his degree in the less prestigious Tapiola University. He got his doctorate by working on a project as part of a graduate student team—he did the least work of anybody, but the examiners, friends of his father, took pity on him and let him pass."

"So this was enough to get him a job as an academic?"

"Right. He took a post as assistant professor at Tapiola but was intensely frustrated. It seemed as though everybody in the small academic community measured his shortcomings against his father's achievements. Finally he decided the only way out was to escape. He figured that Americans don't have a clue about Finnish universities and their respective reputations and would automatically attach prestige to anyone with a European background."

"But he would have needed publications to get a job here," I said.

"When Einar Salo, an accomplished violinist, came to Tapiola to do his graduate work, Paavo encouraged him, acted as his mentor, and listened with interest as Einar described his 'quatrain theory.'"

"The relationship among 4-measure phrases in works from the Classical period."

"I'd always wondered what that was about. Einar apparently had been thinking about this for years, and had written pages and pages of notes, which he showed to Paavo, who saw this as his ticket out of Finland."

"So Paavo took the work for his own, submitted it to the Journal of the American Musicological Society, which published it to considerable acclaim, and murdered Einar, arranging it to look like an accident."

"Well, we don't know that, but it certainly seems to fit."

"Paavo must have been worried when Einar's posthumous article turned up in the *Finnish Music Quarterly*."

"But he was pretty safe. How many musicologists read Finnish?"

"So on the basis of this groundbreaking article, Paavo was offered a position at Brook. Without any original idea of his own, he mechanically applied what he understood of Einar's theory to one composer after another, publishing a fair number of articles and giving papers based on the same material."

"I've got to say though, Axel," she continued, "there's something that's still puzzling me."

"What's that?"

"How is it that your investigation has led to the departure of Lewis Mack, George Collins, and Seth Nelson, the three faculty members who voted to deny you tenure the last time you came up?"

"Poetic justice, I guess."

"Aside from removing obstacles, Axel, what have you gotten out of all this?"

"Well, it's a relief to get Viola's name cleared."

"But what about you?"

"It's funny. People have been talking to me in a different way."

"And?"

"I think about Erda in Wagner's Ring Cycle, coming up out of the earth to tell people the truth."

Maureen chuckled.

"Erda wasn't very popular. She was immortal, but nobody liked her much."

"And what about Axel?"

"I think I'm through with grand schemes. I read somewhere that you should aim at changing 10% a year: any more than that is unrealistic but any less is unprofessional."

"That's not a bad goal—after five years you'll have made a 50% difference. Even the most radical reformer would be happy with that."

I said good-bye to Maureen and went downstairs to Viola's studio. Patricia was just coming out the door as I approached. She put her arms around me and gave me kiss. "Way to go, Axel," she said in a half-mocking voice. "I have to get to class. See you tonight."

Viola was seated on the sofa with her bandaged foot resting on a stool. I noticed that she was wearing her Mary Garden brooch. I asked her whether the bookcase had broken her leg.

"The ankle. I have to limp around on these for awhile," she said, gesturing to the crutches on the floor.

"How did you manage to get out from under the bookcase?"

"Bert rescued me. In making his rounds, he noticed that the door to the music library was unlocked; and when he looked in he saw the mess and got me out. I had him call the police. Fortunately there was a patrol car in the neighborhood. They called an ambulance, and a policeman escorted me to the hospital. As far as they were concerned, I was still a murder suspect."

"And Paavo?"

"When the police came to tell me that I was no longer a suspect, they mentioned that Paavo had finally given up trying to explain all the inconsistencies in his story and had just confessed."

"Maureen Chesterton mentioned that both Seth and George are leaving," I said.

"Yes. Seth Nelson has announced his early retirement," Viola said.

"I wonder what will become of his Festschrift."

"The university has agreed to publish it under the university imprint." I sensed the calculating hand of Creighton Manx behind this development. "And George Collins has received a posthumous gift from Edgar. Provided he agrees to participate in an alcohol treatment program, beginning immediately, there's a job waiting for him at the community college in the fall."

"He could have been teaching there all along, if he'd only thought to consider that possibility. Speaking of Maureen, was there anything between her and Paavo when he first came to the university?"

"Whatever gave you that idea?" Viola asked with a nervous laugh.

"The way Maureen responded to some of my questions about Paavo. I suspect that he may have had a card to play."

"Well, Axel, Paavo could be very charming when he wasn't trying to kill people," Viola said, "but that's all I'm going to say on the subject."

"What about you? Aren't you relieved not to be a murder suspect any more?"

"You know, that's just what Freddy Thatcher wanted to know."

"Don't tell me you gave him an interview?"

"Not a chance. I just put my hand on the bust of Mozart and he left."

MURDER

in the

PULPIT

CHAPTER 1

John Armstrong, the senior minister of Allegheny United Church, in what some described as an act of calculated cruelty, had assigned Frances Whelan, the new Minister of Christian Education, to take the family service on Christmas Eve. She'd given it her best shot, organizing a nativity scene and wisely avoiding giving the kids any lines to memorize. But eventually the time came for her to deliver her message, and the bedlam that had prevailed throughout the service scarcely diminished as she began to speak.

For years the Music Committee had been trying to get the church to remove the carpet from the chancel and nave in order to improve the acoustics for music. The ministers wore throat mikes which carried their conversational tones through speakers placed all over the church. The sounds of the organ and choir, by contrast, as well as the singing of the congregation, were immediately soaked up by the rug. Even covering the surfaces of the walls and ceiling with acoustical paint would have been an improvement, but the Property Committee maintained that they already had too much on their plate to consider the proposal, what with the annual problem of repairing water leaks in the tower roof. Anyone listening to the din tonight might have recommended laying down additional carpet.

"Are you all looking forward to Santa Claus coming?" Frances asked, and pandemonium broke loose as the background noise of four hundred children talking turned into outright screaming. A few mothers made half-hearted efforts to bring their charges under control. Fathers who had been drafted to bring the kids to church while their wives prepared dinner simply blocked out the sound the way they might have shut out interruptions to a Sunday afternoon football game. Francis, standing erect in a white robe decorated with gold stripes, her auburn hair carefully coifed for the occasion, consulted her notes.

"Okay," she said loudly into the microphone, trying desperately to regain control, "Who else was born at Christmas?" One could scarcely describe the moment that followed as silence, but no answer came forth. "Who else was born at Christmas?" the minister repeated, beginning to feel as if she'd been set up. Finally a girl in the Junior Choir raised her hand and Frances turned to her in relief. "Yes?" she encouraged.

"I was," said little Noël Stanton, and the adults laughed appreciatively while the children continued talking loudly to each other.

"Jesus!" exclaimed the minister, her mouth too close to the microphone turning the sound into an expletive that caused several mothers in the front rows to look up in surprise.

"Jesus was born at Christmas," the minister went on, trying to recover. "The word 'Christmas' literally means 'Christ's Mass.' In the 4th century ..." One of the elders was heard to moan audibly and the kids went back to their animated chatter. John Armstrong was a master of the microphone but even he knew better than to try to take on this crowd.

Frances Whelan had come on staff in September, replacing the enormously popular Carol Conover, who left the church in frustration over the senior minister's dictatorial leadership style. Whelan inherited a huge Sunday school program (larger than several primary schools in the district) but although she had administrative smarts, she wasn't particularly good with kids.

I got to watch the pageant in the rear-view mirror from my position at the organ console as AUC's director of music. (I'd tried capitalizing that title once and Mae Nolan, the church secretary, had immediately put me in my place. Ordained clergy got the capitals; the paid staff could put up with lower-case.)

From my vantage point I could appreciate the discomfort of James Bellinger, the conservative head usher, who had been roped in at the last minute to serve as the front end of a camel for the nativity scene. During the week he was a salesman at the local Acura dealership and a lower-pressure approach to the job one can scarcely imagine. Fortunately people shopping for Acuras have a pretty good idea of what they're looking for; otherwise I don't know how such an unprepossessing salesman could make a living. But at Allegheny United Church Bellinger had patiently worked his way up the ranks to head usher (I imagine he capitalized the title when he wrote it) and prided himself on the decorum he preserved during services as well as on his own personal dignity. At least it was a camel and not a donkey.

In the congregation behind him I caught a glimpse of Ralph Littlemore, the town's biggest real estate developer, compelled to come watch his daughter in the pageant. I don't know whether I disliked the man more for his fancy suits, expensive haircuts and excessive jewelry or the bullying, sarcastic manner that tended to make people give in just to get rid of him. It looked as if he were writing something on a business card which he passed to the person beside him. Church for Ralph Littlemore was evidently just another opportunity to make business connections. Frances Whelan, determined to avoid sexual stereotypes, had cast the Littlemore girl as a wise man, and was nonplussed when the child appeared at the service made up with a full beard and dreadlocks, courtesy of her mother's Little Theatre Guild make-up department.

My responsibilities for the family service were limited to playing hymns and conducting the Junior Choir. I've had experiences with choirs in which the presence or absence of one key singer meant the difference between a successful performance and a debacle, but what do you do when the indispensable chorister is only nine years old? Cassie, the blond soprano, sang louder than the rest of the Junior Choir put together. All during the fall we'd been rehearsing two-part music for Christmas Eve, only to learn early in December that Cassie planned to celebrate the occasion with her grandmother on the other side of the state. Her mother decided to leave the decision to Cassie and I felt some substantial relief on the Sunday before Christmas when Cassie announced that she'd be singing with us, after all (though I fully expected to hear complaints from Grannie.)

The Minister of Christian Education had also been under some pressure to get the Teeners involved in the service, another example of passing an insoluble problem on to the next person to be hired. For all their energy, creativity and enthusiasm, teenagers don't like to be tied down to regular obligations, in this case, rehearsing for the children's pageant. For that matter, they don't care for doing anything involving younger children, lest their near-adult status be tarnished by association. Through my rear-view mirror I watched in disbelief as the wise men arrived on skate boards, to the accompaniment of rap music blaring from a boom box on the edge of the stage, bearing placards which, when arranged in the proper order, spelled out "Three Wise Guys." It was the kind of stunt Ralph Littlemore's son might have dreamed up before he decided that he was far too mature to have anything more to do with the church.

This wasn't the Teeners' only contribution to the pageant. A heavenly host of little five- and six-year-old cherubs, sporting cloth wings and coathanger-and-tinsel halos materialized in the center of the stage, overshadowed by a two-hundred-pound head angel with waist-length hair. Parmalee Houghton was determined to win the Teener of the Year

award, and if it meant covering her buxom body with a sheet and radiat-
ing an innocence she no longer possessed, she was quite willing to make
a spectacle of herself. Her undisguised ambition had made it difficult to
recruit Teeners to any of the less glamorous jobs in the church. "Why
bother?" seemed to be their attitude. "Parmalee has already wrapped up
the award."

I suspected Parmalee's hand behind the group of Teeners, both boys
and girls, who at the beginning of the fall declared themselves "Virgins
for Jesus" and started sporting "V" buttons, which made the adults
vaguely uncomfortable. You couldn't very well oppose virtue but it
seemed in poor taste to flaunt it. Then a splinter group, just girls, broke
off and began dressing like prostitutes, in emulation of Mary Magdalene,
making the adults even more uncomfortable.

Eventually the family service drew to a merciful close with the lighting of tiny candles and the singing of "Silent Night." I dismissed the
Junior Choir, played a brief organ postlude and immediately set about
preparing for the second service, a relatively child-free celebration of
Holy Communion. The church used to hold its principal Christmas Eve
celebration at eleven p.m. but a lot of the old people complained to the
Care of Senior Citizens Committee so now the services had been set at
6:30 and 8:00 p.m, giving me just a few moments to arrange organ and
choral music in their proper order before it was time to start the prelude
for the next service.

Two Sunday school fathers struck the set from the pageant with Ian
Wetherby, the chair of Ministry and Personnel, directing their efforts.
Wetherby, a tall man with a thin, hatchet-like head, a long nose, and a
prominent Adam's apple, had well-developed frown wrinkles and a life-
long habit of looking down on people (in both senses of the word). On
entering a room he would invariably purse his lips, narrow his eyes and
look about for something amiss. He would have made a great quality
control engineer. The chief purpose of Ministry and Personnel was to
mediate disagreements between members of staff, and ever since the
arrival of a young, female associate minister with a style markedly different from that of the senior minister, the M&P Committee had been
kept busy.

Henry Eldridge checked out the microphone at the behest of his wife
Vera who stood watching nervously from the level of the nave. Eldridge,
thin and balding, wore large black glasses that gave him the appearance
of a displaced raccoon. He owned a private testing laboratory that did

contract work for some of the smaller drug companies that couldn't afford to maintain their own facilities. His wife, torn between her sense of duty to the church and her fear of public speaking, had the misfortune to have her name turn up on the reader list for the biggest service of the year. Her sense of obligation, and unwillingness to make waves, had evidently prevented her from switching for a less prominent occasion.

Stan Rutledge, chair of the Finance Committee, appeared with several canisters of tiny grape juice glasses for Communion. Stan had inherited both the chairmanship and his company, Rutledge Realty, from his father Tyrone, a giant in the industry. No one would ever apply that adjective to Stan, but his plodding, unimaginative nature made him a safe, if uninspired, choice for handling the church's investments. He set the canisters down near the altar then went over to the lectern to inform Henry, quite unnecessarily, that the microphone switch had to be turned on for it to function. Vera retired to a seat in the front pew while Henry, pressed into service as a substitute usher, walked to the rear of the church.

Carmody Talbot, a recent addition to the Chancel Guild, arrived with a tray bearing the minister's water glass which she set beside the pulpit. I remember hearing that she practically burst into tears after being reprimanded by Harriett Bascomb for putting the coffee cups back on the kitchen shelf with the handles facing toward the left rather than the right. A lesser woman, or one with higher self-esteem, might have quit on the spot, but Carmody had evidently survived Harriett's basic training and was now a regular member of the team.

A short time later, as I began the organ prelude for the second service, I heard a bit of commotion in the balcony. A glance in the rearview mirror revealed the large figure of Bud Armstrong, the senior minister's younger brother, guiding the wheelchair of his father Derek, assisted by Henry Eldridge and accompanied by a chorus of murmurs. When John Armstrong first came to Allegheny United, Bud would arrive late, sit in a prominent spot in the middle of the congregation and heckle his brother during the sermon. The ushers, unequipped to deal with deliberate disturbances, didn't know what to do. Harriett Bascomb, head of the Chancel Guild, had no qualms. Armed with her umbrella, she drove Bud from the sanctuary. I hadn't seen him in church since. Derek, his millionaire father, dying of cancer, was not expected to see a new year, but evidently determined to attend one last Christmas Eve service, and mistrustful of the staff at the Valhalla Retirement Home, he must have called on Bud to bring him to church.

The first part of the service unfolded strictly according to plan. The congregation sang the processional hymn, "Once in Royal David's City," Vera Eldridge read the story of the angels and the shepherds in a tremulous but fervent voice, the Senior Choir performed "Glory to God" from Handel's *Messiah*, and the ushers passed the offering plates during the singing of "Hark the Herald Angels Sing." Then the Reverend John Armstrong moved to the pulpit for the Christmas sermon.

Armstrong's small eyes, thick jowls and glad-handing style had made me think more of a used car salesman than a minister when I first met him at my job interview. His high-pitched voice didn't seem to fit his large teddy-bear body. But there was nothing soft about his hold on Allegheny United Church. He had seen many changes during his tenure as senior minister—women in the pulpit, inclusive language in the hymns, a vast increase in the size of the congregation—but his air of authority left no doubt that this was his church as he looked out over the capacity crowd and began his homily.

"Two thousand years ago," he began, "a man and a woman walked the long road to Bethlehem. When they finally reached their destination, they found not a spacious hotel room, or even a modest chamber, but only a cold, dark stable, a place where their donkey felt right at home, but where the man regretted the discomfort endured by his pregnant wife and where the woman feared for the well-being of the child she was about to bear." Someone in the congregation coughed discreetly but the capacity crowd maintained a rapt attention.

The minister paused, took a long drink from the water glass beside the pulpit, and continued. "Our health plans assure that our children will enter this world through the protective portal of a sterile hospital, and a staff of specialists standing by with expensive equipment to deal with any complication in the delivery." A frown came over his face, and he turned to me and said in a stage whisper, "Don't play during the sermon, Axel." I lifted my hands to show that they were nowhere near the keyboard. He shook his head as if to clear his thoughts and returned to his text.

"What mother would not ..." The Rev. Armstrong looked around in confusion and asked, "Where is that music coming from?" Then he rubbed his fingers against his forehead, closed his eyes, as if in extreme pain, bent at the waist, collapsed behind the pulpit, and vomited blood across the chancel carpet. For a moment the entire church sat in stunned silence, as if waiting for the last several seconds to reverse themselves and their spiritual leader to rise from the floor and carry on with his sermon. Then one of the members of the Senior Choir, a physician, rushed forward and took the wrist of the fallen minister. "Call an ambulance!" he shouted. I ran across the chancel and down the hall to the church office, unlocked the door and hastily punched 911 into the telephone keypad. When I returned to the front of the church the posture of the shocked parishioners told me that the call had been in vain. John Armstrong was dead.

CHAPTER 2

I found myself alone on Christmas Day. My romance with Jennifer Guest, a hospital administrator in Pittsburgh who preferred to live in Meadowvale, had progressed to the stage that we spent most nights at one or the other of our dwellings. I lived in one half of a duplex about a mile from the church. Jennifer lived in the carriage house of an estate on St. John's Sideroad, from which she could look out on two different farms. I gave it maybe five years before they were turned into housing developments.

The sight of the items that Jennifer had left in my bathroom gave me a comforting feeling of creeping domesticity and I thought of Christine Rossetti's poem, "Love Came Down at Christmas." She wasn't thinking about romantic love, but I'd had to smile when I looked at the bulletin for Christmas Eve and saw that the senior minister had chosen the hymn based on that text. Of course, we never got to sing that hymn.

The Senior Choir had greeted the news of Jennifer's existence with hearty congratulations, sympathetic smiles, and perhaps a twinge of disappointment from Trish McConnell. But Jennifer and I hadn't reached the point of presenting ourselves as a couple to the world at large, certainly not to her maiden aunt, living an hour north in Clarion. Jennifer had left early in the morning, promising to return as quickly as she could so that we could spend the rest of the holiday together. My only responsibility was to baste the turkey.

As I sat on the sofa, calculating the time until Jennifer's return, I thumbed through a pamphlet that Mae Nolan had given me when I first arrived at Allegheny United Church, *Sizing up a Congregation*, supposedly the most influential analysis of church dynamics published in the last fifty years. The author argues that the internal organization of congregations and the roles of clergy change markedly with different parish sizes, as defined by average Sunday attendance.

In the family-size church of up to fifty worshipers, representing 40% of all churches in the U.S., the clergy's role is limited to preaching and pastoral care, with little or no innovation or growth. In the pastoral-size church, comprising 50 to 150 worshipers, representing another 40% of U.S. churches, the pastor leads the congregation with a "circle of leaders" but the community retains a feeling of oneness since everyone knows each other.

I was momentarily startled by the sound of snow sliding off the roof and crashing onto the flowerbed beside the window. Across the street loomed one of the town's three primary schools. On summer evenings the air would be filled with the sounds of neighborhood children enjoying the large playground. Now they were all indoors celebrating the Yuletide with their parents, though the ruins of a snow fort could still be seen near the fence. I returned to my reading.

Some 15% of U.S. churches attain program size of 150 to 350 worshipers with many cells of activity headed by lay leaders. The pastor plans, coordinates and supports the lay leaders who are the "first line." On the downside, worshipers commonly complain that "we've lost that family feeling," or "the pastor doesn't care—ordinary people minister to me." Allegheny United Church, with some 800 members on the rolls, ranked with just 5% of U.S. churches as a corporate-size church, with three full-time ministers, two full-time secretaries, and countless committees.

John Armstrong, as he was fond of telling the congregation, began as the itinerant minister of a three-point charge, carrying the faith to three tiny congregations each Sunday. The dictatorial leadership style that might have suited the small churches that he served earlier in his career brought muffled complaints from some parishioners at AUC. The church boasted an elaborate committee structure but ultimately the senior minister made all the major decisions and most of the minor ones. Any committee chairperson who expected to last would take the trouble to find out what the minister thought before holding a meeting.

The separation decision was a case in point. In the past two years Allegheny United Church had added more than two hundred families to its rolls. Studies by the national church suggested that potential newcomers get turned off when church attendance exceeds 80% of capacity, a figure we passed some time ago. We also had anecdotal evidence of one long-time AUC member fleeing in tears from a particularly crowded baptismal service when she was unable to find a seat in her accustomed section of the sanctuary.

The church considered the possibility of splitting into two congregations and building a new church, with adequate parking, on a parcel of land in the rapidly-expanding eastern section of the town. Nobody really liked the idea and most people assumed that the church would remain as one large corporate body. Then at a meeting just before Christmas the senior minister had taken everyone by surprise by announcing that AUC would build a sister church. The members of the Long-Range Planning Committee just shrugged and mapped out a schedule for rewriting their policy documents.

The AUC music program had experienced similar growing pains. The previous music director had expanded the position to a full-time job involving six choirs: a Cherub Choir for the youngest children; separate boys and girls choirs for the next age group; a teen choir, the Senior Choir, and a community chorus. Then she went to the Council of Elders and demanded an appropriate salary. On being turned down, she quit.

When I interviewed for the position the Music Committee assured me that they really intended this to be a part-time job that wouldn't interfere with my teaching duties at Meadowvale Prep, but I still had my difficulties with the senior minister. Where else but in the pulpit do you have someone who knows nothing about music talking about it at length? Instead of exploring the resources of the new hymnal, or allowing the music director to do so, he continually recycled the same fifty hymns. And he objected to my announced intention of presenting the repertoire of great organ music during the preludes and postludes, insisting that I devote at least half the time to insipid compositions based on familiar hymn-tunes.

The Music Committee had endorsed my belief in the treasury of church music as a sacred trust that I intended to uphold, and had applauded the integrity of my musical standards. Others in the congregation, displeased with the direction of the music program, carried their complaints directly to the senior minister or to the head of the Ministry and Personnel Committee. Last year Ian Wetherby told me point-blank that my job was to keep John Armstrong happy, never mind what the Music Committee thought. And to make the point clear, he told me that I wasn't getting the annual cost-of-living increase in my salary.

The sound of the telephone interrupted my reverie. It was Shirley Bellinger, a soprano in the Senior Choir, who apologized for interrupting my Christmas celebration but asked whether she could come over and talk with me about a serious matter. At my first rehearsal with the Senior Choir, seeing my bewilderment at all the new names to learn, she had smiled and said "*Surely* you're going to remember my name!" Shirley had more than once guided me through the minefield of personal relationships in the choir. After I had praised the altos for mastering a particularly tricky passage in a Gibbons motet, she had drawn me aside and suggested that I say something nice about the sopranos, and to look in Barb Dawson's direction when I did so. Barb was extraordinarily temperamental but she fulfilled an indispensable role as choir librarian and I would do well to bolster her tenuous self-esteem.

I told Shirley to come ahead, and twenty minutes later she was sitting on my sofa, telling her story in a state of agitation. An attractive woman in her early fifties, Shirley Bellinger belonged to a group from the church who visited the local recreation complex on a regular basis and gathered three times a week for "power walks." She was wearing a simple blue dress with a gold brooch in the shape of two pinecones, matching earrings and black shoes with low heels. A small navy blue purse completed the ensemble. I didn't recognize her perfume but I liked it.

"I'm not sure where to begin, Axel," she said, looking around as if to find comfort in my grand piano on one side of the room, or the floor-to-ceiling bookcases on the other. The contemporary print above the piano, "Blues, Blues, VW Controls," or the abstract "House on Bryant Avenue" in the corner may not have been her style. I prefer to keep things simple and have largely succeeded in avoiding the knickknacks and memorabilia that clutter other people's homes. I like wood floors rather than carpets and take pleasure in the sight of an empty surface. On the other hand, I do have quite a number of books. "I imagine you've been hearing rumors," she said.

"You know, Shirley," I replied. "People don't share a lot of gossip with me. Let me hear the story directly from you."

Shirley looked at her lap, clutched her pocketbook a bit more tightly, then seemed to gain confidence. "James and I have been having trouble in our marriage for the past several years."

"Lot of that going around," I observed.

"For the past year we haven't even slept together. It didn't seem to bother him any but I'm a healthy woman." Then she stopped, as if uncertain how to continue. We'd known each other long enough that she knew I wouldn't interpret her words as a come-on, but the sexually charged nature of the conversation had not escaped her.

"Go on," I said.

"For several months I've been seeing someone—it doesn't really matter who. One day in November when we got together he didn't have his credit card with him so I used mine. James caught the slip when he went over the monthly Visa statement and confronted me. I didn't want to tell him who it really was, so I said I'd been seeing John Armstrong.

You know he has something of a reputation as a ladies man. I never dreamed that James would take him on publicly."

That much I had heard. On the Sunday before Christmas the head usher had approached the Rev. Armstrong after the service and told the bewildered minister, "You're a dead man," or words to that effect. Witnesses' accounts varied but one person reported Bellinger as saying "I'm not going to be cuckolded by that hypocritical bastard." Since then the two men had studiously avoided each other. I had been occupied with a Junior Choir rehearsal at the time so heard only a few bits and pieces of the story.

"So you're upset that your husband found out about your affair?" I asked.

"Of course, but it's far worse than that. The police came to our house this morning and asked James to come in for questioning tomorrow. They said they didn't want to mess up our holiday by taking him in to-day."

"They think he was involved somehow in John's death?"

"That was the clear implication."

"What's he doing now?"

"He locked himself into his den with a bottle of whiskey and refuses to talk to me. When he shouted through the door, 'This is all your fault, you dumb slut!' I decided I needed to talk with someone, and that's when I called you."

"Let me get this straight. The police came out to your house on Christmas Day just because your husband got mad at John Armstrong last Sunday?"

"You don't understand, Axel. They found James' fingerprints on the water glass."

"I'm still having trouble following this."

"John Armstrong died from poison in his water, at least that's what the officer said. They fingerprinted the glass, matched the prints against those the church had on file—you remember last year when John had the whole staff and the ushers fingerprinted "for security reasons"—then came to invite James down the station and to caution him against leaving town."

"Have you talked to your lawyer?"

"When I suggested that to James, he just shouted something like 'They can't convict an innocent man. It's in the Constitution.'"

"You know better than that, Shirley."

"Of course I do, but I've never seen James act like this before. To tell you the truth, I'm a little bit scared."

I'd always considered James Bellinger to be exactly the opposite of scary. Of course, strong drink often brings on dramatic changes. I didn't particularly want to get involved, either in Shirley's marital difficulties or in a death that the police were now calling murder. On the other hand, Shirley had helped me out a lot with the choir, and I've always had a weakness for damsels in distress.

Then I recalled the image of John Armstrong lying on the chancel carpet in a pool of blood. Up to now I'd always regarded him as something of a tyrant—not a particularly useful attitude toward one's boss, I had to admit. I remembered what he had said a couple of weeks back, that he was spending more of his time dealing with music issues than any other matter. Perhaps I owed him a bit of compassion.

"Tell you what, Shirley," I said. "The school is on holiday this week so I can spend some time asking questions, but once James calms down and starts thinking straight I'm sure he'll want to engage a professional."

Shirley didn't hesitate when she got what she was after. She leaned over, put her arms around me, and gave me a kiss. "I feel much better now, Axel," she said. Then she picked her pocketbook up from the rug and departed. As I watched her drive off through the snow I wondered what I was getting myself into. I couldn't share her confidence but reckoned I could at least look into the matter. James Bellinger seemed like a fairly innocuous guy. On the other hand, I hadn't seen his public confrontation with John Armstrong.

An hour later Jennifer returned from her visit and helped put all thoughts of murder out of my mind.

CHAPTER 3

On Thursday morning, the day after Christmas, I called Ben Van Dyk, one of the basses in the Senior Choir. Now a building contractor, Ben had spent more than a decade as a police officer and maintained ties with his former colleagues. He and his wife also operated a catering business and on more than one occasion he had invited me over to his house to sample some new recipe. The anticipation of the annual party he put on for the choir had helped more than one chorister get through the depressing winter months.

"What can I do for you, Axel?" Ben's hearty voice boomed in the telephone receiver. White-haired at fifty, Ben had the barrel-chested frame of a man whose policeman's indulgence in doughnuts had persisted even after he had left the force. When I explained the reason for my call, he expressed some concern. "I don't know, Axel. This is the kind of case that the police aren't going to spend a lot of time on."

"Why do you say that?"

"Well just look at it. The chief suspect publicly threatens the victim with murder. Two days later the victim dies with the suspect's fingerprints on the weapon. The suspect is found to be at the scene. You know the phrase—means, motive, opportunity. The only complication right now is the poison?"

"How do you mean?"

"Evidently John Armstrong died from drinking compound 1080. It's tasteless, colorless, and odorless."

"Sounds like the perfect poison for a murder."

"Yeah, but it's also highly restricted. It was developed to control rodents but the stuff is so toxic that it's been banned for several years now. The police seem to be spending their time trying to figure out how James Bellinger got his hands on it. Once they nail that down, the case will be wrapped up."

"But if it's a banned substance, how would anyone get it?"

"I think there's a bit more to it than that, Axel. But if you want to learn about the poison you might want to give Henry Eldridge a shout." When I expressed my reservations about James Bellinger as a murderer, Ben said, "Murder is a funny thing, especially when it comes to poison."

"How's that?"

"You get somebody killing in fit of rage, a jealous husband, that kind of thing, they'll use a gun, a knife, a poker, whatever comes to hand."

"Yeah?"

"But poison. Now that takes a bit of planning, especially if you're going to use anything more exotic than the weed-killer you find in the garden shed."

"I see what you mean."

"The person who uses poison doesn't have to overpower his victim, or her victim, for that matter. So a man like James Bellinger—if he wanted to kill somebody, poison might be the weapon of choice."

"You may be right, but for Shirley's sake I hope you're not."

I thanked Ben for his help and he promised to let me know if he heard any further details.

I reflected that Allegheny United Church was almost a community unto itself—you could find nearly any professional specialty among its members. The success of the church had been the despair of the other denominations in Meadowvale. Presbyterians or Episcopalians or Lutherans would arrive in town, visit their own churches and then learn about the extraordinary Sunday school at AUC. Soon they'd be drawn into the throng, leaving the Presbyterian, Episcopalian and Lutheran ministers wringing their hands.

Henry Eldridge served with me on the Worship Committee. He wasn't any more supportive of the music program than the rest of the committee but I figured he'd help me out with a question in his own specialty. When his wife Vera answered the phone I congratulated her on her reading of the Scripture on Christmas Eve.

"I was so scared, Axel. Practically the whole town was there," she said. "But I haven't even thought about that, I've been so upset about ... you know." The indelicate manner of John Armstrong's death went beyond her powers of expression.

Her husband showed no such emotion over the death of the senior minister but took a keen professional interest in the poison. "The chemical name is sodium fluoroacetate or fluoroacetamide. The Environmental Protection Agency labeled it as a "super poison" because there isn't any antidote and it takes only 1/500th of an ounce to kill a 150-lb. human."

"That's potent stuff."

"Seems like a pretty poor choice for murder, though."

"Why's that?"

"It doesn't break down in the body, so it's easy to identify. Also, Armstrong showed all the symptoms."

"Which ones?"

"Well I've never seen an actual case before this one, but he displayed all the textbook conditions: auditory hallucinations, numbness of the face, convulsions, vomiting." I thought of the minister's accusation that I had been playing the organ during his sermon and the way he looked around for the source of the music that only he could hear.

"I understood the poison had been banned," I said. "How could anyone obtain it?"

"I can think of a number of possibilities. Of course we'd have no trouble manufacturing it here in the lab, but if a lay person wanted to get it, I understand it's still used out west in livestock protection collars."

"How does that work?"

"Evidently you equip your sheep with a collar containing two reservoirs of the toxin, which kills the coyote when it tries to attack the sheep. Of course, the sheep has to be killed, but I guess it's worth sacrificing one sheep for the good of the herd."

"I suppose so."

"Come to think of it, you could even grow the stuff yourself if you had a mind to: it's a naturally-occurring organic fluoride that you could extract from rat bane."

"Do people actually do that?"

"I've seen people grow stranger things than that, Axel," Henry chuckled. He really did have a macabre sense of humor. Gladys Pinkham reported that he kept a Venus flytrap as a pet and enjoyed feeding it insects. One sometimes wondered where Gladys got her information but I'd never known her to be wrong. I thanked Henry for his time, wished him a Happy New Year, and headed to the church office.

Only a trace of the recent snowstorm remained on the unprotected lawns in my part of town, just enough to say that we'd had a white Christmas. The gold and silver plastic garlands stretching across Meadowvale's principal street had gone up right after Halloween, along with lights and fake fir trees attached to the telephone poles. For the most part the imagination of local merchants extended no further than tracing the outline of their store windows with miniature white bulbs and spraying the perimeter with artificial snow. Commercial Christmas in Meadowvale was an altogether dispiriting sight. Most of the cars in the town sported license plate covers bearing the legend, "Meadowvale, My Kind of Town." Meadowvale wasn't remotely my kind of town, and I frequently made the forty-five minute drive to Pittsburgh for opera, theatre, and foreign films.

I pulled into the parking lot of Allegheny United Church and mused that in a bygone era the adjacent submarine shop would have been located "next to the church." Now when I mentioned that I worked at AUC, people would say, "Oh, you mean that church next to Mr. Sub?" I gazed upward at the ugly yellow brick structure and recalled John Armstrong's frequent reminder that the church was not a building but the people who entered it. I found much to admire in the people of AUC but considered the building itself a real eyesore. It didn't help matters when they erected a billboard in front of the church. The current slogan read, "Jesus is the Reason for the Season." I entered the lower lobby, with its mitten tree decorated by Sunday school children, an enormous hanging quilt created by members of the United Church Women, and a photo montage of the recent Christmas bazaar, and mounted the stairs to the church office.

If anyone could be described as indispensable to the functioning of Allegheny United Church, it would not have been the senior minister but the church secretary. Mae Nolan not only knew everything about the procedures and history of the church, she often served as counselor to those in need. Troubled souls seeking the assistance of clergy would first come upon a plump, friendly woman with twinkling Irish eyes and a non-judgmental manner, and before long they were pouring their hearts out to her. Eventually the church had to install a volunteer receptionist in the hallway to field telephone calls and direct visitors just so Mae and her assistant could get some work done.

Mae's desk was especially crowded at this time of year. In addition to photos of all her grandchildren and the icon that John Armstrong had brought back from his sabbatical visit to the Holy Land Mae had put out a miniature Christmas tree with tiny lights, a glass angel on a clear plastic stand and a revolving brass angel mounted over four small candles. A crèche with hand-carved wooden figures stood atop the bookcase behind her chair.

Mae was no stranger to sorrow. Her oldest son had died in a boating accident several years before and the entire church turned out for his funeral. The incident had added wrinkles to her face and hastened the graying of her hair, but Mae bore no bitterness toward the friends who had been with the boy at the time of his death—rumor had it that some drinking was involved. Nor did she rail at God for taking her first-born from her. But visitors seeking solace in time of death encountered a special empathy when they spoke with the secretary.

Mae didn't think much of James Bellinger as a murder suspect and when I asked if she could imagine anyone who might be considered an enemy of John Armstrong she thought for a moment, then her demeanor turned conspiratorial and her voice dropped. "You know, Axel, in books they always ask *cui bono*—who stands to benefit? The first person who comes to mind is Ralph Littlemore, if you'll excuse an old woman from talking out of turn."

"Why Ralph?"

"The parcel of land where we were considering building a sister church—Ralph wanted it."

"I don't understand. I thought the church owned the property."

"No, no. The church only had an option to purchase the land, and that option expires on January 1st. Ralph wanted to build single-family homes on the property—you know how fast Meadowvale is expanding; he would have made a killing, if you'll pardon the expression."

"Go on."

"With the option due to expire, he just had to wait until the end of the year. Nobody really expected the church to build. Then John announced that we were going to exercise the option. Ralph must have gone crazy."

I reflected on what I knew of Littlemore and concluded that I didn't want to be around when the developer thought he had been crossed.

Mae continued. "But you know, the person you really want to talk to is Fred Carruthers. He's the one who actually owns the land."

The telephone rang and from listening to Mae's side of the conversation I gathered it was the mother of the bride for the wedding scheduled at the church on Saturday. Who was going to perform the ceremony now that the senior minister was dead? She didn't seem at all concerned about the church or its late minister; she just wanted to make sure that everything ran smoothly for her daughter's day of days. She didn't like the idea of having Sarah Beasley, our associate minister, perform the ceremony but under the circumstances she didn't have much choice.

The same woman had called me to be sure that I would play "the wedding march."

"Which wedding march?" I asked her.

"You mean there's more than one?" she wanted to know. I assured her that there were dozens of wedding marches. "Surely you know the one I mean," she persisted.

"Perhaps," I suggested, "you're thinking of the piece that popularly has the lyrics, 'Here comes the bride, six feet wide.'"

"Yes, that's the one! Do you know it?" I told her I thought I could manage it.

The official AUC policy on wedding music was that if you supplied the score, I would play any song, no matter how godawful. Thus I had to learn numbers from *Les Miz* and *Phantom of the Opera* for recent celebrations. I recalled the wedding of two old friends who, after listening to recordings of Bach's complete organ works, asked me to play the Prelude and Fugue in E Flat. I spent a month learning this stupendous piece of musical architecture. The prelude is a tripartite French overture, the fugue a triple fugue culminating in the simultaneous presentation of all three subjects. It set the tone for a splendid musical wedding. When I performed the same work at AUC on Trinity Sunday the only comment came from a former choir member who thought it was too loud.

Mae finally got off the phone and I was going to ask her for further details when Thelma Moore swept into the office.

"Hi, Axel," she said. "I trust I'm not interrupting anything important." Thelma wore a blue ski parka with a fur collar over tight navy slacks. Though she hadn't skated competitively for a number of years she maintained her trim figure with a strict regimen of power walking and aerobics. Recently she'd thrown her energies into nutritional reform and had insisted that the snack table at the Christmas bazaar include vegan chocolate cookies and organic apple strudel.

"Do you have the list of homes to be visited?" she asked Mae, her bright eyes scanning the desk like a chicken searching for a kernel of corn.

"Here are the names and addresses," Mae said, pulling the required document effortlessly from her outbox.

"What exactly do you do with these names?" I asked Thelma. I knew the Outreach Committee made a practice of visiting every new family in Meadowvale, regardless of church affiliation, but I'd never learned the details of their operation.

"Well..." Thelma spun around to face me. "We welcome each new family to the town and we give them a little directory to put by the phone and a list of emergency numbers to put on the fridge with one of these magnets." She held out a blue and gold dove with the initials AUC embossed on the wing.

"What's in the directory?" I asked.

"Oh, all the numbers a new person needs to have: movie theaters, dry cleaners, public and private schools, auto mechanics, dentists, physicians, that sort of thing."

"Do you give preference to professional people who are members of this congregation?"

"Well naturally we have to be selective."

"Sounds like an indispensable resource for people coming to town," I said. "Does the directory include telephone numbers for all the other churches?"

"I'm sure they're in there somewhere," Thelma said vaguely.

"But AUC's number probably appears on the cover."

"And at the bottom of every page," she said enthusiastically. "Well, I'd better be on my way. TTFN!" She flitted out of the office leaving me to wonder whether I was irritated more by people who actually said "Ta ta for now" or those who abbreviated it.

Thelma nearly bumped into Gladys Pinkham who came into the office with a name to be added to the prayer list for Sunday. Though physically frail, Gladys was indefatigable in her efforts to head off change of any sort and had an uncanny ability to derail meetings with her pointed questions and irrelevant observations. Few chairmen had the courage to cut her off. Who wants to get a reputation for being unkind to little old ladies? I numbered her among my strongest adversaries on the Worship Committee. We had a meeting scheduled that evening and I knew from experience that she would like nothing better than to confront me in advance, so I seized my chance and escaped from the office while I could.

CHAPTER 4

I was about to head toward my office when I saw that Sarah Beasley's door was open so I turned the other way and walked down the hall. No light appeared under Frances Whelan's door. No doubt she was still recovering from her Christmas Eve ordeal. When I crossed the threshold of Sarah's office I must have tripped an electric eye mechanism because a set of tiny bells mounted over the door began to bang out "Have Yourself a Merry Little Christmas." Sarah waved a hand apologetically from her desk. "One of Gladys Pinkham's friends installed those last week and I haven't had the heart to take them down."

I considered the appointment of a young woman as associate minister the best thing that had happened at Allegheny United Church since I'd been there. Among other things, Sarha was a natural storyteller who could have made a career as a stand-up comic if she hadn't opted for the ministry.

Recently she began a sermon by saying that in the first week after agreeing to be the night-time response person for the church security system, her husband had been summoned three times. So when her two-year-old son announced that he was going to the church to see Jesus, her husband had responded, "If you do see Jesus, tell him to stop setting off the alarm."

Naturally her success produced mixed feelings on the part of the senior minister, who now had to share the pulpit with her on an alternating basis. During the fall he started pushing for a Sunday evening service, presumably a worship service at which he could preach. But once the notion got proposed, every constituency in the church had a different idea on how the new time-slot might be filled: how about a prayer meeting, or a hymn-sing, or a meditation hour, or how about something avant-garde that might attract the young people?

"Or how about evenings of religious films?" one enthusiastic member of the Program Committee had suggested. "The evangelical church in Waynesboro has been showing religious films every Sunday night and they get two, three hundred people every time, and I've always wanted to see "The Robe" again; you remember that scene where ..." It made me glad that I was only the music director.

Sarah had more than once expressed the belief that the purpose of her previous positions was to provide stories for use at Allegheny United Church. For example, one year just after Christmas the kitchen taps in the Dillsburg United Church manse blew up, which meant that Sarah had to make the long trek to the second floor every time she needed water. It wasn't until the January meeting of the church elders that the question of replacing the taps came up for discussion and the subject turned out to provoke a heated debate. One woman turned to the woman beside her and in a loud stage whisper asked, "Do you get things fixed in your house right away when they break?"

"No," replied her neighbor. "I don't."

"Some things you just have to live with," said the first woman.

"I think this minister expects too much."

"Yes," said the second. "I agree. She is just spoiled."

Before long the discussion had moved from the question of kitchen taps to the question of whether or not the minister was spoiled. When the vote was finally taken, the new taps for the manse were voted down. After the meeting the chief elder took Sarah aside and said, "Go to the Co-op and buy the taps. I'll be over to put them in." It turns out that one of the whispering women was his mother-in-law and he didn't dare oppose her.

Sarah was filing papers when I came in. A short, stocky woman with close-cropped hair, she felt comfortable wearing overalls to the office, a practice which distressed some of the older members of the congregation to the point that they looked up her job description to see whether there wasn't some phrase about "proper attire" with which they could attack her. She knew exactly who they were and they knew that she knew but they weren't about to say anything to her directly so she just gave them an especially bright smile whenever they met and let them stew in their juices.

In addition to theological texts on homiletics, Christian ethics, and patristic studies retained from seminary and a well-worn edition of the twelve-volume *Interpreter's Bible,* the bookcases in Sarah's office held a fair sampling of works on women's studies, grief counseling and adolescent psychology. Her minister's robes hung from a hanger on the coat rack behind the desk along with a rainbow-colored stole, a going-away gift from her previous church. While some older members of the AUC congregation complained about her "touchy-feely sermons," many younger members were grateful to find an understanding heart at the church.

I congratulated Sarah on the success of the recent Blue Christmas service, an annual event that she had inaugurated shortly after her arrival.

"Thank you for that, Axel. A lot of people in this church have given me grief about that service, but if they could only see the faces of those for whom Christmas is a season of pain, maybe they wouldn't be so judgmental."

"I liked having a harpist for the service," I said.

"And here I thought you were just glad not to have to play," she joked.

"No, it gave just the right tone. Save the trumpets for the 'Hallelujah Chorus.'"

Our talk inevitably turned to the death of John Armstrong and Sarah said something that surprised me. "You know, Axel, I'll deny this if you ever repeat it, but while I'm sorry for John's family, I think this may all work out to the good of the church."

"How so?"

"You've been at staff meetings every week. Do you think they're fun?"

"I think that's the last word I'd ever use to describe a meeting that John was chairing." When John was in charge, you had one chance to say what was on your mind as he made his way around the circle of participants. If you thought of anything after that, you were out of luck. "Think of how much easier it was when he took his sabbatical."

"Of course he still haunted the hallways at night, slipping memos under our doors," Sarah recalled. "With no duties of his own, he had nothing better to do than think of more chores for the rest of us."

"Staff meetings became so relaxed and collegial while he was away that it was really tough to return to despotism in the fall."

"And remember his 're-entry from sabbatical?'" Sarah couldn't help laughing.

The senior minister never planned a worship service more than three days in advance, so I was surprised to find, slipped under my door early in the summer, a detailed order of worship for the Sunday of his return. One item entitled "Re-Entry from Sabbatical" evoked images of a space vehicle returning heatedly through the atmosphere, and sure enough, a bit later in the order of service came the hymn "Chatter With the Angels."

Perhaps a more appropriate image, though, might be that of the arrival of a splendid potentate, preceded by the Junior Choir spreading rose petals in his path. The choice of the opening hymn, "Eternal, Unchanging, We Sing to Thy Praise," led Mae Nolan to wonder aloud who the pronoun was supposed to stand for. The conclusion of the first stanza, "who rulest, omnipotent, ever the same," perfectly summed up the way John Armstrong ran his church. There was a committee for every conceivable function, which met regularly and deliberated at length. Then the senior minister delivered his opinion and that became policy.

Came the day of the "re-entry" in August, attendance was less than one might expect for such a momentous occasion, but as the minister ascended the pulpit the lighting technician hit him on cue with a spotlight of beatific blue, the choir swelled in a thrilling, wordless chorus, and a host of cherubs hovered in the air. The minister cleared his throat and a voice like that of Moses filled the sanctuary. "We began our ministry thirty-five years ago today." It couldn't have been the Papal "we" (anti-Papist sentiment runs strong in the United Church in this part of the country), and it wasn't the editorial "we" favored in newspapers. It must have been the royal "we," that of a benevolent monarch addressing his adoring subjects, some of whom were counting the years until his retirement.

I told Sarah that I was surprised by John's sudden announcement that he intended to exercise the church's option on the Carruthers property.

"That was so unnecessary!" she exclaimed. "We just need to do what all the other big churches have done in our situation: hold two identical services each Sunday morning."

"But some people are worried that that will separate us into two churches, the 9:30 group and the 11:00 group."

"Do they think building a new church won't be worse?"

"I see your point."

"You know, Axel, the United Church's greatest strength is its committee structure. If the clergy can get out of the way and let the lay leadership do its thing, there's no limit to what you can achieve."

"That doesn't exactly describe John's style."

"He could never really accept the fact that a corporate church can't be run like a pastoral charge. His ego wouldn't permit it." Allegheny United Church had, in addition to committees in charge of everything you could imagine, a Coordinating Committee to keep track of the other committees and an emergency *ad hoc* committee for use in case of problems with any of the others.

We might have continued this conversation instructively had Abigail Farmer not burst into the office. A voice teacher, formerly a soprano with the Senior Choir, she grew up in Allegheny United Church and saw no reason why things couldn't be just the way they were when she was a girl. A tall, gaunt woman, she was my other nemesis on the Worship Committee. I'd never actually seen her wear knitting needles in her tight, gray bun, but imagined them whenever I saw her as visual symbols for her pointed criticisms. Today she was wearing a light green dress with a pattern of candy canes, but there was nothing sweet about her tone of voice.

"I understand you're taking the wedding on Saturday," she addressed Sarah without so much as a Christmas greeting.

"I'm afraid so," Sarah groaned. Her reluctance to conduct weddings, though surprising for a minister, was well known in the church.

"Well I think it's high time we got the wording of the wedding ceremony straightened out," Abigail went on.

"Straightened out?" Sarah asked.

"That's right. I think we should put the words 'love, honor and obey' back into the ceremony."

Sarah frowned. The battle to eliminate sexist language from the liturgy of the United Church had been hard-fought but, as far as Abigail Farmer was concerned, was far from over.

"Men and women aren't the same, and I say thank God for that!" Abigail continued. "You know what St. Paul said: 'The husband is the head of his wife.'"

This discussion wasn't going to end anytime soon, so I gave Sarah a high sign indicating "good luck" and slipped out of the office.

CHAPTER 5

Fred Carruthers invited me to "come on out to the house" so I drove to his property on the eastern border of the town, reflecting along the way on the transformations that had taken place in Meadowvale even in the time since I had moved there. Once a lazy country crossroads, the town had exploded in population in recent years as one farm after another disappeared into an uninterrupted ribbon of doughnut shops, car lots, strip malls, and rows of tract houses. I used to tell my students, "If you pass a cow, say hello, because it may not be there the next time you pass." Some of the street names betrayed their agricultural ancestry: Willow Farm Lane, Orchard Heights and Grove Terrace. Others came from popular novels of a bygone era, so that one development included not only Ashley Way, Scarlett Mews and Tara Court but even Pittipat Crescent.

The Carruthers apple orchards had been celebrated by a previous generation for the variety and quantity of their output. Old-timers recalled annual expeditions with their children, riding on a tractor-drawn wagon to the rows of trees scheduled for picking that week, shaking the branches to bring down fruit just out of reach, and returning home with baskets full of fresh apples and stories to be retold around the fire. But as imported apples took an ever greater share of the market, Fred Carruthers had begun selling the property, parcel by parcel, to developers. A devout Christian, he sold one tract to the town for considerably less than its market value so that a new school could be built in the neighborhood. Another tract went for a shopping plaza.

As I pulled into the driveway of the old farmhouse that seemed increasingly incongruous in its suburban setting, Fred stepped out on the weather-beaten porch to greet me, his farmer's overalls and heavy workboots providing a sharp contrast to the smart outfits of upscale shoppers a few hundred yards away. I tried to block out the noise of traffic and imagine what this must have sounded like with nothing but apple trees in all directions.

The aroma of apple pies cooling on the kitchen table completed the pastoral picture and I didn't have to be asked twice whether I'd like a piece of pie and a glass of milk. As Fred served I looked about the room at the old-fashioned refrigerator and stove. Decorative plates sat side by side on a narrow rack just above eye level. A cat lay curled up in an overstuffed chair in one corner next to a small television set on a dolly. Clearly this was the center of activity for the house.

After we had exchanged seasonal pleasantries, Fred made a comment on one of the hymns from the previous Sunday and I reminded him that I didn't choose the hymns.

"But I thought you were the music director?" he seemed puzzled.

"I direct the choirs and I play the organ but the minister picks the hymns."

"Oughta let the music director direct the music and let the preacher tend to the preaching, if you ask me."

I asked Fred about his future plans and he told me of his intention to move with his wife to a small cottage on the river out past Coraopolis. I didn't demand details but he hinted that he was in comfortable financial shape due to the sale of other properties and had no hesitation selling the last large tract to the church at a fraction of what he could make from selling it to Ralph Littlemore.

"But now the land will go to Ralph?" I asked.

"I'm afraid so," the old farmer said with a grimace.

"I don't understand. Don't you get a better deal this way?"

"Well ...," he began in the manner I'd observed in other country people. During the pause I studied his strong, gnarled fingers, as weatherbeaten as his house, and the wrinkles in his face, permanently tanned from many seasons of labor outdoors. "I've always had a few reservations about the way Ralph Littlemore conducts his business."

"How's that?"

"Axel, the land that Meadowvale sits on has some of the finest soil in this part of Pennsylvania."

"That must make the homeowners happy when it comes to growing lawns and planting gardens."

"That's just the point. They never see that soil."

"I don't get it."

"When the developers take over a farm, they strip all the topsoil off and sell it. The homeowners get nothing but clay. Then they have to buy sod from the turf farms if they're going to have a decent lawn."

"What a racket. But Ralph Littlemore probably didn't invent the practice."

"No, he's no worse than the others as far as that goes. But there are rumors, hell, it's more than rumors, he's bragged about it himself."

"What's that?"

"You know that phrase 'the circle of life' from the movie?"

"Sure."

"I guess nowadays they call it 'eco-systems.' The point is, everything has a place."

"I'm not sure I'm following."

"The farms you used to see all around here didn't just support cows or apples or sheep."

"Uh-huh."

"There were mice and rats and owls and snakes and all manner of other animals."

"Mm-hmm." I hoped he'd eventually get to the point.

"Now folks move into their new house, they don't want to be setting traps for the occasional field mouse that gets in. City folk are squeamish about stuff like that."

"Okay."

"So rather than deal with individual cases later on, Littlemore saves himself a lot of hassles by just poisoning everything in the development before he builds the houses."

"I see."

"But with so much building going on, the local mice seem to have developed immunity to conventional rodenticides, so Ralph takes stronger measures. Now he knows that Compound 1080 is a banned substance but friends of mine have heard him brag, 'I may not be able to buy it, but they can't keep me from growing my own.'"

"Growing his own?"

"It seems he's figured out how to raise rat bane and extract the poison from it to kill pests."

"Aha! Now this other story makes sense. When his son was busted for marijuana possession and claimed he shouldn't be prosecuted because he'd grown it himself, people at the church were saying 'What's sauce for the goose,' and I never understood what they meant."

"It's nasty business, if you ask me. I hate to say it after all these years, but I'm glad to be getting out of here."

I'd heard of a case like this, a farmer who remained on the family homestead even as suburbia surrounded him on all sides. When asked whether the encroaching sprawl bothered him, he had maintained that he was just living on his farm out in the country. Increasing deafness had evidently made it easier for him to block out what he didn't want to notice. Fred and his wife seemed to be in better touch with reality.

I thanked Fred for his time and the pie but before I could leave he had a suggestion for me. "You know what would be great, Axel? Have the Senior Choir perform an evening of show tunes. You could call it 'Broadway Melody.'"

"That's an idea," I said a bit dubiously.

"And you could have them sing 'O What a Beautiful Morning.' The wife and I went to New York, they didn't call it The Big Apple back then, for the original production of 'Oklahoma,' and let me tell you ..."

I let him tell me for fully ten minutes then returned to the church. Actually, an evening of show tunes might not be a bad idea, I reflected. It might get some of those people off my back who complained that I performed nothing but "high-brow" music. It bore thinking about.

As I backed out of the driveway I looked around at the several dozen bare apple trees on the property, the last remnant of a once prosperous plantation, and made a mental note to return to see them in apple blossom season, assuming they hadn't already been sacrificed to the devouring maw of development.

On the way back to the church I passed an enormous inflated gorilla atop one of the car dealerships announcing a "Monster End of Year Sale." This wasn't the first time I'd spotted the oversized primate; evidently one dealer would rent it for a week or two then pass it on to the next. The building opposite, under construction for several months, had now finally revealed its identity: yet another doughnut shop. Doughnut shops and car dealerships seemed to make up the bulk of Meadowvale's tax base, and lately the two concepts had begun to merge as one after the other of the doughnut shops introduced drive-through service. I wondered whether I wouldn't be happier living in the city and commuting to Meadowvale, reversing the daily pattern of most of its inhabitants.

CHAPTER 6

Clancy Davis, a tenor in the Senior Choir, chairperson of the Music Committee and a successful realtor, could probably give me more information on Ralph Littlemore and when I telephoned he invited me to stop by his office, a short walk from the church. So I locked my door, waved to Mae Nolan as I went past the church office and headed up to Meadowvale's main street.

The AUC Music Committee, whose self-image as a bunch of renegades probably wasn't that far from the perception of the rest of the church, had won plaudits last February for the First Annual Potluck Supper and Variety Show, held on Leapnight, a kind of United Church Mardi Gras. We'd also received acclaim for the Music Workshop for Sunday school teachers in which we had five different people come in to demonstrate action songs, percussion instruments, cassette recordings, and other aids to getting kids to sing.

I dodged a spray of water as a car traveling at rather above the local speed limit plowed through the slush and sent a wave up over the sidewalk. While Christmas decorations remained in the shop windows—the gingerbread house in Mary's Flowers and Sweets was beginning to look a bit bedraggled—the carols had utterly disappeared. It had felt strange to be hearing "Joy to the World" in stores in early November but now that the liturgical season of Christmas had just begun, the secular world had no further interest in carols. There were plenty of pedestrians about, probably picking up last-minute items for New Years festivities.

Technically the Music Committee was a subcommittee of Worship, a group as far from renegade as one could imagine. Last year we appealed to the Coordinating Committee for independent status, but that would have meant according committee status to Adult Education, a subcommittee of Christian Education, and nobody wanted to do that. Since each Elder is required to serve on at least one committee (subcommittees don't count), full committee status would have made it easier for the Music Committee to recruit members.

The December Music Committee meeting failed to draw a quorum to hear the chairman say that work pressures compelled him to resign. I pointed out that if he resigned the committee would fold, and wondered whether there weren't some more graceful way of handling the situation. We recalled the strategy offered to, and unfortunately rejected by, President Johnson in the midst of the Vietnam War: declare victory and withdraw.

"Splendid idea," the chairman declared. So the Music Committee announced that it had achieved all its objectives and would hereafter convene as circumstances required. We reckoned that circumstances might require us to convene maybe two or three times a year, under which conditions the chairman happily agreed to carry on.

I entered his office, wiped my feet on the welcome mat and hung my coat on the rack beside the door.

Clancy Davis maintained the fun-loving demeanor of a tuba player in the University of Michigan marching band, and though his hairline may have receded somewhat since university days, he still acted as if he'd be happy to go out for a beer or a pizza at the drop of a hat. He wore the required business suit but managed to look as if he'd just come back from a pep rally.

In contrast to the teams of representatives tending most of the real estate firms in town, with little alcoves containing stainless steel chairs and polished tabletops surrounding the main office like chapels in the great cathedral of home ownership, Clancy ran a one-man operation out of a modest single room. Recently he'd felt compelled to affiliate with the ReMax system, but his business retained the homey atmosphere of a man who knew his customers and cared about them as individuals.

When I asked Clancy about Ralph Littlemore he said, "That guy's a piece of work." He laughed when I told him what Fred Carruthers had told me about Ralph Littlemore's home-grown rat bane. "That's small potatoes compared to the schemes that fellow has carried out in the past," Clancy told me.

"Really?" I asked.

"You understand that this doesn't go outside this room," he cautioned. "I sometimes have to deal with these guys."

"Mum's the word," I said.

"You know that mansion he lives in just outside town. That didn't come from the land deals in Meadowvale. Mind you, he still makes a good living as a respectable businessman, but the big money came from some of the scams he pulled off in another state."

"Like what?"

"One of the most lucrative deals involved getting phony appraisals from a tame appraiser then taking out multiple loans on the land or the house before the lenders caught on. He not only managed to avoid going to jail but he even kept the money. I imagine everybody kept passing the buck and the insurance companies ended up covering the losses."

"Goodness!"

"In another state he pulled the old forged deed con."

"How does that work?"

"You hunt around for an unoccupied house or an undeveloped piece of land." Clancy was obviously warming to his subject. Our Music Committee meetings had often been enlivened by his anecdotes of life at AUC. "Then, posing as the owner, you bring in a legitimate appraiser. You forge the deed and take out an improvement or development loan on the property. Nobody's living in the house so the actual owner isn't even aware of what you've done. By the time people figure it out, you've taken the money and moved on."

"How do you know all this?"

"Oh you know how it is; word gets around. But as I say, Ralph played it very cool by quitting when he was ahead. He's legit now, a member of the church, and all the rest. Since coming to Meadowvale he hasn't done anything worse than property-flipping."

"What's that?"

"Two unscrupulous realtors get together and sell properties back and forth, artificially elevating their market value with each transaction so that the eventual legitimate buyer ends up paying far more than he should. But what's your interest in Littlemore, anyway?"

I explained the case against James Bellinger, the unusual poison that killed John Armstrong, and Littlemore's boasts of home-grown rat bane.

"There's no question he's going to turn a tidy profit on the Carruthers property—you knew he held the second option, right? But it would be pretty hard to pin a murder charge on him. Littlemore's a very slick operator. On the other hand, if he ever did commit murder, it would be in just such a flamboyant public way."

Clancy had such an easy-going manner that one might imagine he led a trouble-free existence. On the contrary, he had for many years endured the burden of a wife in such a state of clinical depression that she seldom ventured outside the house. He would bring her to church a couple of times a year, as he had on Christmas Eve, but for the most part she remained housebound, facing inner demons that even the most potent drugs seemed helpless to dislodge.

"I don't want to dash your hopes, Axel," Clancy continued, "but I think you need to consider seriously the possibility that James Bellinger really did it."

"But why?"

"Try to look at it from his point of view. He's making a modest living selling Acuras. Hell, Shirley's probably making more money than he is."

"Okay."

"In other words, the guy doesn't have much. Marrying Shirley was probably the best thing he ever did for himself, though I'm not sure his wife would agree."

"So?"

"So now the only thing he has gets taken away from him."

"Shirley wasn't planning to leave him."

"Yes, but I'm asking you to look at this from Bellinger's point of view. And taken away by the most powerful man in his little world: John Armstrong. How do you think a guy is going to react in a situation like that?"

"He might just give up and get depressed."

"Or he might snap."

"Uh-huh."

"You remember the movie 'Network' where Peter Finch says 'I'm mad as hell and I'm not going to take it any more'?"

"Right."

"That could easily be James Bellinger."

"I see your point." I thanked Clancy for his help and he told me he'd see me at choir rehearsal in the evening. Bellinger again. Clancy seemed to be echoing Ben Van Dyk's sentiments. I wasn't getting much support in my campaign to clear Shirley's husband.

CHAPTER 7

Worship Committee meetings took place the last Thursday of every month and the old biddies who made up the committee had no intention of letting the Christmas holidays spoil their monthly complaint session. In previous meetings they had debated the resolution that the organist plays too loudly and had expressed the opinions that the purpose of the organ prelude was to make people feel good and that I played too much Bach. They objected when the choir sang in Latin or in any other foreign language and in November one member had asked me pointedly, "Are you a Lutheran or something?"

The members took their seats and Gladys showed us a Christmas gift made for her by her grandson: a pair of white face masks, one happy and the other sad, mounted on a wooden stand. Sarah Beasley, sitting in for John Armstrong, thanked Gladys for sharing, then reported that there had been complaints about all the fund-raising efforts after worship. More people lined up for the Teeners' "Bowling for Dollars" program than for the church's official stewardship campaign. Gladys asked whether something couldn't be done about children crying during services. The committee discussed how to run the elevator: a suggestion was made to have the elevator key chained to the cage, but what would happen if the power failed? Gladys asked whether something couldn't be done about applause during the service. The committee discussed whether the announcements shouldn't come after the Prayer of Confession rather than at the start of the service. Gladys announced the scripture reading for the coming week on the theme of purity and Henry exclaimed, "Not again!"

Abigail Farmer launched her monthly Junior Choir rant, wondering whether the children couldn't file more neatly from their seats to the chancel stairs. Back when she was in the Junior Choir, she reported proudly, the music director used to make the kids practice marching so they could process as smartly as little toy soldiers, and she gave a meaningful glance at the slovenly incumbent.

In last month's rant, Abigail had asked why the children in the Junior Choir had to wear white cassocks. Couldn't they wear colors, and wouldn't it be nicer to have ruffled collars and maybe hats? She remembered that when she was a chorister, much earlier in the century, everyone wore matching hats.

Gladys asked whether the organ prelude could be softer and more spiritual. Henry Eldridge asked the same for the organ postlude. Abigal thought the hymns could be softer, too. Gladys said that she and a number of her friends were troubled by the increasing number of children wearing bonnets at baptism. Henry Eldridge reported that the new altar candles were burning at an alarming rate.

Various issues surrounding baptism had vexed the Worship Committee for more than a year. Each such ceremony brought in a crowd of people never seen in the church before or after having their children "done." In addition to the parents and the infant, there would be a flock of family members, outsiders who had neither knowledge of nor interest in the procedures of worship at AUC and who often disrupted the service by departing noisily as soon as the water had been sprinkled. In the end the Committee recommended that the number of baptisms be limited to five per month. At one point I made the mistake of wondering aloud whether anything could be done to limit the number of births, and cited the example of the Virgins for Jesus.

In addition to the noise factor, the Worship Committee had devoted considerable time to the baptismal cradle crosses which, until recently, had been wrought in silver by the same artisan who had perpetrated the enormous Christmas mural hanging in front of the organ pipes. When poor health prevented him from continuing to supply the crosses, the committee had to consider alternatives, including wooden Dutch crosses.

Sarah congratulated me on a successful Carols by Candlelight service earlier in the month and I made a mental note to tell her in private of disaster averted. A member of the Worship Committee had been assigned to pick the readings; I was to select the music. The Worship Committee member went to Florida for a spell, promising to supply me with readings on his return in early December. On December 8th he called to ask what I thought of an inspirational poem, which he proceeded to read over the phone, about the organist being absent at Christmas and an old drunkard, reeking of gin, rising from the congregation and staggering to the console to offer his services. Perhaps I could play appropriate organ selections while the poem was being read. I did what any sane person would do under the circumstances and suggested he run the idea by the senior minister. Next day the chap called again to say that on reflection he favored the Christmas story according to St. Luke. I commended his choice and went on to select the rest of the readings myself. John Armstrong wasn't all bad.

One would think that in a church as large as AUC any kind of Christmas concert would succeed but I had unsuccessfully tried music with brass, an organ recital with choral interludes and a choral concert with organ interludes before hitting on the idea of a service of carols illuminated exclusively by candles. A member of the Senior Choir had designed a prototype candleholder that could be attached to the pews to bear a candle capable of burning for an hour and a half. A crew of men got together in his basement shop one Saturday in the fall to turn out the hundred or so candleholders necessary to illuminate the church.

Meanwhile, under the supervision of the fire marshal, a special ushering team practiced dealing with any mishap that might arise from a wayward candle. (A simulation had already shown that the candles would not set off the church's sprinkler system. They thought of everything.) Some of the Teeners volunteered to serve as "victims" and by the time of the performance the fire team could reach any spot in the church within ten seconds and wrap a burn victim in a smothering blanket.

The magical glow from these candles was ruined the first year by an usher who thought that adding "just a little bit of electric light" would improve matters. The following year we printed the program in 16-point type and gave strict orders that no electricity would be permitted. Since then the event had become so popular that we had to give two performances. Members of the Meadowvale community who would never have considered coming to a church service found this little touch of nonsecularity the missing soupçon for their seasonal festivities.

Abigail couldn't stand to let the meeting end on a positive note so she brought out a copy of the repertory list that I had distributed to the choir at the beginning of the season and complained, "This schedule contains works by lots of great composers—I'll be the first to admit it—but nearly all of them are dead." When Henry pointed out the anthem that we had recently performed by living composer Violet Archer, Abigail made it clear that this wasn't the kind of music she was talking about. What she wanted was schmaltz (her word). I promised to take another look at the repertory list and after a closing prayer the meeting broke up.

I drew Gladys aside and asked her about Henry's surprising behavior. She looked around discreetly then leaned toward me and said in her grandmotherly voice that there were rumors about the way his laboratory disposed of toxic wastes. For an old girl, Gladys didn't miss a trick.

CHAPTER 8

I went directly from the meeting room to the choir loft for the weekly rehearsal of the Senior Choir. The group had begun to sound pretty good, once they made it clear to me that the sopranos didn't like to sing above a D, that nobody wanted to sing in foreign languages, and that they didn't like unfamiliar carols at the Carol Service. I had even negotiated an agreement with the two tenors who insisted that in complicated music they would each sing every other note.

As the singers gathered I heard Thelma Moore, who had been serving as a temporary secretary in Henry Eldridge's lab, describing her employer's rage when she had opened an envelope that arrived at the office. "And all it had in it was a blank sheet of paper," she said with a tone of prim self-righteousness.

"But why would anyone mail a blank piece of paper," asked one of the altos.

"Could have been they just forgot the letter," suggested a soprano.

I asked Thelma idly where the envelope had come from, and the woman, proud of her attentiveness to details, said, "202 Morningside Drive."

Shirley Bellinger commented, "Why, that's in my neighborhood, but I don't think there is any 202. At least, not yet. Our new house is 188 and the last house on the road is 198. The next houses are still under construction."

"You're not living on Partridge Lane anymore?" came another voice.

I managed to get the rehearsal started. After we had run through a few vocal warm-ups I congratulated the choir on their performance at the Valhalla Retirement Home. Half the audience had been semiconscious; the rest wished we had come at some time other than Christmas. "Everybody wants to sing for us at Christmas and the rest of the year they forget we exist," one old gentleman had complained. Shirley commented on the excessive heat, Ben on the excessive dryness, and Trish McConnell, one of the altos, giggled as she recalled the image of the piano gliding away from me as I tried to accompany the singing, probably due to an overenthusiastic lubrication of the wheels.

Trish had come to my rescue, holding onto the wayward instrument, just as she had rushed to retrieve my music on the morning that one of the basses jacked up the fans so that they blew my music off the rack in the middle of the postlude. A slender girl with shoulder-length black hair, Trish had a plain face, when considered as a separate feature, but her animated personality and self-confidence led one to take in her trim figure and athletic build and consider that this was quite an attractive young woman.

We practiced the anthems for the next several Sundays then I excused the choir early; they all had families waiting for them and I appreciated their coming out during the holidays.

CHAPTER 9

I returned to my office to find Ben Van Dyk waiting for me. He was examining the little doll that Trish McConnell had given me after the choir's performance of Handel's *Messiah* the previous spring: it wore a choir robe in the AUC colors and bore the inscription "Mouse-siah." At my request the church had installed a file cabinet for my organ music. The room also served as the choir library, with rows of labelled boxes containing scores filling the shelves of one wall. The only other decoration was a lithograph called "Fifty-One People and a Tree," a title which invariably made visitors stop to verify the count.

"I talked to one of my friends on the force this afternoon," he reported. "They're still trying to figure out where Jim Bellinger obtained the poison."

"Perhaps I can ask you to wear your other hat for a moment," I said. "I heard a couple of odd things this evening."

"Go ahead," Ben said.

"At the Worship Committee meeting Henry Eldridge got quite upset when Gladys announced that next week's reading would be about purity. When I asked her to explain after the meeting, she hinted that he might have been disposing of toxic wastes improperly."

"What's the other thing?"

"Just before you came into the choir rehearsal Thelma Moore said that Henry flew into a rage when she'd opened an envelope containing a blank piece of paper. She noticed the return address, but according to Shirley Bellinger there isn't a house at that address yet. It's just a hole in the ground."

"I'd heard about something like that," Ben mused, "but I didn't think anyone would actually be so bold."

"How do you mean?"

"People are always tossing things into holes at construction sites. Some mornings we have to haul out old tires or somebody's garbage before we can get to work."

"Can't you hire guards?"

"That gets expensive, especially when you're building a lot of houses at the same time. You know the way this town is booming—we can't keep up with the demand."

"So you think Eldridge may have been using the construction sites to get rid of illegal chemicals?"

"It's a possibility. Where did you say this took place?"

"202 Morningside Drive was the return address on the envelope."

"That's one of Ralph Littlemore's developments. I wouldn't put it past him to make a little profit on the side helping Henry Eldridge dispose of his wastes."

"But why would Henry have to do that?" I asked.

"He's getting squeezed by the competition of rival laboratories overseas and probably cuts corners wherever he can. Now he's stuck: if he gets reported to the Environmental Protection Agency his firm risks fines that would bankrupt him, but he can't afford to use a legitimate disposal site and still remain competitive—both the transportation and dumping fees have tripled in the past several years."

"Then the blank piece of paper could have been a signal. There wasn't any message in the envelope but the return address told Eldridge where he could get rid of his chemicals, probably just for that night before the construction company actually laid a foundation."

"It's stuff like this that gives the rest of us a bad name," Ben said. "You say the words 'contractor' or 'real estate developer' and people almost automatically put the word 'crooked' in front. Take Carl Rutledge."

"Who's that?"

"Stan's brother. He's visiting for the holidays. He has a reputation as one of the biggest, but also one of the dirtiest building contractors in Colorado. That kind of thing hurts us all."

"Perhaps I'd better plan a visit to the Eldridge lab," I said. We chatted about how good the choir was sounding and Ben invited me over to try a new mushroom recipe, but I hadn't seen Jennifer all day so I thanked him and took a rain check.

Just as I was about to leave the phone rang again; it was Fred Carruthers.

"Glad to catch you, Axel. I wasn't sure you'd still be at the church."

"What's on your mind, Fred?" I asked.

"Well." Again that long pause. "After we talked I thought of something else that might interest you. Could be nothing, but then you never know."

"What's that."

"Every evening Trey and I go out for a walk. It's not as long as it was in the old days, but then I'm getting older and so is Trey."

"I see." Fred had his own style of telling a story and there wasn't any point in trying to hurry him along.

"Now all that's left is the property around our house and the tract I was saving for the church."

"So you saw something on your walk?"

"Nothing happening on either of those two tracts, except for the occasional raccoon. Trey's learned to live with the squirrels but he still gets pretty excited when he sees a raccoon."

"I can imagine."

"But of course the tract I sold to Ralph Littlemore last year adjoins the other two."

"Yes." Now we were getting somewhere.

"And that new road—Morningside Drive, I think it is—runs right down to the boundary of the church tract, at least that's what I call it even if the church isn't going to build there after all."

"Yes?"

"So the other night Trey and I were out there, and as I say, I've trained Trey not to bark at strangers, so we don't attract a lot of attention. In fact, I don't think they even knew we were there."

"Who's that?"

"Why the Littlemore boy and the Houghton girl. That's what I've been trying to tell you."

"What about them?"

"At first I thought they were just playing around, but after they left I went over to investigate and it appears they were serious."

"What did they do?"

"The first night they disabled a backhoe."

"And then?"

"The next night they came back and disabled a steamroller. After that Ralph hired a night watchman to protect his equipment."

"What do you think they were after?"

"Well, from what I've heard about the Littlemore boy, he doesn't have a lot of admiration for his Daddy's line of work."

"Did he imagine he could stop a whole development?"

"You know the way teenagers are. They start out on a project full of enthusiasm without calculating its size."

"Yes."

"I reckon it wasn't the night watchman that scared them off. I kind of figure they realized Ralph's operation was just too big for them to shut down, just the two of them."

"You're probably right." I could easily imagine Parmalee recruiting the Littlemore boy to the ecological cause. If anyone were to reproach the young people, Parmalee would no doubt quote Henry David Thoreau at them. Whether the ideas came from philosophers or from *People* magazine, it all carried the weight of scripture to some of these kids.

"I don't know whether this helps at all but I thought I'd tell you anyway."

I thanked Fred for calling and filed the information away for future reference. It was raining when I left the church, which made the town's Christmas decorations seem even shabbier than usual, but when I got home I found that Jennifer had turned on the gas in the fireplace and lit candles all through the house. I briefly considered telling her about my investigation then decided it could wait for another time.

CHAPTER 10

On Friday morning Mae Nolan called me at home to say that Derek Armstrong had died during the night and asked whether I would be available to play for his funeral the following Tuesday. When I told her I was free she said that she would leave the musical requests in my mailbox. Ordinarily for funerals I played a selection of Bach and Brahms chorale preludes but recently had come upon a nice arrangement of "The Lord Is My Shepherd" that I wanted to try out.

I decided to drive out to the Eldridge laboratory unannounced. I didn't think Henry would refuse to see me, but I preferred not to make him suspicious by calling in advance. I hadn't counted on the school bus problem. Pennsylvania state law calls for drivers in both directions to come to a stop whenever a school bus halts to pick up or drop off a child. On major roads the traffic has ample opportunity to get past the bus between stops but on this narrow, winding road with frequent pauses for waiting schoolchildren the bus served as a rolling obstacle, with several dozen cars backed up behind it and nearly the same number held up in the other direction. Anyone not familiar with the daily routine would have suspected a major accident or a police roadblock.

The Eldridge laboratory was so inconspicuous that I almost drove past it. Nestled among tall oak trees at the back and sides and protected from casual view by a thick row of fir trees in front, the low one-story building seemed to have been designed to avoid notice. I found a place for my car in the single slot marked "Visitors" and walked along a cement sidewalk to the front entrance. A peculiar odor greeted my nose: it didn't smell noxious exactly but it wasn't pleasant either and it didn't smell like anything that occurred in nature.

Thelma Moore was not in evidence as I approached the reception desk. Evidently the regular secretary had returned to duty. I announced my name, she repeated it into a hidden microphone, and a moment later directed me to Henry Eldridge's office at the end of the hallway. The plastic Christmas tree in the lobby, decorated with red lights and some rather shopworn packages, had presumably been through this routine every year and was probably looking forward to returning to the quiet and safety of a storage box.

Henry Eldridge's office seemed pretty modest for the head of a corporation: a plain wooden desk, a row of filing cabinets, a couple of extra chairs and a tired looking rubber plant where you might have expected a coffee table, a sculpture, an ebony credenza or some other indication of the inhabitant's status. Henry rose from his desk and beckoned me to one of the chairs.

"What brings you out here, Axel?" he said. "I thought we'd covered just about everything on the agenda last night."

"Actually my visit does tie in tangentially with the Worship Committee," I began. "I noticed that when Gladys announced the readings for next week you seemed to get rather upset."

"Oh that was nothing," he said dismissively.

"Something about the topic of purity that gets under your skin?"

"What are you talking about?" he asked defensively. Then he tried to laugh it off. "Actually, I confess that the choice of readings does seem to have been a bit one-sided recently."

"How do you mean?"

"Well, let's see. Two months ago we had 'Cleanse yourselves, ye that bear the vessels of Yahweh.' Isaiah, I think that was. Then last month it was 'Who shall stand in his holy place? He that hath clean hands, and a pure heart.'"

"Psalm 24. The choir sang an anthem on the text."

"Then it was 'Blessed are the pure in heart, for they will see God.' Then we had 'For God did not call us to be impure, but to live a holy life.'" Henry became more animated with each successive verse. "He was doing it on purpose!" His voice had risen to a shout. Then he recovered himself and his eyes narrowed as he asked me, "Just how much do you know?"

"Pretty much all of it, I think."

"How did you find out?"

"I figured out how Ralph Littlemore told you where to dump the stuff."

"I'm glad none of my drivers talked. I'm paying them enough to keep it quiet. But how did John Armstrong find out?"

"You're convinced that he was using his sermon texts to provoke you?"

"He was just toying with me, pushing me to 'come clean,'" Henry said bitterly. "But what does this have to do with the Worship Committee?"

"It doesn't."

"But I thought ..."

"Henry, as far as I'm concerned, this toxic waste business is between your conscience and the EPA. What I'm seeing is a lot worse than that?"

"What are you talking about?"

"If you really believed that John Armstrong was threatening your livelihood, you had a strong motive to murder him."

"Murder? Now wait a minute ..."

"You were there at the Christmas Eve service. You would have no difficulty manufacturing the poison—you told me so yourself. If your drivers are as close-lipped as you maintain, once he was out of the way you were safe."

"You can't be serious."

"Right now the police seem to be content with James Bellinger as the murderer. But if they look at who stood to gain from the death, you seem to have a lot better motive than he does."

"It wasn't me, Axel. You have to believe that. It's true, the sermons were driving me nuts, but when I complained to Ralph, he said he'd take care of it. I never thought he meant this way." Henry looked more and more like a sick puppy.

Littlemore again. Now it looked as if he had two reasons for wanting to get John Armstrong out of the way. Henry didn't strike me as having the nerve to commit a murder, but he was still a chemist and could easily have furnished the poison to his ruthless partner. On the other hand, why would Littlemore need Eldridge if he could grow rat bane on his own? This supposedly rare poison was becoming a good deal too available for my liking.

"If you don't mind my asking, how did you and Ralph Littlemore get hooked up, anyway?"

"Last year the dump jacked up their fees again," Henry said with a touch of bitterness in his voice. "My driver hadn't heard about the increase and didn't know whether he was authorized to go ahead, but he couldn't very well return to the lab with a full load."

"Uh-huh."

"Then his partner spotted a construction site and had the idea of dropping it into an excavated site."

"But I suppose it would be too dangerous to try that on a regular basis."

"Actually they did try it again and that time they got caught."

"What happened?"

"The next day I got a phone call from Ralph Littlemore. He gave me a choice between prosecution or working out a deal with him. It wasn't a difficult choice." He sounded thoroughly defeated.

I told Henry I had no immediate plans to talk with either the EPA or the local police about his transgressions, but suggested that I didn't think his scheme for disposing of toxic wastes would remain secret much longer.

Eldridge made a half-hearted effort to get up and see me to the door but the weight of his burdens seemed to be too much for him; as I left the office he slumped forward and rested his head in his hands. The world was changing fast and seemed to have no place in it for those who couldn't keep up.

CHAPTER 11

When I returned to the church Friday afternoon I found Mae talking with Lewis Hartley about the arrangements for the elder Armstrong's funeral. Hartley served as attorney not only for the church but for a sizeable proportion of its members. A tall, slightly-stooped man with silver hair, he wore a dark suit and a tie whose pattern of stripes suggested some fraternal organization. His avuncular style and deep-set brown eyes communicated the perfect blend of reassurance and intelligence. The conversation fell within my domain, at least tangentially, and Hartley made no objection when I sat down to listen.

After the two had nailed down all the details for the service, I asked Lewis as casually as I could, "I suppose the old man's fortune goes to Bud now."

He looked at me oddly, then said, "I guess there's no harm in telling you this, but the terms of Derek Armstrong's will have always bothered me."

"How's that?"

"He insisted on leaving all the money to his 'eldest surviving son.' Evidently there had been another Armstrong brother who died some years back. In any case, his clear intent was to leave his fortune to John."

"I remember when he visited the church a year ago," Mae interjected. "He knew even then that he wasn't going to live long, but he said 'John's been poor as a church mouse long enough.' He seemed to take it as a personal insult that John wouldn't invest in IRA's, like any red-blooded American, but insisted on tithing to the church."

I recalled the disdain with which the senior minister spoke of his parishioners retirement investments. His concern for social causes was entirely genuine. He'd spent many an evening on the Meadowvale Planning Committee arguing for subsidized housing on town-owned land while Ralph Littlemore argued no less vigorously in favor of condominiums.

"His appearance caused something of a stir, as I recall," Lewis said.

"That's right," Mae replied. "It was the first time he'd set foot in the church for nearly ten years."

"What made him leave?" I asked.

"That's a story in itself," Lewis chuckled. I waited for him to go on but when he gave no signs of continuing I glanced at Mae for enlightenment.

"He had a famous row with Harriett Bascomb. This was before your time, Axel, but you need to know that the church looked quite a bit different before we built the Sunday school wing."

"How so?"

"It was great," Lewis rejoined the conversation. "There used to be a gymnasium and even a bowling alley."

"You're kidding," I said.

"No, it's a fact," Mae said. "The Teeners used to get tips for serving as pinsetters."

"I suppose that made it something of a social center," I observed.

"Well that, too," Mae said, "but that wasn't Derek's interest. He'd organized a seniors bowling league that drew in people from all over the town. Three nights a week you couldn't even play if you didn't have gray hair."

"So how does Harriett come into this?" I asked.

"When they drew up the plans for the new wing, given the size of the property something had to go." For an attorney, Lewis seemed surprisingly reluctant to go into adversarial relationships.

"And the bowling alley was it?" I asked.

"By that time the town had grown a lot—not as much as today, but still a lot bigger than before—and a new bowling alley with automatic pinsetters had opened out by the mall," Lewis said.

"So why didn't Derek move his operation out there?" I asked.

"It wasn't going to be the same," Mae replied. "At the church he ran the entire league. The new alley organized its own leagues and he would have been just another player."

"But what about Harriett?" I persisted.

"Well you know how Harriett can be," Lewis said vaguely.

"She turned the issue into a personal fight, making it look as if Derek was standing in the way of the Sunday school. The way she framed it, you had to choose between old men with bowling balls and little kids eager to hear Bible stories. Derek never forgave her."

"He made an anonymous gift to upgrade the senior minister's study—I guess it's all right to disclose that now," Lewis said, "but except for the visit Mae mentioned and Christmas Eve, he never returned to the church."

The death of two Armstrongs in such a short time period raised an interesting question of timing. If John Armstrong had died after his father, in the normal course of events, the Armstrong fortune would have passed to his wife and children, presumably with some provision for his impecunious brother. But as events had played out, Bud would inherit it all.

Lewis interrupted my reverie with a gently put but direct question. "Axel, something has been bothering me. I have great admiration for your musical talents, but don't you think a murder investigation is a bit of a stretch?"

"I assure you, Lewis, I would rather be doing almost anything else, but Shirley Bellinger has asked for my help and so far James has forbidden her to call a lawyer."

"Do you know the phrase 'Methinks the lady doth protest too much'?"

"Shakespeare, isn't it?"

"Hamlet." Lewis nodded. "I know you're fond of Shirley and all, but in my experience the simplest answer is usually the best."

"And in this case?"

"James did it. He may be an ordinary man but he's not stupid. He hears John Armstrong preaching Sunday after Sunday about purity and then learns that the man is banging his wife, if you'll pardon the expression," he said, turning to Mae. "Does it seem so unreasonable for him to blow up at John and then, when that didn't alleviate his anger, take stronger measures?"

"You could be right."

"Keep it simple, Axel. That's my advice," Lewis said as he gathered his coat and departed.

I stayed behind and pressed Mae for more details on John Armstrong's relationship with his brother.

"That's a sad story," she said, "that two brothers should live in the same town yet be so far apart."

"Where does Bud live, anyway?" I asked.

"Out in the township beyond the Meadowvale city limits. He supports himself on unemployment, welfare, and the occasional odd job. He doesn't make much but then he doesn't need much. He lives in the trailer that John gave him when his children went off to college and he no longer required it for family vacations. And John has found other ways to get money to Bud from time to time."

I shared with Mae the ideas I had regarding the timing of the two Armstrong deaths. "One brother killing another? Ah, now that would truly be terrible," she said.

"Well, he was here the night of the murder and he had a great deal to gain. Perhaps he resented John for his success and even held his generosity against him."

"They say that no good deed goes unpunished."

"I wonder about the poison, though."

"Everybody makes so much about Compound 1080 being a banned substance. If you go out to the township, you'll find it readily enough," Mae said.

The telephone rang. It was the mother of the bride again. Evidently she didn't like having her daughter's wedding on the same day as the minister's funeral. Wasn't there some way they could postpone the funeral for a day or two. After all, a girl only got married once. Mae rolled her eyes as she listened to the conversation and I left her to deal with the distraught woman.

CHAPTER 12

Friday evening saw me at the organ console for the first time since Christmas, and as I practiced I recalled the words of the president of the American Organ Guild, writing in *The American Organist*:

"I've had some nice jobs in nice buildings in my life so far. I don't think I would last more than one day in a church I heard about this week, where the hymns on Palm Sunday included "When Jesus came riding into town, Hurrah, Hurrah," to the tune of "When Johnny comes marching home," and "We have a king who rides on a donkey and his name is Jesus," to the tune of "What shall we do with a drunken sailor." I know I'm a snob, an elitist, and a prehistoric reactionary, but I've come to the conclusion that I'm proud of it; that kind of insulting trash would send me out of this profession instantly." You may not be surprised to learn that he was writing about Allegheny United Church.

My eyes glanced upward toward the great mural of Mary, the baby Jesus and Joseph, painted by a member of the congregation. In this version, Mary was a hulking Amazon, built like an ox, easily capable of carrying Joseph, Jesus and the donkey, too. My principal objection to the mural came on acoustic rather than aesthetic grounds. Despite my objections the Visual Arts Committee insisted on hanging the thing directly in front of the organ pipes every Advent, muffling the organ throughout the very season when its power was most needed.

The present pipe organ had long since exceeded the expected lifespan of its leathers, to the astonishment of every organ builder who visited it. Charged with the responsibility of formulating a long-term plan, the Organ Assessment Committee found itself completely deadlocked between the four of us who wanted to improve the instrument (whose pitifully weak pedal division had confounded one organist after another) and those who refused to countenance anything more expensive than duct tape and bailing wire.

How I would have loved an instrument like the Von Beckerath organ recently installed in the Roman Catholic cathedral in Pittsburgh. I'd attended the inaugural recital and should have been warned by the decoration on the program cover, a representation of a keyboard with alternating black and white keys instead of the proper pattern. The organist's playing wasn't bad so long as he stuck to the repertoire, but late in the program he got into some wretched improvising followed by a hymn in which the audience was expected to participate. Unaccustomed to the delay time between the sound of the instrument and the sound of the congregation, the organist slowed down to give them a chance to catch up. The audience responded by slowing still further and the resulting vicious cycle left me wondering whether we'd ever finish the hymn.

Others at AUC had directed their energies toward solving the parking lot problem. From time to time the manager of the bank whose parking lot adjoined that of the church threatened to close off the passage between the two lots, and while Lewis Hartley advised us that the bank could not unilaterally block a right-of-way that had been in existence for more than thirty years, the Administration Committee wasn't taking any chances and wanted to build a "window to Tyler Street." This window wouldn't come cheaply, since the sharp drop in elevation would require relocating underground electric and telephone lines. Right now, the smart money was betting on the parking lot over the organ by odds of 4 to 1.

As I returned to my office after practicing I ran into David Moore, the treasurer of AUC, just leaving an emergency meeting of the Ministry and Personnel Committee called to decide whether Sarah Beasley's title should be changed to "Acting Head Minister."

"Hi, David," I said. "Heading for the kitchen?"

"As a matter of fact, yes, but how did you know?"

"Just a wild guess."

Then he saw my eyes resting on the book in his hand, *Drink More Water*. Last week it had been *Your Thirsty Body* and the week before that *Drink Water or Die*. "Axel, did you realize that your body is 70% water and that ..."

"David, we've already had this conversation," I broke in. "Give it a rest."

"But if you don't drink eight glasses of water a day... You know, your skin is looking a bit parched, Axel."

I thanked him for the advice and continued on to my office. It was his wife Thelma's fault, really. She had bought him a treadmill and started him on this "eight glasses a day" regimen and now he was preaching with the enthusiasm of the new convert. He claimed to have lost ten pounds and gained inner peace but he also drew a chorus of ill-concealed giggles every time he showed up in the kitchen to maintain his quota.

As I put my organ music away I recalled my last run-in with the Ministry and Personnel Committee. For years before my arrival on the scene, the good people at Allegheny United Church fretted that their children didn't sing "Jesus Loves Me" around the house the way they used to when they were little. Like any organization they decided to resolve the problem by simply writing it into the job description of the next person to come on board. Surely someone should have realized that I couldn't very well be in church Sunday mornings playing hymns on the organ at the same time as I led 150 kids singing "Jesus Loves Me,"but nobody said a word.

For three years John Armstrong asked what we (meaning I) could do to get the kids to sing "Jesus Loves Me." At my annual evaluation meeting with Ministry and Personnel, Ian Wetherby told me, "I know that Jesus loves me, and the reason I know it is that from the time I first went to Sunday school I sang "Jesus Loves Me." We hired you to get our kids to sing "Jesus Loves Me" and frankly we haven't been getting our money's worth." He went on to tell me that my salary for the coming year would be reduced as a result.

The Ministry and Personnel Committee went to Coordinating with the request that an ad hoc committee be struck to deal with the problem of kids singing (or not singing).

"What's the problem?" asked one person on the Coordinating Committee.

"The kids don't sing enough," came the reply.

"But I was in Sunday school leading them singing just last week."

"Well, they don't sing enough new hymns."

"But I taught them three new ones."

"Well, they don't sing enough old hymns."

"But last month Brad led them in a whole bunch of old hymns."

"Well, there's a problem here and we need a new committee to handle it."

So the ad hoc committee was duly struck, a blue ribbon panel including the entire Music Committee, the Sunday school superintendent, a representative from the parents, a representative from the Sunday school coordinators, a representative from the Worship Committee, a representative from Ministry and Personnel, the senior minister *ex officio*, an experienced chairperson in the form of Lewis Hartley, and the music director.

During a previous staff meeting, while the senior minister was away, we brainstormed ideas on children singing and I worked up a report outlining some half a dozen activities that had been tried before, along with their advantages and disadvantages, followed by ideas for current consideration. I took this to Lewis Hartley who suggested that I submit it to all the committee members prior to the meeting to serve as a basis for discussion.

Come the night of the meeting, Hartley invited the senior minister to offer a prayer then suggested that we use my report as a basis for discussing how we were going to get the kids to sing "Jesus Loves Me." No sooner had the words left his mouth than Ian Wetherby, the Ministry and Personnel representative, intervened and announced that he could not continue to serve on this committee if this is how we were going to proceed. He said that he expected us to be discussing a 1987 document outlining the philosophy of music at Allegheny United Church. The senior minister said that no mention of any such document had been made when the ad hoc committee had been struck. "Well," said Wetherby, "I'm only here as a facilitator in any case." His idea of facilitating a meeting evidently being to stop it dead in its tracks.

After a good deal of hemming and hawing we went through my report then set another date to consider the 1987 document along with, perhaps, my job description. In the corridor three children went by singing "Jesus Loves Me."

The jarring ringing of the telephone brought me back to the present. Vera Eldridge no longer sounded like the scared mouse who had talked with me a few nights before.

"Axel, I've never complained when you played the hymns so fast that I couldn't get a breath between verses."

"I appreciate your forbearance."

"But this is too much."

"You sound upset, Vera."

"Henry's the one who's upset. He told me you'd come to visit him but wouldn't tell me what you said."

"I see." If Henry wasn't going to tell her I wasn't about to fan the flames.

"Henry's not a strong man, Axel, and you've got no business interfering in people's lives this way."

I attempted to explain but Vera would have none of it. "The church is paying you to make music," she interrupted, "not to bother God-fearing folk."

I tried to placate the woman as best I could and ended the conversation. As I drove to Jennifer's house I mused that Sam Spade never seemed to get complaints from spouses when he rattled the cages of suspects in Dashiell Hammett's novels.

At the carriage house on St. John's Sideroad Jennifer had prepared a late dinner of salad, green peas, and a casserole of spaghetti and leftover turkey that she called "turkhetti," followed by fruitcake from her maiden aunt in Clarion. I looked admiringly across the candlelit table at the girl in a cranberry ribbed sweater and gray woolen skirt and thought about how we might disport ourselves after dinner, but Jennifer wanted to hear details about my recent activities. I described my progress so far in trying to learn who had strong motives for John Armstrong's murder.

Jennifer frowned as she nibbled on a bit of fruitcake, then she said, "You know, you may want to try looking at this from the other end."

"Which end is that?"

"You know he was poisoned and you know what kind of poison was used. Now if the murderer can be caught by tracking down where the poison came from, the police will probably do that."

I observed that determining the availability of poison seemed to be the last step before James Bellinger was arrested.

"But you may be in a better position than they to ask the right questions, if you can think of them."

"What are you suggesting?"

"Why not start with trying to find out how the poison got into the glass?"

"You know, I saw that glass being put in place at the pulpit."

"How did it get there?"

"Carmody Talbot, one of the members of the Chancel Guild, brought it in on a tray."

"So she's probably somebody you want to talk to."

Then Jennifer asked whether I would give her a back massage, and the rest of the evening passed without further reference to troubles at Allegheny United Church.

CHAPTER 13

The church was filled to capacity for the funeral of John Armstrong on Saturday morning. The entire balcony area was occupied as well as all the pews in the nave, and ushers had been compelled to set up several rows of folding chairs in the narthex. During the organ prelude the worshippers observed a respectful silence except for one old woman, brought in from the Valhalla Retirement Center for the occasion, who insisted on telling her embarrassed escort the details of her recent gall bladder operation followed by the latest scandal involving one of the interns. The rest of the congregation alternately leaned back to block out the offending noise and forward to catch a fascinating tidbit, producing the ecclesiastical equivalent of the stadium "wave."

The late senior minister had, of course, planned the service down to the last detail, with every hymn and scripture reading chosen to suggest the passing of a potentate. Bud had wanted to offer a few remarks of regret on his brother's departure but the last wishes of the deceased overruled him and instead we heard a triumphal summary of John Armstrong's accomplishments followed by a maudlin recitation of his unfulfilled dreams.

At the reception in the Fellowship Room I found myself standing beside Harriett Bascomb, head of the Chancel Guild and the daughter of an Episcopalian Altar Guild head. Harriett had moved to the United Church in deference to her late husband's wishes but she retained her mother's unswerving allegiance to protocol beyond all other virtues and the members of the Chancel Guild trembled before her. Last year she single-handedly raised the money for new stained glass windows in defiance of an order from the Coordinating Committee, who wanted to keep all fund-raising activities under the aegis of the Stewardship Committee. Even John Armstrong would hesitate before taking her on directly.

Now she had lent her support to the Steeple People. The great hurricane of 1937, in addition to leveling much of the Meadowvale's tiny downtown area, knocked the steeple off the Allegheny United Church tower. For years a hardy band of sentimental souls had urged that it be restored, arguing that the cost of rebuilding the tower would be less in the long run than the perennial repairs due to improper drainage. The rest of the church never took the Steeple People seriously but with the backing of Harriett Bascomb they were suddenly a force to be reckoned with.

"I've just received good news, Axel," Harriett said, her eyes gleaming. "Bud Armstrong has just pledged the money to replace the steeple."

"I thought that was a pretty expensive undertaking," I said.

"Not for a new millionaire it isn't," she replied.

"Does that mean they're going to take down all those ropes and cables that have been lying around up on the roof for the annual repairs?"

"Water leaks are going to be a thing of the past," she announced triumphantly, and moved on to share the news with the other members of her team.

I glanced into the kitchen to see three small armies of women at their tasks. The reception was being catered by an aging group of United Church Women who specialized in funerals. It was becoming increasingly evident that their ranks would soon be so depleted by their own funerals that there would soon be no one left to carry on, but the group had handled this responsibility for so long, and with such a flair, that no one knew just how to institute a change. Each UCW group had its own character but none was more distinctive than these ladies, mostly from the South, who began their meetings not with a hymn or a prayer but by singing "Dixie." So far no one had the nerve to tell these daughters of the Confederacy that it was time to pass on the torch.

The second group was the Chancel Guild, cleaning up after the service itself. You could distinguish them by the white gloves that Harriett Bascomb insisted they wear whenever on duty. She didn't actually make them march, but in every other respect this was a highly drilled team. I looked for Carmody Talbot in their midst but was unable to locate her.

This was perhaps the last appearance by the third group, the apron-clad dishwashers. The debate over installing an electric dishwasher in the church kitchen had raged for years. One side argued in favor of the "fellowship" of washing dishes together, the other pointed out that it wasn't the "fellows" who actually had to wash the dishes. The senior minister, for his part, observed that more evil occurred in the kitchen than good in the pulpit, what with the gossip that flourished there during dishwashing. In the end the modernists prevailed and an industrial machine capable of completing an entire cycle in less than 90 seconds was due to be installed after the holidays.

CHAPTER 14

I tried telephoning Carmody Talbot but received no answer. I had barely laid the telephone down when Ralph Littlemore stormed into my office. The information I had learned in the past few days about his unscrupulous business dealings did nothing to endear him to me. Littlemore didn't appear to care much for me either, judging from his narrowed eyes and mean expression as he approached my desk.

"A lot of people in this church don't like you, Axel," he began. "They say you play the organ too loud and don't choose music they enjoy. I don't give a damn about that. As far as I'm concerned, that's your job and you do it."

"I appreciate your support."

"But when you start interfering in my business, that's something else. Henry's told me how you've been meddling in our affairs, and if it doesn't stop right now you can kiss this job good-bye."

I detest being shouted at, and in other circumstances I would have found some appeasing words just to get this angry man out of my office. But I thought that this time I might hold an edge.

"I'm glad you stopped in, Ralph," I said as calmly as I could manage, "because it saves me the trouble of finding you. I've been asked to look into John Armstrong's death, and the things I've learned in the past two days make you a strong suspect for murder."

"Why you little twerp!" Ralph's face went purple with rage. "How dare you talk to me like that?"

It took all my concentration to maintain a calm demeanor but I plunged ahead. "When John announced that the church was going to exercise its option on the Carruthers property—a move you'd been fighting for months in the Long-Range Planning Committee—you realized that you had to act before January 1 and so you poisoned him with home-grown rat bane."

"That's it!" Littlemore's emotions had turned to a cold fury. "You're going to wish you'd never set foot in this church." He spun on his heel and stalked out of the office, leaving the door open behind him.

I don't think I'd faced so much direct anger since the notorious Music Survey the first year I came to AUC. One hundred ninety people filled out the form that I inserted into the Easter morning bulletin, by far the largest response ever received to a questionnaire at Allegheny United Church. Though multiple check-offs sometimes produced percentages adding to more than 100, the results were clear enough: 66% liked the direction of the current music program, 22% didn't, 12% had no opinion, 75% liked to learn new hymns, 21% didn't, 62% liked classical organ music, 61% preferred medleys of old hymns. Two things emerged from the exercise: people felt very strongly about music in their church; and nobody agreed on what that music should be like. Unable to please everybody, I decided at least to please myself, and so continued to follow the repertoire of great organ and choral music that had so distressed Abigail Farmer.

But Ian Wetherby told me that he had opposed my appointment from the start. "This man is going to tear the congregation in two," he told the members of the Music Committee who had conducted the search for a new music director. From the looks of the survey, the congregation was deeply divided even before my arrival, and I wasn't sure how to mend the divisions.

I was about to grab a quick lunch at the restaurant across the street when the telephone rang.

"I have wonderful news," came a familiar voice: the mother of the bride. Perhaps the wedding had been cancelled? No such luck.

"Karen's old roommate from college is going to be able to come after all."

"That's nice," I said, utterly confused.

"She was supposed to be away on business but they got finished earlier than expected and she just flew in this morning."

"Well."

"Anyway, she'd like to sing a solo at the wedding."

I tried to explain that it was customary to rehearse before giving a performance.

"Never mind that. I'm sure she knows the music. This way she can be seen."

"I'm sorry?"

"We'd already set up the bridesmaids and groom's attendants. We couldn't add her now because her dress wouldn't match and besides the numbers wouldn't be even."

I guessed that made a certain amount of sense. From the office window I could see children sledding on a bit of snow that the shade had protected and rather wished I were out with them rather than in here.

"Don't you see? This will give her an opportunity to show off her dress."

"But I thought ..."

"You know, for a church organist, you sure don't understand much about weddings."

I made no demurral but agreed to meet with the late addition to the program a few minutes before beginning the organ prelude.

CHAPTER 15

When you play upwards of fifteen weddings a year you tend to forget all but the most remarkable. Merely to have the bride reserve the church for one hour and print another on the invitation doesn't produce a really memorable occasion, though it does cause a fair amount of confusion. The couple who brought in a pair of friends with guitars and amplifiers to perform an air-headed country-and-western number will happily soon be forgotten, along with the bride and groom who gave each other high-fives instead of a kiss while the congregation whistled and cheered with vulgar abandon. (The senior minister was inspired to call his next sermon, "A High Five for God," in a service that featured a kitchen sink and a toilet paraded across the chancel to advertise the Fall Bazaar. At least the Episcopalians have liturgy as a last line of defense against the incursions of TV mentality; AUC embraces secularity with open arms.)

But I shan't soon forget the August wedding in which a soloist, untrained but enthusiastic, sang the recessional march. Perhaps march isn't quite the operative term, though the bride and groom did make their exit at this point. Maybe bossa nova would be more appropriate. You know the rhythm. Actually, you might recognize the tune, too, a snappy, upbeat number by Beethoven, sometimes called the Ode to Joy. The soloist's score gave no such attribution, listing only "Spanish Lyrics and Music by Orbe-Waldo de los Rios". So a thin but sincere soprano voice bleated out the English text, "Come sing a song of joy, of freedom tell the story." Earlier in the ceremony, while the bride and groom signed the register, this same soprano offered the words "As it was in the beginning , is now and till the end, woman draws her life from man and gives it back again," leaving the listener to choose whether to be offended more by the sexist sentiment or the false rhyme.

I may hate to play this stuff, but I don't have to be embarrassed by it. If they insist on sentiment, I'll serve it up with the treacle fairly dripping. My rendition of Orbe-Waldo de los Rios' magnum opus lacked only maracas.

On Saturday afternoon, Sarah Beasley gave me a nervous little wave from the hallway before entering the chancel to begin the ceremony. I could never fully comprehend Sarah's fear of performing weddings. Morbidly frightened of forgetting her lines, she had even consulted a professional therapist and adopted her suggestion of keeping a copy of the text in her hand at all times, to no avail. If the bride or groom were nervous, they had nothing on the poor minister.

Yet she had provided wise counsel to many a young person, both here and in her previous churches. In one sermon she recounted the story of a teenager in a tiny town who wanted to get married. Sarah suggested that she wait until she'd had a chance to go to college and see something of the world. The girl had looked up at her in disbelief and asked, "But why would anyone want to leave Dillsburg?"

Most professional actors hate working with children and animals, knowing that they will inevitably be upstaged. Despite the advance planning by her mother, this afternoon's bride hadn't foreseen the error of being preceded by both a flower girl and a ring-bearer, each so abominably cute that the bride herself seemed like a superfluous after-thought.

Sarah somehow managed to get through the ceremony without a misplaced word and maintained her aplomb even when the best man presented her with the two rings still stapled in place in the presentation box. And she didn't even trouble to clear her throat when the groom, instead of giving the bride the traditional peck at the appropriate point in the service, put his arms around her and pinned her body to his for a prolonged soul kiss.

Ben Van Dyk, a cousin of the groom, came into my office after the ceremony before heading on to the reception. "Mae told me you'd been asking questions about Ralph Litttlemore and Bud Armstrong and I thought you might be interested in a link between them."

"I'm all ears."

"Have you ever wondered how Bud supports himself?"

"Mae said he takes odd jobs and lives in the trailer that his brother gave him."

"Would you say that he looks like a bum?"

"Torn sneakers, faded jeans, a T-shirt that reads 'Redneck and lovin' it,' a stolen biker jacket: I'd say that 'bum' pretty well sums it up."

"It gets better," Ben went on. "He gets paid to dress like that. Bud Armstrong isn't just a bum, he's a professional bum."

"I don't get it."

"Here's the way it works. Suppose you're a realtor. You pick a neighborhood that you want to flip, you install Bud into a vacant house, or else you buy a house at well above its market value and put Bud into it. Bud never acts antagonistic or confrontational—it's impossible to get him into an argument—but he tosses beer cans over the neighbor's fence, plays country-and-western music late at night and parks a rusty pick-up truck in the driveway. You avoid people who might know the town by-laws well enough to put a quick end to the shenanigans, but you're a pretty shrewd judge of character and you know who can be intimidated."

"What happens then?"

"Bud just gets worse and worse until one of the neighbors decides to sell. This is where you use your gimmick: 'Buy this house and I'll buy yours for cash.' Once they consider selling, it's easy to get them out. You may intimate that one of Bud's friends will be occupying the house next door and soon other nervous homeowners on the street decide that perhaps it's time for them to sell, too."

"But it's hard for them to get a good price."

"Right. Bud has a special routine for when people come to visit houses in the neighborhood, so the victim isn't likely to get an offer from another agent and will gladly settle for your low bid. After a few people have left and you've bought the houses, you move Bud out, do a little bit of upgrading and soon you can sell the houses at a much higher price for a tidy profit."

"What a great racket."

"Now for Bud, it's all a game, like 'treat or treat.' He's actually a pretty gentle guy, despite his intimidating size. But you dress him up like one of the Hell's Angels and let's say you give him a motorcycle along with the pick-up. He just sits drinking beer on his patio in a sleeveless T-shirt that reveals a tattoo of a snake on his arm. It's a fake, but it's persuasive."

"I'm impressed." I heard cheering from outside the church and concluded that the bride and groom must have finished their post-ceremony photo shoot and retired to their limousine for the three-block trip to the wedding reception.

"Now who do you suppose would think up an operation like this?"

"Ralph Littlemore?"

"You got it."

"And here I thought he'd decided to go legit when he came to Meadowvale."

"Are you kidding? That guy couldn't draw a straight line from A to B if you gave him a ruler."

I wasn't sure how this gave Bud a motive for murdering his brother, but it helped explain Ralph's rage at my interest in his operations. I let Ben get to his reception and I went home.

For once I'd been able to come to the office on foot and I was relieved not to have to drive through the center of town on a Saturday afternoon. Meadowvale's main street also served as a state highway, still heavily traveled despite the construction of the interstate several miles to the west. Whenever anyone proposed using the parking lanes to enlarge the road, local merchants claimed that such a move would put them out of business. Whenever the town council tried to consider building a bypass the developers, who essentially took the place of city planners in Meadowvale, nixed the incursion on their domain. As a result, every weekend the single traffic light in the center of town caused enormous line-ups in each direction.

On foot I could appreciate Meadowvale's menagerie at sunset: the whimsical bronze cats that a local sculptor had added to the tiny park near the church, the spooky metal birds, praying mantises and frogs on sale, but seldom sold, in the same artist's studio, and the placid snow-covered stone lions at the memorial near the Roman Catholic Church.

At the town's main intersection a bit of debris still remained from the latest accident. Scarcely a month went by without a fender bender at this spot. For some reason the traffic lights permitted a protected left turn in only one direction and varied that direction depending on the time of day. Impatient drivers, seeing that they weren't going to be given an opportunity to turn safely, turned when they could, and fragments of glass, plastic and metal in the middle of the road bore witness to their folly.

As I walked I thought about my situation at Allegheny United Church and the contrast between the adversarial relationship I'd had with John Armstrong and Ian Wetherby and my monthly ordeals with the Worship Committee, and the cheerful, collegial relationship I enjoyed with Sarah Beasley and Mae Nolan. Perhaps I'd invited confrontation by taking such a strong position on what church music should be when I first took the job. I wanted everyone to be clear about where I stood. I remembered Jennifer's advice, "Doing a job is pretty simple, Axel. You find out what your boss wants and then you do it." Perhaps that was the problem: I didn't regard this as a job but as a vocation. Then I thought back to the words of the president of the American Organ Guild, a man I knew and respected: "I don't think I would last a day in a place like that." What did it say about me that I'd managed to survive four years at AUC?

I turned the corner toward home and saw the sunset in all its glory, not an overwhelming Big Sky sunset this evening but an array of horizontal streaks of orange and purple between narrow bands of cloud. I stopped and watched for a few moments as the colors turned darker in shade and then faded. "Thank you, Lord," I muttered under my breath and proceeded on my way. "You choose your focus," a photographer friend once told me. Her words referred to holding on in a difficult relationship but applied as well to finding beauty in a community seemingly bent on extending ugliness.

I suppose I shouldn't have been surprised that Jennifer didn't feel like talking the case over with me. Instead she sent me out for a pizza and a video, "something romantic and Christmasy," she suggested. I returned with Cary Grant and Katherine Hepburn in "Holiday." We put on pajamas, turned on the gas fireplace, and pretended we were snowbound.

CHAPTER 16

When I turned on the organ Sunday morning I was greeted by a cipher: not a cute, furry creature but a persistent note that wouldn't go
away. I climbed up into the organ chamber, grateful that we'd persuaded the Visual Arts Committee to cease storing all their off-season
decorations in the entry way, and cautiously made my way along the
ranks of pipes until I came upon the offending note. I didn't have the
expertise to repair the problem but by removing the pipe from its hole I
could prevent it from disrupting the service until the organ tuner had a
chance to come and address the situation properly. I was grateful that
this unpredictable glitch had come today and not on Christmas Eve.

The entire Senior Choir was present except for Susan Scollard, and
they acquitted themselves well in singing "In Thee Is Gladness," in English. Happily Bach's organ setting of "In dir ist Freude" didn't require
translation, though it would have been more impressive if we'd had a
decent rank of reeds in the pedal.

After the service I was on my way to a rehearsal with the Junior Choir
when Trish McConnell, Susan Scollard's best friend, expressed concern
over the girl's absence. Susan had a lovely pure soprano voice and had
sung several songs of Stephen Foster, Pittsburgh's local musical hero, at
the Strawberry Sunday last spring. She seldom missed a rehearsal, but
singers often had commitments around the Christmas holidays.

"She didn't show up for Christmas Eve or for Thursday night's rehearsal," Trish persisted.

"Perhaps she's visiting her family over the holidays," I suggested.

"Ordinarily she would tell me if she were going out of town," Trish
countered.

"I'm sure it's nothing to worry about," I said. "She'll probably be back
after New Year's."

"I would agree with you except for something Susan said before
Christmas." Trish sounded genuinely worried.

"What's that?"

"A lot of her co-workers were upset because they didn't get a Christmas bonus this year. Susan had been planning to use hers to take a winter vacation in a warm climate. She told me she'd taken steps to get
back at her boss and when she told him about it at the office party, he'd
been really angry, so she felt vindicated."

"Where does Susan work?"

"Rutledge Realty."

"I still think she's probably out of town, but if she doesn't come to the next rehearsal, I'll give her a call." I don't think Trish was entirely relieved.

The Junior Choir rehearsal after the service was what you might expect when you give thirty five- to ten-year-olds a sudden infusion of sugar. It wasn't candy canes this time but goodies from the Teeners bake sale. The Teeners had been acting a bit weird ever since Teen Confirmation Sunday got messed up last spring. Allegheny United Church has trouble finding places on the calendar not just for liturgical celebrations but for the far more important quasi-religious occasions such as Mother's Day, Boy Scout Sunday, or Sunday school Recognition Day, which this year managed to pre-empt Transfiguration Sunday altogether.

There just don't seem to be enough Sundays to go around. The crunch comes at the end of the year. Teen Confirmation Sunday was booked fully a year in advance in order to avoid the problems that occurred last time when a change in schedule meant that several kids couldn't attend because of family commitments. But Senior Citizens Sunday had to be at one end or the other of National Senior Citizens Week. Why couldn't it be put forward a week? Because that was Father's Day Sunday and the senior citizens wanted a Sunday of their own. It got worse. The Choir Reunion & Church Picnic never made it onto the official calendar at all but was allowed to roll about like a loose cannon. When the Church Picnic finally came to rest on the first Sunday in June, it displaced the carefully scheduled Teen Confirmation Sunday and the whole calendar went haywire.

Fortunately I had two choir parents helping with crowd control, so after we'd practiced pieces for the following Sunday and sung "Happy Birthday" to Noël Stanton, I accepted requests from the kids for favorite songs from our repertoire. Cassie suggested "If You're Happy and You Know It (Clap Your Hands)" and after that came requests for "Happy Wanderer" and "The Johnny Appleseed Song." (I drew the line at "Little Rabbit Foofoo.")

I really enjoyed working with these kids. In the fall they had rehearsed a dozen pieces from a *Songs for Kids* book put together by the Music Committee then given up a Saturday morning to record them. We combined the booklet and cassette into a package which became a favorite stocking-stuffer item at the Christmas Bazaar. The congregation enjoyed the Junior Choir, too, and their applause at each appearance of the ensemble had led to many a wrangle in the Worship Committee. I tried to think of something special for the Junior Choir each month. In September they had taken turns ringing the church bell at the beginning of the service. In October we gave them a Halloween Party and in November I had taken them up into the organ to take a look at the pipes, at least all of them who dared climb the tall ladder into the organ chamber.

"Hello, Mr. Crochet," Parmalee Houghton called from behind a long folding table where only a few lonely pastries remained. "Would you like to buy a cupcake?" I wondered how such a childlike voice could come out of such a whalelike body.

"Perhaps another time, Parmalee," I said.

"It's for a really good cause. We're raising money to send kids to camp." She'd traded in her white sheet for a tent of a dress but I recalled the image of a haloed hippo from Christmas Eve. No one knows what angels really look like but I had to hope they didn't like look like Parmalee Houghton.

"You mean poor children from the city?" I asked.

"No," Parmalee frowned as if someone had just passed gas. "One of the kids from this congregation. After all the money has been collected, we draw lots for it."

"That's nice," I said as I continued toward my office, thinking of the Roman soldiers who cast lots for Jesus' mantle.

After the rehearsal I tried again to reach Carmody Talbot and learned that she was away visiting her aunt. Then Sarah Beasley appeared to summon me to a special meeting.

CHAPTER 17

When the Sunday school Superintendent moved her office downstairs next to the classrooms, a space opened up in the main hallway containing the church office, and the offices of the Minister of Christian Education, the associate minister and the senior minister. Between church meetings and rentals to outside groups the room was in constant use, but no one had come up with an appropriate name for it. Some called it the meeting room, some the Upper Room, some just "the other room."

A mural depicting a bearded, benevolent, decidedly Caucasian Jesus doing good works and performing miracles decorated one wall. The long table topped with plastic veneer, the chrome seats lightly padded in green or red, the gray industrial carpet and the overhead fluorescent lamp could have come from any office. To this room Lewis Hartley assembled a few key leaders of the church to an extraordinary meeting: Ian Wetherby, chair of Ministry and Personnel and a representative of the Long-Range Planning Committee; Harriett Bascomb, head of the Chancel Guild; Stan Rutledge, chair of the Finance Committee; David Moore, the church treasurer; Frances Whelan, Minister of Christian Education; Sarah Beasley, recently named "acting head minister," and myself as music director.

"I'm not going to trouble you with all the details of John Armstrong's will," Lewis began in his resonant voice. "The bulk of his estate naturally goes to Mrs. Armstrong, including the house, the car, and a small annuity. You may also be aware that the church maintained a substantial life insurance policy on the senior minister with his wife as beneficiary. These details needn't concern us here."

"Then why bother mentioning them?" David Moore whispered in my left ear.

"However there is one aspect of the will that has a direct bearing on the administration of this church and it is for that reason that I have asked you to come here today."

"Can't he talk plain English?" Sarah Beasley whispered in my right ear.

"As it happens, the terms of the Rev. Armstrong's will are presented in fractional proportions of the estate rather than in fixed dollar figures. According to the terms of the will, subject to certain stipulations, the senior minister has left 25% of his estate to Allegheny United Church."

"What does that come to in dollars?" asked Ian Wetherby, who whistled when Hartley pronounced the figure.

"That's a lot of money," said Stan Rutledge, who had a genius for stating the obvious as if it were some great discovery.

"Evidently old man Armstrong had been looking out for John's welfare without his knowledge," Lewis explained.

"Let's hear the stipulations," said Harriett Bascomb, always wary.

"The will specifies," Lewis went on, "that the church will receive the money only under the following conditions: first, that the entire proceeds from the next church bazaar and silent auction be donated to the Salvation Army for the purpose of supplying clothing to the poor; second, that any properties to which the church currently holds title shall be donated to the town of Meadowvale with the proviso that the land be used for low-income housing; third, that any monies collected for the purpose of restoring the physical plant of the church be disbursed through the local Food Bank."

A stunned silence followed the completion of the list as each leader calculated the effect of these stipulations on his or her fiefdom. "There is one last pertinent section that I should perhaps read to you," Lewis continued, "though you are probably already familiar with it."

"'Then the righteous will answer him, "Lord, when was it that we saw you hungry and gave you food, or thirsty and gave you something to drink? And when was it that we saw you a stranger and welcomed you, or naked and gave you clothing? And when was it that we saw you sick or in prison and visited you?" And the king will answer them, "Truly I tell you, just as you did it to one of the least of these who are members of my family, you did it to me."' (Matthew 25: 37-40)"

"Now hold on just one minute here," said Stan Rutledge, evidently the fastest thinker of the lot. "The proceeds from the bazaar normally go to the national church for the Mission and Service fund. If we give the money to help local poor people, how are we going to meet our M&S commitment?"

Ian Wetherby chimed in, "We can't give up that property: it's intended for the new parking lot."

"What property?" asked Harriett Bascomb, incredulous that there might be some detail of church business to which she was not privy.

"Two years ago the town passed an eminent domain resolution to build a sidewalk along Tyler Street," Ian explained with a slightly guilty expression on his face. "Ever since, nobody has wanted to buy the houses on that street, so as they've come on the market, the church has quietly purchased them in order to tear them down and put in a proper parking lot."

"Wait a minute," interjected Frances Whelan, "We were counting on converting at least one of those houses into Sunday school classrooms."

Harriett Bascomb didn't let her finish before demanding, "That restoration clause—does it apply to funds collected to date or only before John Armstrong's death?"

"What's that all about?" whispered Sarah Beasley.

"She's thinking of the steeple replacement," I told her. "Before John died, she'd only collected a few thousand dollars, but yesterday Bud pledged an amount sufficient to cover the whole job. I don't see Harriett letting that go without a fight."

"Does this fall into the current fiscal year?" asked David Moore. "I just finished closing the books."

"Sounds as if we're the only ones who aren't upset by the announcement," I commented to Sarah.

"Does this feel familiar?" she responded, "The iron hand of John Armstrong controlling the church even from beyond the grave."

"I especially liked that phrase, 'The king shall answer them.'"

In the confusion of voices that ensued I could make out only disjointed phrases. Lewis Hartley finally restored order by announcing that under the circumstances he thought it appropriate to ask Coordinating to appoint a special committee to study the situation and its ramifications in detail. As I left the room I thought of T.S. Eliot's poem, "The Difficulties of a Statesman": "The first thing to do is to form the committees: the consultative councils, the standing committees, select committees and sub-committees. One secretary will do for several committees." Unfortunately I wasn't in a position to follow the advice at the end of the poem: "Resign, resign, resign." Instead I drove to the city with Jennifer for dinner and a play at the Pittsburgh Public Theater.

CHAPTER 18

Monday morning I found a note under the door of my duplex from the realty company that owns the building informing me that my lease had been cancelled. Ralph Littlemore didn't utter idle threats. I left a message for Lewis Hartley, asking what I should do, then finally got in touch with Carmody Talbot, who invited me to her house.

Unlike the newer developments with their tiny saplings protected by fences and anchored to the ground with cables, the old section of Meadowvale was graced by distinguished tall trees arching benevolently over the streets. Carmody Talbot lived in an attractive brick house with a porch on two sides. As I pulled into her driveway I could see an old inner tube still hanging from a tree in the backyard, a reminder of children long since departed from the nest. The remnants of a snowman could be seen in the yard next door, its carrot nose jauntily challenging the sun to do its worst. In Carmody's front lawn the snow remained untouched.

The widow Talbot, her hair done up in a neat bun, her dress a seasonal green with red holly-berry accents, was one of those people who try so hard to put you at your ease that you end up feeling thoroughly uncomfortable. I could easily imagine her nervousness as a new member of the Chancel Guild trying to avoid making a mistake in front of the intimidating Harriett Bascomb.

She invited me into her living room, a testimonial to the transforming power of Christmas. Every surface not already covered with framed photographs of family members bore a painted porcelain Santa, an oversize red candle, a sprig of holly, or a glass globe that produced a miniature snowstorm when inverted. A red crepe paper streamer pinned with Christmas cards outlined the archway leading to the dining room. While Mrs. Talbot prepared tea and coffee cake I recalled her role in last spring's Strawberry Sunday.

Remember the old Strawberry Social, where folks would gather at the church for ice cream and strawberries while a strolling barbershop quartet in white slacks, red-and-white-striped jackets and bowler hats would provide entertainment, perhaps with the odd banjo as a change of pace? I thought it might be fun to have a Strawberry Social at Allegheny United Church and figured that the hard job would be teaching the choir forty-five minutes of show tunes and for me to find time to get forty-five minutes of Joplin and Gershwin into my fingers.

I was wrong. That was the easy part. The hard part was the food. "Strawberry Sunday," as we billed it, was scheduled for the last Sunday in May and fresh strawberries don't appear in these parts before late June. And did you say ice cream? "Who's going to scoop ice cream for all those people? And what if it melts?" came the protests from the United Church Women.

So we followed AUC procedure for dealing with any situation by forming a committee, headed by Carmody Talbot, which experimented with four possible desserts—strawberry shortcake, strawberry crepes, strawberries on sponge cake and another concoction I have difficulty describing—by trying them out on the Senior Choir one Thursday evening after rehearsal to general satisfaction. In keeping with the United Church philosophy of inclusiveness the committee decided to serve all four desserts at the event. They transformed the social hall with strawberry mobiles, streamers and baskets of flowers and 130 people enjoyed Strawberry Sunday.

After we had finished our repast, I asked Carmody to describe the preparations for Holy Communion on Christmas Eve.

"Well let's see. First we had to estimate the bread cubes. You figure maybe two hundred and fifty for a normal Sunday but this being Christmas Eve we had to estimate a good deal higher."

"Uh-huh."

"Then somebody poured the minister's water glass and Harriett asked me to take it to the pulpit."

"How did you know it was the minister's water glass."

"It was precisely three quarters full."

"Why was that?"

Then I saw something I hadn't observed recently, a sixty-year-old woman blushing. "Well you see, it all started last summer when one of the other Chancel Guild members filled the glass to the brim. I don't know whether I should be telling you this," she actually giggled. "The Rev. Armstrong reached for the glass and spilled the water right in the middle of his sermon on Onan spilling his seed. Of course everybody laughed but the Rev. Armstrong didn't think it was at all funny. So the word went down that we were never to fill his glass more than three quarters full."

In the hallway the grandfather clock I had passed on the way in sounded the hour in sonorous tones. It occurred to me that this clock might be Carmody's only companion in the house, for I had seen no sign of any pets. One might have thought that such an intrusive reminder of the passage of time would be disconcerting for a woman in the twilight of her life; then again, perhaps she took comfort in its imperturbable regularity.

"Okay. Now when I saw you near the pulpit the glass was on a tray," I continued.

"Well of course. That's the way Harriett told us to do it."

"Let's get back to the kitchen for a moment. You picked up the glass and put it on the tray."

"Oh, no. I couldn't do that. You see I already had the bread container in my other hand."

"Then how did the glass get onto the tray."

"Mr. Bellinger was in the kitchen preparing the grape juice containers and he put it on the tray for me."

And put his fingerprints on the glass. At last this was beginning to make sense. I had begun my organ prelude at 7:45 and saw Carmody, white gloves and all, put the glass at the pulpit a few minutes later. At that point Henry Eldridge was up in the balcony helping Bud Armstrong with his father's wheelchair, so both of them would seem to be in the clear, but Bellinger and Littlemore were still viable suspects. I thanked Carmody for her help and for the coffee cake and was about to depart when she took my arm and asked whether I'd be willing to listen to a musical suggestion.

"What did you have in mind?" I asked.

"I think you should organize an old-fashioned hymn sing," she said.

"A hymn sing?"

"That's right. It would be a chance for us to sing all the old hymns that we never seem to sing on Sundays. Why don't you ever choose the old hymns?"

"The minister picks the hymns, Carmody; I just play them."

"Well there are a lot of good old hymns."

"Did you have a particular piece in mind?"

"Do you know 'The Little Brown Church in the Vale?'"

I confessed that I hadn't sung that hymn since I was in grade school and asked whether she had a copy of the music. Carmody instantly produced a faded volume of "Songs Americans Love to Sing" that she said had belonged to her grandmother. Whether out of gratitude for her help on the case or in the spirit of the season I agreed to sit down at the piano and sing it with her right then and there. Carmody hadn't sung in the

Senior Choir for years but the venerable hymn evoked her former musical skills and she belted out the refrain with an enthusiasm that belied her years.

As I drove back to the church I speculated that a hymn sing might not be a bad idea. For once we wouldn't have to worry about conflicting opinions. We could just put out a suggestion box and sing the hymns that got the most votes. I filed the idea away for future reference.

CHAPTER 19

Ben Van Dyk phoned to say that the police had interviewed one of James Bellinger's associates at the Acura dealership. It seems Bellinger had described in detail how he'd like to kill Armstrong after learning the identity of his wife's supposed lover, though the weapon mentioned had been a tire iron. An arrest was expected soon, as the ring of circumstantial evidence closed tighter.

Then Lewis Hartley called. "I've talked to the attorney for the realty company that owns your building, Axel, and I think your lease is safe."

"Thank goodness for that."

"But Axel, ... I'm not sure exactly how to put this."

"Yes?"

"You really don't want Ralph Littlemore for an enemy. The law is obviously on your side but, not to put too fine a point on it, that hasn't always prevented Ralph from reaching his objective."

"What do you think he might do?"

"Do you play poker, Axel?"

"I know how the game works but I can't say I'm a big fan."

"But at least you understand the phrase 'raise the ante'?"

"Certainly."

"Then you know how disconcerting it can be to face an opponent who has no apparent limits?"

"Yes."

"Ralph Littlemore is such an opponent."

I told Lewis I would try to be careful and thanked him for his help. Abigail Farmer called to thank me for choosing one of her favorite hymns at Sunday's service. I reminded her that I don't choose the hymns and she asked me whether the Junior Choir couldn't stand with the tallest singers in the middle and the others arranged by descending order of height on either side, since it bothered her to see a short person standing beside a tall one. I told her I'd think about it.

The Episcopal churches with which I'd been involved had different problems: the choirmaster who became too friendly with the choirboys; the gay priest who moved his partner into the rectory; the divorced priest who took up with an 18-year-old girl, moved her into the rectory and then married her. By contrast, there was no sex in the United Church, just energetic committees and captious busybodies with too much time on their hands.

The phone rang again. This time it was Shirley Bellinger.

"The police have been around to question James again. I'm really getting worried."

"And your husband still won't consider getting a lawyer?"

"He's awfully stubborn, Axel."

"Well, I think we may have some good news for you soon. The evidence that I've gathered points pretty strongly toward Ralph Littlemore." I explained Littlemore's connections with Henry Eldridge and Bud Armstrong, his access to the poison, and his compelling motive. "All I really need now is someone who saw him in the church kitchen after the early service on Christmas Eve."

There was a long silence at the other end of the line and I began to wonder whether Shirley had hung up on me. Then she spoke in a very quiet tone. "Axel, it wasn't Ralph."

"You think everything I've just told you is wrong?"

"Ralph may be a crook, but he didn't murder John Armstrong."

"How can you be so sure?"

"He came with me right after the early service."

"I don't follow."

"Axel, Ralph is the man I've been sleeping with, not John Armstrong."

"But why did you tell your husband ..."

"Because I know Ralph. I was afraid that if James confronted him he might kill him."

I guess I could understand why Shirley, finding herself stuck in a monotonous marriage with James Bellinger might look elsewhere for a bit of excitement, but couldn't she do better than Ralph Littlemore? Maybe she saw something in the man that I couldn't. If she were telling the truth, my investigation was far from over. I thanked her for calling and told her I'd let her know if I discovered anything new.

Monday evening was my turn to cook and a venerable crock-pot had been laboring in the kitchen the entire day on my behalf. A simple salad, a bottle of wine, and we were in business. Over dinner I filled Jennifer in on what I had learned, explaining how James Bellinger's fingerprints had appeared on the fatal water glass.

"Unfortunately, that doesn't make him innocent," I concluded.

"What you really need is a better picture of just who was in the kitchen on Christmas Eve," Jennifer said.

"You don't understand how that church operates," I said. "There were probably a couple of dozen people in and out of the kitchen what with preparations for communion."

"Is it all that complicated just to put on a church service?"

"It is at AUC. Their motto seems to be never to let one person do something if you can involve five instead."

"So who would have been there?"

"First you have the Chancel Guild. Now most United Churches don't make a big thing of this, but Harriett Bascomb comes from the Episcopalian tradition of the Altar Guild, and everything had to be just so."

I described the Sunday of my audition. As I played the organ prelude one of the Chancel Guild members entered from the left, walked to the altar, and moved the flower arrangement a half inch to the right. A few minutes later a different woman came in from the right, walked to the altar, and moved the flower arrangement a quarter of an inch to the left.

"So we've got a lot of Altar Guild ladies scurrying around. Who else?" Jennifer asked.

"In the Episcopal Church the congregation comes forward one by one to sip wine from a common chalice."

"Sounds pretty unsanitary to me," Jennifer said.

"That's the way the United Church feels about it," I explained. "Instead they use tiny glasses filled with grape juice."

"I thought they were supposed to be re-enacting the Last Supper. Don't tell me Jesus drank grape juice," she said.

"Nobody has ever given me a good theological explanation, but that's the way they do it."

"I'm beginning to get the picture," Jennifer said. "With a common chalice you just fill the thing with wine and let the people come to you. If you have to furnish several hundred individual glasses, it's going to take a bunch of people to carry them, even if they are tiny."

"Exactly. And I guess because of the weight, carrying the metal containers full of glasses has always been the responsibility of the ushers."

"Which explains what James Bellinger was doing in the kitchen."

"Not just him. There would have to be two or three other men to carry all the containers upstairs."

"Anybody else?"

"You also have the United Church Women's group putting cookies and squares on plates for the reception after the service. And since the kitchen is the social heart of the church, you could have had any number of other people just passing through, asking whether they could help but really just looking for an opportunity to chat."

"No wonder the kitchen is so big."

"And out of that crowd, I have to figure out who poured the poison into John Armstrong's water glass. As of this moment, all my suspects have been eliminated except for James Bellinger, the man I'm trying to clear."

"Is there any chance he could really have done it, after all?" Jennifer asked.

"That's what I'm beginning to ask myself," I said. Had Shirley's desperate request on Christmas Day just been an act? More than once I've been called naïve, and I don't mind erring on the side of trusting people, but I didn't like playing the fool if this was all just some kind of charade.

CHAPTER 20

I greeted Stan Rutledge, the chairperson of the Finance Committee, who was leaving the church office as I arrived Tuesday morning.

"Nice day for New Years Eve, Stan," I said.

"Three hundred fifty seven more days until Christmas," he responded brightly.

Rutledge oversaw the church's sizeable endowment fund, much of which had been invested in a local real estate company, presumably a prudent choice given the booming market in the Meadowvale region. There were some who thought he could be getting the church a better return for its dollar, but on the whole it was thought better to err on the side of caution. I had intended to ask him about Susan Scollard but he said that he was in a hurry to get home, what with his brother visiting over the holidays.

But her name came up soon enough. David Moore was busily revising the church's end-of-year financial statement in a little alcove off the main office and he'd evidently been awaiting my arrival.

"Axel, can you tell me how I can reach Susan Scollard?"

"I think she may be out of town. She was absent on Christmas Eve and again on Sunday, and she didn't come to the rehearsal on Thursday night."

"She had some disturbing things to say when she came to see me just before Christmas. You understand that this is in confidence."

"Of course."

"According to Susan, Stan Rutledge has been using church funds in an irregular fashion."

"How do you mean?"

"It's a little complicated. We knew that he was putting the bulk of the church's endowment money into a real estate company, but according to Susan he owns the company himself."

"But where's the problem? If he does well, so does the church."

"That's not exactly the way it worked, as she reported it. Apparently Stan would invest in some fairly risky speculative schemes. If they panned out, he'd take the lion's share of the profits. If they failed, he'd write it off as a loss to the church."

"So that's why the church's net profit always seemed so modest. I thought he was just investing judiciously."

"I imagine that's what a lot of people thought. Anyway, I plan to check out her story, but I was hoping to get a few more details before I proceeded. For example, if Stan had so little imagination, where was he getting the information on these speculative deals?"

"Sounds as if he had someone feeding him leads."

Our conversation was broken by the arrival of Gladys Pinkham who popped in to suggest adding "a young woman in her 70's" to the list of recipients for the church's floral arrangements. The interruption gave me a chance to reflect that the situation could be a good deal more serious than our treasurer imagined.

"How many people know about Susan's story?" I asked David when Gladys had departed.

"I don't know how many people she told, but I haven't mentioned it to anyone but you," he replied.

"Her friend Trish McConnell evidently knew Susan had something up her sleeve, but I don't think she had any of the details." I was trying to reconcile this new picture of Stan Rutledge, speculator, with the rather boring plodder that I knew from committee meetings. "So Stan inherited his position as the church's investment counselor along with the family business?"

"That's right. Tyrone Rutledge was a legend in Meadowvale real estate, building up a huge network of satisfied clients, and eventual repeat customers, through hard work and an impeccable reputation for integrity. I haven't heard anything one way or another about Stan."

David took a long drink of water from a plastic bottle and I kidded him about avoiding the trip to the kitchen.

"It isn't that. Those women in the kitchen are so efficient that the minute you put a glass down they've washed it and put it away."

"Aren't you exaggerating a bit?"

"Not at all. On Christmas Eve, for example, I poured myself a glass of water, took a drink of it, turned to exchange pleasantries with James Bellinger, and when I went to pick up the glass, it was gone. I guess I'm better off carrying my own."

"How much of the water did you say you drank?"

"Oh I don't know. Maybe a quarter of a glass. But you have to drink eight full glasses a day to keep your body from drying out."

"Was Stan Rutledge there, too?"

"I don't recall. No, wait a minute. Sure, he was down on the floor taking measurements for the new dishwasher. I remember, he informed me that it would sure speed things up."

Suddenly the image of Christmas Eve in the church kitchen spun 180 degrees and I found myself looking at it from the other side. Suppose Harriett had seen David Moore's glass on the counter, three-quarters full according to her protocol. She would have told Carmody Talbot to take it up to the pulpit. The inexperienced Carmody, trying to carry two things at once, had asked James Bellinger's assistance in putting the glass on her tray then had taken it up to the pulpit. Suppose the poison was already in the glass at that point. Then the intended victim might not have been John Armstrong at all, but David Moore.

David turned pale when I shared my thoughts with him. Then he recovered and said, "I guess I can imagine the possibility of Stan Rutledge scamming the church, but it's hard to picture him as a murderer."

"There may be someone else involved," I said. "But if we're looking at this the right way, both you and Susan are in real danger."

"You mean Stan might try again?"

"Look at it from his point of view. The wrong man died on Christmas Eve, and no one suspects him. On the other hand, you're still alive and you represent a threat to him. He's counting on you to be cautious and methodical about checking out Susan's story, but he needs to act fast. He can't very well come over to your house and ask to pour poison in your water glass. I don't suppose he put anything in your bottle when he was here just now?"

"It was capped the whole time," David said with a nervous glance at the container.

"As things stand, we don't have a bit of proof, and we're not likely to find any unless Stan tries again."

"What am I supposed to do? Wait around until I'm poisoned?"

"Tonight. The family New Years Eve party. Most of the church community will be here. I'll watch Stan and perhaps we can catch him in the act."

"You mean you want me to act as a staked goat?"

"As long as you don't drink anything you'll be fine. You don't imagine Stan is going to bring a gun or a knife to the party, do you?"

"You're probably right. He's not a very imaginative man. He'll probably try to go with what he knows. But won't you be in danger too?"

"I think I'm in better shape than Stan is. But let's keep our eyes open and back each other up."

David now acted considerably more confident than he had at the beginning of our conversation. He seemed to enjoy the possibility of real action as opposed to clerical competence. We agreed to meet at 8.

Derek Armstrong's funeral was a far more upbeat affair than his son's had been. In recent years cancer had kept the elder Armstrong from his customary social rounds but several of his old cronies regaled the congregation with tales of an inveterate gambler who would not hesitate to wager huge sums of money on the most outlandish propositions. Bud Armstrong looked resplendent in a three-piece suit—someone had obviously taken a proprietary interest in his haberdashery—and Harriett Bascomb sat beside him wearing the expression of a cat that has just swallowed the canary. The old man had left specific directions for the music and I was pleased to discover that he had remarkably good taste.

I prolonged the postlude until everyone had left the sanctuary, then gathered my music together, shut off the organ, and was about to roll the heavy cover over the console when an unfamiliar voice said, "I can see having one keyboard for each hand, but what on earth are those rowboat oars doing down there?"

I looked around to see the large ingenuous face of Bud Armstrong. It occurred to me that this might be the first time in his life that the man had actually taken a good look at a pipe organ, so I withheld any impulse to crack a joke and said, "That's the pedal board. It's like another keyboard for the feet."

"You're putting me on!" he exclaimed jovially.

"No, really," I said, but guessing that he wasn't going to accept my word for it I turned the organ back on, pulled out a pedal flute stop, all the while wishing we had a reed, and played a brief accompanimental figure on the pedals."

"Well I'll be," was all he could say. "That's the darndest thing I ever saw."

"Would you like to try it?" I asked.

"Could I?" he asked incredulously.

"Sure thing." I hopped off the organ bench and watched Bud cautiously edge his hefty body into position as if he were sitting on a carton of eggs rather than a solidly-constructed piece of wooden furniture. From the side I kicked the toe stud labelled "Full Organ" so that every time Bud touched a key or a pedal the church resounded with the none-too-powerful sound of the *organo pleno.*

"This is unbelievable," he said as he produced a series of discords that would have gotten me in hot water with the biddies of the Worship Committee if it had been I instead of him.

"Could I ask you a question?" Bud turned to inquire. "Do you think you could play 'Abide With Me' sometime?"

"I don't choose the hymns," I said out of force of habit, "but I could play a prelude on the tune. Why don't you come next Sunday?"

"That would be great," Bud said, "but don't play it too softly, okay? Let her rip."

I told him I'd do my best. Bud sidled down to the end of the bench, dismounted, and shambled to the back of the church as I shook my head in disbelief that I could have thought this overgrown kid capable of murder. I decided that among the twenty-seven volumes of hymn preludes in my file cabinet there must be some decent pieces and resolved to comb through them in search of wheat among the chaff.

As I was returning to my office I heard Harriett Bascomb and Ian Wetherby engaged in a heated conversation. They'd evidently moved into the protection of the choir room but their angry words carried to the hallway.

"... and so it looks as if you're going to have to give up the money for the steeple," Wetherby was saying.

"If you think I'm going to put the stomachs of a bunch of lazy good-for-nothings ahead of this church, you've got another think coming," Harriett said firmly. "And what about your having to turn over all the property to the town of Meadowvale for low-income housing? Bunch of knee-jerk liberals," she muttered.

Wetherby sounded as if he'd worked out all the angles. "It turns out that the properties aren't actually in the church's name. They've been put into some kind of holding company—evidently someone gets a tax benefit, I don't know all the details—but Lewis Hartley seems to think that we may be able to escape John's stipulation."

"You mean to stand there and tell me that you're going to get that stupid parking lot while my steeple gets eaten up by a bunch of welfare cheats?" Harriett's voice had risen several notches.

"It looks that way," Ian said smugly.

"Ian Wetherby, you have picked the wrong woman to tangle with." Harriett had lowered her voice now and sounded more dangerous than ever. "That announcement Sunday caught me by surprise, I'll admit, but I've been doing a little checking on my own, and it seems that the parking lot isn't the only thing that's benefiting from these secret real estate deals."

"What are you talking about?" Ian said, his tone no longer as confident as before.

"You know perfectly well. You stand to turn a tidy personal profit from these little transactions."

"How did you …"

"It doesn't make any difference. The point is," and now it sounded as if she were speaking through clenched teeth, "that you personally and the members of the committees you serve on are going to throw your support to the Steeple People." The phrase didn't sound at all silly the way she said it.

"But …" Wetherby sputtered.

"What part of that do you not understand?" she said as if addressing a small child.

Wetherby tried to regain his balance. "Well of course I'll have to …"

"How you do it is your affair. Are we clear?"

"Yes," he managed to choke out the word then quickly left the room. I got out of sight before Harriett emerged but if this had been a western she would have been blowing the smoke off her pistols.

After lunch I called I called Clancy Davis and told him I needed a bit more information.

"You want more dirt on Ralph Littlemore?" he said with a chuckle.

"No, right now I'd like to learn more about Stan Rutledge."

"But Rutledge is small potatoes."

"How do you mean?"

"You know the name Nathan Rossiter?"

"Of course, his face is everywhere."

"That didn't happen by accident. He hired a whole stable of associates to help him earn the Century 21 Realtor of the Year award, which he plastered on billboards and bus benches. "#1 Salesman in the Country.""

"I've seen it."

"Stan Rutledge's name would never even appear on the charts. Given the real estate boom in this area, it's difficult to see how even a mediocre realtor wouldn't succeed, but between laziness and a complete absence of people skills, Rutledge scarcely makes a living at it. It's a shame, too. When his father was alive Rutledge Realty was at the top of the heap."

I could understand that Stan Rutledge would want to protect his little scam at the church—he obviously wasn't making a lot of money as a businessman—but the picture that Clancy had painted didn't seem to go with murder. Still, I was sufficiently concerned about Susan Scollard to give Trish McConnell a call. I asked her to meet me at Susan's apartment and she gave me the address, saying she could be there at two o'clock.

CHAPTER 21

Susan Scollard lived in a townhouse, or "town home" as the real estate ads insisted on calling them, halfway between the church and one of Meadowvale's two high schools. The developers had managed to squeeze half a dozen townhouses into a tiny tract of land too small for single-family homes with the expected backyards. Meadowvale boasted houses to fit families of all sizes but had little to offer single people. Susan had been lucky to find such a place.

Trish joined me at the appointed hour and we rang the doorbell to Susan's unit. Not surprisingly, there was no answer. I asked Trish if Susan had ever entrusted her with a key and she shook her head. The stained glass pattern in the vestibule window, a nice touch that Susan must have installed herself, prevented any view of the interior so we walked around to the back of the complex. "That's Susan's car!" Trish exclaimed as we approached the rear of the building. Each resident had a numbered space near the doors affording back entry into the units. Susan's rear door was also locked but I spotted a bedroom window just above her car that might get us in.

"If I boosted you up, do you think you could see whether that window will slide open?" I asked Trish.

"I think you're too short to lift me high enough," Trish eyed me dubiously.

"We won't start from the ground," I said. "I'll stand on the bumper of Susan's car. Good thing she parked so close to the building." Trish mentally re-calculated the height and nodded. I hopped up on the car bumper, followed by Trish, who then placed her foot into my clasped hands, put one of her hands on the top of my head for balance and lifted the other hand until she could reach the window sill.

"Can you lift me any higher?" she asked. I raised my hands slowly to around waist level. "It's sliding," Trish said excitedly. "I think I can get it open."

"The question is, can you make it through the window?" I asked. Trish gave no answer but boosted her body over the sill with athletic ease and disappeared into the bedroom. A moment later the back door opened and she led the way into Susan's apartment.

"Come to the bedroom," Trish said. She sounded worried. We mounted the stairs to the second floor and as we entered Susan's plainly-furnished bedroom I could understand why. Hanging over the door knob was a brown handbag, not a fancy dress-up purse but the kind of everyday accessory that a woman might expect to have with her at all times when she was out of the house.

We found nothing out of place in the bedroom, no signs of a struggle, no indications of mayhem. Susan evidently considered neatness a virtue: the ruffled bedspread was tucked evenly across two pillows, with another pair of throw pillows carefully placed, not thrown. A variety of toiletry objects, a few perfume bottles and a jewelry case sat on top of a low dresser. A dreamcatcher hanging in front of the window and a rather bland painting of a southwestern scene constituted the only decorations in the room.

A search of the rest of the apartment—living room, kitchen, dining alcove, bathroom, laundry room, hall closet—gave no reason to suspect foul play. Susan Scollard had simply vanished. I promised Trish that I would not sleep until I had some answers. She left looking more worried than ever.

The first flakes of the snowstorm we had been promised appeared as I headed home.

CHAPTER 22

The Fellowship Hall had never seen so many balloons. Entering guests walked through a balloon archway into a room whose ceiling was virtually paneled in balloons, with balloon centerpieces at each of the two dozen round tables. A bandstand constructed at one end of the room was marked off by pillars of balloons while a balloon border on the refreshments table seemed designed as a buffer to inhibit the movements of the youngest children as they stretched their arms to grab another treat.

The snow, which might have led to the cancellation of school or scout meetings, could not prevent the people of Allegheny United Church from bringing in the New Year in their own way. At one side of the room Sarah Beasley was calling out the numbers for Bingo. On the bandstand Clancy Davis, Henry Eldridge, Lewis Hartley and Ben Van Dyck were playing a lively Dixieland number on trumpet, clarinet, drums and bass, respectively. At the other end of the hall Frances Whelan, assisted by a simpering Parmalee Houghton, was trying to persuade a group of nine- and ten-year-olds to watch "The Littlest Mermaid" rather than "Cheerleaders in Trouble." Harriett Bascomb was well in command of a "Monopoly" game, with deeds to all four railroads in front of her along with complete sets of green and red properties. She was just purchasing "Boardwalk" as I walked past the table. Fred Carruthers and his wife played bridge with Carmody Talbot and Ian Wetherby in the corner. Jennifer, not particularly comfortable with this crowd, had volunteered to help out babysitting the youngest children. I'd promised to make a brief appearance at the party, after which we would go out to celebrate properly on our own. I hadn't told her what I planned to do.

David Moore came over to me as I entered and told me that he had checked out Susan Scollard's story: the Horizon Development Corporation was wholly owned by Stan Rutledge. I saw Stan come in with his brother and asked whether I might have a word with him. Carl lumbered off to find a drink and Stan and I moved to a relatively quiet corner of the room.

"Stan, I think the jig is up for you."

"What are you talking about?"

"You were the one who put the poison in John Armstrong's glass. I suggest that you confess to attempted murder. That way James Bellinger will be off the hook."

"You can't pin anything on me." For a mild man, Stan had a defiant side.

"What about Susan Scollard?" I demanded. At that Stan's face went white. I'd evidently struck a nerve and decided to press my advantage. "This is too public a place. Let's go to my office."

As I walked down the hall I told Stan how I'd figured out his scheme but allowed that he could hardly be charged with premeditated murder, since the wrong man had died. If he turned himself in, any decent lawyer should be able to get him off with no more than manslaughter.

But when I opened the door, it wasn't Stan who followed me into the office but his brother Carl. The contrast between the puny realtor and the hefty building contractor couldn't have been greater. With his huge neck, bullet head and massive upper body, Carl in a shiny purple shirt and gray dress slacks resembled a circus animal that someone had put into a costume to amuse an audience. Carl himself didn't seem the slightest bit amused. I placed myself on the other side of the desk and waited to hear what he had to say.

"So you think you have it all figured out, eh, organist?"

"I guess I hadn't realized Stan was so clever?"

"Stan! You think Stan worked this out? You're even dumber than you look."

I just shook my head and waited for him to continue.

"Where do you think Stan got the scam he's been pulling on the church for all these years? A few years ago he came to me complaining about not having enough money and I passed along a scheme I'd heard about from some friends."

"Apparently you passed along some speculative deals as well."

"It wasn't enough I gave him the scam—I practically had to hold his hand to make it work," Carl said contemptuously.

"What about the poison?"

"You think he dreamed that up? You're crazy. I got him the poison and coached him all the way through it."

"What about Susan Scollard?"

"You'll never see her again. Of course, they're going to have a tough time finding you."

I tried to assess the situation. If I reached for the telephone Carl would surely fall on me. He hadn't shown a weapon, which I counted as a plus. On the other hand, if he ever laid his hands on me I'd be as good as dead. The man moved toward me around the desk but I'd been expecting that and dodged around the other side and headed for the door.

I figured that he might have posted Stan at the other end of the hall, and I didn't like my chances trapped between the two brothers, so I headed up the stairs to the connecting Sunday school rooms under the eaves. Carl followed, breathing heavily. He might be strong but he didn't seem to be used to stairs. As I threaded my way through the child-size chairs I tipped over as many as I could to impede his progress, but it was like trying to flee from a charging bear: you could slow it up some but you weren't going to stop it.

In the second of the two garret rooms I took a few seconds to overturn the tables then made my way as rapidly as I could to the door at the other end. Again I had a choice. Stan, down on the second floor, knew the layout of the church as well as I did. If I rushed blindly downstairs I might be heading into an ambush. I decided in favor of the known over the unknown and ran up the last flight of stairs to the roof.

The air was cold and the snow coming down heavily as I pushed open the door to the outside. The clock tower a block away could scarcely be seen through the curtains of white. The roof was covered with a tangle of ropes and cables left by the workmen assigned to repair the leaks. There wasn't really any place to hide. I just hoped that my greater agility could hold off Carl's greater size and strength until I could either attract attention or escape back through the door, but as I looked over the low railing toward the street below I couldn't see anyone who might help me and the muffling effect of the falling snow made it unlikely that my voice would carry far.

Carl came through the doorway. One on one I still had a chance to survive. If Stan came through the door, I was in real trouble. Carl had a nasty smile on his face as he drew closer. I could imagine that he had been in a fair number of brawls and had already sized me up as a pushover. I edged down further toward the corner of the tower. Carl moved toward me. I made a break for the opposite wall and Carl stood facing me with his back to the railing. He couldn't see that I'd gained anything by the maneuver because he was still closer to the door than I was.

I studied the maze of cables on the snow-covered cement surface. Carl seemed happy to catch his breath, confident that I wasn't going anywhere. With my eyes I followed the confused path of the rope closest to Carl's feet as it wound over and under the other ropes. I'd only get one chance at this. I dropped to my feet, grabbed what I prayed were the right ropes, and yanked on them with all my might.

The loop closed around Carl's ankles and pulled his feet out from under him. His height, the slick surface and the suddenness of the movement prevented him from grabbing the tiny railing and he went over the edge of the tower. I hadn't been planning to let him fall, only to trap him, but the force of his weight pulled the slippery ropes from my hands and I heard his cry grow more distant as he fell three stories to the concrete pavement and his death.

A few minutes later Jennifer ran through the doorway, followed closely by David. "What the hell do you think you're doing?" she shrieked at me. "You might have been killed!" She came over and put her arms around me.

"I guess the idea of backing each other up didn't work out the way we expected," David said lamely.

It might have been the snowy night air or the impact of realizing what nearly happened, but I began to shiver and suggested we move inside.

"You two leave now," David said. "None of us has been on the roof tonight." I thought he'd been watching too many old movies but a look from Jennifer made me follow his lead. We'd leave this death entirely to the police. The storm increased in intensity as we closed the roof door behind us.

CHAPTER 23

On Wednesday morning Ben Van Dyk called me at home to wish me a Happy New Year and to report that Stan had confessed to the plan to kill David Moore. The district attorney still hadn't decided exactly what charges to press. Stan was distraught at his brother's death and couldn't figure out what he'd been doing up on the tower roof. I hoped that the snow had covered our footprints by the time the police reached the scene. Evidently Carl hadn't told him how he was planning to take care of me and had simply told Stan to keep an eye out for an opportunity to use the poison on David. Stan was too occupied with his own affairs to think much about me.

The next call came from James and Shirley Bellinger, talking on separate extensions. They thanked me for helping to clear James and told me that they'd been talking to Sarah Beasley about marital counseling.

"I'm glad to hear that some good has come out of this," I said.

"Sarah suggested that after we'd concluded our work with her she would conduct a Rededication of Marriage Vows service for us."

"What a nice idea," I said.

"But we can't take forever to get our act together," James chipped in.

"Why's that?"

"Sarah's planning to submit her resignation effective in June, so we have to finish up before then," Shirley explained.

"Sarah's leaving?" I asked in surprise.

"She told us that Dillsburg was too small but AUC was too large. She's going to look for a church in between," said her husband.

David Moore phoned to be sure that I was all right. He sounded a little disappointed not to have been able to participate in the rooftop drama. I tried to explain that it was hardly my idea of fun, but ever since realizing that he had been a potential murder victim, David had begun to see the whole affair in terms of a suspense movie.

"You remember in Hitchcock's *Vertigo* when James Stewart is hanging on to the roof with one hand?" he asked with some excitement.

"David, that's a movie. The actor is never more than a foot or two off the ground."

"I still wish I'd been up there with you," he insisted. "But I do have some other news to report."

"What's that?"

"Harriett Bascomb got wind of Henry Eldridge's problem—you really stirred up the pot in this one, Axel—and decided to take an interest."

It struck me that any time Harriett Bascomb took an interest the alterations were not likely to be minor. "What has she done?"

"It turns out that Carmody Talbot used to be a CPA. Henry's a fine chemist but a pretty poor businessman. So Carmody is going to try to get his day-to-day operations straightened out."

"What does that do for his business in the long run?"

"That's where I come in," David announced proudly. "Harriett has persuaded Henry to accept a Board of Directors for the business and I'm going to be on it."

"Who else is going to serve?" I asked.

"I think Bud Armstrong is going to be a member as well," he said. "The plans call for Henry to redirect his efforts away from toxic wastes and toward environmental impact studies."

That would presumably deliver him from the nefarious arrangement with Ralph Littlemore.

The presbytery hadn't wasted any time in dealing with the leadership vacuum at Allegheny United Church. After consulting with Sarah Beasley, who assured them that she had no interest in becoming senior minister, they appointed the Rev. Adam Baxter as interim senior minister until a full search could be carried out.

Baxter sounded friendly enough when he talked to me on the telephone and liked my suggestions for a hymn sing and an evening of show tunes. I told him that, given the diversity of musical tastes at Allegheny United Church, we might do best by offering as much variety as possible so that worshippers could leave each service having heard at least one thing they liked.

"I'm going to have my hands full just mastering the committee structure at this place," he said. "Suppose you pick the hymns."

About the Author

Arthur Wenk loves music, mathematics, movies, mountains, mysteries, magic and marathon running. He has published books and articles on Debussy, music and the arts, music history and bibliography, programming graphing calculators, and the bookstores of Toronto. In the summer, he enjoys hiking in the White Mountains of New Hampshire. Wenk's teaching career has taken him to southern California, Boston, Pittsburgh, Québec City and Southern Ontario, where he has founded a succession of a cappella choirs and served as a musician in addition to academic duties. Axel Crochet represents a nod to Claude Debussy's alter ego, Monsieur Crochet, the dilettante-hater.